SATAN'S LEGIONS

Book 1: **Love**

by

Philip G. Brown

Satan's Legions. Book One: Love
Copyright © 2015 by Philip G. Brown
All rights reserved.

Published by Swanford United Books
All contacts to be made through:
swanfordunited@aol.com

ISBN 978-0-9932461-3-5

Acknowledgements

I'd like to thank my copy-editor Jane Hammett, an Advanced Professional Member of the Society for Editors and Proofreaders, for her sterling work on my books.

To my friends pictured within.

1: Friday, 4th January. Evening, Pear Tree Cottage, the Ropewalk, Swanford.

ROBERT

Caught in the glow of the single street lamp, snowflakes were blowing in icy flurries across the Ropewalk and piling up into small dunes along the pavement on the other side. Maybelle Crittenden stared out of her son's bedroom window.

"It's very... quaint, isn't it?" she said – 'quaint' being the most complimentary word she could think of.

She drew the curtains across, wafting cobwebs in their wake.

"This whole place needs a good vacuuming!"

Maybelle didn't want to be disloyal to her husband, but she couldn't help but contrast this poky, damp old cottage, set in a poky, damp old lane, with her spacious, beautifully furnished home in Tyree, Oklahoma.

Mother and son had been in England for just thirty-six hours, and the journey from Heathrow to the small market town of Swanford had taken almost as long as the journey across the Atlantic. They were both still seriously tired.

Robert Crittenden stood by his single bed, on which lay three full carrier bags. His feet were cold. The heating was on, but the old stone building, known as Pear Tree Cottage, hadn't fully warmed up yet.

"My feet are like blocks of ice, Mom." He wriggled his toes, watching them through his threadbare white socks. He had no slippers, and he wasn't allowed to wear shoes in the house.

"Well then, hurry up and get changed into them things your daddy bought you. There are dress shirts and underwear in the closet. When you're done, come down and let's see just how handsome our son looks in his new uniform."

After his mother had left, Robert unpacked the carriers, laying out each item neatly on the bed. There was a black blazer, two pairs of charcoal grey trousers, a belt and a

1

maroon-and-grey tie. The yellow school badge on the top pocket of the blazer caught his eye. At first, he thought of the RKO Radio Pictures mast which came on at the start of some of the old black-and-white movies his mother enjoyed. Then he realised it was a lighthouse. Which is odd, he thought, as the sea is miles away.

"Omnibus optium," he read out loud, "which means..."

The boy decided to look it up later on his new laptop.

***

"Well aren't you a picture?" said his mother, as he entered the lounge. It was warm and cosy in here, thanks in no small measure to the DRU gas fire which complimented the central heating and glowed brightly in the subdued lighting. This was the largest room in the cottage by far, having been extended at the back, and his father intended to use it for entertaining clients, as well as being their main living space.

"You'll be a credit to us, I know," said his father, seated by his wife on a floral sofa in front of the fire. When he was standing up, Francis Robert Crittenden, known as Frank, wasn't much taller. A slight man with a skin tone and beard much darker than his son's, their only shared characteristic was their black eyes. Otherwise, the boy had acquired the pink complexion and orange hair of his mother's side of the family – and their height, for at fifteen he was already three inches taller than his father.

"What about my shoes?" asked Robert.

"Well, go put them on, boy; we'll forget about the rule for once."

Robert scurried into the passage to retrieve his only pair of suitable shoes. He knew they were wrong.

"They're brown," he said, on returning. "They don't match."

"And what would you know about matching?"

2

"Enough. Mom, they don't match." He didn't usually answer his mother back, but he was concerned about how he would appear on the first day of school.

"Now, son," his father admonished.

"Sorry, sir, sorry Mom, but they don't match," he insisted.

"Hmm, well, the boy's probably right, May, don't you think?"

"But that'll be another fifty dollars, Frank."

Robert often wondered, but never questioned out loud, why his family always seemed to be living from hand to mouth. After all, his father was a highly experienced and qualified engineer. He had worked for the same company, Burnoco, for twenty years, and was often on secondment to one or another of their international subsidiaries. The boy was proud of his father: he knew that colleagues thought him 'a safe pair of hands' and admired the way he was able to schmooze clients and smooth ruffled feathers.

This was Frank's second assignment to England and the first to Burnoco's UK head office in Swanford. It was also his first ever extended contract, planned to last for two years, with a possible extension of six months beyond that. This meant his family were expected to relocate with him, about which both mother and son had been equivocal. But they had to accept that the career of the breadwinner was paramount, and Maybelle made it known that she was kind of looking forward to the 'entertaining' part of the contract.

"You think I could get a Saturday job, sir? That'll help a little."

Frank squeezed his son's shoulder.

"That's a great idea, Robert. But you take your time and settle in and don't worry. Maybelle, you can drive the boy to the retail park next weekend; there'll be money enough in the housekeeping account by then."

"Thanks, Dad," said a grateful Robert. "Where is the retail park?"

Having been in Swanford since before Christmas to make the arrangements for their extended stay, Frank was already familiar with the area.

"Prestleigh; it's about five and a half miles north-west of here." He smiled. "You'll feel right at home up there, I'm sure. Now, you go and get ready for dinner. Your mother and I have important matters to talk over with you."

"What's for dinner, Mom?" asked the boy, his mouth watering.

She made a fluttery gesture with her hand. "You men and your stomachs! We got meat loaf, mashed potatoes with sour cream, green beans, biscuits, and gravy and, for afters, apple pie and ice cream."

"Oh, yummy!"

***

"Great God, giver of all that is good, accept our praise and bless our food. Grace, health and strength to us afford, and I thank You specially on this day, the first in our new home, for delivering my precious family safely to me. Through Jesus Christ, our blessed Lord. Amen."

"Amen."

"Amen." Robert looked up and began to unfold his napkin. "That was nice, Dad, thank you."

"You're welcome, son. We don't spend enough time having family meals."

"Your daddy is off to Scot Land tomorrow, honey."

"Gee, Dad, on the rigs?"

"It looks like it. Think of me being sea-sick for a week."

"Oh, Frank, please, not at the table!"

"Sorry, May. Can you pass the biscuits?"

"There'll be terrible winter storms up there. I read all about England on the plane."

"Actually, son, Scotland is a separate country from England. You wouldn't believe how messy this tiny island is."

Robert smiled through a mouthful of beans.

"I wanted to thank you for my laptop, Dad. It's what I've always wanted."

"It's a company computer, son, just like mine, connected to the internet via their servers and safely filtered."

"I am so pleased about that, Frank," said Maybelle.

"I would prefer it, son, if that was the only one you used. Even school computers allow indecent content to pollute the minds of the young."

"Sure, Dad. I shan't need any other."

"It's a real neat little package," beamed his father.

"Is this the important matter you wanted to talk to me about, Dad?"

"Not really, son." he turned to his wife. "Do you think it's time for the boy to hear our advice, or should we leave it till our meal is finished?"

"Can't hear it soon enough for me," said Maybelle.

Frank directed his attention back to Robert. "We know how much you will miss your old home, son: your friends, school, sports, the choir, your whole family in Christ. Your mother and I have talked a great deal about how you will manage in this new environment, and there is much you need to know and understand."

The boy rummaged through his mashed potato with his fork, listening carefully. Then he gazed at his parents.

"I'm ready," he said, his black eyes sparkling in the amber glow of the room.

"I talked to Pastor Dunn before we left Tyree, Robert," said Maybelle, "and he has given me a whole sheaf of information. England has become a Godless country. It is our ancestral home, but now the people have turned against the Lord and sin has become the norm, and decay will surely follow."

"But why, Mom? I thought England was a bastion against Satan."

"It was son, it was, but the ways of the Beast are mighty subtle and he has worked his magic on the people. I am not going to pollute your mind with stories of its decadence, just to say that not one-third of the population are regular worshippers, and they treat the Sabbath day as no different to any other. Some weeks, may the Lord God forgive us, even your father is forced to labour on a Sunday."

"I make my feelings known, May."

The boy attacked a piece of meatloaf, as if it were an apostate. "They that defy the Ten Commandments do so at the peril of their immortal souls," said the boy, stuffing the morsel into his mouth.

"Manners, Robert!" chided his mother.

"Sorry, Mom," he smiled at her, "but it is so delicious."

She smiled back. "Why, you've got your father's silky, sweet-talkin' tongue all right."

"Son," said his father, "we are guests in this country and, benighted though it is, remember that ours is not to condemn our fellow men. We are all sinners. There are still many good and righteous people in this land, but all have been affected by the scourge of socialism, so that they have become weak and many are unable to resist the forces of darkness."

"What should I do, sir?"

"Be on your guard all the time. Satan never sleeps. Do not let him insinuate himself into your life. Remember, he comes like a wolf in sheep's clothing."

"But how will I recognise him in this place, Dad, among all this strangeness?"

Maybelle took her son's hand.

"Oh, Robert, he is too subtle, even for your father and I. No human can withstand him. You must trust in the Lord, keep close to God. He will wash Satan's influence from your mind, if you recognise your sins and repent of them."

"On Sunday, you will meet Pastor McKellan," continued his father. "I'm told he's a little more reserved than Pastor Dunn, but a fine man nonetheless. He will be our spiritual guide while we are here. The church fathers back in Tyree have sent a generous donation to the pastor, on our behalf, so that he has been able to start up a regular Bible study class

6

every week on a Wednesday, at 6.30 p.m. We shall expect you to attend, Robert."

"Yes, sir."

"That was a fine dinner, Maybelle," said Frank, leaning back in his chair, his plate cleared. "Thank you."

"Now, would anyone like a slice of my home-made apple pie?"

"Yes, please, Mom!"

His mother rose and began to clear the dishes. "You all can continue your talk. I shan't be long."

Frank smiled at his wife, then rested his arms on the table and clasped his hands together. "The school I chose for you is the better of the two in this town; even so, it is built on the shifting sands of moral relativism. You know what that is, don't you, son?"

"Yes, sir. That there is no objective truth. That God's laws as stated in the Holy Bible can be changed by the whims of man."

"And we know they can't. You may find a level of degradation at this school which you have not encountered before. Young people of your age who swear and smoke, drink alcohol and are lewd and promiscuous. Do not let a girl use her wiles and talents to charm you, Robert. Remember the story of Samson. Keep yourself clean and free from sin for the day that you marry. Allow no Delilah into your heart, for she will cut off your locks and weaken you."

"Yes, sir."

Frank paused while his wife placed the golden crusted apple pie on a serving mat.

"Fresh from the Aga," she said. "I do like that sweet little cooker."

"Yummy," said the boy, his eyes straying to the three large slices of pie his mother was cutting.

"Pay attention, Robert, I haven't quite finished," his father said. "You may think the words I am about to say to contradict what I have just said, but listen carefully and you will understand.

"You must obey your school teachers; there can be no question of that. You must develop good, but not intimate, relations with your fellow pupils. And if, in the course of your studies, you can bring a benighted soul to the Lord, you will have done Him a great service. Remember: To the weak became I as weak, that I might gain the weak: I am made all things to all men, that I might by all means save some. Build your foundation on the rock of God's will, Robert, by daily obedience, service, Bible study and prayer. In that way He will deliver you from evil."

"What do you mean by intimate, Dad?"

"A good question, son. I mean, keep your relationships at arm's length. Your real friendships are with our people back home in Tyree."

"I understand."

Robert finished the last mouthful of apple pie and ice cream, laid his spoon on the under-plate, wiped his mouth on the napkin, folded it loosely and placed it on the left side of his bowl. "Thank you, Mom."

"You're welcome, dear, and now your daddy is going to say a special prayer for you and, afterwards, you can relax in this lovely room while I wash the dishes. I must say, I am beginning to feel a good deal more content."

"Yes, ma'am."

They joined hands and Robert bowed his head and closed his eyes, replete.

"Dear God, our Heavenly Father, keep our son, Robert, safe from harm in the months and years ahead. Do not allow him to become prey to Satan's schemes. Let him see through the camouflage of the Enemy. Protect him from the unrighteous and the Godless. Let him not be led into temptation by Satan's minions. Give him the strength of your sword and shield to fight the legions of demons. Keep him pure and chaste so that he may better come to know Your everlasting glory. We ask this, Great God, in the name of your son, the blessed Lord Jesus Christ. Amen."

***

2: Monday, 7th January. 8.45 a.m. Swanford Community School.

JACK

Under the gleam of a watery sun, the snow had thawed during the weekend and the morning dawned dry, crisp and cold. It was the start of the spring term. Jack Moseley, Year Ten, sauntered in through the school gates, where Charlie Masefield was waiting for him with a triumphant smile on his face.

"Hey," said Jack. "Good Christmas?"

Charlie said nothing, but thrust a screen in front of his eyes.

"Christmas present?" Jack asked, quite impressed.

"Look!"

"Oh, which porn site did you get that off?"

"It's not porn, it's my girlfriend."

"Which porn site does your girlfriend work for?"

"That's not porn, that's her breasts."

"So your skanky girlfriend allowed you to take a video of her breasts?"

"She's not skanky; she didn't know I had my camera on. It was sweet: I was rubbing them, she had her eyes closed and the camera whirred."

"You're sick."

"Guess who my girlfriend is?"

"A cocaine-snorter from the sleaze school."

"She's in our class."

Jack's interest was suddenly piqued. With a twinge of jealousy, he looked harder at the three-second clip on the handset and blew a frosty breath.

"It's crappy, it's dark, it's out of focus."

"It's not out of focus; my hand was shaking."

9

"Did you know, when normal people take pictures of their girlfriends they usually aim the camera at the head?"

"She hasn't given me head... yet."

Charlie laughed at Jack's expression.

"I have got a proper one of her, but I want you to guess who it is first."

"From her breasts?" Jack shook his head. The picture seemed to interest and repel him in equal measure. "Linda Woolley."

"Tuh, please!"

"Carol Manning."

"Get serious."

"Joan Field."

"Nope."

Jack was working his way up through the hierarchy of girls in his class.

"Surely not Mandy...?"

"Mandy...? Of course not!"

Now Jack was getting worried, because this was clearly not one of the usual suspects or even the not-so-usual ones.

"You know, if she finds out, she'll dump you straight away and you'll never get a proper girlfriend again. You'll also get suspended or even moved to another school, if a teacher finds out, and do I have to remind you that your dad is a policeman?"

"I know, I know. I'm going to delete it once you and Max have guessed."

Jack took the longest shot he could think of. "Barbara Carter."

Charlie's face fell. "How did you know?"

You're joking, Jack thought, but knew his friend wasn't.

"Because I had her on Saturday night," he said, with a nonchalant air. "Took her to my bed and we fucked like jackrabbits."

Charlie's jaw dropped.

"You know," Jack continued, leaning confidentially towards his friend, "she told me she was really concerned about your small dick not giving her any satisfaction."

Charlie appeared to be about to weep, but then his expression changed, as it dawned on him that he had been the one with Barbara on Saturday night.

"You fucking liar, Moseley!"

"Your face...!" Jack screamed, doubling up with laughter.

"You arsehole!"

"Morning, girls." Max Seddon, the third member of the three live wires, as they were known to some in the staff room, joined the pair. "Why is Jack creasing himself?"

"Because he's an arsehole," said Charlie.

"I know that, but what's up with him?"

Charlie stuck the handset in front of Max's face.

"Oh yes – Barbara Carter, very nice."

By this time, Jack was all but rolling around on the frosty ground.

"Bastard!" Charlie exclaimed. "How did you know?"

Max clapped Charlie on the shoulder. "Because I saw you and her on Saturday night, smooching in that flea pit we call a cinema."

"Oh..."

"I should delete it now," said Max.

"Arsehole has already told me that."

"Good advice."

"What's going on over there?" asked Jack, wiping his eyes and peering at the small crowd which had gathered in front of the school. In their midst was a tall, smart-looking boy with a ruddy complexion and a head of tightly curled ginger hair.

He joined the periphery of the group, which mostly consisted of little sprogs from Year Seven, wondering why the stupid dork was letting these insects harass him.

"Where do you come from?"

"A town called Tyree in Oklahoma."

"Do you know Buzz?" a boy asked excitedly.

The centre of their attention smiled. "Not personally."

"Don't be stupid," the first boy's companion chided, "Buzz lives in Michigan."

"Don't worry, little fella, I didn't think it was a stupid question."

What a weirdo, Jack thought, he's actually enjoying himself. Still, I may as well hang around to listen.

"Do you live in a log cabin?"

"No, sir, there aren't many trees where I come from. I'm not really used to all this greenery yet."

"Have you got a gun?"

"No, but my dad taught me how to rifle-shoot."

"Do you get rattlesnakes?" questioned a girl in a bright purple coat and furry mittens.

"There have been a few. It's hot and dusty enough in summer."

"Do you get snow?"

"We don't get snowfall that often where I live, but some places in the state get truck-loads every winter. We also get tornadoes and lots of hail and thunder."

"Wow!"

American, obviously, thought Jack, and that southern drawl makes him sound a bit thick. Keeps his mouth open too, when not speaking. Holds himself stiff and upright. Not really one of those 'jock' types, but more like a jock than a fat burger freak. What's he doing here in Nowheresville? No coat and a new uniform. Must be here to stay. That backpack's seen better days; he must have brought it with him. Kind of like it, though. Kind of like him, too, in a goofy sort of way, but he's probably Year Eleven at that height.

Jack turned to go, but stopped when he spotted Miss Chawner, the school secretary, marching down the steps and cutting a swathe through the gaggle of moppets.

"Robert Crittenden?" She spoke as if that was going to be his name, even if it wasn't.

"Yes, ma'am," he replied.

"Follow me, please."

For a moment, the American stood and looked around the circle of faces, as if he were lost in a dense forest rather than surrounded by children.

"Say, how d'ya get out of here?"

Jack laughed at the crack, though no one else did. The American shot him a glance and their eyes met. Very dark, very deep, thought Jack, and smiled, lifting his chin in greeting. The boy nodded and smiled back.

"Robert!" Miss Chawner spoke sharply.

"She who must be obeyed!" whispered Max, his voice quavering into Jack's right ear. "Where is she taking the poor boy? How soon will it be before he becomes a shrivelled, dehydrated corpse... like the rest of us?"

***

3: Monday, 7th January. 9.05 a.m. Swanford Community School Class, 4S.

JACK

"This is Robert Crittenden, class, he is from the United States of America and will be joining us for the remainder of this school year and all of the next. Is that right, Robert?"

"Yes, sir, that's exactly right." The accent, the lilt, brought forth a few titters.

"Like your shoes, Yank... not!" called out Henry Adams.

Robert blushed.

"Did you have carrots for breakfast?" asked another joker.

Mr Colt, their form teacher, put up his hand.

"Please, class, show the same consideration for a new pupil that you would hope to get for yourselves. Just imagine yourself in a foreign country and what it would be like for you on your first day at school."

"Ah! The old empathy trick," whispered Jack, smirking at Max, who occupied the adjacent desk.

"Mr Moseley, since you are smiling so sincerely, perhaps you would like to take Robert under your wing and show him the ropes."

"Well, I would, sir, but I've got a hot date." This brought forth the required subdued laughter and derisive you wishes in equal measure.

The teacher peered over his glasses at the dark-haired boy.

"Jack Moseley, the day you get a hot date will also be the day that hell freezes over."

There was more laughter, and Jack grinned. He liked to banter, especially with someone as dry as Mr Colt, and, with acute and perhaps surprising sensitivity, he always let the old man have the last word.

"Go on Robert, sit next to Jack, he'll look after you. Max, find a spare desk somewhere, will you?"

"Like at home, sir?"

"If you wish, but how we would miss your delightful company..."

"Come and sit next to me, Maxxy," called Mandy Simpkins from the back.

"Oh, crikey!" cried the boy.

Mr Colt watched the manoeuvres indulgently for a few moments before opening the register. "Since we have less time than usual, while I undertake this chore, please get out the text of our favourite play and turn to Act 2, scene 3. Mr Moseley, perhaps you'll guide Mr Crittenden into the Forum. Mr Adams, because of your little outburst earlier, you are Several Citizens. Begin!"

Forty-five minutes later, the lesson finished.

"Exeunt Colt and assorted Romans," said Jack.

"I don't think I understood much of that," admitted Robert.

Max plodded over. "There's only one thing to understand," he yawned. "It's a load of shite."

Charlie Masefield closed his eyes and rested his forehead on the edge of his desk. "Jesus H. Christ; Corio-fuck-my-anus, what a sodding bore."

Jack noticed the American's look of disapproval at Charlie's comment.

"Do all Americans chew gum?" Mandy asked, her stick-like figure coming to stand just behind Robert.

"I'm not allowed to," he said, half-turning in his seat.

She pulled a string of illicit gum out of her own mouth. "Would you like some of mine?"

"Er, no thank you, ma'am."

She let the gum back into her mouth. "Why did you blush when old man Colt was talking to Jack?"

Robert tilted his head and smiled shyly at her. "I'm just not used to teachers using the H-word like that, I guess."

"The H-word?" she repeated back at him, "What the fuck is the H-word?"

"Hell," said Robert quietly, glancing round, as if the word might conjure up the devil himself.

Mandy nearly swallowed her gum. "Hell!" she cried. "Are you fuckin' religious, or something?"

"Yes, ma'am, I believe the Lord Jesus Christ is our saviour... Those persons who come to Christ will surely know the Kingdom of Heaven."

Her mascaraed eyes went wide and she sat down heavily on Robert's desk, crossed her legs and folded her arms. "Are you trying to convert me?"

Robert swallowed. "I believe everyone can be brought to the true path."

"You know I'm a good Catholic girl, don't you?"

There were snorts from around the class, most of whom were enjoying the show.

"You lot shut your gobs," she chided. "I was going to be a bride of Christ when I was young."

"More like 'Bride of Frankenstein'" said Charlie.

"You're a fuckin' cunt, Masefield, and I know full well you can't get it up, because Barbara's told me."

"Lies!" said Charlie, and turned to Barbara: "Tell them!"

"Mandy," called Stewart Henderson, "Will you uncross your legs for me like that woman did in that film?"

"Henderson, you jug-eared Nazi, it wouldn't do anything for you even if I did. You see, I'm just an ordinary girl, and I haven't got a tattoo of bleedin' Hitler on my fanny, like you've got on your tiny little dick."

She allowed herself to slip down from the desk, and took a deep breath.

"Thank you, Mandy," said Max. "That was a lovely performance. We'll let you know if you've got the part by second-class mail."

The girl stalked towards the door, holding her middle finger up, while trying to remain balanced on her platform shoes.

"Do all the girls talk like that?" Robert asked in a low voice.

"Oh, no," replied Jack. "Mandy is one of the refined ones."

Jack waited for Robert's response and for a few seconds the cogs seemed to be whirring furiously beneath the tight thatch of ginger hair. Then the boy scratched his forehead and, for the first time, smiled. "That's English humour, isn't it?"

Jack nodded sagely, but then his face broke out into a big grin.

"Yes, it is! Robert Crittenden, you have passed your first test." He rose. "Come on, we've still got ten minutes before maths; I'll show you around." He turned to Max and Charlie. "See you guys later."

***

Outside in the corridor, Jack paused at the lockers to get his maths books. "Do you prefer Robert, Rob or Bob?"

"Just Robert, please."

"And I'm just Jack."

The American offered his hand and they shook.

"Welcome to the wonderful world of Swanford Community School," said Jack, feeling the firm grip of the American. "That's a big hand," he said, with a grimace that turned into a grin.

"And you've got cold hands, which means a warm heart," replied Robert, blushing when he realised what he'd said.

"Ha! And here's me assuming it was because it's fucking freezing in this corridor. Oh, sorry, you don't like swearing, do you?"

"I'm not used to it."

"You looked daggers at Charlie."

"I saw you notice my reaction. That was blasphemy, Jack, against the Lord Jesus Christ."

"We'd better watch what we say, then," said the English boy, half-seriously.

"I would be a hypocrite if I told you it was all right by me, but I can't lay the law down."

"That's good, because swearing is fucking endemic at this school." Jack smiled at his joke and the use of the word endemic, which he had recently picked up in geography.

Shortly, they reached a pair of swing doors, one of which was propped open with a bucket and mop.

"And this is the canteen."

They paused on the threshold.

"Dinner hour is between 12.30 and 1.15 – and don't say it, I know that's not an hour."

"This is OK," said Robert.

"Yes, it's new. Potted palms and some comfortable seating. Won't last, though. Are you packed lunch or dinner?"

"Dinner. How's the food?"

"I expect you'll think it's crap, but it's not bad. We all have it."

"Why do you say I won't like it?"

"Because it's not super-size portions and we never have steak."

"At home, I get steak about once a month."

"Have you come to live in England for good?"

"No, my dad's on a two-year contract, he works for Burnoco."

"Oh, right. You must be rich."

"No..." Again, Robert found himself wondering why this English boy's assumption was incorrect.

"We're not rich, either. My dad works for the council and my mum is part-time in the post office."

"Hey, you!"

They turned to find two Year Eleven boys bearing down on them. The more assertive of the two was barrel-shaped with short greasy hair and the shadow of a beard.

"Why Ben, how nice," said Jack, adopting the tone of his form teacher.

"Shut up Moseley, you moron. So, you're the American kid, right?"

"Robert Crittenden from Oklahoma. How d'you do."

Ben brushed aside the pleasantry.

"Bout time you Yanks nuked some of them A-rabs. Getting too big for their boots."

"I expect Robert will report your opinion to the President immediately, Ben," said Jack.

"Fuck you, Moseley, you pinko pussy boy."

The bell rang for next period, much to Jack's relief, and Ben and his companion loped off. It was maths, which was held in a first-floor classroom in the science block, quite a distance from the canteen. The boys picked up their pace, so as not to incur the wrath of Mrs Gutteridge.

"Who was that belligerent type?" asked Robert.

"You know Stewart, the little kid with the jug ears in our class? That's his brother."

"They don't seem much alike."

"There's five in the Henderson clan, each dumped by a different mother, so people say."

"Out of wedlock?" asked Robert with a frown.

"Well, I think he's married to one of them."

"Who was the other boy?"

"You mean Jason Spriggs, the silent one."

"He seemed out of it."

"Probably high, but he's pretty harmless. His brother Lucas is in our year, but in 4T."

"Complicated."

Jack chuckled. "Robert, will you be taking your GCSEs here?"

"I guess so. Are they difficult? That Shakespeare was hard to understand."

"It's the way Henry Adams reads it."

"He noticed my shoes. They don't match."

Jack looked down and frowned.

"Haven't you got any others?"

"I'm getting a new pair on Saturday."

"I'd bin them, then," advised Jack, "they're horrible."

The American boy's face turned scarlet, his shoe discomfiture complete.

"Robert..." said Jack.

"Yes?"

"They don't match, but there's nothing wrong with your shoes."

Robert's cogs whirred into action and he looked at Jack.

"You were kiddin' me again, right?"

"Right," said the boy with a broad grin. "You'll sit with us at dinner time, won't you, despite our swearing and blaspheming?"

"Sure, I'll be glad to. Thank you, Jack."

The English boy grinned again at the American's formality.

"Say, how does that tall girl get away with it?" Robert asked, as they walked out of the main building into the cold morning air.

"That's where we're going." Jack pointed towards the side door of the three-storey science block, the highest and newest building on site. "Who, Mandy?"

"She's... overpowering – and that short dress and all that make-up!"

"And the swearing?"

"I've never in my life heard a girl talk like that."

"She gets away with it, because she gets A stars in every subject. She'll probably go to Oxford or Cambridge."

"You mean it's an act?"

"No, Mandy's Mandy." They clattered up the dog-leg stairs which overlooked the playing fields. "She's taken a liking to you, you know."

"It didn't seem so to me. In any case, how can you tell?"

"She sat on your desk – that's a sure sign. You'll never see her sitting on Henry's desk, for instance. Also, you stood up for yourself and treated her with respect. If you wimp out on her or, worse, try to slap her down, she'll flip you off. "

"Jack, you are a very astute person."

They had reached Mrs Gutteridge's room and could hear her commanding the class to be silent. Jack allowed Robert through the door first. He may be a strait-laced goof, but I quite like him, he thought.

***

4: Monday, 7th January. 3.50 a.m. Leighton Lane.

__ROBERT__

A frosty evening in Swanford, and the setting sun cast oblique shadows across Leighton Lane. Maybelle Crittenden had already been parked for fifteen minutes when her son opened the car door.

"Gee, I need my coat and gloves, Mom," he said, blowing into his hands. "Is this the company car? It's kinda neat."

"Put your belt on, dear," she replied absently, for the streets of Swanford were narrow, congested and had many junctions, requiring concentrated thought for an American, unaccustomed to driving on the left.

"Ready, Mom."

Gingerly, Maybelle engaged first gear and took her foot off the clutch.

"Hey, there's Jack – sound your horn, Mom."

Maybelle was much too busy dealing with the manual transmission as well as peering into the dusk to sound her horn. Robert knocked on the window and waved, but was not sure whether Jack had seen him or not.

Once back in the cottage on the Ropewalk, Robert changed out of his school uniform, which he hung neatly in the closet, then joined his mother in the lounge for coffee and chocolate chip cookies.

They sat down in front of the fire. "Why can't they have roads that go in straight lines, like any normal town?" she asked, handing him a plate and a napkin from the coffee table.

The boy stretched out his socked feet towards the hearth and relaxed into the sofa.

"I love these cookies, Mom, it's just like home."

"Your father didn't get off until this afternoon, Robert; a colleague drove him to the station. They finally cleared the line, though goodness knows what took them so long."

"Dad said that the English only do things by halves. Half an inch of snow means half the country comes to a halt, because they've only got half a snow plough here, half a pile of grit there. Still, it was good that he was able to go to church with us on Sunday."

"What about that building, honey? So historical! The pastor told your daddy that it was built in 1848, when Queen Victoria was on the throne of England."

"And to think Tyree was just open prairie then," said Robert, remembering sepia-toned photographs he'd seen from the 1890s when the town was new.

"I found Pastor McKellan and his wife a very charming couple."

"I'm still confused that he doesn't actually belong to our church."

"Your daddy saw his résumé and, take it from me, his theology is sound."

21

"I'm looking forward to Bible study on Wednesday," said Robert, dunking his cookie in the coffee, then glancing at his mother to see if she would disapprove.

She waved a finger at him. "Remember, not when we have visitors!"

"No, ma'am," he said with a smile.

"And how was your day, hon?"

"All those British accents made my head spin. And some of those words they use, like pudding for dessert, which they shorten to pud. We laughed a lot at that. My form teacher, Mr Colt, was just like the one in the film we saw on Sunday night."

"Mr Chips? Well, I never!"

"Oh, but Mom, the cussin' and blaspheming are rife!"

"I knew it would be, son, you just got to keep your ears closed to such filthiness and trust in the Lord. Now, who was that boy you mentioned on our way home?"

Robert smiled. "His name's Jack Moseley. He only lives just up the road from the school. Mr Colt kinda handed me over to him to show me around."

"And does this boy swear and hold the Lord's name in vain?"

"He swore a lot, but not like he was cussin'. He said swearing was endemic in the school, but I didn't know what that word meant."

"You'll have to look it up; we don't want you fallin' behind."

"He seemed kinda nice. A lot of the kids seemed friendly but, as far as I know, none of them are saved."

"That's why your real friends will be at Bible study, Robert. Meanwhile, you should set yourself a mission to bring all your classmates at school to Christ."

"That's a big job, Mom."

"Start with a single soul and others will surely follow."

"I gotta lot of homework. I thought they'd be easy on us on the first day back, but I gotta write a 250-word précis on

Coriolanus, that's a play by William Shakespeare, and twenty questions on algebra."

"Better get started then, hon."

"What's for supper, Mom?"

"English muffins, eggs over easy, cheese and bacon, with fruit salad for dessert."

"Hmm, yummy!"

***

5: Wednesday, 9th January. 6.05 p.m. The Ropewalk.

ROBERT

His bedroom in Pear Tree Cottage was becoming more like his own space and less a room where a visitor might spend a few days. His football helmet was on the dresser, as was a small silver-plated cup for winning the under-15s 100-metres freestyle race at the Tyree schools swimming gala. A white cross, which glowed electric blue in the dark, hung above his bed, and an Oklahoma State Cowboys pennant adorned the wall opposite. On the bedside cabinet was a 1980s Mickey Mouse two-bell alarm clock, inherited from a great-uncle. The old table which served as a desk had on it a Bible; a blurry, framed photograph of his parents holding a baby; a diary notebook, and a holder for pens and pencils. The centrepiece, though, was his laptop: its desktop image was a screenshot from Google maps of his home in Tyree.

Robert had studied the route from the cottage to the Baptist church on Westbury Avenue, judging that it would take him seven and a half minutes to traverse the distance, which meant he had another ten minutes to finish his geography homework.

At 6.20 p.m., he left the house with the route etched firmly in his mind. What he hadn't taken into account was the difference between a series of images taken at midday in springtime and the reality of a dark, midwinter's night. A

23

shortcut, across a small playground that looked simplicity itself, turned into a panicky search for the exit on the other side. Once he had found his way onto the maze of roads outside, he began to gather speed, ignoring the slippery ground, until on Westbury Avenue he was actually running. With one minute to spare, he opened the lychgate and trotted breathlessly up the path to the porch, where a grimy lantern shone a desultory light.

The main body of the church was in near-darkness, but a glow came from the vestry. Quickly, he crossed the nave, making his way up the north aisle to the open door, where he paused on the threshold. It was a drab room of unplastered limestone coated in beige emulsion. In a tight semi-circle around Pastor McKellan sat two girls and three boys, none of whom he recognised. On a side table lay a jug of orange squash, plastic tumblers and a plate of digestive biscuits. A vintage cast-iron radiator provided heat, with accompanying clangs from the pipework.

"Good evening, Robert."

"Good evening, Pastor McKellan."

"I thought you might have shown a little more enthusiasm on your first evening and got here in good time. As it is, we are about to start."

"Sorry, Pastor." Robert blushed, catching the eye of a fat-faced, pink-cheeked boy with a mop of curly hair, who patted the vacant chair next to him. The American went over and sat down.

"It is my intention that each of you will choose a subject or passage in the scriptures for you to present to the meeting, after which we shall discuss your findings..."

"Excuse me, Pastor, I have not yet been introduced to the other members of the group," said the American.

"Robert," the pastor said sharply, "it is not customary in England to interrupt a speaker who has the floor. We call it good manners. If you have a point to make, you should put your hand up. However, since you are new to the country, I shall make an allowance and answer your point. If you had managed to get here a few minutes early, there would have been time for such niceties. As it is, your five colleagues already know each other and they know who you are. Now, if you'll allow me to continue..."

"Ooo, tut!" murmured the pink-faced boy, his lips puckering into a smile that Robert found disconcertingly suggestive.

"....we shall do this in alphabetical order so that next Wednesday, Mary, you will begin. Do you have any particular subject in mind?"

Mary was holding a handkerchief to her nose and sniffing. Her eyes, behind a pair of dirty, round spectacles, were puffy and red-rimmed, as if she had been crying.

"I thought I'd do the miracle of the two loaves and five fishes," she responded, withdrawing the handkerchief just far enough away from her face for the words to be intelligible.

The American put up his hand.

"Yes, Robert?"

"Sorry, Pastor McKellan, but I think Mary means the miracle of five loaves and two fishes."

"That's what I said," she mumbled, this time not bothering to take the handkerchief from her face.

"Shall we get on?" It wasn't really a question from the pastor. "So we come to 23rd January, which will make it Jane's turn to choose."

Jane had been picking her nose incessantly with quick flicks of her thumb. It was just a nervous reaction, the American realised, but it made him feel queasy. Now, at the pastor's behest, the thumb stopped in mid-air.

"The story of Jesus and the centurion's servant."

"Ah, yes, Luke 7, an interesting choice... And so on to 30th January, Robert, what do you have in mind?"

"To be honest, Pastor McKellan, I haven't given any thought to a subject, because I wasn't aware of what we'd be doing. I've only just started to settle in, you see, and I have had a lot of school work." The American was feeling decidedly uncomfortable. Making excuses was not a pastime he enjoyed.

"Very well, let us go on to James."

James was clearly the eldest in the group, probably seventeen or even eighteen. His sallow face, his complexion made worse by acne, was framed by a tangle of long black hair that curled about his collar. He slouched rather than sat in his chair and appeared to be barely able to keep his eyes open. He shook his head at the pastor, but didn't speak. Robert noticed that the youth's fingernails were black with dirt and stained with tobacco, and the shoulders of his dark jacket were covered in flakes of dandruff."

"I'm sure James will have prepared a subject by the date fixed for him," said the pastor, seeming not to mind the boy's casual dismissal of his itinerary. "Callum, you will be on the 13th February."

This youth had the least mobile face of anyone Robert could think of. His eyes, too, had a curious blankness. Like Mary, he wore glasses, though his had silvery metal frames and were polished to a reflective shine.

"The betrayal of Jesus in the Garden of Gethsemane."

"I had in mind doing that whole subject during March, as a lead-up to Easter."

Callum nodded. "In that case, the Ten Commandments."

"Excellent! And, finally, Kieran?"

The pink-faced boy smiled.

"Well, Pastor McKellan," he said in an affected whisper, "I really want to look up a passage, but I can't decide between Sodom and Gomorrah."

James laughed quietly, the first sound he had made, but the pastor seemed completely unfazed and instead rose from his chair.

"I have some small business to attend to, so you may as well have your refreshments. I shall be back in ten minutes or so."

Kieran hurried to the side table and took up the jug of orange.

"Robert, will you give out while I pour?"

"Sure."

He took the first tumbler of squash to Mary.

"Are you all right?" he asked. She beheld him through the dirty glasses and red eyes and took the handkerchief away from her face.

"I did say five loaves and two fishes."

Before the American could reply, Kieran interrupted.

"Actually, Mary dear, Robert is right; you did say two loaves and five fishes."

The girl slumped back in her chair, as if she had been struck, then leaned forward and presented a thin wrist to the American, drawing up the sleeve of her cardigan as she did so. Robert almost dropped the tumbler he was holding. Stipples of bloodied flesh, like a zip fastener, were ranged up her arm.

"You're very naughty, Mary, frightening the poor boy like that," Kieran admonished, waggling his finger at her, then, making a gesture with his wrist that Robert had seen his mother make a thousand times, he added: "She's lactose, you know..."

"Allergies," elucidated Callum.

"She's allergic to everything!" Jane snickered, flicking her nose.

Mary took the beaker off him and gave a wan smile.

"They test me regularly at the clinic, but it's no good. Sometimes I wish I was already in Heaven."

When the rest of the orange and biscuits had been given out, the American sat back down next to Kieran. The pink face regarded him with an expression of surprised amusement, as if he knew some secret about him which he didn't know himself.

"Tell me, Robert, what state of the Union do you come from?"

"Oklahoma," he replied, trying to make his voice as deep as possible.

"Oh, and I thought that was a musical!" Kieran giggled, making that wrist gesture again and touching Robert lightly on the knee.

"Do you fancy him, K?" James interceded.

Kieran's face fell. "Am I being too..."

"Obvious?" said the older boy.

"Sorry, Robert," whispered Kieran, "but you are very nice."

The American could barely believe what he was hearing. He stared at the fat pink face with a mixture of incredulity and distaste, but said nothing.

Pastor McKellan re-entered the vestry.

"I'm afraid I'm going to have to end this session early," he said. "My wife's been taken ill."

Outside, the group of five hurried away into the night, leaving the American standing alone near the lychgate. He pulled out his gloves and slid them onto his hands. Overall, it had not been the experience he had either expected or wanted. He blew out a frosty breath and lifted his gaze to the stars shining brightly overhead, wishing they were above his home town of Tyree.

The porch door clanged shut and a key turned in the lock. A few moments later the pastor whisked by him.

"Goodnight, Robert. Do try to be on time next week."

"Yes, sir," he said automatically then, thinking himself impolite, called out, "I hope your wife is better soon."

***

6: Tuesday 15th January. 3.20 p.m. Swanford Community School.

ROBERT

This game is so lame, so disorganised; there's no strategy, everyone just runs round. There are too many players on the pitch and you can't even pass the ball forward!

The coach had just blown the whistle at the end of their half-hour practice game of rugby. 'Coach' was probably a rather grand title for Mr Harris, who was also their PE teacher, a big man, made even bigger by being at least a stone overweight, whose preferred way of teaching sport was 'do as I say' not 'do as I do'.

"How did you find it this week?" called Jack, trotting down the pitch towards him.

Robert took out his gum shield, which was another bone of contention. Was this and shin pads the only protection allowed?

"A bit better," he answered doubtfully.

"You're doing OK. You've got height in the line-outs and strength in the scrum. If you go on like this, you could make the team."

No, thanks, thought the American. Jack grinned at him and they began to walk towards the changing rooms.

"I've got an interview at Fruit and Flower on Saturday morning," said Robert.

"An interview? That sounds a bit highfalutin for the local veg shop."

"Do you know it?"

"Course, it's next door to the post office where my mum works, that's only five minutes on a bike from my house." The English boy paused. "Hey, would you like to hang out sometime?"

Robert knotted his brow. "I'd like to, but..."

"You could always come with us to the gym on Thursday nights. There's a session for teenagers, and we meet up at the Jewel Café afterwards and sometimes on Saturday mornings too, and maybe see a film in the evening..."

"Listen, can I give you a rain check on that?"

"Sure," said Jack in the nearest he could manage to an American accent.

They were last into the changing rooms and had to step over discarded boots, pads and kit to get to their places.

"Get your stinking teenage bodies into the showers," screamed Mr Harris above the din. "Moseley, Crittenden, you're dawdling like a pair of geriatric grandmas. Get a move on!"

"Very PC, isn't he?" said Max, throwing his rugby shirt into a supermarket bag.

"Probably got a date with Burger King."

"Forget Burger King, just show him the field of cows."

Jack and Max walked off together towards the showers, each with a towel over their arm, leaving Robert still in shorts and boots. This communal bathing was a new and really embarrassing experience for him. In his American school there had been cubicles and curtains, and some students had actually showered in trunks, while these English boys didn't seem to have any self-consciousness at all.

Last week, he had been first in and first out and very careful to avert his eyes at all times. The steam had helped. This week, he had intended to be last in, last out, but he had not taken into account Mr Harris, who now lumbered towards him like an angry hippo.

"Crittenden, you sorry excuse for a human being, why are you still not out of that kit? Are you married to it or something?"

"Sorry, sir. I was dreaming, I guess."

"Dreaming, boy? Not on my time you don't!"

Mr Harris tapped his foot, waiting with hands on hips, belly bulging against the black material of his tracksuit, while Robert, now blushing with shame, quickly stripped off the remainder of his kit, tied a towel round his waist and, eyes front, made for the shower room.

A gaggle of boys met him at the entrance, towels safely wrapped around themselves. He let them pass, then went into the tiled room of water, steam and bantering adolescent voices. It occurred to him that, in his rush to get away from Mr Harris, he had forgotten his shower gel, and he dithered at the towel rack, wondering if he should go back.

"Do you need some of this?" a familiar voice said. He turned to see Jack, naked and dripping, holding out his own bottle. "I've done that a hundred times."

Robert nodded, trying not to look at anything other than Jack's face, but his eyes had other ideas. First they strayed to the boy's nipples, were quickly averted to the bottle of Sanex, then descended in wilful disobedience past his navel to his genitals. But worse was to come, because there his eyes became transfixed, and the American's mouth, already open, dropped a further half-inch in astonishment. It has skin right to the end! His father's words came back to him: it's a real neat little package. He almost said them out loud.

"What's up?" cried Jack, checking himself out, fearing that something was wrong.

Robert, in confused panic, grabbed the bottle of gel from Jack and sped away into the watery ranks of naked bodies, his towel still wrapped around his waist.

***

7: Tuesday, 15th January. 3.50 p.m. Outside Swanford Community School, Leighton Lane.

JACK

Leaning back against one of the pillars that supported the school gates, Jack waited, determined to show Robert that he wasn't offended by what happened.

"Hey!" he said when the familiar figure emerged onto the pavement.

Robert jumped and his cheeks coloured.

"How did you get dry?" asked the English boy, grinning.

"I didn't, I'm all wet... Listen, Jack, I'm sorry, you must think I'm a pervert."

Jack laughed. "What happened in there?"

"At my old school in the States, we didn't shower together like you do here."

"Yeah, but you've seen a dick before – you've got one of your own."

Robert was so guilt-ridden by the whole incident that he hid his head in his hands.

"Jack, I can't talk about this. It's sinful. I looked at you and I shouldn't have. Satan is working within me."

"We all check each other on the sly; it doesn't mean anything."

"It does to me."

"Forget it," said Jack.

Robert looked at him. "I gotta go."

His face had such a tormented expression that Jack wanted to comfort him.

"OK, see you tomorrow and don't worry about it."

Jack watched Robert cross Leighton Lane and head for one of the side roads, and it occurred to him that he had never found out where he lived. Though Jack had spent his whole life in Swanford, there were parts on the south side of town that he didn't know at all.

**

8: Tuesday, 15th January. 4 p.m. 15 Leighton Lane.

JACK

"Hi," said Jack, entering the kitchen, which was really a kitchen diner and – unusually – situated at the front of the house. His mother, Pamela Moseley, known to all as Pam, was standing at the sink as usual, and his two brothers, Mikey, aged six, and Dan, aged thirteen, were seated at the table, where the family took most of their meals.

"Hello dear," said his mother. "Have you had a nice day?"

He shrugged and slung his bag down by the door.

"Jack Moseley, go and empty your kit into the washing machine this instant!"

He chuckled to himself at this familiar Tuesday evening ritual. "Oh, Jesus, I get home from a hard day at school and then you put me to work straight away, like I'm a slave or something, and I've got to do my paper round and I've got masses of homework..."

"Jack," piped Mikey.

"What do you want, squirt?"

"Dan's got an important match tonight."

"Oh, yeah?"

Dan looked up at him, nodding apprehensively. He was fairer than Jack, with fine, golden-brown hair cut short, a high forehead and a friendly smile which currently showed off a set of wire braces.

"Got a text from Coach Brennan saying that there'll be scouts from Woolgrove Wanderers Academy there tonight."

"This is your big chance then, LB."

LB was short for little brother, which Jack had always used as a term of endearment.

"Hey," he exclaimed, "we could all go up to the ground and support you!"

"Will you?"

"Yeah!" squeaked Mikey, looking at his mum.

"Now just hold on," said Pam. "As you just said, you've got your paper round and homework and the kick-off isn't until six-thirty and so it'll be way past Mikey's bedtime by the time we get back..."

"But, Mum," answered Jack, "just think – there we are on the terrace while LB is on the pitch running with the ball towards the goal. The scouts are just below us with their binoculars trained on this impressive young star of Swanford United Under-14s, and they hear us shouting, 'Go, Dan Moseley! You're the best, Dan Moseley! You're a star, Dan Moseley!' They've got to be impressed... even if we don't mean it," he added, grinning at his brother and receiving a metallic smile in return.

"And," he continued, "we could tie Mikey to a long pole and wave him above our heads, like a mascot. Then, at the end of the game, we could hammer the pole into the ground and leave him there."

"Yeah!" cried Mikey.

"Oh, don't be so mean to your little brother," scolded Pam.

Jack went to the sink and filled a mug with water, which he gulped down. He sensed his mother was wavering.

"Got to go. I'll get the paper round done quick. I should be back by six."

"I'll speak to your father," said Pam, "as he'll be the one doing the transport, if it happens."

"Great! See you..."

As he picked up his bike from the front garden, he heard his mother shouting from the door: "And what about this dirty kit, Jack Moseley?"

He grinned and pedalled away.

***

9: Tuesday, 15th January. 4.25 p.m. Ray's newsagent, the high street.

JACK

Mr Ray had been born in England, but was of Bengali extraction. His first name was Satyajit, but because of the difficulty in pronouncing such a conglomeration of vowels, most locals, including Jack, called him Mr Ray. His newsagent shop was situated in the high street about a hundred yards down from the post office.

"Good evening, Jack my boy, I hope you have had a very pleasant day."

Depending on his mood, Jack found the constantly repeated and unpunctuated use of Jack my boy either irksome or mildly amusing.

"Hello, Mr Ray."

"I've just had three miscreants from that damn Morcross School in here. They asked if I had anything for a penny, but all they wanted was to steal my Haribos."

"What happened?"

"I pointed to my sign 'Only two under-sixteens at any one time', then ushered them out with my broom."

"Did they go quietly?"

"They gave me the finger, but I've got them on my CCTV now, so they'd better be careful or I'll report them to our Crime Commissioner. I wish my shop was near your school, Jack my boy, where the nice children are."

"Mmm," replied Jack, doubtfully. In fact, Morcross, at the bottom of Church Lane, was almost as far from the newsagent's as his own school.

"Mr Green from number 25 has been complaining that you don't push the newspaper all the way through the letterbox, but that half remains out to get soaked by the rain."

"I try to push them all the way in, but some of those letterboxes are like gin-traps."

"That is very true; nevertheless, I don't want to risk losing customers on a technicality."

Jack nodded, having got the message.

"Now, Jack my boy, I make a humble request. My number-one son, Sandip, is having eyeball trouble, and has a doctor's appointment tomorrow night. Therefore, he won't be able to deliver the weeklies, which is a very important contract for me. Can you step into the breach and do a double?"

Eyeball trouble? You mean he can't keep his eyes open! Sandip was in Year Eleven at Swanford Community and had a reputation as the idlest time-waster in the school. Jack pictured him snoozing in the doctor's waiting room. Still, this would give him the opportunity to earn another fiver. Since starting the round, he had managed to accumulate almost £800 in his Post Office account, though that included £75 he had received in Christmas tips and £200 in gifts from relatives.

"OK, will I get a huge bonus for standing in for him?"

"Of course you will, Jack my boy."

This was a complete fabrication on Mr Ray's part, because he had never paid a bonus to any of his paper boys, ever, and Jack knew it, but he did enjoy asking.

***

10: Wednesday, 16th January. 6.10 p.m. The corner of the high street and Westbury Avenue.

<u>JACK</u>

It was a chill, foggy night, water vapour glistening on every surface. Rush hour, such as it was in Swanford, was over and there was little traffic and few pedestrians about. The south-east quadrant, as Mr Ray liked to call it, was a mixed, middle-class area of new developments, built in cul-de-sacs, and old-style ribbon housing running along Westbury Avenue, with large gardens sitting behind stone walls and privet hedges.

Jack locked his bike to the railings on the opposite side of the road to the church and slung the first of the two bags across his shoulder. He had considered carrying both sacks, but the weight of sixty copies of the Swanford Mail plus inserts would have been too much. Still, though the area was unfamiliar, it was routine work for him; the papers went through every door and so there were no numbers to consider.

Jack came parallel with Church Lane and looked across, noticing a group of five young people sauntering up towards the junction with Westbury Avenue. Immediately, he recognised the tallest member of the group. It was James Edison, famed among the youth of Swanford as the local drug dealer, with a reputation as a stoner. Strictly small-time, he normally only dealt in marijuana, but occasionally had been known to get his hands on amphetamines. His favourite haunt used to be the bushes around by the youth club, but when that closed, he moved his business to the alley beside the gym on Thursdays and the waste-disposal area behind the Roxy Cinema on a Saturday.

As the group came closer still, Jack was convinced that the rest were a contingent from Morcross House, a children's home, next to Morcross School, the bane of Mr Ray's life.

I expect they're going somewhere to have a smoke, he thought; well, more fool them! He was fairly certain that both Max and Charlie had sampled James's wares, but just the thought of the mixture of dope, dirt and dandruff made him want to vomit. He moved on quickly down Westbury Avenue, not wanting to become involved with them, and soon found himself on unfamiliar territory.

He stood before a pair of dilapidated wooden gates, painted green with insets of fleurs-de-lis in canary yellow. The front garden was overhung by the tangled branches of mature trees, their fallen leaves left to rot in thick piles on the driveway. The house itself had an unaccountably sad air, as if it pined for more youthful days. It's haunted, Jack thought, walking quickly down the drive towards a huge asbestos garage which stood at the side of the house. He made a sharp left and stepped onto the red tiles of the open porch, where he pushed a folded copy of the Swanford Mail through the letterbox. It dropped onto what sounded like a substantial pile of post and newspapers already lying there.

Half afraid, he pushed open the letterbox and peered inside. The hallway was dark and silent, but just within his field of vision he could see papers scattered over the polished floor.

I'll have to tell Mr Ray about this one, he said to himself, wondering why Sandip, or the postman, or someone hadn't made the effort. He made a mental note of the number: 41, then hurried back up the drive to the well-lit safety of Westbury Avenue.

"Jack!"

His imaginings of ghosts and hellhounds dissolved at the sound of the voice. Emerging through the mist came the smiling face of Robert Crittenden, encased in a knitted trapper hat.

Suddenly, he felt happy.

"Robert! Where are you off to?"

"I'm on my way to Bible study. I didn't know you lived here..."

"Don't be daft; you know I live on Leighton Lane." He showed the American his bag of newspapers.

"You're a delivery boy?"

"Yeah."

"You know, in the States, the paper boys throw the papers onto the front lawns."

"Imagine doing that here." He pointed back with his thumb to number 41. "That is one creepy place."

They stood for a few seconds just smiling at each other.

"I'd better go!" said Robert, "I got told off last week and I wasn't even late."

"Hey, give me your number," said Jack, fishing out his smartphone.

"But I haven't got a cell. My dad said he'd get me one, though."

"When you get that job at the veg shop, you'll be able to buy one of your own."

"If," corrected Robert, with a shy smile.

"You'll walk it, I know. And I'll make sure my mum comes and buys stuff from there."

"Jack, I'll talk to Mom about us hanging out, I promise. It's just a bit awkward for me."

The English boy grinned happily, knowing that, whatever else happened, Robert Crittenden would keep a promise.

"See you at school tomorrow then, buddy..."

***

11: Wednesday, 16th January. 6.25 p.m. Westbury Avenue.

<u>ROBERT</u>

The American reached the lychgate and looked up. Droplets of condensation hung in the air, sparkling in the glow of the street lamps. For some reason, he was elated. Tonight, whatever Pastor McKellan said to him would not bother him.

His thoughts returned to his meeting with Jack. I should try to bring him to Jesus Christ; he needs to be saved! But, even if I can't, he's still the most... Robert tried to think of a suitable word, but all the ones that kept popping into his mind were either too corny or inappropriate for one boy to think about another. Eventually, he settled on likeable, but allowed himself to put buddy on the end, as Jack had done. They were buddies, and he couldn't believe his mom wouldn't like Jack if they met. There was a lightness in his step as he entered the church.

***

12: Wednesday, 16th January. 8.15 p.m. Pear Tree Cottage, the Ropewalk.

ROBERT

"I'm home," he called, going to sit on the stool in the passage to take off his new black shoes. They were wet, so he set them by the radiator, hoping they would dry by the morning. I ought to have worn my brown ones to Bible study, he thought, peeling off his socks.

On passing the lounge he heard a familiar voice.

"Hi, Dad," he said, putting his head round the door. "You're back early."

"Hello, son; come on in and join us."

"I've just got to change my socks. It was a bit wet underfoot."

He scuttled up to his room, tossed the wet pair into the laundry basket, found a pair of quarter-length socks in his sock drawer and, without drying his feet, sat on the bed to pull them on. They felt uncomfortable.

It was then that he noticed the airmail letter on his desk. It was postmarked Oklahoma City, January 10th, and addressed to Robert Crittenden, Pear Tree Cottage, The Ropewalk, Swanford, England. He smiled. No zip code, and no county, but it got here just the same!

He opened it carefully and found, between the folded single sheet of paper, a ten-dollar bill. He held it up and smiled at the familiar sight, then slipped it into the empty note compartment of his wallet. The letter was, as he knew, even before opening it, from his Auntie Una, his mother's sister and the black sheep of the family.

Dear Robert,

I hope you are well and settling into life in little old England. I enclose a small gift in lieu of Christmas, when I didn't have cash enough to send anything.

I shall give you my email address and cell phone number so that if my skinflint of a brother-in-law ever buys you a cell, or – Heaven forfend – one of them new gadgets that does everything except pass water, we can keep in touch.

Your cousins Barney and Susie send their love.

We are quite well, and Tom and I have both found jobs with the City. I am now a School Crossing Guard; ain't that something?

Your loving aunt,
Una

PS Are you breaking any of those English roses' hearts yet?

Robert booted up his laptop and copied the email address and telephone number into his Windows contacts. Then he returned the letter to its envelope and filed it away in his 'home' folder.

By the time he got downstairs, his mother had made him a hot chocolate and set out a plate of biscuits.

"They're called jammie dodgers," she explained, as he eyed them suspiciously. "The lady in the supermarket said that English children love them."

He sat down on the sofa next to his mother and took one up, holding it between thumb and forefinger.

"May I?" he asked.

"Go ahead," said Frank, eyeing him from the armchair. "I can see standards have slipped since I've been away."

Robert smiled and dunked the biscuit in the chocolate milk, before biting off a good half.

"Hmm, not bad," he said.

"And how was your study, hon?" his mother asked.

The boy nodded. "Good, we did the five loaves and two fishes." He didn't mention that he could hardly hear Mary, as she read the text while sniffing and wheezing through her handkerchief, or that Jane had been sick after drinking the orange juice, or that Kieran had touched him on the leg again, or that James and Callum had said barely a word throughout the session.

"We discussed whether the account in Matthew of the seven loaves is actually the same event reported twice."

"What do you think, son?" asked his father.

"There are great similarities, but I think that the feeding of the five thousand is more poetically told."

"There is no doubt that the miracle occurred twice! Remember that the Biblical texts are infallible, and thus the feeding of the four thousand must have been different to the feeding of the five thousand."

"That's what Pastor McKellan said."

"He is a wise man, then."

"Did the pastor say how his dear wife is?" enquired Maybelle.

"He didn't mention her, Mom."

"And you didn't see fit to ask?" his father admonished.

"No, I didn't, sir, I got the feeling he didn't want to talk about it."

"We shall enquire again on Sunday," said his mother, firmly.

Robert took another biscuit and a drink of chocolate before broaching what he knew was a touchy subject.

"I read Aunt Una's letter."

His parents' faces clouded.

"When did that come?" asked Frank.

"Today," said Maybelle. "I had half a mind to throw it in the fire. However did she get our address?"

"She's still got friends in Tyree, Maybelle, and some of those friends are our friends too."

"Well, they wouldn't be if I knew who they were."

"And what has my sister-in-law got to say for herself?" asked Frank, turning to his son.

"She sent me ten dollars," the boy replied, trying to hide his pleasure, "and gave me her email and cell phone number."

"Well, you won't be needing those!" said his mother firmly.

"Now, Maybelle," said Frank. "Robert has always had a soft spot for his aunt, haven't you, son?"

"I guess."

"Only because he doesn't know the half of the shame she caused us."

"We must never forget, Maybelle, Una took him in, like the Good Samaritan in our time of strife," said Frank. "You email her back, son, and thank her for the gift."

Before Auntie Una had moved to Oklahoma City, she had lived only four blocks from her sister in Tyree and there was at least a familial cordiality between them. When Robert was ten, he had stayed with his aunt for over a month and they had formed a lasting bond. Her great rift with his parents had come a year later, when Una left the church and went to live with a man she was not married to. This was the Tom mentioned in the letter, and by whom she had since conceived Barney and Susie, his first cousins. But Robert was also aware that there was another, much older issue, between the family which had never been resolved. What did surprise him, though, was that when it came to Auntie Una, his normally strict and unyielding father was the more malleable of his parents.

"Mom, Dad, do you think I could invite a school friend over one night?"

His parents exchanged glances.

"Who is it, hon?" asked his mother.

"His name's Jack Moseley, I've mentioned him before."

"Has he accepted Jesus Christ as Lord and saviour?"

"No, sir."

"Do you think you could bring him to Christ?"

"I am willing to try."

Frank turned to his wife.

"Do you see anything wrong in this, Maybelle?"

"It's a pity it can't be one of your Bible study class, but I have no objection, as long as he is a nice, clean-living boy."

"His mom works in the post office."

"Hmm," said Maybelle, meaning that she was going to do a little checking up on her own account. "Would you like to invite him to supper?"

"That would be great. What day?"

"Your daddy and I will be doing some entertaining next week. Some important clients from Japan, which I shall have to plan and prepare for. Shall we say a week Saturday?"

"I'll check with Jack tomorrow to see if he can make it. Thanks, Mom."

"I'm afraid I won't be here to meet your friend, Robert. From next Thursday, I shall be escorting these clients around our sites."

"How long for, Dad?"

"Until just before they get bored, son."

***

13: Thursday, 17th January. 9 a.m. Swanford Community School.

ROBERT

The pupils of 4S filed into the classroom and, because Mr Colt had not arrived yet, there was a cacophony of noise. Robert sat down at his desk, in the second row, adjacent to Jack and Charlie.

"What are you looking so pleased about?" asked Max, who was already perched on the desk, feeling that he still had partial rights to it.

Robert looked up at Max as if to say, what are you talking about? Then he leaned in towards Jack.

"Would you like to come to my house for supper – not this Saturday, but the Saturday after, if you can make it?"

"Well, I'll have to consult my diary," he answered casually, though his beaming smile told a different story.

"Consult your diary, Moseley? That won't be difficult," said Charlie. "Blank, blank, blank, blank."

"Why is everyone listening in to our private conversation?" asked Jack.

"Because you didn't put a sign up saying private conversation, that's why."

"Is it evening dress?" asked Max. "And are we all invited?"

"No," said Robert and, having picked up a little on the English way, added, "and no."

"I think Jack would look good in a dress," said Charlie.

"The trouble is, you would start getting horny for me," replied Jack.

"And pigs might fly."

"Maxxy!" a voice cried from the back of the class.

"Oh, crikey! Coming, Manners."

"Manners!" said Charlie. "Where did that come from?"

"The same place as the checked trousers and cravat he was wearing on Saturday at the Jewel," said Jack. "The poor boy's in love."

Max sniffed. "Miss Simpkins and I have a relationship based on mutual understanding and intellectual respect."

"In other words, she can twist him round her little finger."

"I prefer to have relationships based on my cock," said Charlie, his eyes roving to Barbara in the row behind, who – fortunately for him – was deep in conversation with Alice Crabtree.

"I don't wish to continue this discussion," declared Max, rising from the desk.

"And neither do I," said Robert.

Mr Colt entered the room with a pile of exercise books, which he set down in a teetering stack on the corner of his desk.

"I'll let you know about Saturday week, for absolute certain, tomorrow," whispered Jack, as silence fell.

After registration, their form tutor once again took up the books and began an apparently random walk around the class.

"I asked you to write a 1,000-word essay on our pre-1914 poet, entitled, 'In what way did the life and times of Mr A. E. Housman affect his poetry?' It was to have been based on your own research, using whatever media you chose. Well, for better or worse, I have marked these singular works and in no particular order I am returning them.

"Miss Carter, B plus. Some interesting points, though I detected an overall lack of commitment. Mr Masefield, B minus – an improvement on your last effort, which, I confess, isn't saying much. Miss Simpkins, A star – but I expect no less. I was particularly impressed by your astute comparison between the poetry of Mr Alfred Edward Housman and the music of Sir Edward William Elgar, both Worcestershire men and both afflicted with a high degree of melancholy."

Mandy shrugged. "It's all on the web."

"Excuse me, sir?"

"Mr Crittenden, you have a question?"

"Didn't Sir Edward Elgar write that piece of band music we play when we graduate?"

"Robert, I'm afraid you seem to have forgotten which country you're in, but if you could perhaps, quietly, sing a few bars of this band music, I might be able to assuage your curiosity."

"La, la, la-la, la, laa, laa. La, la, la-la laa, laa..."

Mr Colt allowed the performance to go on for fifteen bars before holding up his hand.

"A fine rendition, Robert. I'm sure Mr Williams, our esteemed music master, would be delighted if you made your voice available to him. And you are correct: that is indeed the trio section of Elgar's Pomp and Circumstance March No. 1 in D, better known to we British as 'Land of Hope and Glory'."

"They play that at my dad's political meetings," said Stewart. "Loud."

"Hmm, I'm not at all surprised by that, Mr Henderson, but I'm not entirely sure that Sir Edward would approve. Now, back to business. Mr Seddon, an astounding A minus..."

"Crikey!"

"Yes, it seems sitting next to Miss Simpkins has allowed some of her shine to rub off on you. Mr Moseley, also A minus, scatter-brained, but not without merit..."

And so it went on through a further nineteen names until, finally, Mr Colt went back to his desk with one book still in his hand.

"Mr Crittenden, did you find particular difficulty with this essay?" He peered over his glasses at the American.

"I couldn't find anything about him, sir, except a few of the poems."

"Robert, we have something, upstairs, called a library. A library, a place for books: are you aware of its existence?"

"Yes, sir."

"Did you know that the school also has a room full of those modern technological marvels known as computers, packed with information and at your disposal?"

The American hung his head. "I'm sorry, sir, I just used my computer at home."

"And is your computer connected to the internet?"

"Yes, sir."

"It probably filters out fag poetry," said Stewart.

After a few titters, the class went silent. Mr Colt sighed, then sat back in his chair for a few moments, staring at the back wall, while his fingers beat out a funereal drum roll on his desk. Everyone sensed that the axe was about to fall.

"Mr Henderson," he said, in a calm voice that was nevertheless laced with menace.

"Sorry, sir," said Stewart, beginning to have doubts about his outburst.

"Mr Henderson, I have sent creatures like you to the headmaster for less."

"Oh, sir, please..."

"Your words would at least merit a detention with the redoubtable Ms Lane."

Most pupils considered a detention with the equality counsellor even worse than a meeting with the headmaster, and Stewart was no exception. He visibly blenched.

"...But, I think, in this particular instance there may be a kernel of wisdom in your vile and inappropriate words."

"Sir?"

Mr Colt turned his attention back to the American.

"Robert, will you see me at the end of the lesson? Don't be alarmed; you are not in trouble."

"Yes, sir."

"Now, Mr Henderson, you have a choice..."

"Oh, sir, I thought you'd let me off, for my kernel!"

"Don't be silly, Mr Henderson. As I said, you have a choice. Either an hour with the redoubtable Ms Lane, on a day that will suit you least, or you can learn one of Mr A. E. Housman's poems by heart and recite it out loud to the class tomorrow, after registration."

There was a look of panic on Stewart's face. He had gained a C in the essay which was about the average level of his achievements in all subjects, except for PE, in which, despite looking like a twelve-year-old, his wiry physique and natural agility made him an above-average athlete.

"I can't learn lines, sir."

Mandy Simpkins raised her hand.

"I'll help him, sir."

Mr Colt smiled.

"There you are, Mr Henderson, surely an irresistible offer?"

"Will you, Mandy?" asked Stewart, excitedly.

"Don't get any ideas, Jugs, this is purely business."

"Let us say eight lines. I'll leave the choice to your discretion."

At the end of the lesson, Robert waited patiently for Mr Colt to collect up his books and wipe down the board. When the classroom door closed on the last of the pupils, the form tutor sat at his desk and looked at his latest charge.

"Robert, have you been forbidden to use the library and computer facilities at school?"

"Not forbidden exactly, but my parents prefer me to use my own computer."

"Do you understand that restricting your access to information on any subject will have a deleterious effect on your prospects for the GCSE examinations next year?"

"I do understand, sir. I want to do well, but I don't want to disobey my parents."

"Robert, I haven't marked this essay, because there's nothing to mark. It would be an automatic F in an examination. I would like you to have another go at it. Are you willing to ask your parents to revise their edict, or would you like me to speak to them?"

"I shall speak to them tonight, sir."

"Good, thank you, Robert." Mr Colt handed back the exercise book. "I'll see you tomorrow."

***

14: Thursday, 17th January. 6.45 p.m. Pear Tree Cottage, the Ropewalk.

ROBERT

"This is delicious, Mom."

"Very nice, Maybelle."

"Cajun shrimp with fettuccine. It has lots of parmesan and cream. I am trying out dishes for our guests from Japan next week..."

"I will have to cut down on school dinners at this rate," said Robert, eyeing the peanut butter pie for dessert.

"It'll be back to scrambled eggs soon enough," replied his mother. "What does your friend, Jack, like to eat?"

"Almost anything, I think. He certainly likes his puddings, as he calls them. I'll know for sure tomorrow, Mom, about a week on Saturday."

"Frank, have you had enough? There's plenty more..."

"An excellent sufficiency, thank you, my dear."

"Dad, I'm having difficulty finding information on the laptop for an English literature essay, and my form tutor, Mr Colt, was asking if it would be OK if I could use the school computers."

Frank Crittenden put down his napkin.

"Robert, if you cannot find information on your computer, then there must be something wrong with the subject of this piece of writing."

"Everyone else has completed the assignment. Even Linda Woolley and Stewart Henderson got Cs. Mr Colt said that if I didn't repeat it, I would be given an F, which is the lowest grade."

"Tell me the title of this essay."

"'In what way did the life and times of Mr A. E. Housman affect his poetry?'"

"I have not heard of this man Housman – have you, Maybelle?"

"I only know the poetry of our beautiful hymns: 'Throw out the lifeline across the dark wave, Oh, grasp the strong lifeline, for Jesus can save....'"

"What do you know about him, Robert? Is he one of these modern, vulgar poets who use profane language and can't rhyme to save their lives?"

"No, he's an old English man. Mandy Simpkins, she's an A-star student, compared him to Sir Edward Elgar, who wrote our high school graduation march..."

"Well, you think no more about it, Robert. I'll deal with this Mr Colt and his poetry essay."

***

15: Thursday, 17th January. 8 p.m. 15 Leighton Lane.

JACK

There was no one in the kitchen when Jack arrived back from gym. He threw his bag down by the door, took off his shoes, got a drink from the fridge and walked through to the lounge. Mikey was in his pyjamas on the settee, having a bedtime story, Crocodile Boy Goes Down the Drain, read to him by his mum, while his dad was on the carpet by the TV, fiddling with a pair of old headphones which allowed him to hear the sound, without disturbing anyone else.

"I'm home," said Jack, throwing himself into the spare chair.

Roger Moseley looked up and gave him a distracted smile, then went back to his fiddling. He was still the tallest member of the family by an inch or two, but his broad shoulders, which both his eldest sons had inherited, didn't seem quite so broad as once they had, now that his hips and abdomen had filled out. His dark hair, another endowment to his eldest son, was greying at the temples and he would have had a noticeable bald patch on the top of his head if he hadn't decided one day to keep his hair permanently short, à la Bruce Willis.

Pam got to the end of a paragraph before addressing Jack.

"Have you put your kit in the washing machine?"

"Can't I have five minutes rest first?"

Mikey pushed himself against his mother.

"Go on," he squeaked.

"Where's Dan?"

"Upstairs in his room doing his homework, which is what you should be doing."

"Duh!" exclaimed Jack. "Can't this family chill for once in its life?" Then he added: "Are we doing anything on Saturday week?"

"Not as far as I know," his mum replied. "Are we, Rog?"

"What was that?" he answered, removing the right-hand earphone.

"Jack wants to know if we're doing anything on Saturday week?"

Roger shook his head, abstractedly, as if they never did anything, ever.

"I've been invited to spend the evening with a friend."

Usually friends were either Max or Charlie or their wider circle, and the word 'invited' was never mentioned. They just did things together.

"Jack's got a date," said Mikey.

"Shut up, squirt."

Pam looked at him as if to say, it would be lovely if it was a date, and you can tell us because we'll raise no objections; and how soon can we meet her; and are you going to get married; and when can I hold my first grandchild?

"It's not a date," he said, feeling the colour rising in his cheeks.

"Jack's gone red," said Mikey, holding his bare feet in his hands and rocking himself gently.

"Squirt, tomorrow I'm going to take you to that haunted house and dangle you through the letterbox, so that the starving dog can chew your toes off."

"Jack!" said his mother. Mikey giggled.

"What did Mr Ray say about that house?" enquired Roger, having finally given up on the headphones.

"Said he would inform the authorities."

"So, what about this date?" continued his dad, casually.

Jack sighed heavily. "It's not a date. His name is Robert Crittenden, he's an American, he's only been here a few weeks, OK?"

"Oh, that's nice dear," said his mother, then she became thoughtful. "There was a very statuesque American lady in the post office today. Flaming hair and done up to the nines; she was very polite, just like someone out of Gone With The Wind."

Could be his mum, thought Jack: statuesque, flaming hair and very polite, but I wonder if she's got the same goofy smile?

Pam put down Crocodile Boy Goes Down the Drain.

"Come on you, time for bed!"

"But you haven't finished the story yet!" protested Mikey.

"The story is that it's school tomorrow and you need a good ten hours' sleep."

"Night, squirt."

"Give your brother a kiss," ordered his mother.

Jack grimaced as Mikey climbed onto his chair, put his arms round his neck, then licked him on the cheek.

"Disgusting!" cried Jack and blew a wet raspberry on Mikey's forehead. They began to giggle then, as they tried to outdo each other in slobber. It was a favourite ritual and went on until Pam decided enough was enough and whisked the six-year-old into her arms and carted him off upstairs.

When they had gone, Roger sat down on the sofa and eyed his eldest son.

"You know he's going to twig one of these days, don't you?"

Jack grinned evilly. "When he's twenty-two, probably."

"He's not daft and you don't want to hurt his feelings."

The boy rocked his head and raised his eyes to the ceiling.

"OK! I'll try not to call him squirt quite so often."

***

16: Friday, 18th January. 8.55 a.m. Swanford Community School.

ROBERT

Half an hour with Mr Colt, then maths; Friday assembly; break; history and double science in the afternoon. Robert put his timetable back in its folder. Not too bad; only four real work periods, though he found double science got a bit tiring towards the end.

Jack entered the classroom and sidled over to his desk.

"I'm OK For Saturday week," he said with a grin. Robert was about to reply when Mandy's voice cut through the din, silencing everyone.

"Right, listen up you lot. Jugs and Maxxy are putting on a little performance after register..."

"For one night only," murmured Max, while Stewart looked around, hoping everyone was paying attention.

Robert exchanged glances with Jack, as if to ask, what's this all about?

"So," continued Mandy, "I don't want any sniggering, interrupting or general fucking about from you ignorant lot of tossers, and at the end I want appreciation."

"How will we know when it's finished?" asked Linda Woolley.

"Because, you slapper, I've printed out twenty copies of the bleedin' poem and all you need to do is listen for the last line."

"Why have you gone to so much trouble for Henderson?" asked Henry.

"Adams, if it's any of your business, I'm trying to kill him with kindness."

"I think it's because Mandy is quite a nice person at heart," drawled Robert.

Jack sat down, laughing to himself, as Mandy's eyes narrowed and her lips pursed and unpursed several times in quick succession. Finally, she wandered casually towards Robert and made herself comfortable on his desk, folding her arms and swinging her long legs gently to and fro.

"Crittenden..." she said at last, looking down at the American.

"Yes, ma'am?"

"Don't yes, ma'am me, you smarmy git. You come over all sweet and Jesus-y, but in actuality you're a fuckin' clit-teaser on the quiet, aren't you?"

Robert was baffled both by the remark and the effect it had on the rest of the class. He looked at Jack, but he was doubled over his desk, his shoulders shaking with mirth.

Mandy stood up.

"And what's the matter with you, Moseley, are you having a wank under that desk?"

The door slammed. Mr Colt strode to the front of the classroom. His face had a red tinge, his jaw was working furiously, his eyes glared. He slammed a book down on the desk.

"Be quiet!" he ordered. "Miss Simpkins, get back to your desk immediately. I will not tolerate this uproar!"

Mandy scuttled back to her seat while the rest of the class sat bolt upright in shocked silence.

"After registration there will be five minutes of quiet contemplation while I set you a twenty-minute précis on Coriolanus, which will be carried out without any talking."

Stewart Henderson's face fell. He had worked for nearly three hours on the poem with Mandy and Max. They had even gone to Max's house after school to rehearse which, if truth be told, he had enjoyed more than he could have imagined.

Mr Colt's eyes scanned the class, then came to rest on Robert, where they froze into orbs of ice.

"Robert Crittenden..."

Robert blinked nervously, and his mouth fell open.

"Yes, sir?"

"Get out a pen and paper."

Knowing he was in trouble, but not knowing why, Robert did as he was told, but in the complete quiet, every scrape and scratch he made seemed like a provocation.

Mr Colt drummed his fingers impatiently. "Hurry up, boy!"

"I'm ready sir," he said, holding his pen in a trembling hand.

"Here is the title of the essay you are to write in substitution for the one you were set yesterday. 'Compare and contrast the poems 'London' by William Blake and 'Upon Westminster Bridge' by William Wordsworth.'... Have you got that?"

"Almost sir, sorry." He swallowed nervously. "You said 'On Westminster Bridge' by William...?"

"'Upon Westminster Bridge' by William Wordsworth!"

Robert's normally neat writing became a spidery scribble as he set down the essay title before it disappeared from his mind.

"I shall expect one thousand words by first thing on Monday morning. Is that clear?"

"Yes, sir."

"And I hope you are satisfied," said Mr Colt, half to himself. He turned, meaning to go to his seat, but out of the corner of his eye glimpsed Jack leaning into Robert in order to whisper something.

He whirled round and roared: "Moseley! What did I tell you about talking?"

The boy looked up, wide-eyed with shock.

"Well, are you deaf or just plain stupid?"

The boy rocked back in his chair, his shoulders hunched. He had never been spoken to like this, and certainly not by his form tutor.

"Stand up!" ordered Mr Colt.

Jack struggled to his feet and those nearest him could see that his eyes had filled with tears. And those nearest to him included Mr Colt, whose expression of concentrated fury changed in just a few seconds to one of self-absorbed abstraction and then to a calm awareness of what had just happened.

"Jack," he said.

The boy laboured to meet the gaze of his teacher, but eventually their eyes met.

"I'm most profoundly sorry. Please, resume your seat."

Jack wiped his eyes quickly on his sleeve, but didn't immediately sit down.

"Sir, is everything all right?"

Mr Colt smiled, more to himself than at the boy in front of him.

"Bless you, Jack, for showing an old fool how to behave with grace in a trying situation. Everything is much better now, thank you."

Form 4S gave a collective sigh of relief, as the storm clouds passed.

"I think it would be better for us all if, after register, I left you for the remainder of this period..."

Mandy raised her hand.

"Excuse me, sir, you've forgotten about Jugs' – I mean Stewart's – punishment."

Mr Colt looked hard at Mandy and then at Stewart and did not see the expressions he was expecting.

"Miss Simpkins, are you up to something?"

"No, sir. It's just that after sweating blood over Stewart's poem, it would be a shame not to hear it."

"Very well. Are you agreeable, Mr Henderson?"

Stewart nodded.

"And Max, sir."

56

"Mr Seddon?"

"Oh, crikey, yes me, sir."

"How intriguing."

After the register had been taken, Mr Colt retired to the back of the class, while Stewart and Max went to stand together at the front. At least in height, they could have been man and boy. Mandy handed out the copies of the poem and when she had finished she eyed the audience.

"You lot remember what I said, or there'll be consequences..."

Then, in her role as prompter and director, she took a seat along the eye line of the performers and nodded for them to begin.

Stewart cleared his throat and in a nervous, but clear, voice began.

"When I was one and twenty, I heard a wise man say..."

They turned to face each other and Max waggled his finger at his little protégée.

"Give crowns and pounds and guineas, but not your heart away; Give pearls away and rubies, but keep your fancy free."

Stewart turned back to the audience and shook his head.

"But I was one and twenty, no use to talk to me..."

Mandy nodded encouragingly and mouthed the beginning of the next line, which the boy took up.

"When I was one and twenty, I heard him say again..."

Max bore down sternly on Stewart.

"The heart out of the bosom, was never given in vain; 'Tis paid with sighs a plenty, and sold for endless rue."

Stewart faced the class now, his eyes forlorn, his hands gesturing defeat, and in a sad voice intoned: "And I am two-and-twenty, and oh, 'tis true, 'tis true."

The class didn't need Mandy's threats. It erupted into applause, whistles and cheers. The three stars bowed low in acknowledgement and then like true actors joined hands and bowed again. Mr Colt beamed at them and clapped as loudly as anyone. At last, he returned to the front and raised his hand for silence.

"I am humbled," he said. "Class, this morning you have given me a lesson I sorely needed, and restored my faith in the goodness of humanity. Mr Henderson, eight lines exactly: you are absolved. Please resume your seat."

The class settled and Mr Colt looked at the clock. It was 9.28.

"I would suggest that the three of you consider a similar performance in the end-of-year concert. I'm sure Mr Williams, our esteemed musical maestro, and organiser of that fête de l'humanité, would be only too pleased to offer you a spot. Now, I think it time you made your way to the science block and into the stimulating hands of Mrs Gutteridge."

Of all the bodies in that room, only Robert felt that he was not part of that moment of celebration, of togetherness. As he sat and thought about what had driven Mr Colt to such uncharacteristic rage, it became clear to him what must have happened. The fact that he felt guilty about it meant that this alien culture had a certain allure for him, even as his parents had predicted it would. He realised that it would have to be fought against, if he wasn't going to succumb to its temptations. He must find sanctuary in the teachings of the church, in the love of his family and most particularly in prayer.

***

17: Friday, 18th January. 10.50 a.m. Swanford Community School.

JACK

For once, assembly had not overrun, and class 4S were at break, along with another fifteen classes. The downside was that it was raining and they were all cooped up in the same hall where the assembly had taken place. Most pupils were arranged around the periphery, some leaning back against the walls, while others sprawled on the floor.

"How dreary it is," said Max, spooning strawberry yogurt into his mouth. "Even for one so full of grace as you."

"Shut up fuck features," retorted Jack. "You two were really good though. I didn't realise Stewart had it in him."

"I shouldn't be at all surprised if Manners isn't hot-footing it to Welsh-Williams' door to propose an encore at the school concert. She's a bit show-bizzy, you know."

"With Stewart panting after her."

"I'm afraid he's in a much lower division than she," said Max. "In fact, we probably all are."

Charlie bounced up to them, crunching a Club orange. "You'd better watch it, Maxxy, I think your girlfriend has the hots for the Yank."

"You mean the clit-teaser?" stated Max. "Ah, talk of the devil."

Robert was weaving his way towards them with a serious look on his face.

"Where have you been?" asked Charlie.

"To pray," answered the American.

The three friends looked at each other, then back at Robert.

"In the middle of the morning?" enquired Charlie. "And we've just had assembly..."

"I had some questions," answered Robert.

Max stopped spooning. "And did you get answers?"

"Some..."

"Lucky you; the best I've ever had is empty silence."

"That's because you don't accept Jesus Christ as your saviour."

"I would accept him, but I don't think he would accept me."

"He accepts everybody as long as they repent their sins and are saved."

Max licked his spoon clean.

"Do you ever sin, Robert?"

"Yes, but I ask forgiveness."

"Is being a clit-teaser a sin?" enquired Charlie, crunching the last bite of his Club biscuit.

Robert looked at him. "I don't know what that word means."

"Maxxy!"

"Oh crikey, it's Manners. Must go, chaps. See you next period."

"And I've got to see a man about a dog," said Charlie, giving them a wave, before making for the exit.

The American watched him go with a puzzled expression on his face.

"I don't understand half the things he says."

Jack sat down on his haunches. "He's going to the toilet."

There was a long moment of silence between them, then Robert sat beside him.

"My dad got Mr Colt to change my essay."

"How did he do that?"

"I don't know exactly."

"But why?"

"Because A. E. Housman was a pervert; a homosexual."

Jack looked at Robert. "He was gay, but does that make him a bad person?"

"In the eyes of God it does."

"Is that what your church teaches you?"

"No, it's what the Bible says."

"How did you know all that, if you couldn't find out anything about him?"

"Because I went against my parents' wishes and looked it up on the school computer just now, and that's why I prayed for forgiveness."

"Are you going to tell them?"

"I expect so."

"Do you tell your parents everything?"

The American shook his head. "Some things are too shameful. Then, I have to pray to our Heavenly Father and hope he will forgive my wickedness."

Jack shook his head. "You're not wicked, Robert. You're the least wicked person I've ever met."

"Will Mr Colt forgive me?"

"Depends how good your essay is," said Jack with a smile. "I've never seen him so angry."

"He nearly made you cry," said Robert. "I hated that."

"Thanks for reminding me," said Jack testily, but inside he was quite touched by the words.

"Jack, what is a clit-teaser?"

"Oh, Robert, it sounds really dirty when you say it. Say it again!"

The American blushed. "No! It's swearing, isn't it?"

"Have you never done sex ed.?"

"Yes – we learned that sex before marriage is a sin, and anything that promotes sex before marriage is a sin."

"But do you know what sex is?"

"Yes, it's when you plant your seed inside a woman."

Jack began to giggle and then to laugh. "That sounds more like gardening!"

Robert looked away.

"If you're offended by what I just said, I'm certainly not going to tell you what a clit-teaser is."

"Please, Jack."

"Only if you look at me first and smile." The English boy pitched his voice an octave higher. "Come on, Robert, give Jack a smile, please."

The American raised his head. "Don't be so lame," he said, trying to sound annoyed, but when he caught sight of Jack's grin, he couldn't help but smile himself.

"That's better. Now, this is your first real sex ed. lesson. You know what a clitoris is?"

Robert shook his head.

"A clitoris is like a very small penis inside a woman's vagina. It's what turns her on. When it's rubbed it grows erect..."

The bell rang to signal the end of break. The American held his head.

"I don't want to know any more, Jack. All those disgusting words."

"It's not disgusting, it's natural."

Robert picked up his bag and got to his feet.

"It makes me feel sick."

***

18: Monday, 21st January. 8 p.m. 15 Leighton Lane.

JACK

Two taps on Jack's door made him pause the games console and take off his headset. He was glad, really, as he had been playing for an hour and his eyes were beginning to smart. In addition, he had yet to start a 500-word essay on 'the role of the plebeians in Coriolanus with contrasting examples', and it was due in tomorrow.

"Come in, LB," he called.

The boy padded in barefoot, managing to avoid the debris of clothes, magazines, games, sweet wrappers and bottles strewn across the floor.

"What you doing?"

"Stuff," replied Jack, swivelling in his chair to face his brother. "Actually, I've just crossed to the Isle of the Dead where I've been sent to find the Landburger's treasure chest."

Dan sat on the bed, his face downcast.

"Coach just texted. No practice tomorrow: snow and ice on the pitch."

"That's not why you're down in the dumps."

"I thought I'd have heard by now, if it was going to happen."

"Dan, it's been less than a week."

"We're top of the league after Saturday. Surely they know how good we are? Any one of us could make the Academy."

"Patience, my son, girt not your sword and shield just yet, as the Landburger said to me earlier."

Dan smiled, crossed one leg over the other, and began massaging the toes of his right foot. "Actually, I'm quite glad we've got no practice tomorrow, it'll give these time to heal." He removed the hand so that Jack could see how red and swollen the toes were. "I was stamped on by their bastard of a full-back."

Jack held out a packet of Black Jacks, but Dan shook his head. "I can't wait to get these braces off, then I'm going to eat a zillion sweets."

"Yeah, but I won't offer then."

"What are you getting Mikey for his birthday?"

Jack crossed over to his computer and brought up a screen.

"How about this? I ordered it yesterday."

"I like it," said Dan, "Can you get me one for my birthday?"

The transparent piggy digital coin counter stared out at them from the screen.

"With the battery, postage and card, and a few coins, it comes to about £12."

"God! I can only afford a fiver, especially as your birthday's in three weeks."

"Don't worry about me, LB," said Jack, "a packet of Maltesers would be great."

"Guess what Mum and Dad are buying him?"

"Does it begin with P and end in O and is it available on Blu-ray?"

"Correct; that boy is so camp. I wonder why your birthdays are so close and mine falls in September."

"Well, if you work back nine months, you might find out. I think you were a Christmas present."

Dan blushed.

"I'd never thought of that."

Jack chuckled.

"I don't think there's any reason for me and Mikey."

"I definitely want a bike for my next birthday, then I won't have to borrow yours."

"That'd be good, if they can afford it."

"I think we're going to Malaga at Easter, so there must be some money somewhere."

"I quite like that idea," said Jack, and thought how great it would be if Robert could go too.

"Better shove off," declared Dan, "still got homework to finish."

"Me too. Good to chat, LB."

***

19: Wednesday, 23rd January. 7 a.m. Ray's newsagent, the high street.

JACK

"I'm very sorry Jack my boy."

"Huh?"

"Local Hero Saves Pensioner," ran the headline in the latest edition of the weekly Swanford Mail, above a picture of a beaming Mr Ray and his son Sandip. The article went on:

"A paper boy on his round in Westbury Avenue had the wit and foresight to realise that something was seriously wrong at the home of Mrs Elspeth Chambers (83), when he discovered the house in darkness and a pile of newspapers on the floor..."

"Jack my boy, the main thing is that between us we managed to save the life of poor Mrs Chambers."

"So why is it that I'm not mentioned at all, whereas Sandip, who wasn't even there, gets his photograph taken with a sack of newspapers around his neck, as though he was the paper boy concerned?"

"You know what these terrible rags are like. Never let the truth get in the way of a good story. I'm afraid your contribution got lost in translation. In any case, the reporter with the camera, Mr Little, a very nice man, said he had a deadline to meet."

Jack shook his head in disbelief, slinging the bag full of thirty morning dailies around his neck.

"I'll see you later, Mr Ray," he said.

"Mind the ice, Jack my boy, it's treacherous underfoot."

***

20: Thursday, 24th January. 6.05 p.m. Swanford Health and Fitness Club, Malton Road.

JACK

Jack padlocked his bike to the rack and sauntered up the steps at the entrance to the gym. Junior night usually garnered around fifteen to twenty of Swanford's youth, with eighty per cent being boys. Charlie, Max and Jack had been members for a little over a year, and it was as much a social evening for them as a chance to improve their fitness. They all considered it a step up from the barking of Mr Harris, their PE teacher.

Jack passed his card to the woman on reception, who swiped it on her till.

"Anyone else here yet?"

"Just the Henderson boys." she answered with a knowing look. "Code's ten sixty-six."

"Thanks." He took the card and made his way to the dry changing rooms, where he found Stewart Henderson sitting alone on the tile benches.

"Hey, you OK?" Jack hung up his bag and began to undress. A week ago, he would have ignored, or just not bothered to notice, the skinny, unprepossessing figure with the prominent ears: after all, he was a Henderson.

Stewart looked up at him, wondering why he was being talked to by a class hot-shot. His right eye was still half-closed and purple-yellow from 'walking into a door', as he had

65

explained to Mr Colt on Monday. He half-smiled in case it was a tease, and gave a little shrug.

Jack took off his shirt and noticed that his armpits smelled sweaty. That's through not having a shower this morning, not changing when I got home, and then rushing through my paper round with a nylon parka on. He took one step away from Stewart, then realised it would probably seem like an unfriendly gesture.

"Sorry, I'm a bit sweaty," he said.

The small boy nodded, then smiled admiringly. "I wish I was as built as you."

Jack did not consider himself 'built'. All he saw when he examined himself in the mirror was an expanse of white, punctuated by dark tufts of hair in his armpits, small, dark pink nipples, some shadows of ribs and a hollowed-out navel.

"Thanks, but my little brother's got more muscle than I have."

Max and Charlie blew into the changing rooms, their chatter echoing off the walls.

"Move over, Jugs," said Charlie, throwing his bag down.

"Hey, do you mind, we were talking!" said Jack, pushing the bag back at his friend.

"Sor-ree," said Charlie, snatching the bag and finding another spot.

"Stewart, who punched you in the eye?" asked Max, which was the question everyone had avoided asking at school, even though it was the week's most popular gossip. "And don't tell me it was a bloody door."

The boy shook his head and looked down at his feet.

"Come on then, Stewart, get changed," said Jack, "we're nearly ready."

"They don't want me in there," said the boy.

"Who?" asked Max.

"My brothers."

"No offence to your shared genes, but who cares what a bunch of Neanderthals say. Just come in with us. They won't dare try anything on while Si's around."

Si was Simon Hazeldene, the fitness instructor. He was respected by all the young people and most of the more elderly ones too, not least because he was six feet three inches tall and weighed fourteen stone, and did not have an oversized gut.

"There's always afterwards, though," warned Jack.

"After the session, they'll be too stoned to care."

"I'd better not," said Stewart, "thanks all the same."

The three friends left the changing room and made their way down the corridor to the gym. Charlie punched ten sixty-six into the keypad and they entered.

The room smelled of hot bodies, despite the air-conditioning. Five video screens lined the wall above the rank of cross-trainers. Four of the channels required headphones to hear the audio, while the fifth was a bespoke pop video station which blared out music into the room. Barbara Carter waved at them from the treadmill, where she and Alice Crabtree were burning calories. The Hendersons were all in the weights area, which they pretty well monopolised throughout the session. Charlie went for the treadmill next to Barbara, while Jack and Max went to warm up on the two rowing machines.

They both input 1200 metres at resistance setting 5, the midway point, the competition being who could do the distance fastest.

"You all right, lads?" Simon greeted them.

"Si," said Max, turning to face him. "Stewart Henderson is in the changing rooms and he won't come into the gym because he's afraid his brothers will bully him. I think one of those bar-stewards has already given him a black eye, though Stewart says he walked into a door."

The fitness instructor nodded slowly as the tale unfolded and his eyes narrowed.

"Why?" he asked.

"Probably because he gave a poetry reading in class," answered Max, blandly.

"OK, leave it with me."

Ten minutes later, Jack was pulling twenty kilograms on the Radiant machine by the door, when Si came back in with his arm draped around Stewart's shoulders. The slight boy had on an oversized black T-shirt, faded to grey; baggy blue pyjama shorts and a pair of plimsolls without socks. He was visibly trembling.

"Derek!" called Si. "Can I have a word, please?"

Exercise stopped, chatter ceased. The only sound was the background music as all eyes turned to the eldest Henderson. At the age of eighteen, Derek was dark, lean and muscular and cut an intimidating figure, which was precisely the image he and his father wanted to communicate. But when he came to stand before Si, he was half a head shorter and an arm's width narrower.

"Why did you leave Stewart in the changing rooms? You know it's against the rules."

"No, I don't."

"Well, you do now. So, why did you leave him in the changing rooms?"

"Because he's a fuckin' minge."

"Keep it civil, Derek, or you won't be in here again."

"Because we don't want him near us."

"How did he get this black eye?"

"He walked into a door."

"No, he didn't. As part of my course, I do medical training, and I can tell you that this black eye is the result of a punch. Am I making myself clear, Derek?"

"You can't pin anything on me!"

"That is true, and since Stewart won't tell me what really happened, I have no evidence to pin it on anyone. However, I also noticed when your brother was getting changed that he had bruises on his stomach and kidney area."

"As I said, I know nothing about it."

"Well, Derek, perhaps you'd be good enough to tell all your family members that I shall be writing a report about this. Next week, if Stewart doesn't turn up, or has further marks on his body, I shall inform both the police and the social services department, is that clear?"

The eldest Henderson stood for a few moments, weighing up his options. First, he looked up at Si and then down at Stewart. Finally, he turned to his brothers.

"Let's sling our hooks, boys," he said. "There's more fun to be had elsewhere."

Though there was disappointment among the three siblings, Derek's word was law.

"You come too," he said, pointing at Stewart.

"No," said Si. "I haven't finished talking to him yet."

When the door closed on the four Henderson brothers, there was a spontaneous round of applause and Max, uncharacteristically demonstrative, punched the air and shouted, "Way to go, Si!"

The remaining half hour passed quickly. Now that the weights and bench area were free, for once, most boys took the opportunity to have a go. Max had Stewart lie on his back on one of the benches and watched over him while he attempted to lift two four-kilogram weights vertically into the air. He managed eight before tiring, while Jack and Charlie easily doubled those scores without feeling any strain.

Back in the changing rooms, Stewart shyly slid off his T-shirt, revealing the yellowing bruises on his front and back.

"Is that why you missed games on Tuesday?" asked Jack.

The boy nodded.

"Bastards," said Max. "We're meeting Manners at the Jewel in fifteen minutes – do you want to come?"

Stewart's eyes lit up for a moment, then went dim.

"I haven't got any money."

"You don't need any money," answered Jack. "We'll chip in for you."

"Why are you so thin?" asked Charlie with his usual tact. "You look like you've been in one of them camps they told us about in history."

"I'm just not hungry most of the time."

They showered and dressed and were outside the gym in no time, where a familiar sweet scent permeated the frosty air. From the dark alley that ran by the side of the fitness centre came the sound of laughter and four tiny pin-pricks of orange light which dimmed and grew bright again illuminating a haze of marijuana smoke.

"Wankers," whispered Max, "they couldn't be more obvious if they did it in the middle of the high street."

"They don't usually let Alan smoke," murmured Stewart.

Alan was the youngest known Henderson, a boy of thirteen. Short, stocky and blond, he was the only fully legitimate member of the clan, since Councillor John Henderson Snr had married Lisa, the boy's mother, some fifteen years previously in a bid to gain some political respectability. The birth had been like a good omen for the family because their star had risen dramatically both in terms of wealth and influence, particularly in the past two years, since John Henderson Snr's defection to the newly formed UK Majority Party. At the last local elections the party's representation had quadrupled, and was now the dominant force on the council. This made him the favourite to become the first elected mayor next year.

"Hey, boys!"

They turned to see James Edison walking out of the shadows. Unusually, he wasn't touting on his own tonight, but had a girl with him.

"Got some good stuff," he said. "Half a gram for five, quarter gram for three."

I expect that includes seeds, stalk and dandruff, thought Jack. I'd rather eat worms. But he could see that Max and Charlie were tempted.

"Hello," he said to the girl, hoping he could divert his friends' attention.

"Hello," she sniffed, keeping the handkerchief she was holding firmly attached to her nose.

"This is Mary," said James, "she's my muse."

In the distance a police siren sounded.

"Sounds like your dad's coming, Charlie," said Jack.

"Some other night, perhaps," said Max, pointing back down the alley with his thumb. "When those twats aren't around."

James waved his finger in a semi-circular motion around his temple and as quickly as he had come faded into the night with Mary tagging along beside him.

"I've not seen her before," declared Charlie.

"I have," said Jack. "I think she's from Morcross House. I saw them coming up Church Lane when I was on my round."

"Is that when you found the old lady?" asked Stewart.

"I'll tell you all about that when we get to the Jewel," answered Jack.

"Oh, no!" exclaimed Max. "He's got a new audience for his hard luck story."

***

21: Thursday, 24th January. 7.25 p.m. The Jewel Café.

JACK

Although the high street was the main shopping area of Swanford, the geographic centre was the square, a paved rectangle planted with silver birch trees under which park benches had been placed. On the east side was the council building where Roger Moseley worked, and among the premises on the west side was the Jewel Café. A family-run enterprise, it had been in the Crabtree family since the 1970s and had managed to keep up with passing fashions without losing its character. It was now a strange hybrid of tea shop and American-style fast-food outlet, and was successful in catering to young and old alike. Sam Crabtree – brother of Alice – and Andy Venables, both year thirteen students at Swanford Community School, shared the waiting table duties.

Warm air and the smell of freshly ground coffee enveloped them as they entered from the ice-sheened pavement. Except that the café did not have a licence to sell

71

alcoholic drinks, you might have been walking into the lounge bar of a typical English pub. Instead of beer pumps and optics to dispense spirits, there were soft drinks on tap and espresso and milkshake machines behind the green-tiled bar. In the back, through a swing door, was the thoroughly modern kitchen, where Ilona or Richard Crabtree prepared the food for which the café was renowned. However, to most people what made the Jewel a little bit special was the three antique crystal chandeliers which hung in sparkling decadence from the roof and gave the café not only its ambience, but also its name.

Half the booths were already taken. Mandy Simpkins was sitting in the most secluded one around the corner of the L-shaped room, drinking a banana milkshake through a straw. The only drawback to being in this booth was its proximity to the door to the toilets, whose opening and closing in busy times would cause a continual draught of disinfected air to waft over the occupants.

"Maxxy," she said, patting the seat next to her, "and Jugs too! What are you doing here?"

The boy gave a languid smile and shrugged, slipping into the place opposite her, a little colour coming to his cheeks as he gazed admiringly at the girl.

"He's been having a spot of bother with his brothers," explained Max.

"A lot of bother, actually," said Jack, as he and Charlie joined Stewart on that side of the booth.

"Perhaps, Manners, we could start calling him by his proper name, too?"

She leaned forward.

"What would you like me to call you, Jugs?"

The boy looked at Mandy and his colour heightened.

"Stew," he said.

Mandy sat back. "Stew it is, then."

"Hi, guys, can I get you anything?" Andy Venables stood in his black waiter's shirt and trousers, pad and pencil in hand.

"Coke and fries, please," said Charlie.

"Same," said Max.

"What do you want, Stew?" asked Jack.

"Tea."

"OK, one tea, and I'll have a strawberry milkshake and a toasted EBLT cut into four with fries."

"Blimey, you're splashing out, Moseley," said Charlie.

Andy totted up the bill. "That's £2 each for the Coke and fries, and Jack's comes to £6.50. It'll be about ten minutes."

"No rush," said Max as he and Charlie handed over loose change, while Jack fished in his wallet, drawing out a £10 note. Andy gave them their change and then went off to sign in their order.

"James Edison was outside the gym," said Max. "He'd got a girl with him."

"Maxxy, I hope you're not going to go all vampire-eyed on me."

"No, Manners, I can handle it."

"Tell me about the haunted house," said Stewart.

Jack grinned and waited for his friends' reaction.

"Oh, look," said Charlie, fortuitously noticing that his girlfriend had just walked into the Jewel with Alice Crabtree, "there's Babs, I'll see you later..."

"Whisper some sweet nothings to me, will you, Maxxy, while Moseley tells his enthralling story for the thirty-fifth time."

"Crikey, Manners, can't we just make out for ten minutes."

Jack had finished his tale of woe and was taking questions when their food and drinks arrived, along with a tray of condiments.

"And where is the house exactly?" asked Stewart.

"It's on Westbury Avenue. Number forty-one. It's got a pair of old green and yellow gates and bats flying round the roof." Jack grinned.

"Masefield!" called Max. "Food!"

Charlie broke off a long and very public snog with Barbara, but was still clenched up close to her.

"Has he finished?" he asked out of the corner of his mouth.

Max nodded.

"Shall we go upstairs?" suggested Alice, who had been playing unwitting gooseberry during the session and had spent the time texting and looking at photographs on her phone.

Barbara straightened her rumpled clothes.

"OK. Can I stay over?"

"S'pose so," answered Alice.

"Does the silly whore like being called Babs?" scoffed Mandy as Charlie retook his seat.

"She does when I call her it," answered Charlie, then added, almost as an afterthought, "And Babs is not a whore."

"Where've they gone?" asked Jack, taking one of the four squares of the toasted sandwich and pushing the plate towards Stewart. "Help yourself."

Stewart hesitated then, seeing that no one was taking any notice, dug in.

Charlie sprayed tomato sauce onto his fries.

"She and Alice have gone upstairs to do girl stuff."

"They've gone to suck each other's muffs," said Mandy, blowing through her straw in the dregs of the milkshake to demonstrate the noise.

"What a lovely turn of phrase," said Max.

Egg yolk squirted onto Stewart's fingers as he bit down on the toastie, and he licked it off with relish.

"If we get dressed up as soldiers that would be really good..."

"What?" demanded Max.

"I like it," responded Mandy, already on the same wavelength as the boy. "And you two could be sitting in a shell hole, with just a spotlight on you."

"We'll both need a bayonet, a rifle and a cartridge belt. It'll be just like Call of Duty," exclaimed Stewart.

Max had finally twigged what they were talking about.

"It is an anti-war poem, you know."

Stewart continued unabashed. "Do you think Mr Williams will be able to get us the kit?"

"What are those three on about?" asked Charlie.

Jack took a few fries, then pushed the plate right in front of Stewart.

"You finish it, Stew, I'm not as hungry as I thought." He turned to Charlie. "It's their pitch for stardom in the end-of-year concert."

"Oh, the Swanford's-Not-Got-Talent-Show."

Mandy gave Jack a sideways look, as if to say, I saw what you did...

"Wouldn't it be nice," she said, "if you could persuade the Jesus freak to join us, Jacky-boy. It would make our little group complete."

The same thought had already occurred to Jack several times.

"I have tried to make him come..."

Charlie snorted and nearly lost a mouthful of fries.

"That wouldn't surprise me!"

"Shut up, jerk-off..."

"Now, boys," said Max. "So, what's his problem?"

"Let me guess," said Mandy. "The Fifth Commandment..."

"Manners, you've been genning up on the Bible so you can throw awkward questions at Robert, haven't you?"

"Might have," she replied.

"Honour thy father and thy mother," said Stewart.

All eyes turned to the skinny boy, who had finished his meal, and had a ring of egg yolk and tomato sauce around his mouth. Max handed him a serviette.

"How do you know that?"

Stewart wiped his mouth on the serviette, then with the back of his hand.

"My dad has a big old Bible and sometimes he'll read it to us. He says that, of all the Ten Commandments, that one is the only one worth keeping."

"Figures," said Mandy. "I expect 'thou shalt not commit adultery' has a fairly low priority with him – no offence, Stew."

"I don't mind." He relaxed back into his seat and closed his eyes, a drop of moisture oozing from the bruised one. "I thought tonight was going to be really bad, but it's turned out to be one of the best ever."

"Almost time to go," said Jack, breaking the silence.

"Where do you live, Stew?" asked Charlie.

"Up past the school," he replied, smiling sleepily. "You know, I could just stay here all night."

"I don't think Andy would go for that," said Max.

"Where up past the school?" enquired Jack.

"Edward's Lane."

"That's quite a way. I deliver papers round there."

"I know, I've seen you."

"Do you want a lift on my bike? I can take you halfway. I live on Leighton Lane."

"Would you?"

"Course!"

It was nearing half past eight when they left the warmth of the café and stepped out onto Weymouth Road. The lights in the square were already switched off and, despite the glow of the street lamps, the winter constellations shone brightly overhead. After saying their goodbyes, Mandy and Max made off arm in arm down the road, while Charlie, gloved and hooded, walked briskly away in the opposite direction.

Stewart hunched his shoulders and shivered, waiting while Jack unpadlocked his bike from a lamppost. No coat, no hat, no gloves, no socks for him.

"Take this," said Jack, unwinding his scarf.

Pedalling with Stewart on the bike was hardly more strenuous than having Mikey in the saddle. The skinny boy held on around his waist, though Jack gained the impression it was just as much for warmth as for balance. It only took ten minutes for them to come to a skidding halt outside 15 Leighton Lane.

"Is this where you live?" said Stewart, as if making a mental note for himself.

Jack nodded.

"It's not as big as your house."

"I'd rather live here," Stewart replied without thought, and began to unfurl the scarf.

Jack stopped him.

"Give it me back tomorrow."

The boy nodded.

"It's been good," said Jack with a grin.

The boy nodded again absently, as if absorbed in storing up memories of the evening.

"Well, go on then. I don't want you freezing to death outside my house."

The boy smiled at him, then turned and trotted off down the road. Jack stood for a few moments, watching the small figure recede into the darkness, suddenly glad that his name was Moseley and not Henderson.

***

22: Saturday, 26th January. 9.30 a.m. 15 Leighton Lane.

ROGER

Roger Moseley sat at the kitchen table, chuckling over his cereal at his copy of the Swanford Mail. "I expect Sandip's smiling face will be in the paper again when he gets a certificate of good citizenship and a reward from the old dear when she gets back her marbles."

"I've a good mind to write to the editor of that so-called newspaper. Poor Jack!" Pam sat down beside her husband, cradling a cup of coffee in her hands.

Roger laughed again.

"You can never be too young to learn about the foibles of the Fifth Estate."

"In any case, I heard in the post office that Mrs Chambers is far too frail ever to go back to that huge old house."

"Turn it into flats and she could make a good living out of it."

"I expect the nursing home fees would take care of that and more."

"She's probably got thousands stashed away in cupboards."

Jack came in, wearing loose tracksuit bottoms and a hooded top.

"Who's got thousands?"

"Mrs Chambers is going to leave all her money to Sandip," chuckled Roger.

"Ha, bloody, ha!" exclaimed Jack.

"Language, young man," said his mother. "Sit down and have some breakfast."

"Why are you up so early?" asked his dad, eyeing him suspiciously.

Jack went to the fridge and pulled out a fresh container of milk.

"We need some oranges, don't we?"

"Do we?" replied Pam, "Since when have you been interested in oranges?"

"I like freshly squeezed orange juice," Jack stated, putting a tea bag into a mug and filling it with boiling water.

"OK, I'll get some from the supermarket this afternoon."

"Shouldn't we be supporting the local shops, instead of buying everything from the supermarket?" Jack sat down with his mug, and helped himself to a bowl of Crunchy Nut Cornflakes.

Roger and Pam exchanged glances.

"I could go and get some after breakfast," he said shovelling cereal into his mouth with his right hand while spooning sugar into his tea with the left.

Pam and Roger looked at each other again, then at Jack.

"Are you feeling all right, dear?" asked his mum.

"Course I am." He gulped down some tea.

"Not lacking in vitamin C or anything?" enquired his dad.

"I just think it's high time this family had some fresh fruit, instead of all that processed stuff, and we bought it from local stores."

"My son, the eco-warrior," said Roger, sceptically.

"All right," agreed Pam, reaching for her purse. "I'll give you £3. See how many oranges you can buy with that, then we'll compare the result with how many we can get from the supermarket for the same price."

"Sounds complicated," he said, pocketing the money. "Better go."

A moment later he was by the door pushing his feet into a pair of old trainers.

"Jack!" said his mother, her hand sweeping over the table to the bowl with a puddle of milk at the bottom, a half-empty mug, and a teaspoon caked in sugar. "Can you tell me why I'm expected to clear up your mess?"

"Duh!" replied her son, raising his eyes heavenward. "Because it's woman's work, that's why!" He dashed out with a laugh, half-expecting his cereal bowl to be thrown after him.

"Well, at least he's in a good mood," said Roger.

"He's going over to see that American boy tonight."

"Let's get my mother to take Dan and Mikey, then we can have a little time to ourselves?"

"What are you suggesting, Roger Moseley?"

"Hmm," he smiled. "I think you know what I'm suggesting..."

***

23: Saturday, 26th January. 9.55 a.m. Leighton Lane.

<u>JACK</u>

Jack swung right out of Leighton Lane across the oncoming traffic into the high street and pedalled furiously the hundred yards or so to the little row of shops, which included the post office and Fruit and Flower. He dropped his bike onto the pavement and went to gaze through the window. Robert was by the till at the back of the shop, weighing out some potatoes for a customer. He had on a knee-length butcher's apron, black trousers and a loose-fitting white shirt with silver sprung sleeve garters.

I like the look of those armbands, Jack thought; they suit him. He doesn't look quite so buttoned up as he does at school. Jack continued to stare until Mrs Annesley, the owner, came into his field of vision, eyeing him disapprovingly. He smiled disarmingly at her, hoping she hadn't noticed his blush, then sauntered into the shop, giving her another sheepish grin as he passed her at the till.

Fruit and Flower was like a mini-supermarket with all the produce arranged in trays, boxes, or buckets for customers to help themselves before going to pay at one of the two tills. Jack went straight to the oranges, the scent of ripe fruit filling his nostrils. There were two sizes: small for twenty-five pence and large for thirty-five.

"Can I help you, sir?"

Jack turned, trying to appear superior, but unable to completely suppress the grin that stole over his face.

"I'd like some oranges, please, my man."

"And how many would sir like?"

"I've got £3, so I could have..."

"Twelve small ones."

"That's just what I was going to say. Where did you get those armbands?"

"But the big ones are juicier, trust me," drawled Robert. "They're called arm garters and I got them back home in the States."

"I do trust you, but that means I can only have..."

"Eight with twenty pence change."

"You seem quite good at this job. Have you ever thought of making a career out of it?"

"I can't answer that in the way I'd like, sir, because the customer is always to be treated with courtesy."

"If I buy eight large ones, can you give me a discount of five pence on a small one?"

Robert turned to the owner, who was watching them from her till by the door.

"Mrs Annesley, this gentleman wants me to sell him eight large oranges and one small for £3."

"Is he a friend of yours?"

"I guess."

"All right, then. You're Pamela Moseley's boy, aren't you?"

Jack nodded, but Mrs Annesley's attention had already been diverted to another customer.

"Would sir like a bag?"

"Please."

Robert handed over the oranges in a supermarket carrier and took the money.

"Is there anything else I can do for you?"

I wish, thought Jack. "No thank you... but I am looking forward to tonight."

"Seven o'clock, sir; don't be late."

***

24: Saturday, 26th January. 5.50 p.m. 15 Leighton Lane.

JACK

The extractor fan wasn't working properly and so the bathroom was full of steam and condensation. Jack wiped the mirror with his towel, creating a circular watery image of his head and shoulders. He looked at himself critically, then stood back so that his chest came into view. Maybe I have got a bit of definition, he thought, but it seems to depend on the light. A drop of water ran down the mirror, cutting his image in two. Jack wrapped the towel round his waist and opened the bathroom door. The chill draught made him shiver and his nipples contracted to hard circles. As he walked along the landing to his bedroom, he saw that the door was ajar.

"What are you doing in here, Pestilence?"

Mikey was sitting on the bed.

"I'm sad."

"I know that, but can you go and be sad somewhere else?"

"Dan and I are being sent to Nanna Moseley's."

"OK, I'll play along. Why does that make you sad?"

"Because she'll make us watch an old film in boring black and white."

"And what plans had you made otherwise?"

"I want to go to Mike's and watch Pinocchio."

"How do you know Nan hasn't got that?"

"It's new."

"It isn't; it's older than Nan."

"It's on Blu-ray."

"The film is even older than Nan, trust me."

"It's my birthday next week."

"So?"

Mikey jumped off the bed, having cheered up for no discernible reason.

"You're going on a date tonight, aren't you?"

"No, I'm not! Now scram, or else!"

Mikey dodged the floor debris, scooted round his brother and reached the door, where he stopped and looked round.

"Jack's got a date; Jack's got a da-ate!" He ran, laughing, feeling the draught of the door as it was slammed shut behind him.

"Pestilence," Jack muttered. Now it was decision time. What to wear? He went to his underwear drawer and picked out a pair of red boxer trunks. That was easy, since no one was going to see them. A rail full of jeans was a slightly bigger problem, but eventually he chose a very light blue pair of standard fit with button fly, to which he added his favourite brown leather belt with a large silver eagle buckle. The full-length mirror in the wardrobe was suitably complimentary and he smiled at himself, mussing his damp hair slightly so that it didn't sit quite so flat. Then he sprayed his armpits with deodorant.

Now, the shirt! He'd got a pretty good idea about it, but he was also aware that it could be very wrong. He'd already decided against a T-shirt (too ordinary), and felt that wearing a top would make him prone to sweat, especially if he was having supper. A white school shirt was completely out, and so this narrowed the field down to six or seven casual shirts. And there it was: the one he wanted, right at the end of the rail. He took it out and held it against himself. It was light cotton – a summer shirt, really, a tailored fit in maroon, white and grey checks, but the really daring part about it was that it was at least a size too small.

He took off the hood and slipped it on, leaving the top two buttons undone and rolling up the sleeves to above his elbows. It was tight, the white buttons straining across his abdomen and chest, and tight too around the biceps. He looked in the mirror. It was just right; just what he wanted. He grinned at himself.

Then he saw his bare feet. Jack didn't like his feet: they were too small, the toes too stubby. Dan, who was a year and a half younger and two inches shorter, already had proper grown-up feet, while Jack's were more like Mikey's, or so he thought. Quickly, he dipped into his sock drawer and pulled out a pair of charcoal calf-lengths, admiring himself in the mirror again as he hoisted them up.

***

25: Saturday, 26th January. 6.55 p.m. Pear Tree Cottage, the Ropewalk.

ROBERT

Another glance out of the window. Perhaps he won't come; perhaps he's forgotten the way; perhaps he's fallen off his bike; perhaps he's in hospital! Robert paced about his bedroom, which was illuminated only by the screen of his laptop. Outside it was dark and had been so for nearly two hours, but at least it was dry and not as cold as previous nights.

Since arriving home from his shift at Fruit and Flower, he had showered, changed, and gone down to the kitchen, where his mom was busy preparing supper. Shooed out of the kitchen for being under her feet, he had laid the table, tried to do some homework, tried to prepare for Bible study class next Wednesday. Now he was just pacing.

The alarm on his Mickey Mouse clock went off with a raucous clanging. He had set it for seven o'clock. Jack was late. A worry pain gathered in his stomach. He went to the window. A darkly clad figure on a bicycle swept round the corner into the Ropewalk and came to a halt outside his house. Robert's mouth opened into a broad smile, and his heart began to beat audibly in his chest. The pain disappeared. He almost ran out of the bedroom, but checked himself. The doorbell rang. He went out onto the landing and flicked the light switch, then at a stately pace descended the stairs. At the bottom he stopped to put on the hall light, just as the bell rang again. What if he gets impatient and goes? Robert scurried to the front door and opened it.

"Hey," said Jack.

They stood grinning at each other, until Robert remembered his manners and stepped aside to allow his guest to enter.

"Can I take your coat?" he asked.

Jack slid the parka off his shoulders and handed it over.

"Shall I take my trainers off?"

The American did not reply. His eyes and mind were elsewhere.

"I like the shirt... "

"Oh, it's just an old one," replied Jack. "Shall I take my trainers off?"

"Please."

I wouldn't have the courage to wear a shirt like that, or those jeans. They probably wouldn't suit me, anyways. Robert glanced at himself in the hall mirror: button-down, dark salmon micro-check shirt, knitted corn-coloured waistcoat, courtesy of his grandma, and beige slacks. Uh-oh, Jack's gone a shade of pink.

"What's the matter?"

The English boy showed the heel of his right foot, where there was a large hole in the sock. "It's the only thing I didn't check."

"It doesn't matter; mine are pretty much all rags."

"But yours are white."

"You can borrow a pair, if you like."

"What size are you?"

"Ten and a half."

"I'm only a seven."

Maybelle's voice called from the lounge.

"Robert, are you going to bring your guest through?"

***

26: Saturday, 26th January. 7.10 p.m. Pear Tree Cottage, the Ropewalk.

JACK

What a dork, not checking my socks! I feel self-conscious now. Robert's got normal size feet too, not like my stupid mini-me ones. Still, he does like the shirt. This is a nice hallway; nice thick carpet. I wonder what the rest of the house is like. Oh, that's his mother calling: do I shake hands? I'm not sure; maybe I'll play that by ear. Must try not to go red...!

Robert opened the lounge door for Jack and followed him in. Maybelle was waiting for him between the sofa and the table.

"Mom, this is my friend Jack Moseley... Jack, this is my mom."

"How do you do, Jack. Welcome to our home."

The English boy waited for a second to see if a hand would be extended and in the meantime gave his own hand a surreptitious wipe on his jeans. When nothing was forthcoming, he gave a small bow of the head.

"Thank you for having me," he said.

His eyes darted this way and that. The room was like something you'd see in a John Lewis window. The carpet had the deepest pile he had ever felt his toes sink into, and was matched by the comfortable sofa and armchairs. The ceiling had polished, dark oak beams which matched the furniture, which included an antique dresser, complete with a nineteenth-century willow pattern dinner service. And then there was the dining table, which was beautifully laid out on a spotless white damask cloth with matching napkins in silver gilt rings, hand-embroidered floral placemats, bone-handled cutlery, crystal glassware and a centrepiece of cream silk carnations in a cut-glass rose bowl.

He suddenly felt out of his depth and very inferior. Mrs Crittenden didn't like the way he was dressed; he could tell that. Her big sculptured hair and statuesqueness made her seem stand-offish. He doubted Robert would be much bothered with him for long, either, being of such a superior status.

"It's a lovely room, isn't it?" said Maybelle. "I have to say I wasn't much taken with the cottage at first, but this lounge helped me change my mind."

"It's very grand," he murmured.

"Would you like a drink, Jack?" asked Robert.

Maybelle made a noise and wafted her hand.

"Goodness me, what must you think of us. Do sit down, honey. Supper will be about ten minutes. I hope you're hungry. Robert tells me you English boys eat like sparrows."

"Some English boys," he smiled, feeling a little better.

"Robert, you try to persuade Jack to try some of our southern iced tea, while I go and get things ready."

"I'd better show him around first."

"OK, dear, I'll call you."

They went upstairs, Robert in the lead. "This is the guest bathroom – I mean, toilet," he said, opening the first door on the left. "It's kinda separate from our bathroom, because there's no bath or shower. We usually call the toilet the bathroom, because they're together in the States."

Jack chuckled at the American's long explanation of something he already knew. It was a small room, newly plumbed and appointed with a bidet and wash basin, though the dark floor-to-ceiling ceramic tiles would have been more appropriate in a hotel than a cottage.

Robert pointed to the other doors along the landing.

"That's Mom and Dad's room, and at the end is Dad's study, but that's really only an overgrown cupboard. This is my room." He indicated the door opposite the guest toilet. "Come and have a look."

Jack took stock. Actually, it was all quite dingy: the carpets were old, the paintwork yellowing and there were cobwebs in the corners. He entered Robert's room and, despite the overlay of personal effects, it too had a feeling of neglect, as though it were overdue for redecoration. There wasn't even a lampshade on the bulb hanging down from the centre of the ceiling. Certainly, he wouldn't have swapped it for his own room at home, which was much more cosy and homely.

Robert sat on the bed.

"I know what you're thinking."

The English boy wondered if he should sit on the bed too. The only other seat was an old chair tucked under the desk.

"What's that?"

The American made a motion with his hand, inviting Jack to sit next to him.

"It's like two different places. The lounge and kitchen downstairs and where we live up here."

Jack sat down on the quilt next to Robert.

"I just expected your room to be more high-tech, and have more things in it, because you're... American, I suppose."

"I've never had that much," said Robert almost apologetically, "though my room in Tyree is better furnished. I guess it could all do with a lick of paint." He turned his head towards his friend and smiled.

Jack smiled back. He had never been so physically close to Robert and in such an intimate space. He was drawn to the warmth that seemed to emanate from the other boy's body and by its solidity. Somehow, he wanted to bridge the small gap that lay between them. His heart had started to beat just a little faster than normal, and there was a nebulous tingling, a vibration, within him as though some electrical current was passing between them... and there was also the vaguest stirrings of sexual excitement.

"Supper's ready!" called Maybelle.

"Coming, Mom!"

"Ah look, baby Robert," said Jack, motioning to the framed photograph on the desk.

The American's face clouded.

"Better wash up."

"Your mum doesn't like my shirt, does she?"

"Probably not, but I do."

"Robert, before we go down, I'm a bit worried about how to behave at the table..."

"But you're a guest. Oh, we hold hands and say a blessing before the meal."

Jack smiled shyly and blushed.

"We hold hands?"

"Only lightly."

"OK, I'll just follow what you do... "

***

"Dear God, our Heavenly Father,
We praise You for Your kindness to us.
Bless us this food, and bless us with Your unfailing love.
Father, we ask this through Jesus Christ, our blessed
Lord. Amen!"

Robert finished the prayer and gave Jack's hand a gentle squeeze of encouragement before letting go. Then Maybelle poured each of them a glass of orange juice.

"Tuck in, boys," she said.

Before them on the table was the starter. Barbecued devilled eggs: a soft-boiled egg, the yolk removed and mixed with smoked pork, mayonnaise, French mustard, salt and pepper, before being returned, and the whole garnished with a sprinkle of paprika and a sprig of watercress.

"That was great," said Jack, noticing that he'd finished way before the others.

Maybelle smiled.

"I'm pleased to see you have a healthy appetite, Jack. It's the mark of a man."

The main course was slow-cooked beef short ribs in gravy with mashed potatoes and a sauté of carrots, small white onions, cherry tomatoes and mushrooms.

"Delicious," said Jack, having left only the bones on his plate.

"Have you got room for one more?" asked Maybelle.

"I'll give it a shot," answered Jack, enjoying himself now, having relaxed in the convivial atmosphere and under the warmth of Robert's smiles.

Maybelle retired to the kitchen with the dishes.

"I've got to loosen my belt," murmured Jack, undoing the top button of his jeans in the process.

"Next time, you'll have to wear something stretchy," said the American.

Dessert was American cheesecake with raspberry sauce: another eight to nine hundred calories. Jack promised himself a good long bike ride tomorrow, an extra special effort at PE at school, and a strenuous workout at the gym on Thursday.

"Thank you very much, Mrs Crittenden, that was better than a Christmas dinner."

"You're very welcome, Jack; there is nothing a woman likes more than being complimented on her culinary skills."

"Mom, I'll take Jack upstairs. I've got a few things to show him."

***

They took up a glass of iced tea each, something Jack had seen on the supermarket shelf, but which he had never really fancied. It was very sweet, but not unpleasant, and not really how he imagined cold tea would taste. Once again they sat down on the bed together.

"Your mum's a really good cook."

"Yeah, she gets a big kick out of that kind of thing. She entertains my dad's clients here; that's why everything is so plush downstairs."

"What's the cup for?" Jack asked, noticing it on a shelf.

"Oh, that was last year's school swimming gala. Hundred-metres freestyle in one minute. I got lucky, I suppose; I'm not that good. Do you swim, Jack?"

"At the leisure centre, not in competitions. My brother's better than me. He's an all-round sporty type."

"I think you could, though. You've got the build for it."

Jack smiled outwardly and inwardly.

"Is that your house in America?" he asked, looking at the desktop image on the laptop screen.

"Yeah! Would you like me to show you my town?"

Actually, Jack would have preferred Robert just to stay sitting next to him, but he couldn't say so, and for the next half hour he was taken on a virtual tour of Tyree and most of the state of Oklahoma.

"Now what have you learned?" said Robert with a smile, shutting down the computer. He pushed the chair back tidily under the desk, then came and sat next to Jack, only this time he allowed himself to fall backwards so that he was lying fully across the bed with his legs dangling. "Go on, tell me something."

"Well, teacher, sir, it's dry and dusty, most of the houses are bungalows, there are an awful lot of churches, and the roads are all criss-cross and boringly straight."

"Would you like to live in a place like Tyree?" asked Robert.

"Only if you were there," replied Jack, without thinking.

He blushed, realising what he'd just said, and was glad that he was facing away from the American.

"Maybe you could come over to visit one day."

The blush quickly subsided and Jack grinned at Robert.

"But you've still got two years of Swanford yet. And in any case, we might not be friends by then."

"Would you like to come to Bible class one Wednesday, Jack?"

The English boy looked away. This was a difficult one. He didn't share either the culture or belief system that Robert had been brought up with. In fact, if he was pressed, he would have to admit to being sceptical about the existence of God.

"Do I know anyone else in this Bible class?" he asked, hoping to sound neutral on the subject.

"I don't think so. I've never seen any of them at school."

"You mean, you don't know anything about who they are? That's weird!"

Robert sat up.

"Well, it's kinda awkward. I know their first names and they know who I am, but I missed the first week's introductions."

"Can I think about it?"

"No problem. Jesus is a patient man."

Jack chuckled, uncertain whether Robert was being serious or not, then decided he probably was.

"Better go," he said, noticing that it was nearly ten o'clock by the Mickey Mouse alarm. "I've had a great time. Will you come and hang out with me sometime? I can't promise you'll get a meal like that, though."

"I'd sure like to."

27: Saturday, 26th January. 10.15 p.m. Pear Tree Cottage, the Ropewalk.

ROBERT

He watched Jack cycle away and when he saw a hand go up in farewell as the bike turned the corner, he waved back, even though he knew it wouldn't be seen. It had been the best night since his arrival in England.

Feeling tired but happy, he joined his mother, who was sitting on the sofa reading a magazine. The house was silent again. He yawned and relaxed back between two cushions.

"Entertaining takes it out of you, hon," she said.

"It's been a great night – thanks Mom."

"You know, his skin is just like porcelain – so pure white you can almost see through it."

Robert looked quizzically at his mother.

"Oh, I wouldn't expect a man to notice such things," she said, touching him lightly on the knee. "He seems a nice enough boy. A little gauche, perhaps..."

"He's asked if I'd like to go over to his house sometime."

"You like him, don't you, hon?"

"Yes, but I remember what you and Dad said about not getting too close to anyone while I was here."

"You just have to be cautious not to let any boy or girl come between you and the Lord Jesus Christ because, if you do, Satan will be there, sure as eggs, turning you off the righteous path and onto the sinful highway."

"So, you think it would be OK for me to go to Jack's house?"

"As far as I am concerned you can, honey, and if it means you can get him on the road to Jesus, that'll sure be a feather in your cap back home."

He looked at his watch. It was after eleven at night. Being out this late on his own made him fearful. The world seemed so alien. All around, a cold, thick fog swirled and eddied as he cautiously made his way further down the alley. To his left and right there were waste bins on wheels and he could hear the pattering feet of rats, scuttling away to hide in corners as he passed by. A yellow stain of light broke through the fog. A street lamp illuminated a door in the side of a building. He looked up. The fog was so thick that he couldn't see beyond the third floor. He pushed on the door. It gave, revealing a narrow passageway and a wooden staircase. In fact, the whole building seemed to be constructed of dark planks, like railway sleepers set on their ends. There was a light, though, white and bright at the top of the stairs, but he couldn't see the source.

Like a moth, he felt himself irresistibly drawn to it. He mounted the stairs, the treads creaking under his feet. At the top, he gazed down a long corridor. At the very end, Jack Moseley was painting the wall white with a roller. He wore the same clothes as earlier, with the addition of black boots with white soles. The light seemed to be coming from that very spot, surrounding Jack in an aura of brightness.

Fancy painting in his best shirt. Whatever is he thinking of? He walked quickly down the corridor. Music from tinny speakers was playing somewhere, but there didn't appear to be any doors in the walls.

"Hey!" called Jack, greeting him by holding up the white paint roller.

Robert strode up to the English boy, grabbed his shirt in both hands and tore it open. The buttons flew in all directions, pattering onto the floor and walls. Against the incredible whiteness of his chest, Jack's nipples stood out like tiny purple balloons. Greedily, the American bent to suck one into his mouth...

Robert woke with a jolt. He was lying on his back, covered in sweat, hot and sticky. This was not the first wet dream he had had, but the others had been short, blurry affairs, the stimulus indistinct, giving rise to not very much. Now the image of this one was seared into his mind, and the orgasmic result had been so intense, so volcanic, the quantity produced so much that his pyjamas bottoms around his groin were soaked.

"Dear Lord!" he cried out loud.

He jumped out of bed and knelt down, holding his head in his hands and resting his elbows on the mattress.

"Dear Lord Jesus Christ, please help me, I have committed a grievous sin. I have had bestial, unclean thoughts. Satan has a hold of me. Please drive him away!"

He reached for the drawer in his bedside cabinet and pulled out a small towel which he kept for this purpose. This was the first time he had had to use it since his arrival in England. Still silently praying to himself, he stripped off his pyjama bottoms and wiped himself clean, but the smell of drying semen was everywhere.

"Dear God, our Father in Heaven, I need your help, please rescue me from this."

He bundled up the towel and pyjamas, and placed them in his clothes basket. He would have to wash them himself tomorrow.

***

28: Wednesday, 30th January. 6.10 p.m. The Baptist church, Westbury Avenue.

ROBERT

A cold, damp day had given way to a colder, dry evening with a stiffening breeze from the north-east, bringing with it the threat of snow for tomorrow. Robert was well wrapped up against the chill, but it was the gnawing coldness around his heart that bothered him. Since the dream, he had shut himself down, distanced himself from social interaction, especially at school and especially with Jack. Prayer was his constant solace, as he strove to redeem himself in the eyes of God. The two attendances at church on Sunday had helped him to focus on His love, and since then there had been no repetition of the dream. What he longed for, though, was a sign of forgiveness. In his darkest hour, he thought that Jesus might have given up on him, that he was destined to become Satan's servant. But the Saviour never gives up on a repentant sinner, and he was truly repentant.

He had come to church early to pray again for guidance that he may know God's will. What he desired most was a test of his faith and of his resolve to fight the sin. But he had no idea how it might manifest itself. If he had been in Tyree, he would have gone straight to Pastor Dunn, confessed his sin and asked how he could seek absolution, but this English pastor was different, almost indifferent.

The church door was unlocked and the porch light was on, which meant that Pastor McKellan was already inside. Divesting himself of his outer garments, which he laid on a pew, Robert went straight to the steps below the altar and threw himself down, clasping his hands together and closing his eyes tight shut.

"Dear Lord, our Heavenly Father, I ask your forgiveness once more for that sin of lust and depravity which I committed on Saturday night. Hear my prayer, please, O Lord, and give me the strength to fight this demon within my soul, that I may be cleansed of this perversion. I ask it in the name of our Lord Jesus Christ. Amen!"

While he had been on his knees, five figures had stolen quietly into the church. One, rotund and pink-faced, on seeing the supplicant, had detached itself from the others and moved cautiously towards him.

Kieran put his hand on the American's back, possibly just a little lower than was commonly decent.

"Ooo, Robert, are you all right?"

It was as if a high-voltage current had been passed through him. He jumped, twisted round and glared at Kieran.

"Get off me!"

The pink face with the mop of curly hair blinked at him.

"But I like you, Robert. You're very attractive – you know that, don't you?"

"You're a pervert!"

"No, I'm not, Robert. I just happen to prefer boys to girls, just like you."

The American stared, his back to the altar steps. Was this the test that he had been praying for: to resist this overweight, effeminate boy? It seemed too easy. Perhaps he had been forgiven after all.

"I don't prefer boys to girls," he said levelly, "and if you touch me again, I'll make sure you regret it."

"Robert!" It was Pastor McKellan, calling him from the vestry door. "Have you forgotten that you are giving the lesson this week?"

"No, sir!"

"Then come along," the pastor said sharply.

The American went to pick up his class notes from his coat pocket

"Don't take any notice of Mac, Robert," said Kieran, tagging alongside him, as if the warning he'd received just hadn't happened. "He wasn't always such a sourpuss."

This is the test, he thought, this is one of Satan's minions. He's like a leech and has no shame. He's trying to corrupt me with his nice-as-pie talk, but the Lord is my shepherd, I shall not want... He restoreth my soul: he leadeth me in the paths of righteousness for his name's sake...

Kieran touched him on the arm.

"Robert, could you tell Mac I've just gone for a Jimmy Riddle and I'll be along in a moment."

When, Robert walked into the vestry, he noticed immediately that the seating arrangement was different. James was sitting on the end next to Mary, then came Jane and Callum.

"At last!" said the pastor. "And where is Kieran?"

"He said something about Jimmy Riddle."

James burst out laughing, Mary giggled behind her handkerchief, and there was even the ghost of a smile on Callum's blank face.

"Oh, this is intolerable!" said the pastor. "Just get on with it, will you?"

Robert cleared his throat.

"I have done a lesson on the Beatitudes, Pastor McKellan, which I would like to share with you all." He looked around at the semi-circle of four young faces for encouragement, but found only blank disinterest.

"Sorry," whispered Kieran, coming in with a swish and the merest brush against the American's thigh. He sat next to Callum, leaving only the end seat vacant.

"What is it, Robert?" he asked excitedly. "What is the lesson?"

"The Beatitudes."

"Ooo, Robert, are they about love?" Kieran pursed his lips into a cupid's smile.

James sat up straighter in his chair.

"K, just chill, will you, please?"

"Sorry."

Robert steeled himself. Why can't the pastor see it? If Kieran had been in his youth group at home... well, he just wouldn't have been. He began to speak in what he hoped was his deepest, most masculine voice. Even so, he couldn't help noticing the sing-song cadence that he always adopted when speaking in public.

"You will know the story of Jesus preaching the Sermon on the Mount to his disciples and followers. Modern Christianity has its roots in these teachings, and among these are the eight Beatitudes found in Matthew, chapter 5. The first is: Blessed are the poor, for theirs is the Kingdom of Heaven..."

"Isn't that the Luke version?" interrupted the pastor.

Robert looked up. He had hardly started, and his flow had already been broken.

"How do you mean, Pastor?"

"Doesn't Matthew say that blessed are the poor in spirit, for theirs is the Kingdom of Heaven?"

"Well, I thought it was the same thing..."

"So, you think that being materially poor is the same as being spiritually poor?"

"Ooo, Robert, you are a naughty boy," murmured Kieran.

The American froze, angry at himself, angry at the pastor, and most of all angry at Kieran for being Satan's minion.

In the silence that followed, James yawned.

"Can we get on? I've got a lot of business to attend to."

Mary giggled through her handkerchief, her eyes even more bloodshot than usual. Jane began to pick furiously at her nose while Callum eyed Robert with clinical detachment, like a pathologist about to perform an autopsy.

Three-quarters of an hour later, Pastor McKellan called time.

"Try to be a good deal more coherent in your next lesson," was his closing remark to Robert, who had managed to stumble his way through seven of the Beatitudes, but had missed out the sixth: 'Blessed are the pure in heart', because his notes had become jumbled. In any case, he felt his efforts had been deliberately destroyed by the continual interruptions of the pastor.

Immediately on stepping out into the night, the cold wind penetrated his sweat-soaked shirt, making him shiver. He wrapped his coat more tightly around him and pulled the flaps of his trapper hat down around his ears. He looked for a bin in which to throw his notes, but all he saw was Kieran sidling up to him.

"Can I walk home with you?" he said, touching him on the arm.

The American looked into the pink face.

"No, you can't you disgusting pervert, and if you come near me again I'll punch you into next week." He bellowed the words, showing more oratorical skill in those few short moments than he had in the whole of the lesson on the Beatitudes. Then his voice grew less strident, but more menacing. "You know that when you die, you'll be consigned to the lake of fire to writhe in torment through all eternity."

Kieran reeled backwards. The words had struck home almost as much as Robert's fist would have done. Then, with remarkable speed, the fat boy recovered, drew himself up and, with hands on hips, retorted: "Oh, Robert, look in the mirror sometime, and take that plank out of your eye, you gormless piece of American pussy," then he turned and, with unexpected alacrity, ran off, towards the lychgate.

When he got home, Robert went straight to his room, only acknowledging his mother's greeting with "Hi, Mom." Minutes later he was in the shower, where he stayed for a good long time. When he had finished towelling himself dry, he dressed quickly, then knelt by the side of his bed.

"Dear Lord, forgive me, for today you know that I threatened violence in your house." Robert hoped his sin might be mitigated, because it occurred in the church yard, not the church itself, and in any case he was fighting for righteousness.

After his obeisance, the American lay down on his bed and fell asleep. When he awoke, his mother was looking at him, cocking her head this way and that.

"Are you all right, honey? You left your door wide open."

"Sure, Mom..." He blinked up at her, sure that she could read him like a book, and continued, "It's just that..."

"What, hon?"

"I hate it here. Why can't we go back home?"

"Oh, darlin', that's just not possible."

"I'll be not far off seventeen when we get back."

"Something's got your goat. You've been quiet since..."

The boy shook his head, gazing up at his mother's concerned face and wondering if he should reveal his anxiety.

"Did something happen tonight at your group?"

"I don't think Pastor McKellan likes me."

"Oh, I'm sure he does, but the English don't act so friendly as we do."

"He never mentions his wife any more."

"I believe he's a very private man." Maybelle sat down on the bed. "But there's something else, isn't there? A mother can tell."

Here was his opportunity. His mind suddenly settled; a steely determination took over. He nodded.

"There's a boy there. He's one of those people that Pastor Dunn talked to us about: unnatural, immoral."

His mother took a second or two to fathom what Robert was trying to tell her. She wasn't used to her son, or anyone else for that matter, talking like this.

"Oh my Lord!" she said at last. "Did something happen?"

"He touched me and asked me to walk home with him..."

This sounded rather lame to Robert and he prayed he wouldn't have to make any embellishments.

"Where did he touch you?"

Robert lifted himself a little way off the bed and indicated the general area of the lower back.

"Did you speak to Pastor McKellan about it?"

"No, he wasn't around, but he doesn't seem to notice what this boy's like anyway."

"What is this creature's name?"

"Kieran."

"And he didn't make any other lewd suggestions, did he, hon?"

"He said he preferred boys to girls and that I was attractive."

Maybelle put her hand to her mouth.

"Oh, Robert, you poor dear."

"I threatened to punch him, Mom, and I did it in God's house."

"No matter. You did right, darlin'. I'm proud of you. I shall talk to Pastor McKellan tomorrow, and I'll make sure you aren't bothered by that pervert again. What is he thinking of, having that sort in his church, and mixing with innocent young people too!"

***

29: Thursday, 31st January. 9.30 a.m. 15 Leighton Lane.

JACK

An unexpected day off ... bliss. Jack lay on his bed eating a slice of toast and marmalade while surfing the internet on his mobile. After doing the morning paper round, which had taken an extra half-hour because of the snow, a text message had arrived.

Swanford Community School regrets that owing to the inclement weather conditions it will be closed today. Parents should make alternative arrangements. All efforts will be made to reopen the school tomorrow. Miss A. K. Chawner, School Secretary.

I'm glad things have calmed down a bit with Robert, he thought. Once the euphoria caused by the events on Saturday had settled, his life had seemed a bit frightening, a bit out of control. Providentially, when he got back to school on the Monday, everyone – including Robert – had been quiet, even subdued, and things had remained that way ever since.

There was a loud knock on the outside door. Jack hoped Mikey might answer it as they were the only two at home, but a second, louder knock dashed that hope. He wandered downstairs and through the kitchen to the outside door.

"Surprise!" said Max.

"Hello," said Jack, looking beyond his friend to the snowflakes still falling from a leaden sky.

"Well, are you going to keep me standing on the doorstep?"

"Come in – help yourself to tea or something."

Max shook off his bobble hat, sniffed and entered the kitchen, closing the door behind him. "Sometimes I think school is specifically designed around the teachers."

"Are you complaining?"

"No, but it's just that we never get to make the decision about whether the school is opened or closed."

"You've been listening to my mum. She was giving me earache on the subject."

"Do you fancy a little sledging on the Hill?" asked Max.

"Not a bad idea, but there is one small problem."

At that moment, Mikey entered the kitchen.

"Ah! And here it is," said Max. "Hello, little irritant."

Mikey scowled, though he was quite used to being treated as an unnecessary appendage by friends of his big brothers.

"Where's the middle one?" asked Max, now making himself comfortable with a mug of tea at the kitchen table.

"Oh, Dan? He's gone to see Justin. He's taken my bike."

"It's my birthday on Saturday," said Mikey.

"Oh, is it? How very interesting." Max swirled his tea.

"I'm getting Pinocchio."

"Mmm, two wooden heads together, then," observed Max.

"Mikey, do you want to go sledging?" asked Jack.

The little boy paused, weighing up his options.

Max regarded him.

"Why can't we just roll him around the garden and leave him here as a snowman?"

"I'll get ready," said Mikey, looking daggers at Max.

"Turn the TV off," ordered Jack, "and get your wellingtons from the cupboard under the stairs. I'd better text Mum and tell her where we're going."

"How very domesticated you are," observed Max, rising to his feet. "Thank you so much for the tea. I thought I'd go up to the barren land that is Edward's Lane and see if Stewart would like to join us."

"Good idea. Isn't Mandy coming?"

"I'm afraid Manners is not a snow kind of person. I won't tell you her exact words, but she is going to make herself especially beautiful, for when we meet at the Jewel tonight."

"Ready," piped Mikey.

"No," said Jack. "Winter coat, gloves, woolly hat to cover the ears, thick socks, and right wellington boot on right foot, left wellington boot on left foot."

"Oh, God!" cried Max. "I'll see you at the Hill. Charlie and Barb... sorry, Babs should be there, and a few others. Don't forget your sledge."

***

His mum replied with a text message, reading: "Be careful, and be home before dark!"

Jack deleted it.

Outside, the air had that distinctive redolence of winter snowfall.

"Put some of this on."

Mikey grasped the offered lip-salve and made a reasonable job of applying it. The sky had evolved into several shades of grey from which just a few flakes were now fluttering. At the kerbside of Leighton Lane, Jack took hold of Mikey's hand.

"When I say cross, cross."

The gritters had been to work, clearing a path in the middle of the road, otherwise all was white, their footprints making little impression on the six inches or so of packed snow. Several cars passed, going too fast, throwing out dirty salted water from their wheels.

"Right, cross!"

Shortly, they turned into Lortas Road, a cul-de-sac lined with 1980s open-plan housing. Here the gritters' reach petered out after only a few yards. Jack threw down their blue plastic, two-man sledge.

"Hop on."

Mikey climbed aboard and they set off again. A car went by gingerly, for there was little to differentiate road and pavement. At the end was a small turning area, where a flight of steps climbed steeply to the top of an old railway embankment, now converted to a footpath.

"Are we nearly there?" asked Mikey, having struggled up the less than child-friendly steps.

"Hop on."

Impenetrable thickets of brambles overlaid with glittering snow lay to either side of the footpath which followed exactly along the line of the old single-track railway. After walking for about another fifteen minutes, in a generally south-westerly direction, Jack realised that they were not far from the Ropewalk, where Robert lived. He gazed over the snowy rooftops of the bungalows below the embankment, trying to judge how far away it was.

In another five minutes, they reached the railway bridge which they needed to cross to get to the Hill. Here, though, was another flight of steps leading down to the long and winding Retford Road.

"We're going to make a short detour," decided Jack, signalling for Mikey to get off the sledge.

"Will you carry me?"

"No."

"I'm cold."

At the bottom, Jack didn't lay the sledge down.

"I think you can walk a bit if you're feeling cold."

"Bloody," said Mikey.

"And don't swear!"

They progressed east along Retford Road for longer than Jack had anticipated, but eventually they turned right into the Ropewalk and were soon standing outside the front door of Pear Tree Cottage. Mikey reached up and took Jack's hand.

"Who lives here?"

"A friend. His name's Robert, he's American."

"Can I ring the bell?"

"Do it."

It was Robert who came to the door. It took a moment to take in the sight of the two well-wrapped figures, one nearly twice the size of the other. Then a broad, goofy grin appeared.

"Jack!"

Maybe it was the surprise, but gone was the aloofness of the last few days; instead, there was the warm fuzziness of Saturday.

"Hey," said Jack.

"And who is this little fella?"

"This is my brother, Mikey."

Robert bent down and shook the little boy's hand.

"Hi, Mikey, you're a cute one."

Mikey was entranced. One of Jack's friends who didn't think he was a mere encumbrance; who treated him like a human being; who spoke quite a lot like Jiminy Cricket.

"Who is it honey?" Maybelle's voice came from the lounge.

"It's Jack and his brother, Mom."

"Well, bring them through and close that door."

Maybelle rose from the sofa when they entered the lounge and looked them up and down. "Now, you boys look as if you need a cup of hot chocolate."

"Yes, please," said Jack, removing his own hat and pulling off Mikey's too.

The little boy clapped his hands.

"I'm cold."

"Well, you sit by the fire, honey, while I get the drinks."

Maybelle went through to the kitchen, while Mikey curled himself up on the sofa, his head on a cushion.

"I like it here," he said.

"Would you like to come sledging?" asked Jack.

Robert made a face. "Sledging? What's that?"

"You know, like in the winter Olympics, the Cresta run – or like snowboarding, only sitting down."

"Sledding!" said the American. "But I haven't got one."

"We've got a two-man."

"I've only got shoes..."

"Please come," said Mikey, sleepily.

"Try the shed, hon," called Maybelle. "You never know."

"I'll get my boots," said Jack.

The large enclosed garden at the back of Pear Tree Cottage had suffered from years of neglect, which even the covering of snow could not hide. A mixture of ornamental trees and shrubs around the periphery formed a matted tangle of branches, into which had grown a mass of impenetrable bramble. What had once been an expansive lawn was now a wilderness of weeds, dry stalks protruding through the snow like fairground organ pipes.

"Mom says she's going to start work on all this in the spring."

"Get a bulldozer," said Jack, who wasn't a natural horticulturist.

They tramped down the garden to a paved area where the shed stood, partly obscured by a trellis. The door was secured by a padlock and peg.

"I've never been in here," Robert said, shivering now because he'd not thought to put on a coat.

"It's more like a little garage," said Jack, shading the grimy glass in order to look inside. "Hey, there's a couple of pairs of wellingtons in here. Have you got the key?"

Robert flexed his toes, which were growing numb with cold.

"I didn't know it was locked."

The English boy gazed askance at the American, then started to chortle.

"You've got a serious face on!"

"Let's go back. I'm stupid. I'm freezing."

Jack went to the lock and gave it a pull and the latch came off in his hand.

"Oops."

The door swung open.

"Come on, misery, you first – we can get the boots at least."

Inside, it was surprisingly neat and tidy, with just a layer of dust and cobwebs to indicate the passing of time.

"It's not like our shed," said Jack, "you have to reach in to get anything and it's full of crap."

"Well, lookie there," slurred Robert through teeth that had begun to chatter. On a shelf below the workbench was a wooden toboggan with steel runners.

"You'd better get it out; my fingers are too numb."

Jack slipped by his friend and passed back the wellingtons.

"Try them on."

Then he reached under the bench and brought the sledge into the light. It was hardly any heavier than his plastic one. He set it down on the bench to examine it.

"This may well have come out of the ark."

"I don't think Noah needed a sled," murmured Robert.

The English boy turned, smiling, at the little joke, and found that the American was now sitting on the dusty floor with one brown shoe off and one green boot on.

"It says size nine and a half, but it seems to fit all right."

"Try the other."

"I'll wait till we get inside. This one feels damp."

The American tried to pull it off, but in the confined space and with such numb fingers he gave up.

"And I thought it was you English who were hopeless in cold weather." He blew out a cloud of frosty air.

Jack knelt and grasped the wellington by toe and ankle, and with one sharp tug removed it along with Robert's sock, sending them both sprawling backwards. The American lay slumped on the floor.

"I'm like a polar explorer who finds they haven't got the energy to move and perishes in their tent."

The English boy took off his gloves and fished the sock out of the boot.

"Lift," he said, taking the bare foot onto his knee. "It's like ice!"

Before he could stop himself, he had begun to gently massage the toes with one hand while firmly holding the foot with the other, finding himself captivated by its shape, size, the neatly trimmed nails and the sprinkling of tiny hairs across the top. It was an intensely erotic experience.

"Jack... please..." said Robert, covering his face.

The English boy realised his action was not only arousing for himself, but was also having a similar effect on the American. It made him feel quite powerful, but also protective enough not to want to distress or embarrass his friend. He took up the sock once more and guided it onto Robert's foot, then did the same with the shoe.

"There," he said, "all done."

***

30: Thursday, 31st January. 1.25 p.m. Pear Tree Cottage, the Ropewalk.

<u>ROBERT</u>

"Now where have you two been?" asked Maybelle, oven gloves on hands.

"The latch broke on the shed door and we had to prop it shut with a rake," replied Jack.

"That garden is going to be my next project," Maybelle said and smiled. "'And they shall say, This land that was desolate is become like the garden of Eden...'"

"We found a sled and some boots." Robert held up the wellingtons, then placed them by the Aga.

"Well, wash your hands, boys. Mikey and I have been busy rustlin' up a pizza for our lunch."

While the food was being dished out, Robert excused himself and ran upstairs to his bedroom, where he knelt by his bed.

"Dear Lord God, I come to you in the name of Jesus. I acknowledge that I am a sinner, and I am truly sorry for my sins and the shame of my life at present. I need your forgiveness for my wicked thoughts and my sexual cravings. Please, Lord Jesus, transform my life so that I may bring glory and honour to you and be a credit to my family. And thank you for sparing your son, Jack Moseley, the sight of my unnatural lust and grant too. I pray fervently that I may soon bring him to acknowledge You as his saviour and that he will undergo baptism by the Holy Spirit. I ask this, dear Father, in the name of our Lord Jesus Christ. Amen!"

After a lunch of pizza, salad and hot chocolate with marshmallows, they set off from the Ropewalk, Robert in his green wellies and two pairs of socks. Mikey had decided that he wanted the American to pull him along on the wooden sledge, but by the time they reached the embankment he had changed his mind, finding the smooth plastic more to his liking.

"Robert, I'm seven on Saturday," chirruped Mikey.

"I think we already know that," said Jack. "In fact, I expect everyone in the world has heard it by now."

The American paused to wipe his nose.

"So, what presents are you getting, little fella?"

"Pinocchio on Blu-ray!"

Robert gave a little whistle and Mikey giggled.

"You know it!"

"Of course I know it, and I know all the songs too."

Jack shook his head. "Don't encourage him."

"Sing one, please," pleaded Mikey.

"Later, perhaps," said Robert, taking the hint.

With two hours or so of daylight left, they crossed the old railway bridge and shortly came in sight of the Hill. Only in wintertime, and then only when it snowed, did this particular piece of land come into its own. Normally an area of common grassland, grazed in the spring and summer by animals from a local farm, it had served as the preferred venue for sledging by generations of Swanfordians. The wide slope started off gently at the top, took a semi-precipitous dip in the middle and then flattened out into a long glide home.

"Golly, I didn't expect to see so many people," exclaimed Robert, responding to the swarm of dark dots milling around in the white landscape.

"What, with a day off school?" responded Jack. "Where else would anyone go?"

The embankment and the Hill met at a tangent where a path through a small copse of trees led to the top of the crowded slope. Max appeared out of the throng.

"Hey," said Jack.

"Hey, yourself, I wondered why you'd taken so long. I see Robert's got the latest fashion in sledges."

"We found it in the shed," replied the American.

"Crikey, you've even got the trad green wellies on as well."

"We found them too."

"Isn't Stewart here?" asked Jack.

"I'm afraid Mrs Henderson said that he was working."

"Working?"

"I get the impression that Stew is like a male Cinderella, put to work while the ugly brothers come out to play. They are around somewhere, including that little blond freak, Alan, with his fancy snowboard."

"Cind'rella is for girls," said Mikey.

Max sniffed.

"Someone wound up the little wooden boy, I see."

"Do you want to ride down the slope with me, Mikey?" asked Robert.

The boy nodded.

"We'll have a race later, shall we?" suggested the American, "me and you versus Jack and Max."

"We'll win," said Mikey, climbing onto the front of the sledge.

"We will if we practise enough," agreed Robert. "Can one of you give us a push, please?"

Jack waited until they were both comfortable.

"Keep a tight grip, Mikey. Ready?"

They nodded and he put both hands on Robert's back and pushed. It took no more effort. The sledge began to accelerate immediately.

"Typical American," said Max, watching them go, "trying to organise our lives; making everything a competition..."

The old sledge was much faster than Robert had imagined. Perhaps the runners had been waxed. It careened down the hill, picking up even more speed on the central section, overtaking many of the assorted plastic sleds, trays and inflatables. Fortunately, it kept a straight path and he knew how to steer with his feet and not to lean. He hung on to the rope – and Mikey – like grim death, flying on into virgin snow at the base of the hill until at last they came to a halt some fifty yards beyond the normal stopping point.

"We'll win," said Mikey emphatically.

"I hope Jack's hair hasn't turned white, like mine has."

On the trudge back up the hill, Robert was suddenly confronted by the barrel shape of Ben Henderson, only in this instance it was with a smile.

"Way to go, Yank!" he said, offering a high five which the American reluctantly returned. "You sure showed that fag where to get off!"

"What's a fag?" asked Mikey, looking up at Robert.

"Shut your rap, runt," said Ben. "This is men's talk, not puking Moseley baby shit."

Before Robert could say anything, the rest of the Hendersons joined them. Derek, the eldest, stepped towards him.

"Listen, Yank, we can do with someone like you on our team."

"What team?"

"Never you mind, just be ready, OK?"

"Mikey!" It was Jack, calling from nearby.

The little boy ran over to where he was standing with Max, Charlie and Barbara.

"You all right?"

Mikey nodded. "The fat one called me shit."

"Robert, are you OK?" called Charlie.

The American raised his hand. "I'm fine."

The Hendersons turned.

"Well look, boys," said Ben, "a line of five faggotards."

"Shut up, Henderson, you greasy skid mark," said Barbara.

"Crikey!" murmured Max, "nice one, Babs."

"Seddon!" shouted Alan, his voice still unbroken. "We heard you called at our house to ask for Stewart to come out to play!"

"Is there a law against it?" asked Max.

"Yes," the blond boy replied, hoisting his snowboard onto his shoulder, "our law!"

Derek made a threatening move towards them. "So, don't ever come to our house again, understand?"

"How is Stewart?" enquired Jack, levelly.

"Why, are you queer for him, Moseley?" retorted John Jnr.

The Hendersons laughed to a man. Derek stabbed his finger at Robert.

"Remember what I said, Yank, and be ready."

He turned to his brothers. "Let's go boys, we got what we came for." Swaggering and laughing, the clan marched off towards the embankment, leaving the Hill a quieter and less threatening place.

"What was all that be ready stuff?" enquired Jack.

Robert shook his head. "I didn't understand what they were talking about."

"Can we have a race now?" asked Mikey.

Towards the end of the afternoon, the clouds thinned and a brumal sun made an appearance, standing low in a yellowing sky. It also grew colder and, when their fifth contest had been run, they called it a day, ready for the warmth of home.

Robert stood near the brow of the Hill, his body casting a long shadow down the slope. There was now just a sprinkling of people left on the snowfield and among them he caught sight of James and Mary from his Bible class. He thought he would go over to say hello, but they seemed intent on what they were doing, surrounded by a small huddle of young people.

"What are you staring at?" asked Jack, coming to stand by him.

Robert pointed.

"Just a couple of the people from my church."

The English boy looked.

"Do you mean the tall guy with the long dark hair?"

"His name's James," said the American, "and there's a girl, Mary."

"I'm cold," said Mikey, taking Jack's hand.

"We'd better go, then."

"What's for tea?"

"I don't know! Probably snot pie, like we usually have on Thursdays."

The group of six left the Hill behind, walking the now well-trodden path back along the embankment. At the steps, on the other side of the old railway bridge, Jack and Mikey bade their farewells and trudged on. Robert paused to watch them go for a moment, before descending the steps in the wake of Max, Charlie and Barbara. It had been a good day.

***

31: Saturday, 2nd February. 4.20 p.m. 15 Leighton Lane.

JACK

Hmm, well, I've done my bit and I'm back in my bedroom. Mikey got into a state when he thought no one would turn up for his party because of the snow, but they all got here in the end – unfortunately. There's only so much seven-year-old enthusiasm I can take. You'd think I was serving them vodka instead of lemonade. I left them playing blindfold balloon stomp in the lounge. Mikey's best friend

Mike Huntley was well into that. No wonder they call him Mad Mike – he's a right little terror. Earlier, I supervised pass the parcel (or parcel-parcel, as we call it because LB misheard it at one of his birthday bashes). When it landed on Mike, he was clawing at it like a velociraptor.

My excuse to leave was homework; a 750-word essay on 'The repercussions for the English navy of defeat in the second Anglo–Dutch war of 1667'. I don't mind history, and I've found an interesting angle on this one, but I have got other issues on my mind ... or, rather, one particular issue – person – Robert. That's why I'm lying on my bed with my hands behind my head, looking up at the ceiling.

For one thing, he's got ginger hair, not red, not gold: a pure ginger, carrot top. Not only that, but it also grows in tight Brillo pad curls. Oh and did I mention he's a boy? That's so gay, isn't it? The trouble is, as soon as I think seriously about him I get a hard-on. It's happening now! I love his ginger hair, his lovely goofy mouth, his lovely dark eyes, his lovely hairy legs, his lovely parts I'm trying not to think about, but failing, not to mention his lovely hairy feet. And I've made a tepee out of my pants...

It's just a crush and it'll pass and I'll meet lots of nice girls and live happily ever after. But I already know lots of nice girls, but none of them interest me in the way that he does. So, what am I going to do? I'm fairly sure he feels something too, but his religion won't allow him to show those feelings. It's bad enough for me, but for him it must be a hundred times worse, especially as he thinks that going to Hell will be the end result. And, anyway, he'll be leaving in less than two years, so what's the point?

The point is, I want to be with him; I want to hold him; I want to rip his clothes off; I want to jump on him!

I am gay, aren't I? There's no other word for it – well, there is, about a thousand – all insults. Am I the only gay in the school? No, I'm not, because there's Andy Venables and Adam Ellis in the sixth form, and that boy with the fringe over one eye in Year 9. No one seems to bother them much at school, as far as I know, though the police had a go at Andy and Adam over that gay bar business. Why can't life be a bit more simple?

Right, I'm not going to think about that any more. I'd better get on with my essay; that'll soon put an end to my stiffy.

***

32: Saturday, 2nd February. 4.40 p.m. 15 Leighton Lane.

<u>JACK</u>

The noise downstairs had subsided. He switched on his computer and took out the history exercise book. Then he noticed he had a saved game from Dagger Coast: Storm of Destiny in which, having recovered the Landburger's treasure chest from the Isle of the Dead, he had now been offered the hand in marriage of the Landburger's beautiful daughter, Esmerelda, and a dowry of 12,000 gold pieces. Though he didn't really want Esmerelda's hand, he knew that to advance in the game the 12,000 gold pieces would come in very handy, especially to enhance his Greatsword of Destruction, which was getting a bit passé at level 16.

He steeled himself against this distraction and began to write: 'The first problem for the Royal Navy was the loss of fifteen ships, especially the flagship Royal Charles, which was captured...'

There were two light taps on the door. Jack sighed and put down his pen.

"Come in, LB."

Dan Moseley entered and shut the door quietly behind him.

Jack swivelled in his chair.

"You're back early..."

It was as far as he got.

Dan sobbed. "Jack!" His head went down, and he began to cry.

"Hey, LB!"

In an instant, Jack was out of his chair and had his arms wrapped around his brother. He could feel Dan's tears wetting his own cheek and just held on to him, letting him weep for as long as he needed.

"Justin's been accepted for the Academy," he sobbed, at last. "He's the only one."

Jack held on just a little tighter, as Dan began to cry again into his shoulder. This was the first time since... who knows when? that he'd seen his brother shed tears. He only rarely got upset. It almost made him feel like crying himself. Jack glanced at his brother and gave him a gentle kiss on the cheek.

Slowly his brother relaxed in his arms, his sobbing subsided and Jack was able to quietly guide him over to his bed, where they sat close together.

"I should be glad that one of us has been accepted..."

"Yeah, but it should have been the right one... you."

Dan closed his eyes, allowing the remaining tears to trickle out.

"Hey, you'd better have one of my special three-ply wanky hankies," said Jack, pulling a tissue out of the box by his bedside and handing it to him.

"It hasn't got any on, has it?" sniffed Dan, wiping his eyes.

"Yes, but it's all right; it'll moisturise your skin."

"Gross." Dan managed a smile and blew his nose.

"Would you like me to go round and break Justin's legs?"

Dan laughed and sobbed.

"Don't give up, LB; this won't be your only chance."

"I feel like packing it in."

"You've got too much talent for that. I bet Coach Brennan is spitting feathers that you didn't get a place."

"He didn't say much, just well done to Justin."

"Have you told Mum and Dad?"

Dan shook his head. "I didn't want Dad to see me like this. You won't tell either of them about this cry-baby stuff, will you, Jack?"

"Never in a million years. Would you like me to fetch you something to eat or drink?"

"Could you just stay with me? Think I'll have a nap."

"Course; you just make yourself comfortable. I've got my history essay to do. I'll wake you up when I've finished."

***

33: Sunday, 3rd February. 10.50 a.m. The Ropewalk.

ROBERT

It was a warm, breezy day under leaden skies and the last of the snow was melting fast. Frank, Maybelle and Robert Crittenden had decided to walk to morning service at 9 a.m. and were now returning to Pear Tree Cottage, where they would have Sunday brunch.

"The congregation was even smaller than last Sunday," said Frank.

"I cannot remember a single word of the pastor's sermon," replied Maybelle, disapprovingly. "And wasn't he a shade offhand with us at the end of the service?"

"It was very bland," commented Frank.

When they arrived home, Robert went upstairs to change and start his history homework essay: 'The repercussions for the English navy of defeat in the second Anglo–Dutch war of 1667'. This was beyond boring for him as he didn't care about the English navy and, anyway, it was too long ago and far away. He had barely begun to collect his thoughts when he was called downstairs. As he descended to the lounge, the intoxicating smell of Sunday brunch brightened his mood. It was American day: pancakes and crispy bacon with maple syrup.

He joined his father at the table while his mom brought in the dishes.

"Yummy," he said, his mouth watering.

"Son, your mother and I are still concerned about your Bible class. We are worried that Pastor McKellan is not showing himself to be the man we thought him to be."

"He's far more strict with me than anyone else."

"Well, that isn't entirely a bad thing; you do start at a much higher level than these other children."

Maybelle sat down.

"At least we've got rid of that pervert. Now, Robert, would you say grace for us?"

"Sure, Mom."

They held hands and bowed their heads.

"Bounteous God, we acknowledge our dependence on You, and our unworthiness of Your benefits. We pray that You will forgive our sins. Please bless us in the reception of this food and enable us to transfer the strength we may derive from it to Your glory. We ask this in the name of our Lord Jesus Christ. Amen!"

"Thank you, son," said his father.

Robert had a stack of five pancakes surrounded by crisp rashers of streaky bacon, over which he poured a generous helping of maple syrup.

"Mom, your pancakes are so much better than the English ones we get at school. They're just silly."

"They're a taste of the home country, hon," she smiled, and exchanged glances with Frank as though they were sharing a secret. Robert noticed, but said nothing.

After brunch, he washed the dishes as he always did on a Sunday, then polished his shoes ready for school in the morning. Today, these chores were as balm to him, because back in his room there was worse: the history essay. He looked around to see if there was anything else that might need doing, but everything was as neat and tidy as always.

By 3 p.m. he had written three hundred words, ending, 'After the war was lost in August 1667, the Navy Board came under scrutiny from the public and parliament alike...' He had copied most of it from Wikipedia; he didn't know where else to turn. He sat back, wishing he could contact Jack and ask him some questions. No, he was dissembling again; he just wanted to talk to him, about anything. Memories of Jack's fingers massaging his toes came rushing into his mind. He began to get excited. No! No! He must concentrate on the second Anglo–Dutch war...

Had Jack known the effect it would have on him? No, how could he? He was blaming his friend for his own sinfulness. This made him feel doubly guilty, and he knew he would have to kneel down and pray for forgiveness.

"Robert, would you come here please?"

His father's voice brought him quickly back into the present.

"Sure, Dad."

He stood up, adjusting his trousers, before going to the door of his bedroom.

Frank and Maybelle were waiting for him on the landing in front of the open study door. There were expressions of delight on their faces.

"We have a surprise for you."

All three squeezed into the tiny room. The screen on his father's desk showed Pastor Dunn's face beaming out at him.

"Robert, it is such a pleasure to be able to talk to you – and to see you."

The boy glanced at his parents, then back at the screen.

"Pastor, this is such a surprise. I had no idea!"

On the periphery of the image were the young people he had grown up with: Tammy, Gregg, Chris and Katie. It made him feel instantly homesick. What was he doing here in this horrible country?

"Robert, we want to congratulate you on the courageous act you performed at your Bible class, and I should like to quote you two passages from the scriptures that seem appropriate to your action. First, Ephesians, chapter 6, verse 11: 'Put on the whole armour of God, that you may be able to stand against the schemes of the Devil. For we do not wrestle against flesh and blood, but against the rulers, against the authorities, against the cosmic powers over this present darkness, against the spiritual forces of evil in the heavenly places.' And, second, from First Corinthians, chapter 6, verse 9: 'Do not be deceived: neither the sexually immoral, nor idolaters, nor adulterers, nor men who practise homosexuality, nor thieves, nor the greedy, nor drunkards, nor revilers, nor swindlers will inherit the Kingdom of God.'"

Pastor Dunn put down his book, while his friends clapped and cheered him. He glowed with pride, though at the back of his mind there was a small voice crying 'hypocrite!'

"You must keep up the Lord's work over there, Robert; I hear you are on the verge of getting your first convert."

"Well, I haven't got quite as far as that, Pastor."

"You must also keep your father informed about our colleague, Pastor McKellan. We have invested resources in him and we should not like to see our good work come to naught."

Robert nodded, then smiled.

"It's nice to see you all. Thank you for your good wishes."

"Here's Tammy to say a few words to you, Robert."

Pastor Dunn moved out of camera shot, allowing Tammy Miller's feline face to move into full frame.

"Hi, Robert." She smiled a wide toothpaste smile.

"Hi, Tammy, how're you doin'?"

"Just fine. You're talkin' real funny."

"How's that?"

Pastor Dunn's voice boomed out. "I think Tammy means that you're sounding more English."

Robert chuckled. "I've only been here a month."

"Missin' you in the choir, Robert," said Tammy.

"Can't wait to get back to a normal life with you folks."

"Lookin' forward to that day."

Pastor Dunn's face appeared like a large balloon in the centre of the screen.

"Robert, we shall leave you with the words of our Lord Jesus Christ, taken from the gospel of St Matthew: 'All authority in Heaven and on Earth has been given to me. Go therefore and make disciples of all nations, baptising them in the name of the Father and of the Son and of the Holy Spirit, teaching them to observe all that I have commanded you. And behold, I am with you always, to the end of the age.' We're going to sign off now, so goodbye and God bless, until the next time."

The Skype connection terminated. Robert smiled at his parents.

"You missin' home, hon?" asked his mother, watching his face.

"I guess."

"If you keep up the good work here, you'll be a bigger and better man when we get back," said Frank. "One day, I can see you in the ministry. Have you ever thought of that, Robert?"

"Not really, sir," replied Robert. "I don't think I have sufficient calling to attend the seminary."

"I know Pastor Dunn feels differently about that, son."

***

34: Sunday, 3rd February. 9.50 p.m. Pear Tree Cottage, the Ropewalk.

ROBERT

I've been slogging over this history essay for over an hour now. Perhaps one day at this English school we'll do a period of history where the USA actually exists!

Heh! I've just had an email. It's from Auntie Una – which isn't surprising, as she's probably the only person, other than spammers, who has my email address.

Oh! This isn't so good...

121

Dear Robert,

I hope you won't mind me writing to you in this way.

I heard through the grapevine that you outed a gay boy to your pastor and got him removed from your church, I am told because he touched you and asked to walk home with you.

I ask you, if a girl had done that, would you have reported her?

You're a very friendly boy, Robert, and sometimes people, especially young vulnerable people, can mistake these signals.

Now, I don't want to make a big issue out of this. I know what your church teaches you, and it's one of the reasons I left it.

But I know you well enough to believe that you are normally above such uncharitable acts, and therefore think you are not entirely happy with your life at the moment.

If you need to talk, you know where I am. It would be great to hear from you.

Tom and your cousins Barney and Susie send their love – and I do too.

Your aunt,
Una

Not entirely happy with my life! What does she mean? And there is no way I'm ever going to talk about Kieran Scott to anyone, period! In fact, it's all nonsense. I'm going to delete it. No, I won't delete it now; I'll read it once more in a few days then delete it. How can anyone living six thousand miles away know how I'm feeling, especially someone who I haven't seen for over a year, and probably won't ever want to see again, given this? In any case, someone like Kieran makes my skin crawl. Disgusting, fat, mincing, effeminate fag.

***

35: Wednesday, 6th February. 8.55 a.m. Swanford
Community School, Class 4S.

JACK

When Stewart Henderson entered the classroom, most
heads, including Jack's, turned his way. Not because of his
black eye or the bruising on his body – which, in any case, was
fading fast – but because he had fainted during rugby practice
the afternoon before and had to be taken home.

"All right, Stew?" asked Charlie.

The boy took his seat, shrugging non-committally.

"You look a bit weird," said Mandy, who was sitting on
Robert's desk.

"I'm OK."

Max walked over to him. "Why did you faint?"

"I don't know; I just felt weak all of a sudden." He bent
to take a book out of his bag, deliberately bringing the
exchange to a close.

"Right," Mandy said, "let's get down to business again..."

"You don't have to put up with this, you know," said
Jack, leaning towards Robert.

"Shut your fucking mouth, Moseley. You enjoy our little
sessions, don't you, Robert?"

"I don't mind, Mandy," he replied.

"Now," she continued, "about this Cain and Abel."

"Cain and Abel were brothers in the Book of Genesis..."

"You don't have to tell me that, I'm not a dipshit. What
you do have to tell me is why God doesn't know where Abel is
when Cain has just murdered him and put him under the
fucking sod?"

"Of course God knows what Cain has done, he's just
testing him," replied the American.

"So, why a moment later does God tell Cain that his
brother's blood is crying out to him from the ground? Why
didn't He just cut to the chase?"

"You're splitting hairs," said Robert.

"Yes, but isn't that what all you Bible-bashers do?"

"I don't."

"Mandy?" interrupted Stewart.

"No, Stewy, I'm not going to uncross my legs for you, because it's pervy!"

"No, I wondered if we could rehearse tonight?"

"I'm afraid Maxxy and I have something planned," she replied, almost apologetically.

"Oh, OK."

"Now," she continued, looking down her nose at the American, "there's an awful lot of fucking going on at this period, isn't there... someone's always begetting this, that or the other little squib, aren't they?"

"If I'd have been around then, I would have been the biggest begetter of the lot," said Charlie.

"You're a gob-shite, Masefield."

"Oh, yeah," said Charlie with a self-satisfied smirk.

"Crikey," said Max, "have you popped a cherry at last?"

"Maxxy, don't be so fucking crude."

All eyes looked at Barbara, who was sitting behind Robert, for confirmation or denial, but she continued to chat with Alice Crabtree, ignoring the banter going on around her.

"If it happened, he's got such a small dick that I doubt any girl would feel it." said Jack.

"Tsk, you needn't talk, Moseley," said Charlie. "Yours is more like a bloody clit."

"No, it isn't," said Robert unguardedly, causing colour to rush to his cheeks.

There was a moment of silence, during which Robert appeared to be waiting for the sky to fall in. Then everyone laughed.

"See, Masefield," said Jack, "Robert is so comfortable with his sexuality that he can be honest about other people and not brag about his fictitious exploits, like some."

"It's not fictitious," said Charlie flatly.

Mandy banged her palms on the desk.

124

"Listen, you lot of sub-adolescent nonces, I'm trying to have an intelligent conversation here about the fucking Bible and all you can talk about are your insignificant little dicks."

At that moment, the clock ticked over to three minutes past nine o'clock and Mr Colt entered the classroom. It took the usual two minutes for class 4S to come to order, by which time their form teacher had arranged his books and taken out the register.

"Mr Henderson, I am pleased to see you here this morning. I understand you gave Mr Harris, our estimable rugby coach, a bit of a fright yesterday?"

"Not really, sir, I just blacked out for a minute."

"Indeed, and are you in the habit of 'blacking out'?"

"No, sir, that was the first time."

"And I sincerely hope it will be the last time, Mr Henderson."

"Excuse me, sir, I didn't get to do the piece of writing you set."

"Well, I think in this instance we can forgive that."

"Thank you, sir."

"But I do expect to have it by Friday morning. Do you think you can manage that?"

"I hope so, sir."

"I hope so too. Can you remember the title of the essay?"

Stewart thought hard. "Write a review of the very last film you saw in no more than 275 words."

At 9.30 a.m. the class left their form room to go to their first lesson, history, with Mr Graham. Few were looking forward to getting their essays back. 'The repercussions for the English navy of defeat in the second Anglo–Dutch war of 1667' had proved a bitter pill for many. Jack stopped off at the lockers to collect a textbook, where he found Ben Henderson in heated exchange with his much smaller brother.

"Everything all right, Stew?" Jack asked.

Ben spun round.

"Fuck off, Moseley, this is between me and him."

"Sounded like it was between you and the whole school."

"One of these days, someone is going to knock your pinko, pansy block off."

"I'm not going," said Stewart, glancing pleadingly at Jack. "I told Derek I've got something else on tonight."

"You liar. A loser like you never has anything else on."

Jack remembered Stewart asking Mandy if they could rehearse and being turned down. "Stew's coming to tea at my house."

"What?"

"Stew's coming over to my place for tea. We're going to go over an essay he missed, because he fainted in rugby."

"You cunt, you just made that up."

"You are still coming, aren't you, Stew?" enquired Jack.

"Yes," said the boy gratefully.

***

36: Wednesday, 6th February. 12.45 p.m. Swanford Community School canteen.

JACK

Jack was quite pleased that Robert was noticeably put out when he learned that Stewart was to have tea at the Moseley household. It made him hopeful that his plan to invite the American over on the last Friday before half term, the day after his birthday, might succeed where previous invitations had failed.

Jack texted his mother:

Bringing Stew round after school. Make sure there's enough food.

She replied:

Who's Stew? Do I get a please??

He texted back:

U no Stew. Ple e e e e e e e e e e ase!

And received:

All right, but tea will just be ordinary.

126

"Has anyone found any beef in this beef stew?" enquired Max.

"I think you got the scrapings," Charlie replied, and held up his dumpling. "Would anyone like this soggy excuse for a Henderson brain?"

"Dumplings and rice – it's a joke," said Jack, making a face.

"It is quite gritty," grumbled Max. "I expect if I complained, though, they'd tell me it's al dente."

"Not a success today, then?" said Charlie.

Max looked hard at his pudding plate. "The pancakes look all right."

"Robert thinks our pancakes are crap," said Jack.

"Having pancakes with bacon and then putting syrup on top is just..." Charlie couldn't think of a word bad enough.

".... Is just a recipe for having a heart attack before he's twenty," concluded Max.

This did worry Jack. He couldn't really understand how Robert could remain so thin with the number of calories he consumed.

"Talking of the opposite, do you think Stewy is getting enough to eat?" he said. "Fainting and all that."

"He's always been wiry," answered Charlie.

Max huffed. "I notice his packed lunch is usually just a sandwich and a Blue Riband."

Robert appeared with his tray and a puzzled expression on his face.

"I just had a strange conversation with Ben Henderson."

"There is no other sort with that psycho," stated Max.

"He asked me again if I was on for tonight. I told him it was Bible class and he just laughed and said that's what he meant."

"Psycho!" repeated Max.

"Whatever it is, Stewy wants no part of it," said Jack.

"And talk of the devil..." observed Charlie.

From the packed lunch section of the canteen, Stewart Henderson was trotting over to their table. He seemed almost out of breath by the time he reached them.

"Robert, you won't go with them, will you?"

"I just spoke to your brother and told him it was Bible class."

This seemed to satisfy the boy, who turned to Jack. "I'm looking forward to tonight."

"We'll go to my house straight from school, if that's all right?"

Stewart nodded.

***

37: Wednesday, 6th February. 4.05 p.m. 15 Leighton Lane.

PAM

Pamela Moseley put down a jug of orange juice and a plate of custard creams in front of her two youngest sons, then went to the sink so she could keep watch out of the kitchen window.

"You don't know Stewart, then?" she asked.

"Not really, I know his brother Alan better," replied Dan. "He's in my year, but in 2T. We do PE and games together. Everyone thinks he's so tough, but without his brothers he's just a wuss, though he has got the best skateboard in the school."

"They're coming up the path now. Goodness! He only comes up to your brother's shoulder."

"Hey," said Jack on entering. "I've brought Stewart – Stew to his friends." He threw his bag down by the door.

"Hello, dear," said Pam. "This is Dan, I expect you've seen him at school, but you won't have met Mikey, he's my youngest son."

Stewart's thin face went slightly pink. He smiled shyly.

"Are you really fourteen?" asked Dan.

128

Jack gave his brother a warning glance.

"I'm seven," said Mikey proudly.

"Help yourself to a glass of orange and a biscuit, Stew." asked Pam.

Stewart nodded.

"Well, sit down, dear."

Jack threw his coat down on top of his bag, then took off his shoes.

"What's for tea? School dinner was rubbish today."

"Dan's just told me that. I thought I'd do sausage, beans and chips. Is that all right for you, Stew?"

The boy smiled at Pam and took a custard cream.

Jack sat down and looked at his brother who in turn was looking at Stewart's dirty hands and fingernails, then at his none-too-clean hair and finally at his ragged clothes. At length, their eyes met and Dan gave the slightest nod.

"So, you're one of Councillor Henderson's sons?" said Pam.

"Yes."

"And you live in Edward's Lane?"

Jack gulped his drink down and stood up. "Right, let's go, Stew, before she starts shining a light in your face and dripping water on head."

They got as far as the hall door.

"Could you take your shoes off before you go upstairs, dear?" said Pam.

"No socks," whispered Stewart to Jack.

"We'll find you some."

Stewart slipped off his shoes to reveal feet in the same condition as his hands.

"Mum, have you got a towel?"

"Yes, they're in their usual place in the airing cupboard."

"LB?"

"Yeah, I'll sort something out for him."

"Am I having a shower?" said Stewart.

"Yes, and when you're done, Dan'll have some clean clothes for you."

***

While Stewart was in the shower, Pam came up to speak to Jack in his bedroom.

"Has he got everything?"

"I gave him a towel, shower gel, sponge, nail brush and clippers, and a toothbrush."

"His family are not looking after him properly. No socks indeed!"

"No boxers either," said Jack.

"What sort of a people are those Hendersons?"

"The other brothers are all psychos."

"They should be reported to social services. I shall speak to your father."

Dan entered carrying a small bundle.

"These are some of the clothes I haven't thrown out because I like them, even though they're too small."

"Thanks LB, I owe you."

"No problem. At least we're getting a decent tea out of it tonight."

Pam gave him the evil eye. "Daniel Moseley, just you be careful..."

***

At six o'clock they were all seated round the kitchen table, tucking into home-made chips, Tesco Finest Cumberland sausages and Heinz baked beans. Stewart had been transformed by the shower and Dan's old green Reebok sweatshirt and blue jeans into a presentable young man. Pam had already informed Roger what was going on before the boys came back downstairs.

"I wish it still fitted me," said Dan, looking sadly at his sweatshirt.

"I had the very same feeling about a pair of pink flared jeans when I was a teenager," said Roger. "Those were the days – when fashion was fashion."

"I wouldn't know – we don't do ancient history at school," said Jack.

"You got an A in history today," stated Stewart, which was not quite a non sequitur, but enough for everyone to give pause for thought. "Most of us only got a C. It was very hard."

"Well done, you," said Pam, patting her son on the arm.

Dan huffed. "No one seems to notice in this house that he is quite clever."

"My son, the historian," mused Roger.

Jack could not deny the pleasure of being lauded so, but he did feel the need for a certain amount of self-deprecation.

"It was only because I found a website that was the daily diary of a man called Samuel Pepys, who lived at that time and worked for the navy."

"It all sounds very interesting, dear. Would anyone like these last few chips?"

"I will," said Dan. "Stew, Jack says you've got to write a film review."

The boy stopped eating for a moment. "Yes, but I haven't seen any films recently."

"What was the last film you did see?" asked Roger.

Stewart became thoughtful, holding his knife and fork poised over a sausage. "*Slime Zombies in New York*," he said at last.

"Sounds dreadful," said Pam.

"Sounds good," said Dan, "was it an eighteen?"

"I don't know – there was no label."

"Stewart," squeaked Mikey who had been listening carefully to the conversation, "would you like to see Pinocchio on Blu-ray?"

"Oh no!" chorused Jack and Dan together.

"What's that?" asked Stewart.

"It's a Disney classic cartoon," said Pam.

"Actually," said Jack, "Coming to think about it, writing a review would be easy for that: 'Pinocchio is the very worst film I've seen in my life..'."

With a pout that would have made Tom of Tom and Jerry jealous, Mikey bunched his fists, in which he was holding his knife and fork, and shook them at his brother. Jack smirked at him in a leisurely and condescending fashion.

"Don't tease," said Pam. "Aren't you supposed to be the mature and clever one?"

"I would go for Pinocchio, Stew," said Roger, "it's quite short and it will be fresh in your mind."

Stewart nodded, then mopped up the remaining tomato sauce with his last two chips and popped them in his mouth. "That was lovely," he murmured, leaning back in his chair and closing his eyes.

***

38: Wednesday, 6th February. 6.20 p.m. The Baptist church, Westbury Avenue.

<u>ROBERT</u>

He arrived at the church early, fearing somehow that Kieran would defy his expulsion from the group and make an unscheduled entrance. Pastor McKellan's car was parked out the front, but inside there was no sign of him – or anyone else. In the vestry, Robert set out the chairs, then noticed there was no drink or biscuits on the side table. It seemed to be a sign that all was not well.

James arrived with Mary at 6.25 p.m. Neither acknowledged his smile, but instead took up their usual places in the seats furthest away from him. After a minute or so of silence, broken only by Mary's sniffing into her handkerchief, James looked across at him.

"Got rid of the fag, then?" he said, conversationally.

Robert was still not particularly attuned to the nuances of English irony and so preferred to take the question seriously.

"He sinned in God's house," he replied, feeling a degree of sanctimony was in order.

"Kieran's pretty sure you're a fag too," said James, matter-of-factly.

Robert coloured up. This was too much. In any case, he had respected James more than any other in the group.

"He revolts me."

"Prefer the more masculine type, do you?"

"I am not a homosexual," said Robert, uncomfortable even using the word.

James shrugged as if it didn't matter one way or the other, then put his arm round Mary's shoulder and whispered something into her ear.

Jane and Pastor McKellan entered the vestry together on the stroke of half past six.

"Hello, everyone," the pastor said quietly. "Jane informs me that Callum won't be joining us tonight."

Robert almost sighed with relief; at least there would be no questioning concerning Kieran's whereabouts.

"Excuse me, Pastor McKellan," he said, trying to keep the sing-song lilt out of his voice.

"Yes, what is it Robert?"

"The refreshments haven't been put out."

"You're right. That was usually Kieran's preserve. Perhaps you could take over that duty?"

Jane sat by him, which surprised and gratified him. She smiled and Robert thought she looked quite pretty, now that she wasn't picking at her nose, and smiled back.

"I'll help you," she said, "if you want?"

He nodded his thanks and began to relax for the first time since his arrival. Pastor McKellan moved to his seat.

"James, it is your turn to take the class tonight. What have you got for us?"

James stood up, taking a piece of paper from the inside of his jacket.

"Mary and I have got to be off at quarter to eight; we're due in town." He scratched his head, allowing a few flakes of dandruff to descend onto his collar. The pastor waved the comment away and so James carried on.

"I thought I'd explore the passage in Romans, chapter 12, verse 19: 'Dearly beloved, avenge not yourselves, but rather give place unto wrath: for it is written, Vengeance is mine; I will repay, saith the Lord.'"

He looked round the small group and his eyes came to rest on Robert, who returned his gaze, staring blankly into James's bloodshot eyes.

Robert had done this passage in Bible study back in home in Tyree and so saw little point in discussing it again with people who knew little or nothing about the subject. The only thing that concerned him was the way James had seemed to connect the passage to him. By seven o'clock, the talk had all but dried up, and so the pastor called for the refreshments to be brought out while he went about his own business.

"Will you walk me home afterwards?" asked Jane, as they set out the beakers. "I'm a little afraid of the dark and there is no one else tonight."

"Sure," replied Robert, "where do you live?"

"I thought you knew: Morcross House, down Church Lane."

"I've never been down there."

"It's not far."

After fifteen minutes the pastor returned but, finding no more enthusiasm to continue the subject than before the break, began a half-hour homily on the dangers of celebrating the largely pagan festival of St Valentine. It was a text he had meant to introduce in his next Sunday sermon, but saw merit in using the time now to rehearse.

At quarter to eight, they all left the church together. James and Mary turned right out of the lychgate, heading for town, while the pastor went straight to his car. Jane paused for a moment to send a text, then she and Robert went left, walking the short distance along Westbury Avenue to Church

Lane. The night was moonless, but starlit, with a gentle westerly breeze. Jane seemed very small and vulnerable to Robert, barely coming up to the middle of his chest.

"What is Morcross House?" he asked.

"A children's home."

"Who do you live with?"

"There are six kids – well, I say kids, we're all over fourteen."

"Does James live there?"

"No, but he used to and the rest of the Bible study group do."

They continued down the lane, walking parallel with the churchyard, which was no longer used for burials, though the headstones of the interred remained. Jane chattered away inconsequentially, allowing Robert to observe his surroundings. Beyond the entrance to Morcross School, on the other side of the road, the lane narrowed to a pedestrian-only path bordered by iron railings on one side and a dense leylandii hedge on the other. Here, the street lamps were old and made only faint pools of light.

"I can see why you don't like walking home on your own," said Robert.

"They like putting children's homes on the edges of places. We're out of the way then." Jane smiled and he realised she was a lot more intelligent than he had given her credit for.

The line of hedging stopped abruptly and was replaced by a new wall made of brick pillars supporting wooden trelliswork. Behind this was a large two-storey house set well back from the lane in its own substantial grounds.

Shortly, they came to a wrought-iron gate.

"This is it," said Jane.

Robert peered between the bars, down a long pathway, wondering what it would be like to live without a proper family. The only light visible was at the front door.

"Do you all live here on your own?" he asked.

"No! There's staff; most are all right. We're not prisoners or anything."

The American saw the front door open and recognised Callum, who emerged, carrying a torch. The distant figure waved and the silver frames of his glasses glinted. Jane waved back.

"I'd better go," said Robert.

"Wait," said Jane, opening the gate.

Two more boys appeared behind Callum, and then Kieran came into view, his bulk almost filling the doorway. Each was brandishing a piece of what looked like sawn-up broom handle. Robert suddenly felt uneasy. Jane stepped around him, blocking his way back. The boys were walking rapidly up the path now, their eyes focused on him, their intentions clear.

"Get out of my way," he said, becoming frightened, but the girl took hold of his coat sleeve. He wrenched his arm away, pushing her to one side, harder than was necessary, for she was as light as a feather and fell over with a little cry. Unheeding, he began to run back up the lane, but the footsteps behind him gathered pace also. He looked over his shoulder to find they were closing in on him.

A sharp pain caught him in the small of the back and a piece of broom handle clattered on the path behind. One of the boys had thrown his weapon, to good effect, for it slowed him a little. He took another glance over his shoulder. Callum was close to coming within physical reach of him, and even Kieran was not far behind, his fat cheeks flushed scarlet.

Vengeance is mine; I will repay, saith the Lord.

He emerged from the narrow part of the lane onto the pavement by the church wall. A transit van turned out of the Morcross School driveway and began to approach. He hoped the driver would see what was happening and do something. A hand tugged at the back of his coat, but he shook it off and put on a spurt of speed. The van went by. He was gasping for breath now.

Another stick caught him on the back of the head. Though his trapper hat cushioned the blow, he saw stars. A squeal like that of an animal went up behind him, but he didn't dare look. Blind panic was the sole factor now driving him on. It was only when he reached the top of Church Lane that he realised he was no longer being pursued. He turned, just as the transit van swept past him, turning right into Westbury Avenue, heedless of any traffic. Stars continued to dance in front of his eyes, and he panted, his hands on his knees. Nothing moved, except for an old black cat which scurried across the lane and jumped onto the churchyard wall.

***

39: Wednesday, 6th February. 10.05 p.m. 15 Leighton Lane.

JACK

Stewart Henderson had left the Moseley household at ten o'clock with Roger, who was giving him a lift home to Edward's Lane in a deliberate ploy to see if he could discover why the boy was so neglected.

Jack came to sit with his mother in the lounge. He was tired and settled comfortably into the settee, closing his eyes.

His mother put the television on standby.

"Did Stew get his homework done?"

"A-ha," replied her son.

"Jack, speak to me in English, please."

He opened one eye. "Yes, he did get his homework done."

"He enjoyed Pinocchio, didn't he?"

"Yes, he's a bit of a retard."

Pam clicked her tongue. "Did you help him with the review?"

"Not much; just got him to concentrate for once."

"Did he say anything about his home life?"

"Only that his brothers pick on him and it's better here."

They fell into silence and Jack closed his eye again and started to imagine what Robert might be doing. He smiled to himself, because all his imaginings were of the pervy sort.

A key clicked in the back door and shortly Roger Moseley entered the lounge. Jack opened both eyes, waiting for his report.

"Well?" questioned Pam.

"Quite warm out," he replied, sitting in the armchair, "for the time of the year."

"Roger! You're as bad as Jack. Tell me what happened?"

Her husband shrugged. "Nothing happened. Nice house, everything shipshape inside and out. Nice car. Very quiet. Councillor Henderson was there with his wife. They recognised me from the town hall; invited me in; gave me a drink." Roger blew out a breath. "One very small whisky with soda. Stewart went upstairs like a lamb. I explained about the shower and the clothes, and they just laughed, saying he was going through a grunge phase."

Jack shook his head contemptuously. "What about the psycho brothers?"

"There was a little blond fellow playing a computer game in front of the telly with headphones, but no sign of anyone else."

Pam frowned. "Well, I don't know. Something's not right."

"Jack will just have to keep an eye on him," said Roger.

"Me!"

"Yes, you – you're his friend."

"Jesus, so now I'm a part-time social worker, unpaid!"

***

40: Wednesday, 6th February. 10.15 p.m. Pear Tree Cottage, the Ropewalk.

ROBERT

I thought I'd be able to get to sleep easily, but I can't. Everything keeps going round and round in my head. How come someone as fat as Kieran Scott can run almost as fast as me? I didn't – couldn't – tell my parents about being chased. All I said was that only three members beside myself had turned up to Bible class. Dad asked me about Jack again and I gave him some lame excuse. I can't lie here with all this going on inside my mind. I may as well get up and do some tidying on my computer, then I'll do a long prayer to calm me down.

That's funny – I can't find Auntie Una's email. I was going to delete it, but I can't delete it if I can't find it. I've looked in all the folders, or at least I think I have. I'm sure I haven't deleted it already. I'll have one more look round...

No, it's definitely not here and neither is her entry in my web address folder. I must be going crazy! This whole night has been like one long bad dream. I wish I could talk to Jack. A prayer for guidance should be my answer, but if I could just talk to Jack, I know I'd feel easier.

This is hopeless! If I don't solve this I won't be able to sleep at all. It's late, but I'm going to have to go downstairs to ask Dad about it.

In the lounge, Dad was reading World Oil magazine and Mom was browsing the new international version of the Bible.

"Hello, hon, aren't you in bed yet?"

"I can't find Aunt Una's cell phone number or email address," I say.

"Well, that's probably a blessing," my mom replies.

"Dad, is there anywhere they could be on my laptop that I might not know about?"

He looks over his shoulder at me.

"No, son. Now, you run along to bed. We've got to be up early in the morning."

I've been dismissed like a child, but I'm fifteen, for heaven's sake!

"But Dad, surely they can't just disappear?"

My father gets up angrily. Sometimes his anger frightens me.

"Don't answer me back, Robert. Now get upstairs and pray to our Lord Jesus Christ for forgiveness. You have broken the Fifth Commandment."

***

41: Thursday, 7th February. 7.30 p.m. Pear Tree Cottage, the Ropewalk.

ROBERT

Weekday breakfast was usually cereal, toast and coffee. But today, as well as Golden Grahams, his mother had made cinnamon French toast with strawberry jam. It may well have been a peace offering and, though his flat refusal to talk about his lost email and address still rankled, he decided to be contrite.

"I'm sorry about last night, Dad," he said, joining his parents at the table.

Frank was wearing a blue pin-stripe business suit with matching tie and a white shirt, which meant high level meetings were scheduled at work.

"That's all right, son, we'll say no more about it. This country is obviously putting us all under strain."

Maybelle patted her son's hand. "Will you say grace, hon?"

"Sure, Mom."

After it was done, Robert had a small bowl of cereal and then tucked into a mound of the French toast. "Yummy," he said, spreading a thick layer of jam onto a slice.

Frank dived into the inside pocket of his suit and drew out a mobile phone.

"Son, I think it's time you had one of these."

He handed it to Robert, whose eyes popped. "Gee, thanks Dad!"

"It's my old company phone. It's connected to the same network as your laptop, but it should do you. Of course, I have replaced the SIM. It's fully charged and you can pay me for the top-up. I believe there is five English pounds worth of credit on there, which should last you a considerable while."

The boy smiled with pleasure. He was very glad now he had apologised, but then a thought occurred to him: any calls or messages he made or received probably would be monitored.

"Robert, a week tonight your daddy and I are entertaining some business folks, so if you want to make plans, that's fine."

"What time are they coming?"

"About six o'clock," said Frank. "They should be gone by nine, but I shall have to go with them. We are all going to Ipswich for a few days."

"Ipswich? Where's that?"

"Oh, it's some little coastal town on the other side of London."

Robert debated whether he would prefer to spend the evening in his room or take a chance and go to the fitness centre with his friends. What bothered him most about the idea was the thought of showering in such close proximity to Jack when the session ended. He had learned by subtle subterfuge how to get lost among all the other bodies at school, but this was much more personal and something he'd have to consider carefully.

"I could go to the gym with Jack. He's asked me several times. It's junior night and afterwards they meet at the Jewel Café."

"That sounds acceptable and maybe you can persuade him to go to Bible class with you," said his father. "In any case, you could do with losing a bit of flab."

Maybelle took this as an indirect criticism.

"Why Frank, there's not an ounce of fat on that boy and, in any case, he's a growin' boy."

"Maybe he spreads the jam just a little bit too thick," said his father.

***

42: Thursday, 7th February. 8.50 p.m. Swanford Community School.

ROBERT

Even before he was through the school gates, Robert noticed the extra level of excitement in the conversations, in the huddles of pupils, in their gestures and expressions.

"It seems," said Max, "that some people with more upmarket phones have been sent a short video recorded last night."

"Have you seen it?" asked Robert.

"I got it on my phone," answered Charlie. "It's called 'Fag Boy in Town'. Quite good quality, since it was shot at night. My dad said it went down a storm at the police station."

"But what's it about?"

"It's about a fag boy in town."

Max elucidated.

"It shows a fat boy running naked through Swanford. At the end there's a close-up of his chest, on which is written in magic marker, 'Beware of the Fag!'"

"I haven't seen it," said Robert, by now certain who the boy was, but unable to figure out how it could have happened.

"Too bad. It's gone," said Charlie.

"Gone?"

"And there it was – gone, deleted, erased, obliterated..."

"Do you know who it was?"

"Not personally," said Charlie. "I don't know any fags. Rumour has it that it's one of the sleaze school's finest."

"Morcross School?" said Robert.

"The same."

"What's going on?" enquired Jack, having just arrived.

"Oh crikey!" exclaimed Max. "You say, Robert."

The bell rang at 8.55 a.m. and with a conditioned response that would have made Professor Pavlov proud, the pupils began to file into school. As he moved through the ranks of slow-moving bodies, the American felt a sharp slap on the back. He turned angrily, only to see the beaming face of Ben Henderson.

"Great work, Yank!"

The youth moved on and Jack gave him a sideways look.

"You seem to be getting very chummy with that anthropoid."

Robert shook his head.

"It's only on his side. I don't know what he's talking about." This wasn't strictly true, because he knew full well that Ben's words were connected to what had happened last night.

They went into their classroom and the American pulled out his mobile phone.

"My dad gave me this."

Jack's face lit up. "At last I can phone you. There have been one or two times that I've wanted to ring you." Though several hundred times might have been closer to the truth.

***

At 9.05 a.m., Mr Colt looked over his glasses at his class.

"Before I take the register, the headmaster has asked me to talk to you about a video which has been circulating among some of you on your mobile devices. I haven't seen it myself, nor do I particularly want to, but I understand the contents to be gratuitously offensive. I would ask anyone who can shed any light on this occurrence to see me at a time convenient to themselves. Anything you tell me will be treated in the strictest confidence." He paused to glance round the class, then continued. "And so to the register, though I can already see that once again you are all here. If you keep this up, 4S will be in line for the Best Attendance award at the end of term."

Jack put his hand up.

"Excuse me, sir, will you get an award too?"

"Of course, Mr Moseley, I shall get a three-fold increase in my salary ... not, as you young people are inclined to say."

Stewart put his hand up next.

"Sir, I've done the film review."

"Excellent! Bring it up to me, and I may get it marked by the time you leave here. Meanwhile, class, you may spend the next twenty minutes reading or even talking quietly – and I mean quietly – among yourselves, though there is to be no moving around the class."

Stewart delivered his book, giving Jack a smile, who grinned in return before leaning towards Robert and handing him a piece of paper.

"This is my phone number and email address. Can I have yours?"

The American had already memorised his own number, and wrote it and his email address out in his neat hand.

"Jack, can you not say anything too personal when we communicate?"

"Personal, like what?"

"Anything you don't want overheard. This is a company network and I think it is monitored." By my father, most likely.

The English boy raised his eyebrows.

"Crikey! As Max would say. We'll have to work out a code."

"My mom and dad are working next Thursday and so I was thinking of coming to the gym with you."

Jack's face fell.

"It's my birthday – we always go out to a restaurant. I wish you could come, but I think it's all booked."

Robert too was disappointed; he didn't feel so inclined to bother if Jack wasn't going to be there.

"Can you come round on Friday night for dinner instead?"

"I'd like to." I'd like to more than anything. "I'll check with my folks and let you know."

"I think you should still go to the gym, though ... pudding."

The American frowned, self-consciously pulling his stomach in, until he saw Jack grinning at him, then they both giggled.

"Mr Moseley, Mr Crittenden..."

"Sorry, sir."

"Sorry, sir."

"Mr Henderson, I have marked your essay..."

"Oh, sir..."

"A minus."

"Oh, sir!"

"Yes, and a more worthy effort than many a professional review written in the darker recesses of our tabloid culture."

Stewart went red. "Jack helped me."

Mr Colt's gaze transferred to the other end of the row. "Mr Moseley?"

Jack shook his head. "I didn't do anything, sir, just showed him a template review on screen. In any case, I'd got my own homework to do."

"I guess the benefit was more psychological than substantial, then." Mr Colt looked at the clock. "Well, since we have five minutes before you are due to go on to our esteemed geography master, Mr Joseph, perhaps, Mr Henderson, you could come up to the front and read your review?"

"Me, sir?"

"Yes, you, sir."

"Go for it, Stewy," called Mandy from the back.

Stewart found the right page in the exercise book, cleared his throat and looked nervously round the class.

Pinocchio: a review.
By Stewart Henderson
"Pinocchio is a Walt Disney cartoon and is 87 minutes long. I saw it on Blu-ray and to say it was made before my great granddad was born it looks great. It's even in colour. Pinocchio is old-fashioned, but in a good way, and is quite scary in parts, but also funny.

It's about a puppet (Pinocchio) made by an old wood-carver who is magicked to life and whose greatest wish is to become a real boy. The other main character is Jiminy Cricket who is actually a grasshopper. He is supposed to be Pinocchio's conscience, but is often one step behind the seductive talk of the villains.

Eventually, Pinocchio finds himself on Pleasure Island, where boys are turned into donkeys and made to work. The most scary sequence though is when Pinocchio ends up inside a whale.

The songs are part of the plot and are not just tacked on. The title song, 'When You Wish Upon A Star', is very famous, and although I can't remember much about my real mum, I know she used to sing it, and just before I went to bed, she would sometimes say, 'Little man, you've had a busy day,' which I didn't know where it came from until now.

Although it wasn't made in 3D, on an HD screen it almost looks as though it was. I think under-5s might find it too scary to watch without a parent, but I saw it with two adults and a seven-year-old and they all loved it. There were also two teenagers present, beside myself, who made fun of it, but I could tell they still liked it.

S. Henderson, 4S

***

43: Wednesday, 13th February. 7 a.m. Ray's newsagent, the high street.

JACK

Mr Ray stood behind his counter tut-tutting and shaking his head.

"Jack my boy, this will never do."

"What's that, Mr Ray?" asked Jack, filling his sack with the dailies.

146

"Yours is a nice school, where the nice children go, but that other one is a den of iniquity."

"You mean Morcross?"

Mr Ray showed Jack the headline on the latest copy of the Swanford Mail: "Police Called To Morcross."

"Here you are, Jack my boy, read it for yourself, it is too shameful for me to read out loud."

"'Last Wednesday night, police were called to Morcross House in Church Lane when neighbours reported a disturbance. An eye-witness stated that the teenage residents ran amok, brandishing weapons and trying to attack passers-by. Two members of staff at the home have been suspended, pending further investigation. In a further development a youth from the home who cannot be named for legal reasons was detained by police after being found walking naked in the town square. It is alleged that video footage of the incident was posted on the internet for a time.

Police and Crime Commissioner Ken Anderson said that the youth in question was a self-confessed homosexual who had been recently accused of touching another boy at a local church.'"

"Morcross House isn't the school," said Jack, wondering why he was defending the opposition. "It's a children's home."

"They are all tarred by a similar brush, Jack my boy."

"Remember I shan't be in tomorrow, Mr Ray." This was at least the fifth time Jack had reminded Satyajit, and he intended to do so again in the evening. "Have you lined up Sandip to take over?"

"Don't worry, Jack my boy, the number-one son is on standby!"

Jack shouldered his bag.

"Better get going, sun'll be up shortly."

***

<u>JACK</u>

His bedroom door was thrown open, there was the sound of running footsteps, then someone jumped onto him and hugged him through his duvet.

"Happy birthday!" said a squeaky voice.

Jack groaned and opened an eye, peering up at the smiley face which was poised just an inch or two from his own.

"Hello, pest. I thought I was going to have a lie-in this morning."

"I've made you a card," said Mikey, thrusting a folded piece of A4 at his brother.

"OK, I give in." Jack pulled himself up and he and Mikey sat together to examine the card. "Happy Birtday, Jack, love from Mikey. Well, the writing's a bit slanty, and there is an 'h' in birthday, but otherwise it's very good. I like the drawing."

"That's you, Dan and me," said Mikey, tapping the picture.

"How is it we're all wearing red shorts and yellow hats?"

Mikey giggled. "Do you want to know a secret?"

"Yes please, I always like secrets."

Mikey put his lips close to Jack's right ear and whispered, "Mummy and Daddy are going to buy Dan a bike, because he didn't get into the Academy."

"That's very interesting – now vamoosh while I get dressed."

When Mikey had gone, he checked his phone and saw that he had eight texts wishing him a happy birthday. There was even one from Stewart, but no message from Robert. Feeling disappointed, he showered, dressed in his school uniform and went downstairs for breakfast.

They were all waiting for him in the kitchen, and he stood and smiled and tried not to be embarrassed while they all sang 'Happy birthday'. Then his mum gave him a kiss while his dad, Dan and Mikey grinned at him from the table.

There was a stack of cards by his cereal bowl, and probably more to come when the postman delivered. He sat down and slowly poured out some Crunchy Nut Cornflakes, watching Mikey growing impatient, then he slowly poured milk onto his cereal while Mikey craned forward, growing ever more impatient, then slowly took up his spoon and began to eat in slow motion, glancing at Mikey every so often until the little boy could stand it no longer.

"Jack!" he shrieked. "Please, Jack!"

"Oh, what are these..."

"Jack, you are terrible," said his mother. "A pity there was no one to torment you when you were seven, then you might know what it's like."

He grinned at Mikey.

"Well, bring your chair round then so we can look at them together."

There was half a minute of scraping and repositioning of chairs, which meant that Jack was able to finish his bowl of cereal. The first one he opened was from his parents, and contained a £50 Amazon voucher. To our eldest son, Jack, our funny Valentine. Happy 15th birthday with love from Mum and Dad.

"Very useful," he said with a grin, "thank you."

The second was from Dan and showed a silver embossed Happy Birthday made up of digital zeroes and ones on a black background. That contained a £10 top-up voucher for his phone. Happy Birthday Jack from LB ~ and thanks.

"Thanks, yourself, LB, you shouldn't spend that amount of money on me, but I'm glad you did." He grinned across the table. "Nice card too."

"What's the thanks for, Dan?" asked Roger.

The boy shrugged. "Nothing."

The next six cards were from generous relatives who together contributed another £120 to his burgeoning Post Office account. Finally, there was a very white rectangular envelope with just his name printed in neat writing on the front, which he instantly recognised.

"That was hand-delivered last night," said his mother, unable to hide her curiosity.

Jack felt his heart beating a little faster as he opened it, then chuckled as he drew out the card which showed the famous First World War poster of Uncle Sam pointing his finger at the viewer, with the message 'I want you for the US Army'. He opened it and felt his eyes begin to smart as he read the message.

To Jack, my very best friend in England (or anywhere), from Robert Crittenden.

What a silly sausage, putting his full name, as if I wouldn't know who it was from. Jack glanced at his brother across the table, who was observing him with a look of benign curiosity.

"Well, who's it from?" enquired his mother.

"Just Robert."

"Oh, that's nice of him. I'm quite looking forward to meeting a real American boy."

"I like Robert," said Mikey, closely studying the card.

"That's because he makes a fuss of you instead of treating you like a pest, which you are." Jack grabbed the little boy at the waist and started to tickle him. Mikey wriggled and laughed and screamed.

"Jack, stop it!" cried his mother, "you'll upset the breakfast things."

Mikey calmed down and leaned heavily against Jack with his eyes shut, pretending to be asleep.

"I'll be out tomorrow night, so I won't meet him," said Roger.

"So will I," said Dan. "We've got a game under floodlights next week and the coach thinks we need to practise."

"Where are you going, Dad?" asked Jack.

Roger frowned. "The parents have been called to a meeting of the Swanford United board. It's supposed to be a jolly, but I've got a feeling it's all about fundraising. I'm going straight from work."

"I hope they don't want you to contribute," said Pam. "There's a lot of far richer people in that club than you."

"I can't very well appear to be a skinflint. You would think that the council environmental services pays me a six-figure salary, to hear some of them talk."

"How much do you earn, Dad?" asked Jack.

"Money and a few words," said Pam. "Now, off you lot go and mind your businesses. Mikey, strip your bed and get those sheets into the wash. Dan, you can help him this morning."

"OK!"

It was 8.15 a.m. and Jack had twenty minutes to kill before he needed to set off for school, the last day before half term. First, he sent a text to Robert: Thx 4 the card ~ J. Then, he decided there was just time to do a bit of searching on the Amazon website, but that plan was scuppered before it had even begun when he heard two taps on his bedroom door.

"Come in, LB."

Dan entered, looking slightly flustered, and sat on his bed.

"Hey, what's up?"

"A small person has just told me a secret."

Jack nodded. "About the bike, you mean. They think Mikey's still three."

"I shall have to act all surprised. When do you think they'll tell me?"

"Probably not today," reasoned Jack. "As it is my birthday."

"I feel quite bad about it, actually. It'll cost at least a couple of hundred, probably three, and all you get is a £50 voucher."

"LB, it's a win-win situation for us. You get a bike and so you won't have to borrow mine."

Dan nodded and smiled at the logic of this.

"What I don't get is where all the money is coming from all of a sudden. My bike; giving money to the club; your birthday; Mikey's birthday; Malaga at Easter."

"They still haven't mentioned anything about that," said Jack, having forgotten all about their prospective holiday.

"I heard Dad talking about it on the phone. Maybe they'll announce it tonight at your birthday bash." Dan went silent for a moment, then looked sheepishly at his brother. "Actually, I've got a little secret of my own."

"Are you going to tell me?" asked Jack.

"Only if you promise not to..."

"I promise."

Dan went to his brother's door, just to check if there was anyone, meaning Mikey, listening outside. The coast was clear and so he came back and once more sat on the bed.

"I've only got practice for an hour tomorrow night."

"And?"

His florid colour heightened.

"Sophie Dale's coming to watch, then I'm taking her to the Jewel afterwards."

"Dan Moseley!" Jack chortled. "You stud!"

His brother's eyes shone. "It's the first time I've asked a girl out. I'm a bit nervous."

"Just be your super-cool self, LB."

"I got her a Valentine's card, too. Have you sent any?"

Jack shook his head, knowing there was one person he would have liked to send a card to. "I'm just a saddo."

Dan looked up at his brother. "There is another thing, Jack."

"You want to borrow my bike, don't you?"

The boy nodded. "Otherwise, I'll have to ask Dad for a lift, which would be a disaster."

"No problem."

***

45: Friday, 15th February. 6.05 p.m. 15 Leighton Lane.

JACK

Jack dashed in through the kitchen door at the end of his paper round, finding Dan already waiting with his backpack on.

"Sorry, LB, got held up at Mr Ray's. He hasn't stopped blaming me for his number-one son's inability to post newspapers through the correct letterboxes."

"Still loads of time," said Dan. "See you later."

"And you be careful and be back by nine o'clock," said Pam. "Have you got your phone?"

"Yes, Mum, remember I'm Dan, not Mikey."

"Sometimes I wonder."

"Hope your training goes well," said Jack with a sly grin. "Stud," he mouthed.

Dan tried to keep from laughing. "When's Robert due?"

"Seven-ish."

"Be good, then."

Jack wondered what his brother meant by that, if anything, but he was already out of the door.

"What's for tea?"

"I know it's not likely to meet the standards of your American meal, but I'm doing a lamb curry and lemon meringue pie."

"Great!" said Jack, then his face clouded. "I can't smell curry."

"That's because I haven't started it yet, and never will if you keep asking questions."

"Can we have it in my room?"

"Is my company not good enough for you, then?"

"When is Robert coming?" asked Mikey, who had appeared in the hall doorway.

"Listen, pest, I don't want you hanging round him like a little puppy."

Mikey glowered at his brother.

"It's time for your tea, young man," said his mother. "Go wash your hands."

"Why can't I have curry and lemon pie?"

"Because it'll be too near your bedtime and two late nights in a row aren't good for a growing boy."

"Must get ready," said Jack, already feeling the nervous tension building inside him.

***

46: Friday, 15th February. 6.50 p.m. 15 Leighton Lane.

JACK

Hello, who's that handsome superhero I can see? Oh yes, it's me, showered and dressed. I've just noticed this wardrobe mirror could do with a squirt of Windolene – and it's not the only thing in this room. Does that make me sound like a gay boy, saying 'squirt of Windolene' or whatever? Would Dan ever talk like that?

I wonder what Robert would say if he knew how much I fancy him? He'd probably call me a deviant and consign me to eternal damnation. Now, I've got to keep calm, there's still ten minutes to go, and I'm nearly ready.

Another mirror study then. Face: worried. Try a smile. No, too forced. Clothes: OK. Charcoal-grey ribbed hoodie with drawstring collar; matching jeans and belt with the eagle buckle. Feet: bare. Put some socks on, quick, and hide those stubby things. Oh no! My room really is a tip. Quick, dump it all in the laundry basket. Look at my unmade bed! Look at that desk! Dust, biscuit crumbs, dried spills. Yuk! Also one mug with the rancid remains of what looks like hot chocolate in the bottom. Take it downstairs and get a cloth. No, put some socks on first! No, that screen needs cleaning; it's barely visible through layers of finger marks. Why am I panicking? Why am I hyperventilating? I could have done all this an hour ago if it hadn't been for Mr Ray and stupid Sandip!

***

<u>JACK</u>

Jack rushed down to the kitchen in bare feet, mug in hand.

"Mum, have we got a..."

That second, his mother opened the door and there stood Robert, smiling, then smiling at him, a big goofy smile. Jack's heart flipped.

"Sorry, I'm a bit early."

"That's all right," he managed to say. "Come in."

His mother allowed Robert to go past her, before shutting the door, then she looked from one to the other.

"Well, are you going to introduce us, Jack?"

"Sorry... Robert, this is my mother... Mum, this is Robert Crittenden."

His mother smiled and held out her hand. "It's nice to meet you, Robert."

"How do you do, ma'am." The American gave a small bow as he took the offered hand, and for one horrifying moment Jack thought he was going to kiss it.

"Your dad works for Burnoco, I hear?"

"Yes, he's been with them for twenty years."

"Is he at the plant or the head office?"

Jack realised that his mother had been doing some research of her own, and wanted to put a stop to the interrogation.

"Let's go..." he said, giving his mother a glare.

"Do you like curry, Robert, dear?" asked Pam, becoming practical.

"Err, I'm not sure. I don't think I've ever had it."

Oh, no! He's not going to like it. It's going to be too spicy, and he's going to be very embarrassed about not liking it, and Mum is going to be embarrassed for him, and it's all going to be terrible! And I haven't got any socks on, and in a moment he's going to notice my awful feet sticking out of my jeans.

Pam put her hands on her hips.

"Jack, where are your socks? It's wintertime, not the middle of summer. And why are you holding that filthy mug?"

"I forgot," he said, not sure which question he was answering.

Jack's heart, which had begun to sink, now plummeted as Mikey entered the kitchen from the hallway.

"Hi," said the seven-year-old shyly.

"Hi, yourself, little fella," replied Robert, going over to him and crouching down. "What you been doing since we went sledding?"

Mikey beamed at the American.

"Will you come and sing Pinocchio, like you said you would?"

For some things, Mikey's memory was razor-sharp.

Jack groaned inwardly and was about to tell Mikey to clear off, when he heard Robert begin to sing 'Hi diddle dee,' and in a moment, the two were dancing in the small space between the table and the hall door.

Oh, no this can't be happening, it's a nightmare. Please make it stop! I don't want to be here. Freaking hell, he does know all the words as well...!

When the word 'gay' came up for a second time in Robert's pleasant baritone, the blush which had been threatening for over a minute suddenly flowered into a fully-fledged beetroot face and he glanced at his mother, who was watching the scene with her head on one side and a Mona Lisa smile on her lips.

When the song concluded, Mikey grabbed Robert's hand and, with a quick look at his brother that said, 'I'm just as entitled to play with Robert as you are', pulled him into the hall and then on down the passage into the lounge where the Blu-ray player was.

"Well, dear," said Pamela Moseley in the maiden aunt tone she used when amused. "Your brother seems to have found a friend..."

She gave Jack a sideways look, which he found disconcertingly suggestive.

"Your face!" She burst out laughing and this time looked hard at him. "Oh, Jack, you're jealous... of little Mikey." She practically squealed this. Suddenly, Jack envisioned his mother as a pig-tailed schoolgirl in the playground, clapping her hands and jumping up and down in shrill delight. Now, even as a woman of forty, he was aware that she never knew when to stop, especially when her assumptions were correct, for he knew only too well that he was suffering from an attack of the green-eyed monster.

"Shut up!" he shouted, slamming down the dirty mug onto the table and flouncing out into the hall, where he was regaled by Mikey's squeals of delight.

"What's going on?" Jack said, entering the lounge where 'it' was playing on the TV. The two boys, one twice the size of the other, were on all fours: a game of chase was in progress. Mikey got up excitedly.

"Robert's Monstro and he's trying to swallow me!"

"I thought we were going to hang out," snarled Jack, annoyed beyond reason. "And you, you little shit, just look at you, you've pissed yourself, again."

Mikey was indeed prone to having accidents, not only at night, but also when he got excited. The little boy looked down at the spreading wet patch on his joggers. Now it was his turn to be mortified. A large tear plopped out of his right eye, then one from the left. Jack had used 'again' to twist the knife in the wound, and now he couldn't stop. He went over to the TV and switched it off.

"First you piss yourself and now you cry. You're just a baby. You should be wearing nappies. Next thing, we'll be smelling turds in your pants."

This was more than Mikey could bear, especially in front of his friend. He screamed and rushed at Jack, punching him on the legs. The older boy swatted him away.

"You're a little piss-the-bed," he taunted.

"Stop it, Jack," said Robert quietly. "Please."

A distraught Mikey rushed from the room and ran upstairs, where they heard his bedroom door slam shut. Next thing, there were hurried footsteps outside the lounge, as his mother went up after him.

***

48: Friday, 15th February. 7.25 p.m. 15 Leighton Lane.

ROBERT

Robert realised when he first arrived at Jack's house that it wasn't the well organised and regimented type of home he was used to. Everything was slightly cock-eyed; everyone seemed to be in a rush. Now, after all that fuss, he wished he hadn't come. Jack stared into space like a forlorn little boy, though he still looked nice standing on those dainty feet.

"Do you want me to go?" asked the American.

The English boy seemed on the verge of tears.

"What a fuck-up," he said.

Robert wanted to put his arms around him, to comfort him, but he just stood waiting for him to come to a decision.

"Only if you want to," said Jack turning to him. "But I doubt we'll get any tea."

"I don't understand what that was all about, Jack."

"That's because you haven't got any brothers or sisters."

The American's face fell and he looked away.

"I'll probably be grounded for a week. Half-term week! Oh, fuck it. Let's go up to my room."

As they ascended the stairs and crossed the landing to Jack's bedroom, they heard Pam's voice reading a story in Mikey's room. Once inside Jack's haven, Robert noticed the amount of stuff compared to his own room at Pear Tree Cottage, not to say his home in Tyree as well.

"Have a seat... the seat."

Robert sat in the swivel chair and twirled round while Jack went to get a pair of socks from his drawer.

"Sorry, it's a tip. I was going to tidy it a bit, but..."

"Don't matter," said the American.

For the first time since his arrival, both boys relaxed a little. Jack sat on the bed and pulled on his socks. "Why didn't you go to the gym last night?"

"Not enough will power."

"What about next week?"

"Could do. Dad says I ought to lose some weight."

"Really, you look fine to me..." They both coloured up slightly at this and for a moment or two wouldn't meet each other's gaze, then Robert steeled himself.

"Jack, you remember me asking you about coming to Bible study?"

"I've been meaning to mention that."

"You have?" exclaimed Robert hopefully, until he saw his friend's expression.

"Do you remember when we were sledging and you saw a couple of people from your Bible class?"

"James and Mary."

"The boy's name is James Edison. Do you know who he is?"

"He used to live in the children's home, but where he lives now I've no idea. I didn't even know his last name."

"Robert, James Edison is the local small-time drug dealer."

The American shook his head again.

"Jack, I don't understand."

"He sells drugs on the street to people like you and me. That's what he was doing while we were sledging."

At that moment, there was a fumbling knock on the door and, when Jack opened it, his mother was standing there with a tray piled high with food. She frowned at him and he stood aside to let her enter.

"No curry, I'm afraid," she said directing her words to Robert, who had stood up out of politeness. "There was no time. So, I've done you some sandwiches and there's a lemon meringue pie and two cans of Coke."

"Yummy," said Robert, "thank you, Mrs Moseley."

"Thank you," whispered Jack, as she passed him on her way out. He closed the door and looked over at Robert with a grimace.

"Still, a bit frosty, then?" smiled the American.

"Deep freeze."

***

The sandwiches were simple ham salad, but nonetheless welcome, and the boys managed to finish every one and eat the whole of the lemon meringue pie between them, so that by the end there were just a few crumbs left on their plates and two empty Coke cans.

"You see," said Jack, "I don't believe in it like you do. Religion just doesn't make any sense to me, and I'd be just be sitting there wondering why I wasn't doing something more interesting, like homework."

His joke fell on deaf ears. Robert couldn't understand anyone not wanting to be filled with the Holy Spirit, to exalt in being close to God, to know that His love would sustain and keep a person, here on Earth and in the afterlife.

"But Jesus Christ loves us all, Jack, and if you accept Him and are saved, you will enter the Kingdom of Heaven."

"I don't see how ducking someone in a pool of water brings you closer to God. And all that stuff in the Bible that Mandy quotes to you, you have to twist and turn to explain it. You're very good at it, but it's just like you've been programmed to say those things."

"You think my belief is just a computer program?"

Jack could sense he was upsetting Robert now, which was the last thing he wanted to do.

"No, I know you're sincere. I wish I could explain it better. To me a lot of these people who proclaim themselves as religious are no better than anyone else, and sometimes worse."

The American felt the hopelessness of his case; that his evangelical fervour just didn't communicate itself to Jack. That he had lost the battle to save him, and to be with him for ever and for always, was disappointing beyond words.

"But you must feel that there's more to life than just a body and brain?" he said desperately. "That someone is watching over us."

"You mean like Santa Claus or the Blue Fairy?" Jack found himself unable to be anything but flippant, when what he really wanted to do was to touch this beautiful boy and hold him and love him.

They stared at each other with a longing that neither could put into words or deeds: the cultural, social and religious taboos were just too great for either of them to bridge.

"I'd better go," said Robert. "I said I'd be back by nine thirty and I've got work tomorrow."

Jack nodded and tried to feel cheerful, but the evening had been a disappointment. His expectations had been too high, his inability to express his true feelings too profound.

"I'll let you know my fate," he said with a wry smile.

As the American was about to go downstairs, he saw a small pyjamaed figure propping open his bedroom door along the landing.

"Shouldn't you be in your bed asleep, little fella?" he said.

Mikey nodded slowly.

"Then why aren't you?"

"I'm not a piss-the-bed," he said, twirling his toes on the carpet.

Robert strode over to him, bent down and kissed him on the top of his head.

"Whatever you are is all right by me."

Mikey hugged the American as hard as he could.

"I wish you were my brother, instead of him!" He pointed along the landing to where Jack was standing at his bedroom door, and stuck out his tongue.

Robert knelt in front of the little boy.

"But you have to be kind to Jack as well; that's what brothers are for."

Mikey screwed up his face and looked down at his feet. After a moment or two of indecision, he gave a curt nod of acceptance, then smiled.

"Will you come again?"

"I hope so little fella. Now, off to bed with you."

Mikey gave Robert a peck on the cheek, then ran into his room. The American stayed where he was for several long seconds, then rose and gave Jack a little wave.

They went downstairs together. Uncertain where Pam was, Robert called out his thanks and received a reply from the lounge. He slipped on his coat and shoes and thanked Jack as politely as if he'd been talking to the pastor after Sunday service.

"Keep in touch," called Jack, watching him walk down the garden path.

At the gate, Robert waved again and was gone.

***

And the day wasn't quite over yet. He filled a mug with water at the sink and drank it down, then rinsed out the mug and put it on the draining board. All this was done noisily in order that it might fool his mother into thinking he was still in the kitchen, while he quickly sneaked back upstairs without being heard, but as soon as he tiptoed past the lounge door...

"Jack, come in here, will you? I want to talk to you."

The boy knew it had to come sometime, and now he was sure the train was about to hit the buffers.

"What?" he asked sullenly, coming to stand in the lounge doorway.

Pam put her reading glasses on the side table and looked up from her magazine.

"Come closer," she said, and waited until he had grudgingly parked himself right next to her. "He's a nice boy."

"Who?"

"You know who."

Jack looked away, sure this was just a preamble to something worse.

"I was about to come in and bawl you out..."

"American expression..."

"Don't be cheeky, Jack."

"Whatever..."

"I was about to come in and bawl you out, when I heard him calm you down."

"You know he's a religious freak, don't you?" Jack wasn't quite sure why he was saying this, because it sounded peculiar even to him.

"Maybe that's what you need."

"Huh," he said softly.

"It was unforgivable – unforgivable! To say those things to a little boy who was just enjoying himself for a few minutes with your very nice and polite friend. Worse, because you know Mikey has a problem with bed-wetting. And you with your filthy language and spiteful mouth. I had intended to ground you for a month..."

Jack was now halfway between anger and tears, and he squeezed his fists and clenched his teeth in order to prevent a show of either.

"...But I know how you and Mikey can wind each other up in an instant, and I didn't read the situation correctly. So, as long as you apologise to him and take him out tomorrow to wherever he wants to go and at your expense, I'm prepared to forget it and will spare your dad the gory details."

This was better than Jack could have hoped for – and probably, he realised, more than he deserved. He nodded curtly his agreement and, just at that moment, Dan's head popped round the door.

"Uh-oh!" he said. "Jack's in trouble, again, isn't he?" giving his brother a big metallic grin.

"No, he isn't," said his mother, "but you are. What time do you call this, and what was that ridiculous text you sent: 'Will be late, don't wait up'?"

"Oh, Mum, all the guys sent that. It was a joke. We went for a drink afterwards at the Jewel and I lost track..."

Jack slipped away to his room. He wanted to phone Robert and tell him the good news; to see whether they could meet up during the holiday; to just talk to him... but he desisted, feeling he should try to control himself at least for tonight.

***

49: Saturday, 16th February. 2 a.m. Pear Tree Cottage, the Ropewalk.

<u>ROBERT</u>

The deep sense of disappointment was like a pain in the pit of his stomach. Not only had he failed to bring Jack onto the road to salvation, but he had also learned of the failings of the remaining members of his Bible study class. James and Mary dealt in drugs. Their sins were now added to those of Callum and Jane, who were part of the gang responsible for trying to assault him, and – worst of all – Kieran was a confessed homosexual and would surely burn in the fiery lake. What was he to do?

He got out of bed, needing to go to the toilet. It was strange that this room wasn't quite like his own and strange that he had forgotten to put his pyjamas on. He went to find the light switch but found it wasn't in the usual place. The bedside light went on; it made him jump. He couldn't remember having a bedside light.

"Hey!" said Jack.

The hairs on the back of Robert's neck prickled. He turned slowly.

The light shone brightly onto the bed. Jack lifted the duvet, revealing his naked body, starkly white and masculine.

Robert tried to cover himself, but his erection was visible above his hands.

"I can't," he said, "I've got to go to work."

The English boy smiled at him and knelt up on the bed. The neat little package between his legs was growing out of the bush of dark hair into a large and fully erect phallus. And as Robert stared it burgeoned still further, becoming obscenely engorged, until the exposed tip was touching the base of his breast-bone. Then, Jack bit down on his bottom lip and grasped the erection, holding it out to Robert, in a lascivious invitation to...

Robert woke with his back arched, his penis poking, fully exposed, from his pyjama fly, tenting his duvet and spraying semen onto himself and his bed. He gasped and moaned in pleasure and in horror. His toes were curled in a febrile spasm. He slumped back into a normal lying posture and threw off the duvet. The cold air made the sticky wetness worse; the sweat on his brow, between his buttocks and under his arms prickled uncomfortably, and he was still hard.

He got out of bed and stripped off his pyjamas. It was on his fingers now. He reached for the towel from his bedside drawer, but it wasn't there. He sank to his knees and clasped his hands together.

"Have mercy on me, dear Lord... "

But the more he tried to pray for release from the torment, the more difficult it was to resist the flood of images of Jack's white, naked body, writhing, tumescent, enticing and seductive on his bed. His penis bucked. He grabbed it and with a few strokes brought himself off again.

The erotic imagery faded at last, but how was he going to clear up the mess he had made without putting the light on? The weight of guilt and self-loathing pressed down on him like the hand of Satan. A paralysis of thought gripped him. The pungent, musty smell was already noticeable.

"Please God help me! I swear on my life that I shall have nothing more to do with Jack Moseley. I shall never go to his house again, I shall never invite him to mine. I shall shun him at school."

A calmness settled on him. Quietly, he put the light on, then stripped the cover from his duvet. Finding an unsullied part, he dried himself as best he could, after which he turned it inside out and, using it like a sack, bundled his pyjamas inside. Next, he pulled on his underwear and went to the door, flicking the light off before going out onto the landing. There was no sound from his parents' room and so, doing his best to avoid the creaking floorboards, he stole downstairs with the bundle of washing.

Once in the kitchen, he worked by the glow of the various LED lights, filling the washing machine, finding a clean duvet cover and pyjamas in the cupboard by the Aga, and dampening a J-cloth to take back upstairs to deal with any remaining marks. Then he stripped off his underwear and washed himself in the sink. Finally, he put on the clean pyjamas, threw his underpants into the washing machine and switched it on. There was no fear of it being heard from upstairs. It all took less than five minutes.

Back in his bedroom, he breathed a sigh of relief. Everything was back to normal and he had managed to do it all without disturbing his parents. He sank onto his knees by the bed and in the darkness began to pray.

"Dear Lord our Heavenly Father, thank you for saving me from the shame of having to admit my unnatural lust. I have made a sacred pact with You which I vow to keep. Jack Moseley is no longer part of my life. I know that I am a sinner, and I have given in again to Satan's demons and do not deserve eternal life. But I ask You, Lord Jesus, please come back into my life, forgive my sins and save me. I am now placing my trust in You alone for my salvation. Amen!"

50: Saturday, 16th February. 6.55 a.m. 15 Leighton Lane.

JACK

Early in the morning, still in his pyjamas, he crept along the landing to Mikey's tiny box room and sat on the bed quietly watching his brother sleeping. Grey dawn light filtered through the curtains and for a few minutes he became lost in thought. Then the central heating clicked on and, as if on cue, Mikey opened his eyes.

"Hello, Jack," he smiled. "What are you doing here?"

He gave the little boy's hand a gentle squeeze.

"I came to say sorry... you know, about yesterday. I was mean to you."

Mikey rubbed his eyes. "Can I come and sleep in your bed?"

"Are you dry?"

Mikey shook his head.

"Well, there are four conditions, if you want to come and sleep in my bed."

Mikey's brow furrowed.

"First you have to go the bathroom and have a big wee."

Mikey giggled.

"Second, you have to put on some clean PJs."

Mikey nodded.

"Third, you have to bring your own pillow."

Mikey nodded again.

"And, last, you have to let me give you a big, wet raspberry kiss for free."

The little boy screwed up his face and shut his eyes tight, while Jack leaned forward and gave him a gentle kiss on his forehead.

"Sorry, Mikey, for being such a div yesterday. Now, scoot to the bathroom and I'll look after these sheets."

The little boy sat up and peered over the side of the bed.

"Will my feet grow as big as yours?"

Jack wriggled his toes. "I expect so. Bigger, probably."

"And will I be hairy all over like you?"

"You're already a little monkey, aren't you, for looking when you shouldn't?"

"But I want to be a hairy g'rilla, like you!" The boy bared his teeth and clawed his hands.

"Come on, King Kong, get a move on, or it'll be time to get up anyway."

On the landing, their mother was just coming out of the bathroom. She smiled at them and wordlessly put a finger to her lips, then passed by on her way back to her bedroom.

***

51: Saturday, 16th February. 6.15 p.m. Pear Tree Cottage, the Ropewalk.

ROBERT

There were seven texts waiting for him when he got back from work that evening, which he deleted without reading. Next went Jack's mobile phone number, then his email address and Windows contact information from the laptop. Then he went online to check his bank account details. He had saved £110 from his work at Fruit and Flower, from which he took £20 to donate to his home church in Tyree. Finally, he looked for a way to block incoming calls, but that didn't appear possible on his handset.

This was going to be a new beginning; a fresh start for him in this Godless country. The danger of corruption was all around: Satan had shown his ability to deprave, even using the people he had called friends to weave his wickedness. Thus, from now on, he would follow only the righteous path of study and prayer without any need to socialise. Yet, to this end, there were still some arrangements to make which needed his parents' consent.

Frank Crittenden was working in his study on his itinerary for the coming fortnight. The week ahead was straightforward, except for the Wednesday, when he and Maybelle would be entertaining visitors from their German subsidiary. However, the following week began with a three-day conference of Burnoco executives in Liverpool which he intended to drive to and from, meaning a very early start on that Monday morning, the twenty-fifth of February. On Thursday he was to make a PowerPoint presentation of the conference to the management in Swanford, then on Friday he was going to take the day off for a video symposium of church elders.

Robert tapped on the door and received an invitation to enter. The small, windowless room was stuffy, given all the equipment that was running, from server to wireless router to printer as well as the primary laptop. Frank was in his shirtsleeves, sitting before his screen in a large leather office chair. The boy set down a mug of coffee for his father, being careful to centre it on the mat.

"Thank you, son. Oh, leave the door open, a nice breath of fresh air is what I need."

"Dad, do you have time to talk?"

"Sure, I'm pretty much finished here. Do you want to fetch a chair, or will this old stool do?" Frank began moving a sheaf of papers off the seat.

Robert adjusted the position of the stool so that his knees wouldn't be so cramped up to the desk, then sat down.

"What's on your mind, son?"

"It's about Bible study. I've been told that two of the group deal in drugs."

His father turned in his chair to face him. "What are their names?"

"James Edison and Mary, I don't know her second name."

Frank wrote the names down on a piece of paper. "That means that the whole class is now tainted. I am very disappointed, particularly in Pastor McKellan in whom we invested a good deal of time and money."

"I doubt the pastor would have known."

"I'm afraid there are other matters relating to that man, Robert, but the details are too sordid to give to you. Tomorrow, when we go to church I shall tell McKellan that you will no longer be attending the Wednesday evening sessions."

This is what the boy had hoped for, and he smiled gratefully.

"To be honest, I'm relieved, Dad. Pastor McKellan is nothing like Pastor Dunn."

"You have done well, son. Now, is there anything else on your mind?"

"Yes, sir. Is there any way I could go back to Tyree for Easter and stay with one of the church families? I should have £300 saved from working in the shop by then, and if I could get another job..."

"Why do you feel the need?"

"I miss them, Dad. Everything is so uncertain, so unchristian here. I would like to attend the services and classes of Pastor Dunn again."

"A spiritual top-up. I understand. Let me think about it and I shall give you my answer in due course."

"There is one last thing. I failed with Jack Moseley he doesn't want to be saved. He is not a true Christian, Dad."

"That's very sad, son. I know you liked this boy, but there are plenty more fish in the sea."

"Is there any way to block calls from him on my phone? I don't wish to have any more contact with him."

"You should always think deeply before giving out your number, son. Leave your phone with me and I shall see to it that you're not bothered by him again. Now..." Frank reached out across his desk and handed Robert a pamphlet, "...you might be interested in this. It's a discussion of the differences between creationism and intelligent design by some of our greatest thinkers. Read it and it should inoculate you against the atheistic, socialist evolutionist you'll probably find teaching at your school."

Robert pointed out which number was Jack's on his phone, then returned to his own room to read the pamphlet, feeling relieved and uplifted.

***

52: Thursday, 21st February. 7.30 p.m. The Jewel Café.

JACK

Six days had passed without any contact. He had lost count of the number of texts he'd sent and was sure his calls were being blocked. The only decent time he'd had over the whole holiday was taking Mikey to the bowling alley in the retail park last weekend, which made him feel like a dork. He eased himself into the seat by Charlie and opposite Mandy who was sucking in banana milkshake through a straw.

"What's the matter with you, Moseley?" she gurgled. "You look like you've lost a pound and found 50p."

"I've been trying to reach Robert all week, but he's not answering."

"Perhaps he died," said Mandy.

Jack's look of horror made the girl smile.

"Moseley, if you're so fuckin' concerned, trying using those two objects below your dick."

"You mean his balls?" asked Charlie.

"Masefield, why do you always have to be such a fuckin' crude cunt?"

"I had thought of going over there, but it just seems over the top."

Sam Crabtree came to their booth with his pad and pencil. "Where's the rest of the gang tonight?"

"On their way," replied Jack.

"I heard that James and that girl got busted," said Sam.

"Sunday night outside the Roxy," confirmed Jack.

"My dad said that Inspector Hammerton ordered out all the Swanford patrol cars to apprehend them and even sent some armed officers." said Charlie, excitedly.

"Could be a bit of overkill, then," observed Jack.

Sam shook his head. "Swanford won't be the same without them."

"Fuckin' useless pricks," said Mandy.

"Can I have two strawberry milkshakes with vanilla ice cream, please?" Jack asked Sam.

"Aaah, are you buying for Stewy again?" asked Mandy, patting him on the head.

"That's £5, please," said Sam.

Jack drew a note from his wallet and handed it over without comment. Shortly, they were joined by Max, Stewart and Barbara, who made a heap of their bags by the toilet door.

"Manners, we're here at last," said Max, kissing her on the lips. "Hmm, banana milkshake flavour."

"Moseley's worrying about the Yankee God-botherer," said Mandy.

Charlie put his arm round Barbara, his hand lightly cupping her right breast.

"It's high time you stopped worrying about other people and got yourself laid, Jack my boy!"

Though 'Jack my boy' had the annoying ring of Mr Ray about it, Jack hardly noticed, for he was thinking, not for the first time, that almost all his friends had paired off, leaving him out in the cold; even Dan, his younger brother, had started talking about his girlfriend Sophie.

"I wish I had someone special," said Stewart.

"You've got Jack," said Charlie.

The boy smiled, noticing neither the sarcasm nor the innuendo. "I mean a girl."

Sam arrived with the strawberry milkshakes and placed them in front of Jack and Stewart, who frowned.

"I can't pay," he whispered.

"All taken care of," said Sam. "Now, what about you others?"

***

53: Saturday, 23rd February. 10.15 a.m. Fruit and Flower, Swanford High Street.

ROBERT

The pedal bike with its rider hove into view as he was wrapping a bunch of new season's Channel Island daffodils for a customer. It was not surprising he noticed it, having been gazing out of the window since the shop opened. Now, the confrontation he had been dreading was about to occur. The next time he looked, Jack was squinting at him through the window, his hand up to mask the sun's glare, a quizzical expression on his face. The glass misted. Robert pretended not to notice. Another customer brought him a bag of pears to be weighed. Mrs Annesley hadn't seen Jack yet; she was too busy chatting with a regular at the front till. His customer handed over the exact money for the bag of pears and now there was no one left to serve. He grabbed a cloth and began wiping the few drops of water that had dripped from the daffodils onto his counter as if they were part of Noah's flood.

"Hey," said the familiar voice.

Robert felt himself blushing. "Can I help you?"

"What's going on?" whispered Jack.

"There's nothing going on."

"Have I done something to make you mad at me?"

Yes, you have, you've made me sin in the eyes of the Lord. "Why would anything you do make me mad?"

"Why won't you look at me?"

Because if I do, I might weaken and Satan will enter my heart. "I don't have to look at you, do I?"

"Why haven't you answered my calls?"

"I don't know what you're talking about."

"Yes, you do! You've blocked my calls!"

In fact, Robert was interested to hear this because he had not yet received his phone back from his father and had put that worry out of his mind.

"Do you wish to buy something?"

"No, I fucking don't. Tell me, what's got into you?"

"Mrs Annesley, this customer is becoming abusive."

Jack stared at him, open-mouthed.

Mrs Annesley marched over immediately. There were relatively few incidents in her shop, probably because of the nature of her wares, but she had a reputation for brooking no nonsense. "Jack Moseley, leave this shop at once. I heard you swearing!"

Tight-lipped, Jack turned on his heel and made for the door. Robert regretted the hurt and upset he had caused, but it couldn't be helped and in the long run this would be the best outcome for both of them. In any case, he had made a promise to God, and his own salvation was at stake.

***

54: Monday, 25th February. 8.25 a.m. Pear Tree Cottage, the Ropewalk.

ROBERT

On his way out, Robert grabbed the phone from the hall table, pleased that it had been left there for him. Unless there were hold-ups on the motorways, his father would be three-quarters of the way to Liverpool by now. The days were lengthening noticeably, especially on a bright, sunny morning like this. The air was cold, but there was no sign of a frost. Since that day in January when he had been sledging, he had worked out that travelling in the opposite direction to the Hill along the embankment would bring him out close to the school. He had looked it up on Google maps and, sure enough, there was a flight of steps which would take him down onto

Leighton Lane only a hundred yards or so from the entrance. It cut at least ten minutes off his journey time.

His plan was to arrive before Jack and the others, so that he might find a place to isolate himself and make it clear he was no longer interested in socialising with them. That's not to say he wouldn't talk or be polite, but there was no question of friendship. In fact, as far as Jack himself was concerned, the less contact the better, which meant rearranging the seating in class. He hoped that Mr Colt wouldn't object to his moving desks around in their form room, though he was of the opinion that he hadn't quite been forgiven over the A. E. Housman poetry essay – though, to be fair to him, Mr Colt had given him a B plus for the revised essay.

He cut through the crowd in front of the school and went round the side of the main building to the grassy bank overlooking the tennis courts with their high wire-mesh fences. Plans to make these all-weather courts had been made and shelved several times, and at the moment the tarmac lay dark and slippery and the nets had been taken away. The American wrestled his bag off his shoulders and crouched down on top of the bank.

***

55: Monday, 25th February. 8.45 a.m. Swanford Community School.

JACK

It was difficult to know why he felt so miserable, so rejected. He had fallen out with friends in the past, but then there had been reasons for the falling out, however trivial. Now there was no apparent reason. But, worse than that, his sense of loss was beyond what he could have imagined. Every time he thought about Robert, he wanted to cry – which was ridiculous for a fifteen-year-old boy. He was acting like a pathetic, dumbass, little girl. It wasn't right that one person could inflict so much pain on another!

Jack ran up to Max and Charlie.

"Where is he?"

"You look terrible," said Charlie with his usual subtlety.

"Who?" asked Max.

"Robert fucking God-arse Crittenden, of course."

Max got the point.

"Are you all right?"

"Of course I'm all right."

"I haven't seen him this morning," said Charlie.

Jack brushed them off with a wave of his hand and started to look for himself.

"Crikey," murmured Max.

"Storm clouds," said Charlie.

Jack found Robert crouching on the grassy bank near the tennis courts. His footsteps on the gravel must have alerted the American, because he looked round and, on seeing him, stood up shakily, for he had been in that position for so long his legs had gone to sleep. Jack noticed the momentary expression of panic in Robert's eyes, and was glad.

"Tell me what's going on," he said, becoming annoyed that Robert refused to meet his gaze.

"Leave me alone. I don't want anything to do with you."

"So all that business about very best friend was bullshit?"

"It was a mistake."

"Why was it a mistake?"

"Just go away, will you?"

"No, I won't go away until you tell me."

Now Robert looked straight at Jack.

"Everything I do is guided by the Lord Jesus Christ."

"So how has He guided you in this?"

"He is protecting me from evil."

"Protecting you from what evil? Me?"

"Yes, if you must know. You're not a Christian, this is not a Christian school and this is not a Christian country."

"Oh, I get it."

176

"What?"

"You faked all this friendship stuff to try to get me to come to your poncey church, and when I said no, you just became what you are: a shallow piece of shit."

"Think what you like."

"Surely faking friendship makes you a fake and your religion a fake."

"My religion is the most important thing in life to me. Belief in Almighty God, and salvation through our Lord Jesus Christ, is all that matters."

"No matter how many people you hurt along the way?"

"Just like you hurt Mikey!"

Jack snorted, enraged. He stepped towards Robert.

"You know fuck all! You're just a spoiled, selfish, American brat. You think Mikey's just a little toy that you can play with and then set down, because you don't know what it's like to have brothers and you don't know what it's like to have feelings. I care about Dan and Mikey and I cared about you, you cunt! You care about nothing but your stupid, ugly, arrogant self and your stupid, ugly, arrogant religion."

Jack turned to go, but he was so incensed he turned back and rushed at the American, shoving him in the chest, catching him off balance so that he slipped and slithered down the bank, eventually falling back awkwardly against the wire fence of the tennis courts.

The bell rang for the start of school, but Jack wasn't listening. He jumped down the bank, raising his fist, struggling not to ram it into Robert's face.

"Don't ever let me hear you talk about Mikey again, you son of a bitch. And you can tell your Lord Jesus Christ that if I see you checking me out in the showers, I'll knock your fucking block off!"

He knew that was below the belt, not to say hypocritical, but there was hatred in his heart. He strode back up the bank, spying Robert's bag, which he picked up with glee, spilling out the contents onto the gravel before throwing it over the wire.

"The courts are locked in the winter, so you'll have to get the key from the groundsman."

***

56: Monday, 25th February. 9.05 a.m. Swanford Community School.

<u>ROBERT</u>

The distant hum of traffic in his ears. The cool breeze on his skin. The brightness of the clouds in the blue sky above him. The tears rolling down his cheeks. It wasn't the physical hurt, though his back ached and his coat and trousers were ripped and there was a cut on his leg. It wasn't even the name-calling or the cruel words, though they wounded him more than anyone could know. It was the fact that Jack had said that he had cared for him. Why should that make him cry? By the time a boy got to be fifteen years old, he didn't cry unless he was one of those effeminate, pansy boys.

"Dear God, I am a sinner and I know I am being punished for my sins. Please let the Lord Jesus Christ into my heart so that he can show me the way out of my unhappiness. I want to serve you and become a better person. I ask this in the name of our Lord Jesus Christ. Amen!"

Robert got to his feet. His bag had fallen just short of the service line on the nearest court. He would have to seek out Mr Peebles, the groundsman, to retrieve it for him. Meanwhile, he climbed the bank and began to collect his books, which were scattered across the gravel.

Then his phone rang from deep inside his coat pocket. He thought he'd switched it off for school, but maybe it had got switched on again when he fell. He fished it out and looked at it. It wasn't a call or number he recognised, but he answered it anyway.

"Hello?"

A woman's voice.

"Frank! Thank Christ it's you. Why haven't you been answering your phone?"

"This..."

"I know it's not a convenient time. It never is. I must see you. I can't talk about it on the phone. Take this address down."

"Could you wait till I get some paper and a pen, please ma'am?" he requested.

"Who is this?"

"I am Robert, Frank Crittenden's son."

There was a click and the line went dead. Only then did Robert realise that he had picked up his father's phone from the hall table.

***

57: Monday, 25th February. 9.07 a.m. Class 4S, Swanford Community School.

JACK

Mr Colt looked up from the register.

"Is Mr Crittenden not joining us on our first day back?"

"I saw him earlier, sir," Mandy chimed from the back, "but not to speak to."

Mr Colt smiled at her.

"Thank you very much, Miss Simpkins, and now if you wouldn't mind, please come and empty the contents of your mouth into the waste basket."

Mandy scraped her chair back. "Gawd, that's what you get for being helpful."

"The road to hell is paved with good intentions, Miss Simpkins, though at least I'm not giving you a detention – this time." Mr Colt closed the register and put down his fountain pen. "I notice in my ocular peregrinations that you, Mr Seddon, have moved back from your situation next to Miss Simpkins to your original position next to Mr Moseley."

"I don't mind, sir," said Max, though in fact he did mind, and it had taken all of Jack's persuasive power and the promise of a free drink at the Jewel on Thursday to finally convince him to move.

Mr Colt continued: "And I'm wondering if the non-appearance of our friend from across the Atlantic and the removal of his desk to the back of the class are in any way connected?"

This rhetorical question was easy enough not to respond to, even by those who knew the answer. In any case, a knock on the door signalled an end to the discussion, for without waiting for an invitation, a blonde woman entered. Unsmiling and business-like, she was striking; not tall but full-figured, in her trademark mauve chiffon dress with a purple ruffled collar.

"Ms Lane," said Mr Colt, standing up, as he always did for ladies (though, of all the female members of staff, this gentlemanly behaviour was received least well by Ms Lane).

"Please, there is no need to get up for me, Mr Colt."

"It relieves the stiffness, Ms Lane."

"Your student, Robert Crittenden. I found him limping around outside by the tennis courts in a somewhat dishevelled state. I'm afraid I had to send him home."

"Oh, shame," interjected Jack quietly, gazing seraphically around the class.

His form master swivelled his head towards him, but said nothing, then turned his attention back to Ms Lane.

"Did you manage to ascertain the reason why Mr Crittenden was in such an unusual state of disarray?"

"He told me he'd slipped down the bank."

"And do you judge that this unfortunate occurrence was an accident?"

"Hardly; his bag had been thrown into the tennis courts and his books were strewn on the ground."

"Well, thank you for that information, Ms Lane."

"I hope to get to the bottom of this matter, Mr Colt. This school has a zero-tolerance policy towards bullying."

"Indeed; a policy I wholeheartedly support."

Ms Lane left in a swirl of chiffon and Mr Colt sat down heavily and looked at the clock. It was 9.25. For a moment he tapped his fingers on the desk, then took off his glasses.

"Mr Moseley," he said at last. "Would you remain behind, please? The rest of you can proceed quietly to your next lesson."

"But, sir, it's only 9.25," complained Henry Adams.

"Mr Adams, thank you for that observation, but would you mind doing as you're told?"

"Yes, sir."

The class filed out, leaving Jack sitting stony-faced at his desk.

Mr Colt paused in taking out books from his briefcase. "Mr Moseley..."

Jack looked up, but wouldn't meet his gaze.

"Mr Moseley, it is customary to make contact when one person speaks to another."

Jack forced himself to look at the old man, and held his gaze defiantly.

"Will you answer a question with your usual honesty and integrity?"

"Yes, sir." Jack knew he was being coerced, but he didn't care. He was still angry with the American, and he didn't care who knew it.

"Did you have a fight today with Robert Crittenden?"

"Yes, sir, I pushed him down the bank."

"Thank you, Mr Moseley, I'm sure your honesty will be taken into account at the disciplinary meeting. You may go to your next lesson."

***

58: Tuesday, 26th February. 9 a.m. The headmaster's office, Swanford Community School.

PAM

Pamela Moseley sat with her legs crossed and her left hand gripping her chin. This was the most embarrassing visit to the school she had ever made, and the one that she least understood. When she had received the phone call the night before from Miss Chawner, she thought at first that one of Jack's friends was pulling her leg. When at last she accepted the school secretary's story, she still couldn't believe that the conversation that ensued was about her son, who happened to be on his paper round at the time.

When Jack had arrived home and shrugged off the matter as if it was an everyday occurrence, she had not become apoplectic – but it had been close. Consequently, Jack had been grounded for three weeks and his mobile phone confiscated; deeds which he seemed to take in his stride, and thus she was tempted to make it a month and sever his internet connection as well.

Pam told Roger what she had done when he got in from work, but he was more sanguine about the occurrence, thinking that boys ended friendships as quickly as they made them.

The headmaster sat behind his desk in a grey suit and tie. He smiled tiredly at Miss Chawner, who was there to take notes.

"Well, Jack, as you know I have no alternative but to suspend you from school for a period of five days, starting today. I don't intend asking the Board of Governors for a longer period, because of your previous good record and your honesty in confessing to your form tutor. When you return you will need to sign a contract of good behaviour. Mr Colt says he wants you back in his class and I shall abide by his judgement, but any repetition of this sort of conduct will not only mean a longer period of suspension, but the removal to another class. Is that clear, Jack?"

"Yes, sir."

"Mrs Moseley, do you wish to make any comments?"

"He needs to be kept working; this isn't a holiday."

"His school work will be delivered and collected every day. Miss Chawner, can you get all the forms and paperwork together? Thank you for coming, Mrs Moseley. Jack, we shall see you back at school at 9 a.m. on Tuesday the fifth of March. Please come and see Miss Chawner, before going to your class."

The headmaster stood up and shook hands with Pam and gave Jack a half-smile. Then, the formalities ended and, with a day's work in Jack's backpack, they were out of school and heading for home.

"You realise I've missed a whole shift at the post office for this totally unnecessary fifteen minutes, don't you?"

Jack shrugged and remained tight-lipped.

"If you could explain to me what is going on in your mind, it might help me to understand."

"Just give me time and don't hassle me," said Jack shortly.

His mother glanced at him while he stared straight ahead. It had begun to rain: a fine drizzle that matched both their moods.

***

59: Thursday, 28th February. 4.10 p.m. Pear Tree Cottage, the Ropewalk.

ROBERT

The return to school, after what he considered to be an unnecessarily long three-day absence at his mother's insistence, had been less daunting than he had imagined. No one had been openly hostile towards him – even Jack's friends only wanted to know the reason for their bust-up, to which he had given non-committal responses. Mandy Simpkins, who he was now sitting next to, hadn't pried too much either, though he considered someone as astute as she was would probably play the long game in trying to find out what had gone wrong in their relationship. There was even less comment from the teaching staff; only Ms Lane had approached him to apologise on behalf of the school and to tell him in no uncertain terms that the school took a dim view of any sort of bullying.

"Hello, son," his father said, taking Robert by surprise. The boy hadn't noticed him, sitting in the driver's seat of his company car, a BMW series 7, parked outside the cottage.

"Oh, er, hi Dad. Did you have a good few days in Liverpool?"

Frank opened the passenger-side door.

"Very productive. Get in, will you?"

"Aren't you working?" Robert clambered aboard, placing his bag on the floor between his legs.

"I did a presentation to the board, and I'm pleased to say it went so well that I was able to get away a couple of hours early."

"I've got your phone here, Dad." Robert handed over his father's mobile, and in return was given his own. He had not mentioned the strange call he had received; in fact, he had not thought about it very much, with all the other turmoil in his life.

"That was a foolish mix-up," commented Frank. "Fortunately, no harm was done."

"Are we going somewhere?"

"We sure are. There's an important person I'd like you to meet."

"Who is it?"

Frank started the car.

"I was very disturbed to hear about the fight you had with that boy at school. Especially after the other incident with the pervert in church. The man I'd like you to talk to is a retired archbishop – not of our faith, but a wise person in Biblical counselling. His name is Nicholas Benn, but you will call him Your Grace. There will be another person there as well: our local Police and Crime Commissioner, Kenneth Anderson; he's a very devout man and takes a personal interest in these matters."

This was the last thing that Robert wanted. Trying to fight against his unnatural lust was a matter he considered best done in the privacy of his own mind. He was not going to confess his sinful nature to total strangers, but neither did he want to have to obfuscate and dissemble his feelings; that would merely make his guilt worse.

"Shouldn't I say hi to Mom first?"

"She knows where we are going."

They turned left out of the Ropewalk onto Retford Road, passing under the old railway bridge. The road veered due south and became the unnamed B3425, running parallel with the Hill before crossing the A998 and then the River Teme at Larch Farm. After a half-hour drive, they came to a pair of open wrought-iron gates on the right-hand side of the road, flanked by two stone pillars and a high wall on which was a sign: The Old Rectory.

The BMW glided down a long gravel driveway lined with cedars of Lebanon that opened out to a gravelled area in front of a large Victorian red-brick house with gabled roofs and tall chimney stacks. Frank parked directly behind a navy blue Toyota Avensis.

"Ah good," he said, "the Commissioner is already here."

They were met at the door by a matronly woman whom Robert took to be the housekeeper. She led them along a dark wood-panelled passage to a pair of sliding doors, on which she tapped lightly. A voice from within instructed them to enter.

Archbishop Benn was a tall man of late middle age, overweight and overbearing in his clerical collar and black shirt and jacket. His eyes were partially hidden behind tinted spectacles. The other man was thickset, but was bearded and dressed in a dark business suit, white shirt and blue silk tie. They rose from their comfortable armchairs in front of the open fire and shook hands with Frank. Robert realised that their manner was not that of strangers meeting for the first time, but of old friends or colleagues.

"And this is the young man in question?" said the archbishop emeritus.

"Yes, this is my son, Robert. Robert, shake hands with His Grace."

The boy quickly wiped his hand on his trousers, but he needn't have bothered because the archbishop's hand was hot and fleshy.

Frank gestured towards the other man. "And this is Mr Anderson, Robert. He is the Police and Crime Commissioner for the area."

"How do you do, sir," said the boy.

The man gripped his hand tightly. "I'm very pleased to hear that you're a chip off the old block. Keep up the good work."

"Would you fetch us some tea, please, Mrs Warner?" ordered Archbishop Benn. "Do you take tea, Robert?"

"Er, I don't mind."

"Sit down, then. Sit opposite me in the armchair."

Robert looked at Mr Anderson, whose seat he had been offered.

"Don't worry about me, sonny," the man said with a smile. "If you'll excuse me, Nicholas, I have a few calls to make. May I use the library?"

"By all means."

The archbishop's chair creaked as he sat back down. The room was getting dark, Robert noted thankfully, feeling uncomfortable and out of place. His father had taken a seat behind him, in the bay of the mullioned windows where the fading daylight shone wanly through the leaded lights. Out of the corner of his eye, the boy noticed his shadow flickering in the fire's glow on the faded red flock wallpaper.

"Robert," the archbishop began, leaning towards him, "you believe that the Lord Jesus Christ is our saviour, don't you?"

"Yes, sir."

"Yes, Your Grace," interrupted Frank.

The archbishop waved aside the breach of etiquette.

"Robert, we are in a battle to save the souls of men. The tide of homosexual immorality has become a tsunami, do you understand?"

"So far."

"The homosexual is threatening our Christian civilisation. You have already shown a stout heart by denouncing one in your Bible class."

"Thank you, Your Grace."

"We have already started the fight back in Swanford, thanks to people like your father and Mr Anderson, not to mention the gallant band of councillors on the local authority and our allies in the press. Shortly, we shall be extending our campaign nationally."

"That's good news."

"Now Robert, when you fought this boy at school, this Jack Moseley, were you fighting another homosexual?"

"I don't believe so..."

"The evil of Satan is subtle, my boy. Did he ever make even the slightest advance towards you?"

The American boy thought about Jack, but all he could bring to mind were images from his own lascivious dreams. He shook his head.

"No, never!"

"Your father has a record of thirty-four text messages sent to you over the course of three days. Most of them asking why you weren't returning his calls. This alone would seem to point to him having an unnatural predilection for you."

Robert shook his head, determined not to follow in the footsteps of Judas Iscariot.

Archbishop Benn shifted impatiently in his chair.

"Why, then, did you give your father your phone and ask him to block these calls?"

"I had a disagreement with him," he said desperately, trying not to blush, but blushing more because he was trying not to. "About a girl, Mandy Simpkins, in our class..."

These terrible lies seemed so transparent that, when he heard audible sighs of relief from both the archbishop and his father, he couldn't believe his luck. He almost felt that God was smiling on him.

"And is this why you were fighting?"

"Yes, sir... Your Grace."

"Well, Robert, what you say is a great comfort to us, isn't it, Frank?"

"I hope you were defending this girl's honour against the Moseley boy," said his father.

"Yes, sir," confirmed Robert, wondering how he was going to extricate his soul from eternal damnation this time.

Archbishop Benn leaned forward again and patted him on the knee.

"You see, Robert, as Christians we are bound by our faith to warn against the homosexual. Those who have taken up this lifestyle, who are but a vociferous and tiny minority, have declared war on us. For too long we have been in retreat against these dark forces, but soon the fight back will begin."

"Yes, Your Grace."

"In the meantime, you must become a Christian soldier fighting the scourge and reporting to your father any suspects, so that they might be investigated."

"I will do my best."

It was almost dark now. Mrs Warner entered with a tray of tea and biscuits which she set down on the Regency occasional table. Then she switched on the four wall lights and drew the curtains.

"Will there be anything else, Archbishop Benn?" she asked.

"Not at the moment, thank you, Mrs Warner. But a glass of sherry before dinner would be much appreciated."

The housekeeper gave a small bob of her head and left the room.

The archbishop poured the tea and handed the bone-china cups around. Robert put in three lumps of sugar.

"A sweet tooth?"

"Yes, Your Grace," he admitted diffidently, accepting a nice biscuit from the plate.

Frank rose from his seat, cup in hand.

"If you'll excuse me, Nicholas, I need to have a few words with Ken before we go. Would you mind looking after Robert for a minute or two?"

"Not at all, Frank. Perhaps you could take a cup of tea in for our most worthy crime fighter?"

Without the presence of his father, Robert felt even more uncomfortable, especially now that the lights had been switched on. He swallowed a mouthful of tea too quickly, which made him splutter.

"Excuse me," he said, clearing his throat.

The archbishop leaned his bulk forward again. "Robert, what advantages does the Christian have over the homosexual?"

"God punishes homosexuals," said Robert.

"Very true. He smites the sinner. He rains down death and disease on all the allies of Satan. The wages of sin are death, Robert: death of the body, death of the soul. It is a proven fact that the practising homosexual dies sooner than a normal man."

A concerned looked came upon the boy's face.

"But not everyone that dies before their time is being punished, are they?"

"Whatever is God's will happens."

Robert didn't understand the reply.

"But good people die young as well, don't they?"

The archbishop squinted at the boy through his glasses.

"As I said, if it is God's will. He will decide who lives and who dies. He decides who has eternal life in Heaven and who is consigned to hell. I know only what the Bible teaches, Robert. The unsaved, the atheist, the unbaptised, the unrepentant sinner, go to the fiery lake to exist in torment through all eternity."

"Amen!" said his father, who had stolen back into the room, unnoticed.

***

PAM

Pamela Moseley walked into the lounge, where her husband was quietly reclining on the settee, watching the television. She had just put Mikey to bed.

"Did you ask Dan to turn that flaming racket down?" Roger asked. "I can still hear it."

"Yes, it's at about half the volume it was, but if you're so bothered why don't you go up and ask him yourself?"

Justin Walker had come over to visit Dan and they were busy talking football and girls while listening to loud music.

Roger set the TV to standby and held up his arm, indicating for Pam to come and sit by him. "There's something on your mind."

She slumped into the settee by his side and he curled his arm around her.

"He's just sitting in his room, staring into space."

"Jack?"

"Who else? If he's not doing school work or playing on his computer, that's what he does."

"Well, at least he's staying out of trouble and not complaining about being grounded."

"It's not natural not to complain about being grounded."

"What do you want me to do?"

"Take him with you when you collect Dan's bike tomorrow. Take him to Pizza Hut."

"If he is grounded, what does treating him to Pizza Hut say?"

"It says we're concerned. Haven't you noticed? He's only eating, he's not hungry."

"Pam, of course I'll take him with us, if he wants to go."

"And see if you can talk to him?"

"What about?"

"About why he's not happy. We never found out why he had this fight with Robert. He seemed such a nice, polite boy."

"They're both teenagers, and teenage boys fight, even the most level-headed ones like Jack. He'll get over it."

"That's what he said."

"Well, then. He'll come round eventually."

***

61: Saturday, 2nd March. 10.20 a.m. 15 Leighton Lane.

JACK

Mikey was pacing the kitchen floor in his green novelty claw slippers watching his brothers getting ready to go out.

"Why?" he asked again.

"Shut up, pest," said Dan, smirking at him. "You're much too young to go to Pizza Hut."

The little boy fumed.

"Dan!" warned Roger. "Any more inflammatory comments like that and none of us will be going."

"Mikey, don't be so silly," said his mother. "If you go to the retail park, you won't be back in time to go to Mike's birthday party."

This was completely irrelevant to Mikey as this was now, and his best friend's party was way in the future – in fact, at 2 p.m. that afternoon.

"He can go in my place," mumbled Jack.

"Yeah!" yelled Mikey.

"You're not helping, Jack. Now get a move on. Have you got the Tesco list, Roger?"

Her husband tapped his top pocket. "All safe."

They travelled westward along Leighton Lane for almost two miles before turning right onto the A998. Here, the traffic built up rapidly and the Saturday-morning queue to get into Prestleigh retail park and leisure centre began about half a mile from the main entrance.

191

Roger parked his Mondeo outside Halfords. Collecting the Carrera mountain bike was just a formality, because he had ordered it online, yet the assistant played his part well and went through the technical points and safety procedures; made sure that the sixteen-inch frame was the correct size for Dan, who was five feet five inches tall; and finally disassembled the bike so that it would fit in the boot of the car.

Jack stayed in the background, watching the pleasure on his brother's face and wishing he could share in it. Several times he had caught Dan watching him, trying to understand what was wrong and why his big brother couldn't – or wouldn't – talk about what was troubling him, not even to him, and not even after nearly a week of trying.

***

62: Tuesday, 5th March. 12.15 p.m. Class 4S, Swanford Community School.

ROBERT

Mr Colt rubbed the back of his neck. He had been on tenterhooks for most of the morning, waiting for any sign that Jack and Robert had either settled their differences or that they were itching to continue the fight. Neither had been the case. Both were subdued and Jack, in particular, on his first day back since suspension, was very much out of sorts.

"I have marked your essays on 'a subject that interests you'," said Mr Colt, casting his eyes over his class, "and, judging by these efforts, I would say that some of you are clearly not interested in anything... Mr Henderson, after your triumph with the film review, this effort is lamentable. Why pick a subject like hang-gliding when you clearly don't know anything about it?"

"I thought I did when I started, sir," said the boy.

Mr Colt shook his head.

"Stewart, a D is not a mark I give too often, as it usually means D for despair, but that is how I felt when I read it."

"Sorry, sir."

Mr Colt sighed and handed back the exercise book.

"Repeat please, and keep it simple."

Stewart looked tiredly at his teacher and nodded disconsolately.

The American leaned towards Mandy and whispered: "I guess showering isn't a subject that interests him either."

"Jack's not been here to look after him," she replied, neutrally.

Mr Colt clicked his fingers at them, then turned his attention to the second row.

"Mr Moseley, I don't wish to add to your woes, but I thought your period in the wilderness would have produced something of quality. Not so, I'm afraid. C plus. I hope this is a minor blip." Jack took the book without comment.

"Mr Masefield, B plus. Your interest in female anatomy is noted." There was a ripple of laughter and Charlie took the book with a smirk.

"On a similar but more elevated level, we have Miss Simpkins, who did an interesting analysis of Plato's Symposium on the nature of love..."

"Crikey," whispered Max.

"A star, and worthy of a Year Thirteen student, if not higher. A pleasure to mark, Miss Simpkins."

"Thank you, sir." Mandy was so used to fulsome praise that she barely batted an eyelid.

"And Mr Crittenden, although your proximity to Miss Simpkins has sometimes made you more garrulous than I would like, it nevertheless seems to have worked the same wonders as it did for Mr Seddon. A star, for an insightful comparison of the first four gospels of the New Testament. Clearly a subject close to your heart."

There was an audible growl from near the front of the class.

"Thank you, sir," said Robert, taking the book with mixed feelings. Jack's absence had relieved him of most of those guilty moments of desire, but now he had returned to school, his old longings were already beginning to stir. There was another problem too, and one connected with his recent visit to Archbishop Nicholas Benn, which would mean a confrontation with his parents.

***

63: Wednesday, 6th March. 4.10 p.m. 15 Leighton Lane.

JACK

The rain poured down from a lowering sky. Droplets bounced on the roads and cars sent up showers of spray. Although there should have been another two hours of daylight left, some of the street lights were already on. Jack picked up his bike from the garden. The chain was rusty, the saddle soaked; water dripped from his hands as he took hold of the handlebars.

"Do you want to borrow mine?" called Dan from the doorway. His new bike was safely tucked in the shed round the back. Jack shook his head, giving his brother a resigned smile before wheeling his bike out onto the pavement.

He reached the newsagent's on the high street and dashed into the dry warmth of the shop. Mr Ray stood dolefully behind his counter, his heavy moustache bristling under the fluorescent light.

"Jack my boy, it has come to my attention that my customers are making pools on my floor, and now my paper boys are doing the same... It may call for the emergency use of a bucket and mop."

"It's raining," said Jack, with a patience he didn't feel.

Under other circumstances, Mr Ray would have probably argued the point, but he had an announcement to make.

"My number-one son, Sandip, has reported a bad leg, which means he is only well enough to do part of his round of the weeklies. Can you fill the gap, Jack my boy?"

Jack shrugged. He had nothing else to do – though having seen Sandip at school earlier he had detected no signs of a bad leg.

"Did it come on suddenly?" he asked, slinging the sack over his shoulder.

Mr Ray wasn't listening, he had thought of something else.

"Jack my boy, you must be very careful not to get the papers wet; there is nothing a customer likes less than soggy newsprint."

"OK."

"When you have finished, my number-one son, Sandip will be waiting for you outside the Baptist Temple on Westbury Avenue with the two bags of weeklies. Is that quite clear, Jack my boy?"

"Yes, very clear." He was going to say 'as mud', but thought better of it.

It took him half as long again to finish his round, because of the extra care he took in not getting the newspapers wet, while he could hardly have been more soaked if he had jumped into a lake. Fortunately, by the time he pushed the last of his papers through the letterbox, the rain had eased to a light drizzle.

He rode up to Sandip, who was sitting on the church wall under an umbrella, smoking a cigarette, the two sacks of weeklies dropped carelessly at his feet.

"You took your time."

"I've been working," said Jack pointedly. "How's your leg?"

"Killin'."

"Yeah, I bet."

"You know what, Moseley? Most people think you're a fairy."

"Really?"

195

"Yeah, really. And you know what they do with fairies in my country?"

"I thought this was your country."

"Smart arse."

Jack picked up one of the bags. If it wasn't for the fact that Sandip looked just like a younger Mr Ray, complete with proto-moustache, he would have been tempted to bop him, despite him being a year older.

"Well, are you coming?" he said.

Sandip flicked ash in his direction.

"Nah, the leg's killin', I told you. Don't worry, though, I'll see you get paid the full rate."

***

64: Wednesday, 6th March. 7.45 p.m. 15 Leighton Lane.

<u>JACK</u>

Jack sat cross-legged on his bed, wearing top, boxers and thick winter socks. A hot shower and a sandwich had restored him physically, but his mind felt dull and unresponsive. He looked at his maths homework, but the numbers and diagrams just seemed to be an incomprehensible jumble. When he had arrived back at the church wall after delivering the first bag of weeklies, Sandip had gone, leaving only the second bag and the butts of five cigarettes on the ground. At first, this made him furious, but by the time he'd finished the round and returned home all he felt was apathy.

Two light taps came on his door.

"Come in, LB."

His brother entered. He seemed to have grown considerably over the past few weeks. His shoulders had broadened, his face had lost some of its puppy fat, and his voice had deepened.

"I've brought you a Fruit Corner – Mum's idea. It's strawberry..."

Normally, Jack loved Fruit Corners, but now the thought of yogurt made him feel slightly sick. "You can have it, if you like."

Dan shook his head and laid it on the bed. "Do you want to hear something funny?"

"Go on, then," said Jack, inviting him to sit on his chair. A diversion from homework – and his despondency – could only be a good thing.

The younger boy took up the seat. "You know how we've been talking about going to Malaga this Easter..."

Jack nodded. "You mean we're not going now?"

"Yes, we're going, but it's not Malaga in Spain, it's Mallaig – in Scotland."

"Scotland in April!"

"Yup! It's a little village on the west coast, in the middle of nowhere. They've booked a caravan, for a fortnight. Just think of it: sleeping by squirty Mikey for two whole weeks!"

"Jesus, that is so crap!" Despite himself, Jack had to smile. "No wonder they can afford bikes and things."

"Actually, I bet it wouldn't have cost them that much more to go to Malaga!"

"LB, that sucks so much, it did cheer me up a bit."

Dan looked concernedly at his brother.

"Jack, you know you can tell me anything, don't you?"

Suddenly, Jack felt tears welling up in his eyes. He looked away and fumbled for a tissue.

"I know. Give me time..."

Dan waited for him to recover, then he stood up.

"And eat your yogurt; you're getting thin."

"Yes doctor..."

***

65: Saturday, 9th March. 10.25 a.m. Fruit and Flower, Swanford High Street.

<u>ROBERT</u>

There was little effort involved in the work any more; if he wanted to, he could smile, weigh, take the money and say goodbye while his mind was elsewhere. And it was elsewhere when he was suddenly brought back to the everyday by a small figure tugging on his apron and smiling up at him.

"Aaron!" he said before he could stop himself. "No – Mikey. What are you doing here?"

He looked round the shop to see who had brought in the little boy, but there was only an old lady chattering away to Mrs Annesley as she was being served.

"When are you coming to my house again, Robert?"

"I... Mikey, who are you with?"

"Mummy."

"Won't she be missing you?"

"Jack's sad," said the little boy, his face serious. "I think he misses you."

"Mikey, I can't come round any more."

"But I want you to come and sing and play Monstro with me."

"Michael Moseley!"

The little boy jumped and turned. Pamela Moseley was standing in the shop doorway. "Come here this instant!"

Mikey scurried over to her. "I was just talking to..."

"I'm sorry..." Pam interrupted, looking round as if she were announcing her apology to the whole shop, then she grabbed the boy's hand and walked on down the street.

Robert watched them go, seeing Mrs Annesley frowning at him out of the corner of his eye. "Sorry about that," he said. "He just seemed to appear out of nowhere."

"She hasn't been in since that trouble with her son. We can't afford to lose customers, you know."

Happily, two more shoppers arrived at that very moment and he was able to knuckle down to some work again.

***

66: Saturday, 9th March. 6.10 p.m. Pear Tree Cottage, the Ropewalk.

<u>ROBERT</u>

As he climbed the stairs, he could hear his father working on the computer in his study. This seemed as good an opportunity as any, if he didn't chicken out. Quickly and quietly, he got changed and went back downstairs to the kitchen, where Maybelle was cooking dinner.

"Hi, Mom, is there anything I can do?"

"You might like to whip up that cream for me, hon. We got pecan pie for dessert."

"Yummy," said Robert, taking the electric hand whisk off its hook.

"You've got that peaky look about you again, dear. You're not sickening for something, are you?"

"Nope, I'm fine."

"I hope you're still not worrying about that awful boy? He hasn't been pestering you at all, has he? To think we allowed him into our house!"

Robert felt a sudden longing in his heart, which he quickly suppressed.

"No, Mom, we're keeping out of each other's way."

He poured the tub of cream into a bowl, then paused and looked at her. The moment had arrived. "Can I ask you something?"

"Why sure, honey, what's on your mind?"

"Aaron."

His mother blenched and stopped what she was doing. "Now, Robert..."

"Mom, I need to know." He looked at her, sorry for the grief and pain he was causing, but desperate for reassurance. "Was God punishing him when he was taken from us?"

"Robert! How can you say such a thing? He was just a little boy."

"But the archbishop said that God punishes people by taking away their life early."

"The archbishop was not referring to innocent children, I'm sure of that."

"Why did he have to die, then?"

"I don't know, dear. A lesson for us all."

Frank Crittenden walked into the kitchen, his face set.

"Why are you talking this way to your mother, Robert? You know it distresses her."

"I'm sorry, sir," replied the boy, "but the archbishop—"

"The archbishop is a wise and powerful counsellor, Robert, but his concern is not with little children. Now come, leave your mother alone and we shall talk and pray about this together."

When they entered the lounge, Frank closed the door and directed Robert to sit on the sofa.

"Before we talk about that, I want to ask you a question, son."

The boy looked up at his father, whose expression was stern, but there was something else there too which he could not quite grasp.

Please don't ask me anything about Jack, please God, nothing about Jack!

"Robert, you received a call on my cell the other day. Why didn't you tell me about it?"

That was unexpected. He had to think back.

"You mean the woman who called?"

"I mean just that."

"It was the day I had the fight."

"Over the honour of that girl."

"Yes. Mandy..." Robert felt exposed and guilty as he spun his web of deceit.

"So, what are you saying?"

"It didn't seem important; there was no message, she just hung up."

His father seemed relieved. He sat down beside his son. The matter appeared to be closed. "You were talking to your mother about Aaron, when you know that this is not a topic open for discussion."

"I'm sorry, sir. I just want to be certain that he is safely in Heaven with our Lord Jesus Christ."

"Of course he is. What more is there to be said?"

"Aaron wasn't baptised." It was the same question he had asked himself a thousand times, but somehow it seemed more important now.

"You know full well that church teaching is that baptism is only necessary to gain the Kingdom of Heaven if the child has reached the age of responsibility."

"But he was seven, Dad – that is the age of responsibility in Oklahoma."

"In a court of law, maybe..." There was silence. His father was not going to continue down this track, and it made him indignant.

"Dad, I want to know why he had to die in the first place!"

Frank stood up angrily.

"Robert, you had better go to your room and gain control of yourself. You're behaving in a very unmanly fashion."

This wasn't what he wanted to hear. Always his enquiries were met with either anger or denial, when all he wanted was to be allowed to talk about their loss. He realised that his feelings of grief were similar to those he was feeling over his separation from Jack.

"Robert!" His father was standing over him. "I told you to go to your room."

"Yes, sir," he said, defeated.

Once he was back in his bedroom, he sat before the blurry photograph on his desk. It was twelve years old and showed Maybelle carrying his newborn brother, Aaron. He could just make out the little hands poking from the white romper suit and the squashy face, the eyes closed in baby sleep. Robert, who had been just three at the time, couldn't remember that occasion, but all his subsequent memories of Aaron were happy and sunlit. They had become buddies, almost inseparable, captivated by each other. Then, at the age of seven Aaron had contracted bacterial meningitis. The end came swiftly. There was barely time to get him to hospital once the diagnosis had been made, and no time for Robert to say goodbye. In fact, it was not until three days after his death that he learned his brother would not be returning home, but instead God had called him to eternal bliss in Heaven.

After the funeral, ten-year-old Robert had been sent to live with his Auntie Una while his parents recovered. It had been a time of pain and comfort for him; the pain of loss and the comfort of his aunt, who had talked to him about his brother when needed, and treated him like one of her very own. When he saw his mother and father again after a month or so, there were lines etched into their faces that hadn't been there before, and – unlike his aunt – they refused to talk about their younger son's life or death. It was all but a mystery to him how he had managed to hang on to this one photograph, because every other item that had belonged to or reminded him of Aaron had been destroyed.

Robert wanted to believe what his father, what his pastor, what everyone had told him: that Aaron was with the Lamb of God in Heaven. But his fears that some other fate had befallen him had been stirred in him again by Archbishop Benn. Aaron had died young … at the same age as Jack's brother, Mikey, was now.

***

67: Wednesday, 13th March. 3.40 p.m. Class 4S, Swanford Community School.

JACK

In the last five minutes of school, and while the class waited to be dismissed, Mr Colt was having an internal debate with himself. It was over a week since Jack had returned from suspension, yet there was no lightening in his mood and his grades, if anything, had got worse. Mrs Gutteridge, his maths teacher, was particularly concerned that the boy had only got a C in his last homework assignment. Though Mr Colt had not experienced any open hostility between Jack and Robert Crittenden, there was a certain tension in the class that remained palpable. It was time, he decided, to take the bull by the horns.

"Mr Moseley, stay behind, will you? The rest of you can go."

It sounded ominous, as if the judge was about to put the black cap on and pronounce sentence.

Charlie looked across at his friend and drew a finger across his throat, for some reason believing this would cheer him up.

Class 4S filed out more quietly than usual, until only Max was left hovering in the doorway. "Mr Seddon, would you mind closing the door behind you, as you leave?"

Mr Colt waited to hear the click, then waited another half-minute, preparing himself for what was to come. Meanwhile, Jack sat gloomily at his desk, his head slightly bowed, resigned to an ordeal by teacher.

But not to Mr Colt coming over and actually sitting on his desk. Startled, Jack looked up. This had never happened. What was going on?

"Don't worry, Jack, I just wanted a quiet talk. Nothing is wrong."

A quiet talk! Listen, I've done my time; I've been no trouble, now I just want to be left alone.

Mr Colt decided this close proximity was to neither of their likings and returned to his desk.

"Jack, I like my classes to be happy. I like my classrooms to be filled with good cheer."

The boy remained motionless.

"Your disagreement with Robert Crittenden, whatever the reason behind it, seems to have affected you very deeply."

Jack sighed in exasperation.

"I expect it was over a girl or some such; it usually is. Especially as you two seemed to be getting along like a house on fire."

Whether this was a question or just musings, Jack wasn't sure, but he felt his teacher was fishing for clues, and an unpleasant heat began to build in his cheeks. He shook his head very slightly, but Mr Colt didn't seem to notice.

"You're fifteen, aren't you?"

Jack scowled resentfully. The old man knew exactly how old he was.

"Being in love at fifteen isn't unusual, and being in love with the same girl is, I'm afraid, all too common. Thus unrequited love, I suggest, is most often the norm at your age."

The boy felt a deep sense of frustration. Why does everyone make assumptions about me? This man has known me for over four years in one capacity or another, yet even he can only talk bullshit.

"Why not try to explain to her how you are feeling?"

Oh please! What is the old duffer on? This is getting too embarrassing, I must shut him up.

"I'm not in love, sir... Robert and I have had a fight. It's over; it won't happen again." He was trying his best to sound matter-of-fact and to speak as a grown-up might speak.

Mr Colt knotted his brow. He had been sure that this was the right tack to take: adolescent love was usually lurking somewhere at the back of teenage angst. But perhaps it was even more serious than that!

"If you need advice, Jack, or perhaps a girl you know needs advice, you can speak to Ms Lane, or the school nurse, or me, in complete confidence."

Now, he's thinking I've got a girl pregnant. Huh! He should be fucking well talking to Charlie Masefield, not to me!

"I haven't got a girlfriend at present," he replied guardedly.

Mr Colt began to feel irritated. The boy's hiding something. It's obvious. Why won't he just say what it is?

"But you're unhappy, Jack: I know you're unhappy. The whole school knows you're unhappy..."

No, they don't, do they? Surely not! They should mind their own fucking business, if they do!

"Jack, you were my sunshine boy. You lit up the school; now you're like a guttering candle flame."

Was I? Am I? Guttering? I don't gutter. Gutters run beside roads!

Mr Colt decided to change direction.

"Next year you take your GCSEs. You may not appreciate how much these exams will affect your future prospects."

What future? What prospects? I don't give a fuck.

"Jack, to be blunt, your work is not up to the standard I expect from you, and your other teachers agree with me. You cannot be fully committed to your studies under a cloud of depression."

What! Depression? I haven't got depression. Old grannies get depression, because they're old!

"Sir, can I go now, please?"

Mr Colt shook his head. He was sweating profusely, and he felt a touch of his old problem, sciatica.

"All right, Jack, you may go. I did my best."

"Yes, you did, sir. Thank you, sir, thank you very much."

For nothing, he thought.

***

68: Wednesday, 13th March. 4 p.m. 15 Leighton Lane.

JACK

Jack stormed into the house, tossed his bag down by the door, threw off his shoes and, ignoring his family, went straight up to his room. After locking himself in and pulling off his coat and school uniform, he got under his duvet and willed himself to go to sleep.

He was woken by a loud knocking on his door.

"Jack! Jack! It's nearly five o'clock – you're late for your paper round. Mr Ray has phoned."

"All right!" he shouted.

His eyes felt baggy, his legs like lead. There was a ringing in his ears. He found an old pair of tracksuit bottoms to put on, picked up his coat off the floor and went downstairs.

Dan and Mikey were with their mother in the kitchen.

"Come on, Jack, shape up please," she said, trying to keep her voice even.

He slipped his feet into his trainers, trying to ignore them all. They couldn't help him. No one could help him.

***

69: Wednesday, 13th March. 5.05 p.m. Ray's newsagent, the high street.

JACK

"Jack my boy, this will never do," said Mr Ray. "I have filled up your bag for you. You know what they say: punctuality is next to godliness."

"No, they don't," said Jack, though he was unable to remember what exactly was next to godliness.

"You mustn't contradict your employer, especially when you are three-quarters of an hour late. I almost had to call on my number-one son, Sandip, to come in and do your job for you."

Jack slung the sack full of papers over his shoulder.

"That reminds me, you haven't paid me for the extra shift I did last Wednesday. You remember, when your number-one son had a bad leg, because it was raining?"

"When you have delivered tonight's papers I shall give you the £2.50, even though Sandip said he hobbled round more houses than you."

"Mr Ray, I did the whole shift. You owe me £5."

"That is not possible. My number-one son..."

"Mr Ray, hasn't anyone ever told you that your number-one son, Sandip, is a dipshit liar?"

"Jack my boy, as your employer I have to give you a verbal warning that your employment will be terminated if you carry on calling my number-one son, Sandip, a dipshit liar."

"Mr Ray, your number-one son, Sandip, is not only a dumbass dipshit liar but he also steals your cigarettes."

Jack took off the bag and hurled it onto the floor of the shop.

"And you can stuff him and your fucking job!"

He turned tail and marched out, glad that he had lost his temper.

***

70: Wednesday, 13th March. 6.15 p.m. 15 Leighton Lane.

JACK

"You will apologise to Mr Ray," said Roger, "even if I have to drag you down there by the scruff of the neck to do it."

Jack gritted his teeth defiantly.

"Perhaps I should make an appointment for him to see the doctor," said his mother. "We can't go on like this."

"He doesn't need a doctor," retorted Roger, "he just needs to buck his ideas up! "

"Hello, I'm here, or have I just become invisible? Perhaps I'd be able to buck my ideas up if people would just give me some space!"

They were all sitting round the table in the kitchen. No one was eating; no one was hungry. They were all staring at Jack.

"We're just trying to help," said Pam.

"You can help by not talking bullshit!" he exclaimed.

"Language!" she cried.

Mikey sobbed and two big tears rolled out of his eyes.

"Why is Jack always sad, Mummy? I don't like it."

Jack shoved his chair back and stood up.

"Where do you think you're going?" said Roger.

"Anywhere but here!" shouted Jack.

"Do you want to be grounded for another three weeks?"

"I don't fucking care. Do what you want!"

"Now, listen to me, young man, what you need is a damn good kick up the arse!"

"Dad!" screamed Dan. "Please leave him alone. Can't you see you're just making things worse?"

Jack fled to his room, where he threw himself on the bed and buried his face in the pillow.

***

71: Wednesday, 13th March. 6.20 p.m. 15 Leighton Lane.

JACK

I am completely fucked up. I am a useless piece of shit. Everyone hates me. I've lost my job, even though it sucked. And everything, everything, is that stupid American's fault! Why did he have to come here? Why was I such a fuckwit as to believe he cared about me, when all he wanted was for me to join his crappy religion? And why do I still care about him when I hate him, and why do I want him to care about me when he hates me? Well, there's one answer to that, Jack

Moseley: it's because you're the biggest fucking, homo, drama queen that ever lived...

***

72: Friday, 15th March. 8 a.m. Pear Tree Cottage, the Ropewalk.

<u>ROBERT</u>

Maybelle put two slices of toast already spread with peanut butter and strawberry jelly in front of Robert.

"Thanks, Mom."

"That's all right, hon. I made it special, because the edge has been taken off your appetite recently."

"The boy can easily afford to lose a couple of pounds," said his father, who – unusually – was working at the breakfast table. A calculator and a number of sheets of paper were spread around him, and in his right hand was his Parker ballpoint pen.

Maybelle swept out of the lounge, saying nothing about that comment. Robert smiled to himself and had a drink of coffee.

"The trip will cost in the order of $2,000 and so I think you ought to contribute fifteen per cent, then you can use the rest of your savings as spending money if you so wish."

"I fly from London?"

"Yes, with Delta. You'll have a stopover in Atlanta. It's a long flight; you should arrive at 2.15 p.m. on the 11th."

"Sounds great, Dad."

"Mr and Mrs Miller are a very generous couple to take you in at very modest cost, not to mention driving all the way to Oklahoma City to pick you up."

Robert began his second slice of toast.

"I'm sure looking forward to seeing all the familiar faces again."

"I certainly think you need this visit, son. Your spiritual batteries are running pretty low. This country has had a worse effect on you than I could have imagined. Still, that's not all down to you."

Three-quarters of an hour later, Robert was sitting at his desk next to Mandy Simpkins in the back row of 4S's classroom at Swanford Community School.

"I'm going back to the States for Easter," he said, pre-empting her usual foray into Biblical controversy.

"Are you coming back?"

"Yes, it's only me that's going."

"Why?"

"I'm visiting some friends."

"Crittenden, do you ever tell the fucking truth?"

"It is the truth," he said, hurt by her suggestion.

"It's not the full truth, though, is it? You Bible bashing Jesus freaks are not capable of giving a straight answer, are you?"

"I always try to be truthful."

"All right, then. Why did you fall out with Moseley?"

There it was, straight between the eyes, the question he had been dreading from her. Asked at a moment of sanctimonious humbug. He knew he had become a habitual liar, deceiving his classmates, his parents and most of all himself. But he was not going to tell her about his inner battle against his dreams and erotic fantasies, any more than he was going to divulge how he felt when he was close to Jack or even thought of him. Instead, he blushed and looked shifty and couldn't hold her gaze. She bit her pen and continued to look hard at him.

"You are fucking with us, Crittenden, I know that."

Mr Colt surveyed his class from the open doorway, an action he tended to do every day now. He hoped for a change; a little lightening of the mood, but he found none.

"Settle down now, please," he said.

Two minutes later he opened the register and began to call out the names, putting a blue tick against those present.

Shortly his pen came to hover beside 'Henderson, S.', but to his salutation there was no response. He looked up to find Stew's desk empty. Strangely, he hadn't noticed that the boy was absent, something he made a mental note of to rectify. Stewart Henderson blended far too well into the furniture.

"Is Mr Henderson not joining us today?" he asked.

Blank stares and shaking of heads, then Henry Adams broke the silence.

"At least the classroom will smell a bit better today."

"Shut your mouth, Adams!" snapped Jack.

"Gentlemen, please," said Mr Colt, pacifically. "I take it that you are all on edge today for some reason."

"It was just a joke, sir," said Henry.

"But a rather cruel one, Mr Adams, if I may say so. Mr Moseley, are you aware of anything untoward concerning Mr Henderson?"

Jack shook his head.

"Stewy has been coming out with us for a while now on Thursday evenings, sir," informed Max, "but he didn't turn up last night."

"It's because Jack hasn't been there to chivvy him along, sir," said Barbara.

"I don't understand, Miss Carter."

"Jack's been grounded for over two weeks now, and Stewy tended to rely on him," explained Charlie.

"Rubbish," said Jack quietly.

***

73: Saturday, 16th March. 3 a.m. 15 Leighton Lane.

JACK

Something had disturbed him, but he wasn't sure what. He was alert, his heart beating rapidly, but he had no idea why. He gazed up at the curtains. The street lights on Leighton Lane were turned off after 1 a.m., and his night vision detected only a dim square of grey. A sharp crack at the window made him jump. He sat up and gingerly moved a corner of curtain aside in order to peep out.

In the moonlight, Stewart Henderson was standing in the middle of the garden, gazing up at his window. Jack knelt on the bed so that his head and most of his torso were visible, and waved. Stewart waved back. What was he to do? Open the window and call out? No, that would wake up the whole house, not to say the whole street. He signalled that he would come down, then quickly stole out of his bedroom and descended the stairs.

When he opened the door, Stewart was standing on the step.

"I've run away," he said.

Jack pulled him inside, only then noticing how badly he smelled.

"Jesus, Stewy!"

Stewart stood trembling in the darkness. He wore an old tracksuit, without a hood, and the same battered trainers he came to the gym in.

"Don't worry, you can stay," whispered Jack, relocking the door.

Stewart didn't seem to react, but then Jack saw tears running down his cheeks. He wanted to hug the boy, to comfort him, but he smelled too bad. The sensible thing to do would be to tell his parents, but that, as far as he was concerned, was not an option. Oh, fuck it! He put his arms round the boy and clasped him tightly to his chest.

"You're frozen," he said, feeling the boy's sparrow-like thinness through the equally thin clothing.

"I need the toilet," whispered Stewart, starting to jiggle. "I need a number two."

"OK, take your trainers off and carry them. We don't want any footprints. Follow me and be as quiet as possible."

Of course, the toilet was right next door to his parents' room, and it would be a miracle if one of them wasn't disturbed by it being flushed. Still that couldn't be helped.

Once on the landing, he took Stewart's trainers from him and watched him go into the bathroom. The click as he shut the door made him grimace, but his parents slept on undisturbed.

The next thing he had to do was to enrol an ally. Quietly he entered Dan's room and gently shook him by the shoulder.

"Huh?"

"It's me," Jack whispered.

Dan turned onto his back. "What's up?"

"When you hear the toilet flush, wait for a minute then come to my room. OK?"

Dan was much more bleary-eyed than his brother had been on being woken, but nonetheless nodded his understanding. Jack returned to the landing and stood waiting for Stewart. The toilet flushed and a moment later the boy emerged.

"Who's that?" a sleepy voice called.

"It's all right, Dad, it's only me," soothed Jack, quickly ushering Stewart into his bedroom. Moments later, Dan entered and his jaw dropped.

"Surprise..." murmured Jack.

Relieved of all the tension, both physical and mental, Stewart could barely keep his eyes open, and as soon as they made room for him to lie down on the bed, he fell fast asleep. Jack covered him with the duvet, then he and his brother sat on the floor.

"He stinks," said Dan. "Where's he been?"

"I don't know exactly what's happened, but he's run away from home."

"What are we going to do with him?"

Jack smiled at his brother, pleased that he had a loyal ally.

"Let's find out what his story is tomorrow, then we'll see."

"Have you got a plan?"

"Not until we work one out."

**

74: Saturday, 16th March. 9.10 a.m. 15 Leighton Lane.

DAN

Wearing pyjamas and dressing gown, Dan entered the kitchen, where he found his mum and dad sitting at the breakfast table.

"Can I make some toast?"

"Shouldn't you get dressed first?" said his father.

"It's Saturday. In any case, I was going to make some for Jack as well and eat it in his room."

Roger looked at him. "Since when have you become your brother's servant?"

"Are you all right?" asked Pam.

"Yes, why?"

"There was a very strange smell in the bathroom."

"It was probably Jack. I think he had a touch of the squits in the night."

"Don't be common, dear," said his mother. "Are you sure he wants toast if he's got a wobbly tummy?"

"Yes, he said he was starving and wanted a bowl of Crunchy Nut Cornflakes, three slices of toast and a mug of tea." Dan put two slices of bread in the toaster, then fished about in the fridge looking for butter. "Isn't it about time we got a four slice toaster or at least one that works properly."

"Buy one then," said Roger, trying to engross himself in the newspaper.

Pam shook her head.

"But he hasn't eaten that much for breakfast since..."

Dan noticed the butter dish and jar of marmalade on the table.

"Since you grounded him for an excessively long period of time."

"It seems to me," said Roger, "that you are excessively influenced by your older brother and you should learn to be

214

more independent. When I was your age, your Uncle Paul and I used to fight like cat and dog, not fawn over each other."

"What are you saying, Dad?" said Dan. "Make war, not peace?"

"There's no need to twist my words."

The boy poured out two large bowls of cereal. "Where's the tray?"

"Under the sink," said Pam, "where it always is."

Two more slices of bread went into the toaster.

"Hi!" said Mikey, bouncing into the kitchen dressed in baggy jeans, a striped jumper and yellow baseball cap.

"Hello, sweety baby," teased Dan as he covered the second slice of toast with a thick layer of chocolate spread.

The little boy glared at his brother and stuck up the middle finger of his left hand at him.

"Michael Moseley!" scolded his mother. "Don't ever let me see you making that gesture again! Now, who taught you to do that?"

The boy sat on his chair, made himself comfortable, and gave her an angelic smile. "Daddy."

Dan sniggered. "Nice one, Mikey!"

"I don't know what he's talking about," said Roger, rustling his newspaper

"I think that's everything," said Dan, having completed spreading marmalade on the last two pieces of toast. "Are you off to Tesco?"

"Yes we are, and when I get back I expect to see all the pots washed and all the clothes in the washer..."

"Yeah, yeah, just chill, will you?"

***

75: Saturday, 16th March. 9.25 a.m. 15 Leighton Lane.

JACK

Jack held the bedroom door open for his brother.

"Good one, LB. I've opened the window."

"Is he still asleep?"

"Dead to the world."

"It's still whiffy in here."

"As soon as they've gone, we'll put him in the shower. Have you any more old clothes?"

"More old than new."

It was a difficult job to wake Stewart from so deep a slumber, but eventually he raised his head from the pillow, leaving behind a little pool of dribble.

"Breakfast, sleepyhead," said Jack.

Stewart swung himself out from under the duvet and sat on the edge of the bed.

"What time is it?"

"About half past nine," replied Dan, handing him a bowl of Crunchy Nut Cornflakes.

Jack frowned at Stewart's grubby feet.

"You have the other one, LB, I'll just have a slice of toast. Stewy, our parents will be going to the supermarket shortly, then you can have a shower and put on some clean clothes."

Dan sat at the desk to eat his breakfast a little upwind of their guest.

"Why did you run away?" he asked.

Stewart glanced uncomfortably at the two boys. "I don't like to say..."

"Finish your breakfast, have a shower. We can talk about it later, if you want to," reassured Jack.

Just after ten, Jack took the tray of empty dishes downstairs to check on progress. His parents and Mikey were in the kitchen, almost ready to go out. There was still an atmosphere surrounding him after what had happened on the Wednesday, especially as he had not yet apologised to Mr Ray.

"How's your tummy?" asked his mother.

That was a question which required some quick thinking and putting two and two together. "Just a bit of the runs in the night; I'm fine now."

"That bathroom stank to high heaven," commented his father.

"It's probably me being cooped up in the house for three weeks, like a prisoner," said Jack.

"Don't be stupid," said Roger.

"Now, you two, don't start," said his mother. "Jack, we're going now, I want this kitchen spotless by the time we get back."

He shrugged non-committally. "When does my sentence end?"

"When you can pull yourself together," said his father.

"Fine, never then!" barked Jack and walked out.

"That wasn't very helpful, Roger," said Pam.

"It wasn't meant to be."

***

It was quarter past ten by the time Stewart got into the shower. As before, he had been wearing no underwear or socks. Dan sorted out some clothes for him and then went to wash up while Jack stripped his bed and took the dirty bed linen and Stewart's tracksuit down to the washing machine.

"I can't do these," he said, indicating the tracksuit bottoms. "They're covered in crap."

"Put them in the wheelie bin," suggested Dan, his hands deep in a bowl of suds.

"Oh Jesus, LB, they're bloody as well!"

Dan stopped washing up and took a quick glance at the soiled garment.

"Freaking hell! What's he been doing?"

"It's not what he's been doing – it's what's been done to him," said Jack. "Either that or there's something wrong with him inside."

"What shall we do? This is beyond us, isn't it?"

"We'll have to talk to him; he needs a doctor or the police or something." Jack bundled up the tracksuit bottoms with his foot and kicked them towards the outside door.

"Don't forget I've got the last match of the season this afternoon."

"No problem, LB. Stewy can stay with us now, at least until tonight. We can just say he came calling."

"But you're supposed to be grounded."

Jack poured a cap of fabric softener into the conditioner compartment and started the machine. "There's two days left. They'll surely cut me some slack over that."

"Dad's still pretty angry at you."

There was a loud rap on the outside door. It made both boys jump. A shadow loomed behind the frosted glass. Dan craned his head over the sink to look out of the window.

"Shit!" he hissed. "It's the Hendersons. Fuck, they've seen me."

Jack went to the door, kicking the tracksuit bottoms out of sight around the edge of the sink unit.

The muscular figure of Derek Henderson towered above him on the doorstep, while John Jnr and Ben stood behind. Their white van was parked at the kerbside and Alan was watching through the passenger-side window.

"We're looking for my brother," said Derek, peering over Jack's shoulder into the kitchen.

"He's not here. He was off school yesterday."

"Yes, he had a bad cold," sneered John Jnr.

Ben took a step forward.

"We think this is the place he's most likely to be, being as he's a faggot and you're a faggot and faggots like to stick together, if you know what I mean?"

"Stewart's no more a faggot than you are, Ben," said Jack.

"Why, have you tried it on with him, Moseley, you pink pussy?"

The three boys laughed.

"Is there anything else I can help you with?" asked Jack, beginning to close the door.

218

"Don't try to get smart with us, queer boy," said Derek, jamming his foot against the sill. "I haven't finished with you yet."

Dan came to stand beside his brother.

"Wasn't it careless of you to lose him in the first place?" he asked.

John Henderson Jnr scoffed.

"Oh look, it's the football failure with his hands covered in Fairy suds. Oh, but where's your Marigolds, sweetie-pie?"

"Fuck you!" said Dan.

"Boys, come closer..." ordered Derek, taking a step into the kitchen. "What can you smell?"

Jack's heart began to speed up, and he felt Dan pressing against him, making a two-man cordon, attempting to block their way.

"He's here!" exclaimed Ben. "I'd know that stink a mile off."

"You're not coming in," said Jack, closing the door as far as it would go.

"Kidnapping is a serious offence," said Derek and punched Jack on the jaw, sending him falling backwards against the kitchen table.

**

Dan's face swam into view. "Can you stand?"

Jack groaned affirmatively and his brother helped him up. "You were out cold."

"Where's Stewy?"

"They took him. He only had a towel to cover himself. He was scared stiff."

Jack sat down heavily at the kitchen table.

Dan's face fell.

"I just stood there like a limp prick..."

"You couldn't have done anything against those three psychos," Jack groaned. "Oh, my head hurts!"

"That's what these are for." Dan handed him a glass of water and two paracetamol. "You've got to rest. You might have concussion. I've seen players with it at matches."

"What are you staring at?" asked Jack, as his brother's face came very close.

"Your pupils – just checking they're normal and oh! They're a bit off, so you may have a slight concussion."

"My brother the doctor. Nice one, LB." Jack swallowed the pills and drained the water. "Is my face swollen?"

"No, just your head, as usual."

Jack chuckled. "Ouch! Better not make me laugh."

"I think we ought to tell Mum and Dad," said Dan seriously.

"I think you're right. Do you think they'll go off like ballistic missiles or try to behave like rational human beings?"

"Probably both... Jack, you know, ever since Stewart arrived you've been more like your normal self, despite everything that's happened."

"I guess dealing with other people's problems is easier than dealing with your own, unless they come and hit you in the face, that is."

"They took the tracksuit bottoms with them."

"Dammit! I'm pretty certain that one or more of those psychos has been abusing Stewy."

Dan's face paled. "Do you think so?"

"What else can it be? Bastards! I hate them."

***

76: Saturday, 16th March. 2.30 p.m. Swanford Community Hospital, Drum Road.

PAM

Pamela Moseley sat in the small A & E department waiting for her son to come out of the examination room. Was this really the same Jack Moseley she remembered from just a few months back? That Jack didn't get into fights, or swear a lot, or have problems with grades at school; he was a level-headed boy, who knew right from wrong, who was good-natured and a generally happy person. What had gone so awry?

The sliding doors opened, allowing in a cold draught of street air. Roger Moseley scanned the stark white room for his wife. The remnants of Friday night's walking wounded had been dealt with by this time, and she was not difficult to spot.

He sat down beside her, giving her a quick hug. "He's in, is he?"

"About ten minutes ago. That's almost a three-hour wait."

"Dan's at football, Mikey's at Mike's house. They're fine."

"What are we going to do with him, Rog?" she asked.

"I don't know. Maybe he needs to see a counsellor or something."

"And the story about that boy Stewart – what do you make of that? After all, Dan confirmed it was all true."

"I've said it before. Dan is just too much under Jack's thumb. It's like hero worship, though I don't know why."

"What do you mean?"

"I mean, if you compare the two, who seems more like a hero?"

"I don't think that's quite fair, Rog."

"Well, I don't feel particularly fair at the moment. He's just being an almighty pain."

"Perhaps the holiday at Easter will do us all good."

"And look at the surly attitude he took about that. Ungrateful wretch."

Jack came out of the consulting room with a senior clinical nurse who had examined his injuries. His left cheek had swollen, giving him a lop-sided look, and there was purple bruising along his jaw. For a moment they all just stared at each other, then the nurse smiled.

"Just a mild concussion, I think," she said, "nothing broken. A day or two off school and no sports for a week. Just keep an eye on him, but he'll know when he's ready."

The drive home through the Saturday traffic was a fairly frosty affair. None of them wanted to speak for fear of stirring up trouble. It was clear to Jack that his parents either didn't believe, or didn't want to believe, his story. The trouble was, it was also becoming unreal to him – as if it had only happened in a dream. Perhaps that was another effect of the concussion.

**

77: Sunday, 17th March. 8.50 a.m. The Baptist church, Westbury Avenue.

ROBERT

The path from the lychgate to the porch was lined with daffodils, bending and bobbing in the south-westerly breeze. The fine weather meant they had walked to church again. Maybelle said it blew away the cobwebs, and set them up for their Sunday brunch when they returned home.

The church was a quarter full, and three-quarters of the congregation were in their sixth decade or more. Frank and his family took their seats some three rows from the front, nodding at the pair of old ladies who always occupied the pew behind, dressed in their Sunday best.

"Such a shame about Pastor McKellan, Patty dear," whispered one of them, making Robert's ears prick up.

"A lovely speaker, and such a gentleman," said the other.

"An unfaithful wife must be a terrible blow to one so devout."

"Oh, Edith! Those stories about her being ill... well!"

"No wonder the poor man has seemed so under the weather recently."

"I do hope his sermon is a little more cogent this week."

"You know, Patty, I wonder if we ought not to send flowers..."

Frank cleared his throat loudly. He had obviously been listening to the conversation too. Robert smiled to himself. There was a certain sinful feeling of schadenfreude learning of Pastor McKellan's misfortune, for which he knew he'd have to atone.

***

78: Monday, 18th March. 8.55 a.m. Swanford Community School, Class 4S.

ROBERT

Robert slipped into the classroom and took his seat next to Mandy's empty desk. She was two rows away, jawing animatedly with Max, Charlie and Barbara. As he sorted through his books, he overheard some of the conversation going on between Joan Field and Colin Messom immediately in front of him. They were talking about Jack, and the words hospital, fight, jaw and broken made his heart thump with anxiety.

"What's happened?" he asked.

Colin turned, always happy to have a new audience. Robert pictured him and Joan as a pair of inquisitive mice, their noses always twitching.

"Moseley was taken to hospital on Saturday. I heard he was beaten up by one of the Hendersons."

"Why?" asked Robert, levelly.

Colin shrugged. "You know yourself what a pain Moseley is; perhaps he bit off more than he could chew."

"Stewart is the odd one out of the Hendersons," said Joan, "He wouldn't say boo to a goose. The rest are a rough lot."

The American was about to ask how badly Jack was hurt when Mr Colt entered the classroom, along with Stewart, who

223

was looking tired, but much smarter in appearance than of late. Immediately, there was an expectant hush and all eyes turned to their form tutor. Mandy tottered quickly back to her seat, raising her eyebrows in greeting at Robert.

Mr Colt directed Stewart to his place then went to his desk.

"Well, I won't keep you in suspense," he said, "knowing that the rumour mill has already made a mountain out of a molehill. Jack Moseley will be back with us the day after tomorrow..." He waited for the news to sink in. "Jack was in an altercation with the eldest Henderson boy. He has a mild concussion. Mrs Henderson, who brought Stewart in this morning, said it was all a misunderstanding, and as far as she is concerned the matter is closed."

***

79: Monday, 18th March. 10.45 a.m. Swanford Community School, science block.

ROBERT

The bell rang for break at the end of Mr Thompson's science lesson, in which he had been attempting to teach his pupils the arrangement of the elements in the periodic table. Robert found the logic in chemistry appealing, and a practical demonstration of the similar properties of sodium and potassium made for an exciting thirty-five minutes, enough to take his mind temporarily off the number-one issue on it.

He made his way down to the toilets at the bottom of the stairs, where he used the urinal, then went to wash his hands. Stewart Henderson emerged from one of the stalls and at first seemed to be making for the door, but when he saw the American, he came over to the sinks.

"Hi," said the American then, noticing the tired look on the boy's face, added, "Are you OK?"

"I will be."

The enigmatic response confounded Robert into silence.

Stewart pumped soap out of the dispenser and glanced at him. "Why don't you like Jack?"

The pat answer came out automatically. "We had a disagreement."

"What about?"

"Just stuff."

"You used to like him, though, didn't you?"

"I guess." Robert felt himself colouring up; this was getting too personal.

"You looked really worried when Mr Colt said Jack had been hurt."

The American went quickly over to the dryer. Had he been that obvious?

"Stewart, what's this about? You don't have to be friends with someone to be concerned about them."

"Sorry," the boy said, shaking water off his hands. "It's just that..."

"What?"

Stewart shrugged. "Jack's a good friend and I don't like to see him unhappy." He gave a little smile and, without bothering to use the dryer, walked out.

***

80: Wednesday, 20th March. 8.15 a.m. 15 Leighton Lane.

<u>JACK</u>

"It doesn't make sense," he said, nestling his head back on the pillow and gazing up through the open curtains at the clouds floating across the sky.

Dan sat on the edge of the bed. "Makes what happened seem even more unreal."

Jack fingered his jaw, which still ached. That was real enough.

"But you didn't speak to him?"

"I didn't get the chance."

"Well, I'll see him today, I suppose."

The bedroom door opened and Mikey burst in. "Hi!" he said, smiling brightly and looking smart in his red school jumper, white shirt and grey trousers.

"What do you want, pest?"

"Mummy says she's got to take me to school now, and if you're both not gone by the time she gets back, you're in big trouble..."

"Yeah, tell her we're shaking in our socks," answered Jack.

"Mummy's squirty little helper can clear off now..." said Dan.

"Love you..." called Mikey as he dashed out of the room and back downstairs.

"I'd better get going. I'm having my braces out this p.m." Dan opened his mouth and bared his imprisoned teeth. "Last time you'll ever see me like this."

Five minutes later, the outside door slammed shut. Jack knelt up on his bed and watched Dan hurrying down the road towards the school. Instead of a shower, he decided on a quick wash. Face, neck and armpits and the hope that he wouldn't smell on his first day back.

It was half past eight by the kitchen clock when he got downstairs, just time for a bowl of cereal. As he dug the milk out of the fridge, he idly flicked the switch on the radio that stood on top of it.

On 95.3 FM this is Radio Swanford, your local station, guiding you through the day with news, traffic reports and music. It's 8.30 a.m. and here are the news headlines: Police have just announced that a fourteen-year-old Swanford boy has been reported missing from his home in the Edward's Lane area. More details in our nine o'clock bulletin...

Jack didn't listen any more, and the bowl of cereal was forgotten too. Within minutes he was running down Leighton Lane, his aches and pains erased from his mind.

He dashed into the melee around the entrance to the school, searching for his friends. There was no evidence that anyone here had even heard the news. At last, he spotted Charlie and Barbara stuck together against the wall that hid the waste bins from general view.

"Hey," he said.

They broke their clinch.

"Thanks for interrupting," said Charlie. "Good holiday?"

Barbara gave her boyfriend a push. "Are you all right, Jack?"

"Fine," he said dismissively. "I just heard on the news that a fourteen-year-old boy has gone missing."

"Who?" asked Barbara, clearly unaware.

"Didn't give a name out."

"You think it's Stewart, don't you?" asked Charlie.

"They said he was from the Edward's Lane area."

"Jesus," said Barbara, "poor Stewy."

Twenty minutes later, Mr Colt addressed his class. There was one empty seat, that normally occupied by Stewart Henderson.

"I probably know no more than you do at this juncture. The headmaster will be making an announcement in assembly and I'm sure if there is any more news by then he will relay it."

Their form tutor scanned the anxious faces in front of him, trying to convey a calm and thoughtful exterior which he didn't feel. His eyes came to rest on Jack and he tried to hide his shock at the gaunt, pasty-faced individual that looked back at him.

"Mr Moseley, welcome back, I hope you are recovered."

"Sir, about Stewart..."

Mr Colt cut him off. "Jack, I know that you in particular will be concerned about Mr Henderson. Any information you can give will probably be best kept to yourself for the time being. I should tell you that, as the police are involved, they may want to speak to anyone who has had contact with him recently. Is that satisfactory?"

227

Jack nodded, and his teacher then began to steer his class back to more mundane matters.

***

81: Thursday, 21st March. 10.45 a.m. Swanford Community School.

JACK

Over the next twenty-four hours, the local TV news bulletin showed Councillor John Henderson and his tearful wife standing next to the Police and Crime Commissioner Kenneth Anderson, who told the press that he was offering his full support in the family's time of trouble and that several lines of enquiry were already being followed up. Jack didn't believe a word of it.

At Swanford Community School a special assembly had been called, with attendance compulsory for the whole school. Unusually, they were allowed to sit down: Years Ten, Eleven and Twelve on chairs, Year Nine on benches and the rest on the floor. The teachers and headmaster were joined on stage by a police officer dressed in a white shirt with black epaulettes bearing two Bath stars. Instead of speaking from the lectern, the head came to stand centre stage to address the pupils. There was no need to make any signal for silence, for a hush had already descended on the hall.

"School, I have to report to you that Stewart Henderson is still unaccounted for as of ten o'clock this morning, which means that thirty-six hours have elapsed since he was reported missing. As time goes by, so the worry for his safety increases, as does his family's distress. For this reason Benjamin Henderson, his elder brother, has not returned to school. We are all hoping and praying for Stewart's safe return, but meanwhile we must keep ourselves safe and give the police as much cooperation as we can. And to that end I should like to introduce you to Detective Sergeant Wills of the Swanford Constabulary, who has some words to say to you..."

Dennis Wills had only recently been promoted to the rank of full Detective Sergeant, having been a beat constable for six years and then spent two years training with the CID. Why Detective Inspector Rains had chosen him, a newbie, for this high-profile case was a mystery to Dennis, but he was determined to do his best. He looked down at the rows of anxious faces, which seemed to recede to infinity at the back of the hall.

"Good morning, everyone. As the headmaster said, I am Detective Sergeant Dennis Wills of Swanford CID, investigating the disappearance of Stewart Philip Henderson. In a school as large as this, many of you may not be familiar with him, and so we shall be posting photographs of Stewart on the notice boards, along with contact numbers, so that if you see him anywhere, you can tell a teacher or get in touch with me directly. This is still early days in our investigation, and I must stress that there is no need for any of you to be unduly alarmed either for Stewart's safety or your own. He is a missing person, which means no one knows where he is.

"As a precaution, we are advising parents not to send their children out on their own for the time being: there is safety in numbers. So from now on, make sure you have at least one pal with you when you're out and about, and that includes coming to school. We don't want you to stop having fun; we just want you to take sensible precautions. You already know to never accept lifts from strangers, and if you think at any time you are being followed, tell someone about it as soon as you can.

"Now, some of you, his friends and classmates, may have information that may help us in investigating Stewart's disappearance. It doesn't matter how much or how little you know about him – if you think you have any information that could help us, we would like you to come forward. I shall be in the office, I think you call it the print room, next door to the headmaster's study for the next hour. If you can tell us anything, however trivial it may seem, please come to see me. By the way, don't think you're going to be questioned like you see on TV: this is not a police station or a courtroom. I promise you there will be no grilling, no third degree, no formalities – just come along and tell me what you know."

It was a rare occurrence for Jack to have any contact with his brother Dan during school hours. For a Year Ten to mix with a Year Eight would have been regarded as beyond sad for both of them, and so they limited themselves to a smile on passing and maybe a hey or a hi. However, today was different and, having been dismissed from assembly, they held a quick conference in the lobby, while their fellow pupils streamed past them on their way to break. It was decided that Jack would speak to the police officer while Dan would offer corroboration if necessary.

There was no queue outside the print room, and so Jack knocked and was called in immediately.

The detective sergeant sat behind a small table that had been temporarily installed for him and the woman police constable at his side.

"Our first customer," he said, standing up and offering his hand. Jack shook it warily. "This is PC Wren, who is my assistant on the case. She will be taking notes." The boy nodded at her and she smiled distantly. During the interview there was a background hum of printing machines and sometimes a whirring as various jobs were queued remotely from distant classrooms.

"You look hung over, if I may so," the policeman said. "Are you all right?"

"Yeah. I haven't been sleeping that well – exams and things," he lied, "and I got into a bit of a fight last Saturday, which is part of the story."

The detective sergeant eyed him in a manner that Jack construed as anything but friendly and informal. He decided then and there to stick only to the facts he knew and not to enter into conjecture, particularly his own far-out conjecture that Stewart had been murdered by his family.

The PC took down his name and address and what his relationship was with the missing boy.

"His father thinks that Stewart has borderline learning difficulties. Do you agree with him?"

"No, he's quite bright in his way, just quiet."

The policeman nodded. "Councillor Henderson also thinks that his son would be easy pickings for anyone. Do you agree with that?"

"I don't think he could put up much of a fight, if that's what you mean."

Detective Sergeant Wills stroked his chin. "Right then, sunshine, tell us what you know."

It took Jack less than five minutes to relate his story from the time that Stewart had been invited to tea after being bullied by his brother Ben, to the punch that Derek Henderson had thrown at him, which had caused a mild concussion.

"And you say your brother, Daniel Moseley, can verify all this?" questioned the detective sergeant.

"The events of last Saturday, yes."

"And he's your younger brother."

"He's thirteen."

"I'm very interested in this bloody tracksuit. You say the Henderson boys took it away with them?"

"That's right."

"And you're sure it was blood?"

"As certain as I can be."

"Dried blood and faecal matter are very similar in appearance."

"It was pretty red," insisted Jack.

"OK, I think we have got everything for now," the detective said, and turned to the PC, who nodded. "We may or may not ask you to make a formal statement at some later date. Meanwhile, thanks for coming in... Oh, and on your way out, can you send in the next person?"

Jack opened the door and looked left and right down the corridor. "There is no one else," he said.

***

82: Sunday, 24th March. 8.20 a.m. Pear Tree Cottage, the Ropewalk.

<u>ROBERT</u>

It was unusual to have the television on before going to church on a Sunday morning, but Stewart Henderson's disappearance still held much of the population, including Robert's mother, in a spell of prurient fascination. The other reason why watching TV was allowed at this time of day on a Sunday in the Crittenden household was because his father was away again in Scotland and would not be back until Thursday.

Robert walked into the kitchen where his mother was standing transfixed by the images on the screen. There was the usual blurry photograph of Stewart Henderson on one side while a local reporter, desperate for the story to go national, mouthed on the other.

"Good morning, Mom."

"Would you like some coffee before we go, hon?" she asked without looking at him.

"I'm fine," he replied without enthusiasm. "I'll just have a glass of water."

"Police have today arrested two Swanford men in connection with the disappearance of fourteen-year-old Stewart Henderson, son of Councillor John Henderson. The men, both in their sixties, live at an address in the Gainsford Crescent area of the town."

"Perverts," said Maybelle. "They should hang them like they would back home."

"A police spokesman told SLTV that the men have not been charged with any offence, but are helping with enquiries."

"We know what that means. Guilty as sin!"

***

83: Thursday, 28th March. 8.20 p.m. The Jewel Café, Swanford town square.

JACK

"Listen to this," said Charlie Masefield, who had just picked up the latest copy of the Swanford Mail.

"Oh, fuckin' hell," said Mandy, furiously stirring her banana milkshake with the straw, "haven't we heard enough garbage already?"

"This is different. It's about that fag from Morcross who was running around town naked."

"Could you possibly be a little more politically correct when you talk about people?" suggested Max.

Charlie made a dismissive noise, then began to read.

"'A fifteen-year-old resident of Morcross local authority children's home, who cannot be named for legal reasons, has been questioned about the alleged abduction of a young boy from the Edward's Lane area of town. Detective Inspector David Rains, who is leading the missing persons case, told our special correspondent, John Little, that the Morcross boy had been in trouble before and was a self-confessed homosexual. "At this stage, we are merely holding him for questioning pursuant to our enquiries," said the officer.

"'He is the twelfth individual in the Swanford area to have been quizzed as part of the ongoing police investigation...'"

"So how do you know he's the same one as in the video?" asked Barbara.

"Babs," chided Charlie, "I know."

"Evening," said Sam Crabtree arriving at their table with pen already poised.

"Where's your friend Andy tonight?" Charlie asked pointedly.

233

"It's not his night," answered Sam. "Are you ready to order?"

"I think I'll be daring and do a Manners," said Max.

"Espresso for me, please," said Barbara.

"Coke and fries," said Charlie.

"Jack?" enquired Sam.

"Nothing for me, thanks."

Sam left to get their orders and Charlie narrowed his eyes as he gazed after him.

"Do you think he is? He could be, the way he walks."

"What is it talking about now?" Max asked Barbara, who shook her head resignedly.

Charlie picked up the Mail again, turned to page three and, after loudly clearing his throat so that he was sure that everyone was paying attention, began to read.

"'On Monday evening, police raided the Orange Lounge public house on Victoria Street after complaints from residents. Police said that one person under the age of eighteen was serving alcoholic beverages without the consent of an adult, and another person under the age of eighteen was consuming an alcoholic beverage. The minors involved, who cannot be named for legal reasons, are thought to be pupils at Swanford Community School. The landlord, Mr Tony Baker, was taken into police custody for questioning. Swanford Constabulary stated that it would be seeking to revoke the premises' licence. Commenting on the police action, Police and Crime Commissioner Kenneth Anderson said that these places are a menace to society and a danger to our young people, and he hoped the council would act with due speed.'"

"So?" said Max.

"Gay bar," said Charlie, "and guess who the gay barman is?"

"Oscar Wilde?" suggested Mandy.

"No, it's our very own Andy Venables, Sam Crabtree's bosom buddy."

"I thought Andy was eighteen," said Barbara.

"Charles, how do you know all this?" asked Max.

"How do you think?" answered Charlie. "And guess who the underage drinker is?"

"Alan Turing?" suggested Mandy.

"No, Adam Ellis!" exclaimed Charlie. "You know, the straight-laced lanky streak in the Lower Sixth, or perhaps now I should say the bent-laced lanky streak..."

"Masefield, has anyone ever told you that you're a cunt?"

Max frowned. "I think you have on numerous occasions, Manners, only this time I'm tending to agree with you."

Charlie gave him the finger, then turned to Jack. "So what does our resident wet blanket think?"

"Moseley no longer thinks; he just exists," said Mandy.

"Crikey," said Max, "what would Descartes make of that?"

"I'm going," said Jack, standing up.

"Aren't we all supposed to be going, two by two?" pointed out Barbara.

"We would if it wasn't all bullshit," retorted Jack, urging Charlie to get out of his way.

"Moseley, you need to produce the body," said Mandy. "Otherwise you're just as bad as these PC Plods."

"Hey, Miss Simpkins!" said Charlie. "You're talking about my dad, you know."

Jack stepped out of the café into the cool air. It was a clear star-bright night with a two-day-old moon setting over the west end of town. Across Weymouth Road the newly formed catkins on the silver birch trees shimmered in the street lights like so many caterpillars hanging by threads. He walked to his bike, which was chained to a lamppost, and noticed a piece of paper stuck into the springs of the saddle. It was a page torn from an exercise book and clearly had been placed there for him to find.

I am at the haunted house. There's an entry round the back. SH.

Jack texted home to say he'd be late then pedalled as fast as he could down to the junction where the Swanford Mail had its offices. Turning left onto Northcliffe Street, he didn't slow up until the empty road curved into Westbury Avenue, where he spotted the narrow path partially obscured by shrubbery. He jammed on his brakes. It was a way he might have noticed before when delivering papers, but it had not really registered in his mind.

There were no lights in the passage and he pushed his bike uncertainly through the darkness. High gates were set at intervals on both sides in the breeze block walls, but which one was number 41 was anybody's guess. His eyes adjusted to the faint moonshine, and he began to examine each gate in turn. Green flaking paint and a fleur-de-lis picked out in yellow gave him the clues he needed. He looked more closely, and saw a small 41 written in pencil next to the latch.

Inside, there was a pergola, taking the visitor through its arches towards the back door of the house. The trelliswork between the posts was covered in the stems of climbing roses, wisteria and honeysuckle which, from mid-spring to autumn, would form a scented tunnel. Jack propped his bike against one of the uprights and closed the back gate, throwing the bolt to lock it.

Effectively screened from view, he made his way down the path to the back door. It stood ajar. He pushed it open and entered a spacious, old-fashioned kitchen. Quietly he shut the door behind him. His colour vision was useless in here and he listened and peered through the deep monochromatic gloom for signs of life. Suddenly a figure stepped out of the deepest shadows, making him jump. It was not Stewart. The hairs on the back of his neck rose.

"Jack!"

It was Stewart's voice all right.

He moved closer. "Stewy?"

"It's me."

Shyly Stewart Henderson walked into the rectangle of moonlight coming through the window. Gone was the dark-haired boy with sticky-out ears. Instead, a fair-haired stranger stood there, with closely shaved back and sides, ears flat against his head, wearing black owl-framed glasses.

236

"Follow me," he said, "I can't put the lights on, so be careful."

Stewart led him out of the kitchen and into a hallway with a long strip of worn carpet along the varnished floorboards. The doors to the three downstairs rooms were half-open, but the boy continued past them to the stairs. Jack paused to look at the frosted stained-glass window in the front door; the very door through which he had, not so long ago, delivered a copy of the Swanford Mail.

At the top of the stairs Stewart crossed the landing to an open doorway. Jack followed him into the pitch darkness. "Close the door and I'll turn on the light," said Stewart.

Jack fumbled for the handle then pulled it shut.

Suddenly the room was flooded with electric light. Jack shut his eyes against the glare. Gradually, he opened them again and looked round. The windows were boarded up and the walls and ceiling painted black. There was little furniture, except for two wooden benches and a square enamel sink that wouldn't have looked out of place in a school laboratory.

"Spooky!" he said. Stewart had brought in a mattress from a single bed, which was neatly covered in a pillow and duvet, and there was also a coat rail on which were hung a few clothes and two large cushions.

Jack watched his friend dispense with the glasses and remove the double-sided tape from behind his ears. "Good disguise," he said admiringly. Stewart stood in the middle of the bare floor with his arms slightly held out, and Jack realised what his friend was waiting for and went over and hugged him.

"Stewy, I'm really pleased to see you. I thought you might be..."

The frail boy trembled in his arms, grasping him lightly around the waist.

"I'm a bit desperate," he said.

Jack squeezed him a little harder and even thought about giving him a kiss, but decided against it. "We're all missing you at school. We want you back."

"I can't come back. I can't go home."

Stewart switched on a two-bar electric fire. "This used to be a darkroom," he said, as they made themselves comfortable on the cushions.

"What's that?"

"It was a way of producing photographs before digital cameras and printers. That over there," he said, pointing to a piece of apparatus that looked like a concertina with a lens on the bottom, "is called an enlarger. It has to be completely dark."

"How do you know?"

"Books; there's loads of books all over the house. I think it was her husband's hobby. You should see the pictures on the walls downstairs. I think they were rich."

"How did you get in here, Stewy?"

The boy smiled. "The back-door key was under the mat."

"Jesus!"

"The police came round once, shining their lights through the windows, but everything was secure so they didn't come in."

"You'd planned all this, hadn't you?"

Stewart nodded. "I had to get away."

"What did they do to you, Stewy?"

Immediately tears appeared in the boy's eyes.

"I can't talk about that, Jack, not even to you."

He sobbed and Jack moved over and put his arms round him again and held him. "Well, if you ever do need to talk..."

Stewart wiped his eyes, but appeared to be content with being held. "I did the disguise to fool the CCTV cameras. I bought some hair dye."

"It's brilliant," said Jack.

"They think I'm thick – that's the advantage I have."

"How do you manage?"

"The electric's on, the water's on. I can have a bath. There was tea and tins of food and even some stuff in the little freezer. I walked to Prestleigh last Saturday and brought back some things."

"You walked!"

238

"I got nothing else to do."

"What about money?"

Stewart's face fell. "I haven't got much left. I stole what I had from my dad."

Jack got out his wallet and gave him £15. "When I come again, I'll let you have my Post Office debit card."

"Thank you." The boy gazed gratefully at him. "Jack, you don't look very well."

"I'm OK."

Stewart took a while before he spoke again. "My mobile got taken, but there's a phone downstairs. I've set it to ring softly, though nobody has." He gave a slight smile.

They exchanged numbers. "If you hear it ring three times you'll know I'm on my way and you can unlock the gate. Don't answer unless it's really important."

"When will you come again?"

"Better not be too often. Say Tuesday." Jack rose. "We'll have a lot to talk about, Stewy..."

The boy followed him to the door. "Don't tell anyone, will you?"

"Of course not."

"I'm much happier now that you know." He switched off the light and Jack made a quiet exit the same way he had come in.

***

84: Tuesday, 2nd April. 7.20 p.m. The Baptist church, Westbury Avenue.

ROBERT

British Summer Time had begun and there was still over half an hour of dusk left when Robert arrived at the lychgate. He entered the church quietly by the south door, finding it in darkness except for the grey light coming in through the windows. Pastor McKellan was kneeling at the altar and, so as not to disturb him, Robert tiptoed between the pews towards the vestry door.

"You!" The pastor's voice rang through the church.

Robert stopped in his tracks.

"Aren't you going to throw yourself down and ask for forgiveness, to subjugate yourself at the feet of the Lord?"

The American turned. "Pastor McKellan?"

The pastor, unshaven, dishevelled, and with a demented look in his eye, pointed heavenward, making a circular motion with his index finger.

"'For they have sown the wind, and they shall reap the whirlwind.'"

Robert stared open-mouthed at him. "What's wrong, sir?"

"What's wrong, sir? What's wrong? I was at Morcross today. Kieran Scott tried to hang himself with a piece of flex tied to the bannister rail."

Robert took a step backwards. For a moment he had thought the pastor might be going to attack him. "Why?" he blurted out.

"Because he is a homosexual." The voice came from the doorway. A man, smartly dressed in a business suit, had entered the church unnoticed and was standing in the south aisle, hands on hips. "Come now, Sandy, why are you intent on denigrating this innocent young man?"

"We are all to blame!" said Pastor McKellan, his face flushed and beaded with sweat, his eyes glazed like marbles. "We shall reap the whirlwind..."

The stranger walked over to the American and clapped him on the shoulder. "You must be Robert Crittenden."

"Yes, sir..."

"I am Gerald Fisher, your new pastor. Pastor McKellan isn't well, and has been relieved of his duties."

"What shall I do?"

"Go home, and I shall see you on Sunday."

As he was making his way to the door, Robert could hear Pastor Fisher talking quietly to his colleague. "Come, Sandy, this is no way to behave in front of the boy. Your time here is over. Go home; seek whatever peace you can in your new-found solitude."

***

On crossing the recreation ground near the Ropewalk, Robert noticed a car glide down the street and pull up outside the cottage. Coming closer, he saw that it wasn't just a car, but a black limousine, complete with flags attached to both front wings. He glanced at the number plate, seeing that it began '123', which meant nothing to him. The liveried chauffeur had ebony skin and was built like a bouncer. Throughout he remained quite still, but Robert could tell that his eyes were following him every step of the way.

He took out his key, but there were shadows approaching down the hallway and so he waited for the door to be opened.

Two black men emerged in front of his father, one thin and tall, the other squat and barrel-chested. Both wore sharp suits and ties, but the taller man also wore a wide-brimmed fedora. Robert stood back to allow them to pass. Neither showed any concern at finding him there.

"You're back early, son," said Frank, standing on the doorstep.

"I've got something to tell you," Robert replied excitedly.

Frank chuckled. "Would that have anything to do with a Pastor Fisher?"

"Why, yes! And Pastor McKellan was there too, and—"

Frank's face lost its look of bonhomie. "I think we should talk about this inside, Robert."

One of the two black men, who had been quietly observing the exchange, now spoke, his voice deep and throaty. "Is this the son you were talking about, Mister Crittenden?"

Robert expected to be introduced, but his father dismissed the men with a wave. "That's him. Now, you boys take care and I'll see you on Friday."

The chauffeur opened the back door of the limousine and stood to attention. Robert found the scene both confusing and incongruous. For a start, he could never remember meeting any black people at home before, and though these two men had all the trappings of power and wealth, his father was treating them as he might junior colleagues.

Robert got changed, then came to sit in the lounge with his father. Maybelle brought them mugs of hot chocolate, then announced she was off to bed, as it had been a tiring day. The boy recounted his meeting in the church, while Frank listened stony-faced. When he had finished, there was a short silence.

"It's a pity that vile boy didn't succeed in what he attempted," mused his father and after another pause: "You won't be seeing Pastor McKellan in church ever again." This was said with the finality of a death knell.

Robert took a drink of chocolate, his mind filled with an image of Pastor McKellan cutting down the body of Kieran Scott. "Why would anyone try to kill themselves, Dad?"

"Suicide is a mortal sin, son, but for the homosexual who already lives in sin, it may seem like a release from the daily torment of his perversion."

Robert took another drink. "Who were those two men at the front door?"

"Oh, a couple of people we do business with in Africa." He waved his hand dismissively.

"They looked important."

"They are influential in their own countries, and they like to have the trappings of power and the symbols of importance, because otherwise they feel inferior. The white man has no need for that."

Robert nodded.

"I shall be flying out to Kampala on Thursday night, and I'm sorry to say I shan't be back to see you off on your trip back home."

"Do you know how long you'll be away?"

"Could be a whole month. I have a meeting in Lagos later on in April, but I shall be back before the general election."

"General election?"

"It's like Election Day back home, son. It's to decide who runs the country for the next five years, only it's in May, not November."

"Gee, does that means you won't even be here when I return from the States?"

"Sorry, son, but we can keep in touch by text..."

Robert made a mental note to look up which African countries Kampala and Lagos were in, as his knowledge of the dark continent was sketchy, to say the least.

***

85: Thursday 11th April. Will Rogers World Airport, Oklahoma City.

ROBERT

The Delta Airlines flight via Atlanta was on time, arriving at Gate 20 at 2.15 p.m. Robert took the escalator down to the lower level, where he collected his suitcase from Carousel 1. As he stepped out of the air-conditioned airport, he paused to send a text to his mother in England and forwarded the same to his father.

Arrived safely. Oklahoma smells of oil and prairie. R.

Just fifteen minutes later he was greeting Pearl and Tammy Miller in the passenger pick-up area beside their Chevrolet Sonic. After kissing them both chastely on the cheek, he put his suitcase and backpack in the trunk and climbed in beside Pearl.

"The man has to sit in the front," said Tammy, leaning forward to straighten Robert's already straight seat belt.

He shrugged contentedly. "It's good to be home, and thank you, Mrs Miller, for your hospitality."

"It'll be nice to have a boy about the house for a week or two," said Pearl. "My girls are always fighting over something these days."

243

"You'll know why when you meet my sister, Robert, she's such a dowdy shrew."

"Why, Tammy! Poor Rosa, you should be more charitable to your little sister."

Robert smiled at Tammy in the vanity mirror. Her dark auburn hair was newly swept up into a loosely lacquered beehive, framing her feline features. She was sixteen years old, though she could easily have passed for twenty. Her mother, Pearl, wore her hair black, her lipstick red and her make-up conspicuous.

They drove north from the airport on Route 35, the overcast sky growing darker until Pearl had to switch on the headlights. Soon a steady rain was beating down on the car and the wipers were going at full speed.

"Familiar?" she asked.

"Yes, ma'am," smiled Robert.

Tammy leaned forward again. "We've had two touchdowns so far this month, but they missed our house by miles."

"I hope we don't get hail," said Pearl. "I don't want my paintwork dented."

They reached Tyree just after 6 p.m. The storm clouds had dissipated, the rain had dried from the roads, and the evening was pleasantly warm. Bruce Miller was home from work, his car already parked in one of the two garages. He met them on the veranda dressed in an open-collared white shirt and slacks. His handshake was firm.

"I bet you're tired, son. How long was the flight?"

"Fifteen hours, sir, but I managed a few hours' sleep."

"Not the same as in a proper bed, though," said Pearl. "Tammy, will you show Robert up to the guest room?"

"My pleasure, Daddy."

Robert retrieved his suitcase and backpack from the car boot, then followed Tammy up the white, winding staircase onto the landing which overlooked the lobby on three sides. This was the first time he'd been in the Millers' house, and he was impressed by its tasteful décor and pristine cleanliness.

His bedroom, with en-suite bathroom, had a king-size bed covered in a golden satin eiderdown, and was four times the size of his room in Swanford.

"Do you like it?" asked Tammy, following him across the deep-pile carpet.

Robert nodded, smiling happily. "It's just great, and I love the bay window seat."

"Are you coming to choir tonight?"

"Golly, Tammy, that'll probably be too much. After dinner, I may just flake out."

"Flake out?"

"In England that means go to sleep anywhere."

"Sounds like them English are surely in need of lessons in English," she replied flatly.

Robert wasn't sure if she was being serious or not. "Is your sister in? I haven't met her yet."

Tammy turned her nose up. "Oh, she's probably peoning in the kitchen with the maid. Would you like me to help you unpack?"

"I thought I'd have a shower and change before dinner," said Robert.

Tammy stood, smiling and unmoving, as if she had been abruptly switched to standby, and so Robert was relieved when Pearl called her to go downstairs.

"She probably thinks we're making out," whispered Tammy, licking her lips with the tip of her tongue.

Robert entered the dining room at the designated time of seven o'clock, only to find the whole family already seated.

"Sorry, am I late?" he asked.

"No, not at all, we're just enthusiastic," said Bruce. "Have you met my youngest daughter, Rosa?"

"Hello," said Robert.

The girl sitting next to Tammy nodded disinterestedly at him, but said nothing. She was certainly not as glamorous as her sister, neither in terms of what she wore nor how she looked, but the boy sensed this was deliberate.

"Would you say grace for us, Robert?" requested Bruce.

"Yes, sir," He was about to reach out, when he noticed that none of the family were doing likewise.

"Rosa does not share our need to give thanks," said Pearl, "therefore by not holding hands we do not exclude her from the circle."

"It makes no difference to me whether you hold hands or not," said Rosa.

"Forgive my little sister," said Tammy. "she is going through a rebellious phase."

Robert bowed his head. "Dear God, Our Father in Heaven, for this meal you have given we thank you from our hearts. May we always give you thanks and praise. We ask this through Jesus Christ our Lord. Amen!"

As soon as the prayer had ended, a black woman entered the dining room, pushing a trolley laden with their dinner: a traditional beef stew in a large blue Spode Italian tureen; chocolate cake with fudge icing, and a jug of orange juice.

"Shall I serve, Mrs Miller?" the woman asked.

"Thank you, Adeline. This young man is Robert Crittenden; he is to be our guest for a fortnight."

The woman smiled and nodded at Robert and he returned the gesture. It was quite a shock for him to find that the Millers employed a cook to prepare and serve their evening meal; he couldn't imagine his own parents being able to afford one, though it occurred to him that Bruce was no more senior in Burnoco than his father.

"I usually drop Tammy off at church for choir, Robert, if you'd like to go with us?" said Pearl after Adeline had withdrawn.

"If you don't mind, Mrs Miller, I'm rather tired," said Robert, between mouthfuls of stew.

"Why dear, of course you are. You need a good night's rest."

"I was thinking of giving it a miss tonight, Momma," said Tammy.

Rosa snorted. "Can't you leave him alone for one second?"

"What an ugly mind you have, sister."

"Tammy that'll be enough. There's no reason for you not to attend choir, and attend you will."

After the meal, Robert retired to his room where he unpacked, hanging his trousers neatly in the closet and laying out his other clothes in the chest of drawers. The sun was just setting when he heard the Chevrolet pull out of the drive with Pearl and Tammy aboard. He sat in the window seat and opened the Bible he had found on top of his bedside cabinet, but the words would not come into focus.

He decided to take a walk in the dusk to collect his thoughts and to become reacclimatised to the Oklahoma air. The house was quiet, except for a quiet hum coming from the kitchen. Not having a key, he was wary about getting locked out, and went to look for Bruce to inform him of his plan, but when he stepped into the lounge it was Rosa he found, reclining on the sofa. Despite being a year younger than himself, he found her rather an intimidating figure; so self-assured, so brusque, so unfriendly.

"I thought I'd take a walk," he said.

"I'm afraid Tammy isn't here to hold your hand, if that's what you're after."

He frowned, and if the room hadn't been in twilight, he probably would have blushed as well. "I was just after someone to tell..."

"So, you've told."

"You don't like me," he blurted out.

She gave her customary snort. "Whatever gave you that impression?"

"Do you treat all guests this way?"

"Only the string of puerile church boys that come through here."

"Are you an atheist?" he asked.

She laughed frostily and sat up. "Does it matter to you?"

"It matters to God."

"Well, I stopped believing in God about the same time I stopped believing in Santa Claus, and it's funny how that seems to matter to a whole lot of people, but I've heard nothing from God Himself."

"You will."

She laughed, this time genuinely amused. "That's quite funny coming from one of the brainwashed brethren, panting for the non-existent afterlife."

Robert was offended both by her manner and her assumptions about him. "I haven't been brainwashed; it's what I believe."

"You believe it because you've been indoctrinated by your parents, school and church."

"So how come you haven't been 'indoctrinated' like the rest of us?"

"Look around you; do you like what you see?"

"Yes, everything's real neat. I wish my room in England was like the one upstairs."

"So you think our mock antebellum house with its mock antebellum furniture, and its mock antebellum servant in our mock antebellum state with its mock antebellum church are 'real neat'?"

"Yes, I do, and you seem comfortable enough here too."

"Only because I see through the sham."

"Fourteen-year-old makes great discovery: Oklahoma wasn't part of the Confederacy," he scoffed, "but we still belong in the South, always have done and always will do, and you still haven't answered my original question."

"Let's just say that I see the people who do the indoctrination for what they are. Self- important spinners of deceit with the gift of the gab, but little else. Then you get hypocrites like my sister with a holier-than-thou exterior and a cesspit inside."

"It sounds to me like your attitude has less to do with God and Oklahoma and more to do with your relations with Tammy."

"You're probably right, Robert," she said, reclining once more on the sofa. "Enjoy your walk."

***

86: Sunday, 14th April. 9.15 a.m. Tyree, Oklahoma.

ROBERT

Tammy had wanted to drive Robert to church alone, but Pearl had insisted on going as well. "It wouldn't be seemly," she said, though Robert had the distinct impression that what mattered more to Mrs Miller was to be part of the 'small celebration' to welcome the return of the lost sheep to the fold.

It was only a two-mile drive down Washington Avenue past the Burnoco plant then right onto Cherokee Drive. They found a parking spot in the shade of the single-storey church building, for the day was already hot and forecast to get hotter still. Except for the cross on top of the building, there was little to distinguish the church from the large residential and retail properties that lined the drive.

The inside was cool, redolent with the smell of floor cleaner and polish that Robert remembered so well. All was peaceful and quiet until they entered the side chapel where the youth group met prior to main service. Here they were met by applause and whoops of welcome. Tammy took Robert's arm, her smile broader than his, as she basked in the reflected glory. They were surrounded by a wreath of happy faces, most familiar, some not, and from their midst came a beaming Pastor Dunn.

Robert took the offered hand and gave the merest hint of a bow.

"Welcome home, son," said the pastor, holding on to Robert's hand. "As the song goes, it's so good to have you back where you belong."

"Thank you, sir," said Robert, colouring at all the attention he was getting.

"And, my, how you have grown! And those broad shoulders!"

249

Robert smiled modestly, but wished his hand would be freed.

Pastor Dunn became more serious. "And you need those broad shoulders to do God's will in that benighted country," he said, to murmurs of approbation. "Your father has told me of the splendid work you are doing in standing up for Jesus against Satan's minions." The pastor beamed again and at last he released Robert's hand. "But we're getting too serious on this happy morning. How are your parents, Robert? I hope you are keeping in touch with them by at least one of these myriad devices we have at our disposal?"

"Yes, sir. Mom is fine, though I know she would like to be back home, and my dad? Well, he's out in Africa on business for a whole month."

"Your father is the nearest thing this church has to a saint, son. For every time he goes away on oil company business he finds time to do church business as well. Like St Paul, he spreads the word of Jesus wherever his travels take him."

"Amen!"

"Now, Robert, I know that normal fifteen-year-old boys do not seek the limelight, but we would like you, just for today, to be youth group leader and answer questions about your stay in England. Are you happy to oblige our fellowship in this manner?"

"I guess so. I mean, I'll do my best, sir..."

"That's all we ask, son." Pastor Dunn turned and raised his arms, projecting his voice expertly to the four corners of the chapel. "But first, a little surprise for our returnee. Come forward, Chris and Katie!"

A gap opened up in the crowd and through it came a trolley pushed by his old friends, Chris and Katie Foster. On it was a sponge cake so large that it overhung the edges. It was covered in icing, decorated with strawberries and the words, 'Welcome back, Robert C'.

"And that's why we were a bit skimpy on breakfast this morning," whispered Pearl apologetically.

The cake was served to all on paper plates and a circle of chairs made around Robert, who felt too much the centre of attention to really enjoy his slice of the confection.

"Could you get me a drink of water, please?" he whispered to Tammy, who passed on the request to her mother.

"You have twenty minutes before service, boys and girls, so make the most of it, and remember to show your appreciation at the end." Pastor Dunn and Pearl then withdrew, leaving Robert standing without water, but with Tammy, who had once again slipped her hand into the crook of his arm.

He cleared his throat and looked around the sea of faces. "Questions, then?" he asked. A few hands went up, including that of his friend Gregory Simmons who, at eighteen, was probably the oldest member of the youth group.

"Greg," said Robert with a tentative smile.

"What's England like?"

"Do you mean what are the people like or the country?"

Greg thought for a moment. "Whatever... both."

"Well, it's pretty cold and damp, but I've only seen it in winter. It snowed and we had some fun. Most of the kids at my school are OK, but they swear a lot and most don't follow scripture..." He looked round, seeing the expected disapproval on their faces. "More questions?"

"Do the people go hungry?" asked a girl.

"No, no more than here," answered Robert, wondering what she was talking about. "Oh, but the portion sizes are real small."

"How do the English people survive the socialist Medicare?"

"It doesn't seem to bother anyone too much."

"Have you met the Queen of England?"

"No, she lives in London."

"Don't you live in London?"

"No, I live about a hundred miles from London."

"Are they difficult to understand?" asked one of the younger boys.

"How do you mean?"

"I mean do you speak their language?" the boy continued.

"No, we speak their language: English."

Tammy huffed. "When are you going to say 'yes' to anyone?"

There were no more hands in the air, and his audience was becoming restive.

"I've got a question," said Tammy loudly. "Is it true they allow perverts to marry now?"

Suddenly the gathering came alive and a hum of conversation rippled around the chapel, which quickly quieted as heads craned forward, waiting for Robert to answer.

"I think so, but I'm not sure how it affects the churches," he said, knowing his reply would be too neutral to satisfy them.

"Are they putting Christians in jail?"

"Er, not that I know of... no one's tried to put me in jail." His attempt at humour fell on deaf ears as the meeting was getting riled.

"Do the homosexuals run England now?" said a voice from the back of the room.

"How do you dare go back to that place of sin?" someone else asked incredulously, before he could answer.

"How did Satan corrupt the Brits, and could it happen here?"

"Why don't the English churches speak out against this abomination?"

"We need to send more missionaries over there," a girl in plaits suggested.

"But Robert is our missionary!" cried Tammy, seizing the moment.

"Yes!" came a cry in unison.

"God bless Robert!" shouted Katie Foster, which was picked up by the meeting and they all started to clap and chant. "God bless Robert! God bless Robert..."

"You see, that's how it's done," breathed Tammy. "You've got to give the audience what they want."

***

87: Sunday, 14th April. 6 p.m. The Miller residence, Tyree, Oklahoma.

ROBERT

"So, you're back then?"

"Looks like it." Robert realised he was being impolite and put down the book he was reading and stood up.

Rosa snorted. "Quite the Southern gen'leman, aren't you?"

"I suppose you'd be insulted if someone called you a Southern belle."

"I'd probably put their eyes out, which would be a pity in your case."

It took a moment for Robert to process this. "You just paid me a compliment."

"Gee, you're fast. I only ever speak the truth."

"You can come in, you know; you don't have to stand in the doorway."

"I'm afraid you'll try to ravish me."

Robert's mouth dropped open and he stepped backwards, scuffing his socked heel on the baseboard under the window. Rosa sniggered and took the opportunity to stride over to the bed and throw herself onto it. "How was your day, then, since you're not going to ask me how mine was?"

"It was good." He slid back down onto the bay seat and began to nurse his heel. "After service, Katie, Chris and Greg took me to the cemetery and we sat under the trees and talked."

"Sounds like fun..." said Rosa, and she began to giggle. "Oh, Robert, sorry. You're so serious you make me laugh."

Offended but not wanting to show it, he continued. "They've invited me to go with them to Eagle State Park a week tomorrow on a spiritual retreat."

"Oh, that."

"What do you mean 'Oh, that'?"

"My sister and I will be accompanying you."

"Oh."

"Well, don't sound too enthusiastic."

"I thought you didn't like..."

"Religious hocus pocus? I don't, but Eagle State Park is quite pretty at this time of year."

"Why, fiddle-dee-dee Rosa, whatever are you doin' in Mr Crittenden's boudoir?" Tammy's head peered around the bedroom door, smiling like the Cheshire cat.

"It's all right, Tammy, you can put your claws away and the phoney Scarlett O'Hara accent."

"Robert, I thought you might like to accompany me to the lounge, where Mommy and I are about to start a game of Pinochle."

"I don't think I know the rules."

"Oh, you can sit with me and I'll show you how to play."

Rosa snorted.

"You know, sister, you are getting to sound more like a hog every day."

***

88: Monday, 22nd April. 10.05 a.m. The Miller residence, Tyree, Oklahoma.

ROBERT

"Honestly, sister, dear, I don't know why you want to accompany us. This is a spiritual day out..."

Rosa plumped the heavy picnic basket down on the hallway table. "I was just dying to do the fetchin' an' carryin' for you good Christian folks."

"Personally, I think you've gone gooey-eyed for a certain Mr Crittenden..."

Over the week Robert had successfully learned how to switch off the exchanges between the two girls, but at the mention of his name, his ears pricked up.

"Need any help?" he called brightly from the landing.

"Enter typical man, stage left," said Rosa, "when the work's all done."

Tammy tiptoed over to the bottom of the stairs on wedge heels, somehow reminding him of Mandy Simpkins. "Robert, now, you just take no notice; my sister has a viper's tongue on her today."

He looked down at her. "Are you sure they're suitable footwear for a national park?"

"I don't want to look like a plain Jane, now do I?" replied Tammy, glancing pointedly over her shoulder. "In any case, I have three gentlemen to support me should I become distressed."

Any further exchanges were cut short by the sound of a car horn as Greg's SUV drew up outside.

Tammy held out her hand. "Will you escort me to our carriage, Rhett?"

Rosa made a gagging motion, then went to open the front door.

"Come on guys, we're wastin' daylight!" cried Greg cheerfully. His seven-seater Cadillac Escalade was his proudest possession. He had bought it with $5,000 of his own money and $10,000 from his father, a present for gaining entry to the Theological Seminary in Kansas City the following autumn.

Chris Foster was seated next to him, with Katie directly behind. Tammy sneaked in beside her, making sure that Robert followed. This meant that Rosa was relegated, along with the picnic basket, to the third row.

They drove through downtown Tyree before picking up Route 60 westbound. There then followed a monotonous sixty-mile journey through featureless, rolling prairie. Greg switched on the radio to KWTH, a contemporary Christian music station which he Chris and Katie would intermittently sing along to, to relieve the boredom. Meanwhile, Tammy slipped off her seat belt and snuggled up close to Robert.

At an unobtrusive junction, they turned left onto state highway 169, a narrow road that took them into a wilderness of undulating woodland and scrub. Soon they dived down into a valley lined with high sandstone and shale cliffs, so uniform that they looked like man-made walls. At last, the valley widened, the cliffs declined into thickly forested hills, and before them was a sign reading Eagle Heights State Park.

The car park could have held two hundred cars, but in this mid-April afternoon there were only about a quarter that number. Around the periphery there were picnic tables set in the grass under the light shade of loblolly pines.

"Shall we eat first and then explore?" proposed Greg.

"But we've not long since had breakfast!" declared Tammy. "I vote we pair off now. I want to show Robert Highpoint Lake. It's so pretty this time of year."

"Shall we all go?" suggested Rosa.

"No, sister, you can go off and play on the swings like a good little girl."

"You come with us, Rosa," said Katie, "Tammy obviously wants to get to know Robert better."

The trail to the lake was steep, leading up through hillsides covered in oak-hickory forest. Tammy held Robert's hand, enthusing over each sighting of grey squirrel or glimpse of a white-tailed deer. They passed on through a gully, still ascending until suddenly they emerged onto a plateau affording a panoramic view across the bowl-shaped lake. The water was a flat blue, reflecting the cloudless sky. There was not a soul about.

"What do you think?" she asked, squeezing his hand.

"Great," he replied. "How far to the other side?"

"Quite a way," said Tammy, "the water goes over a fall."

"I'd like to see that."

"No time," she said, giving him a big smile which showed both rows of perfect teeth.

"Listen!" he exclaimed, hearing a loud trill. "That's a wren."

"Duh!" she scoffed, "wrens are iddy-biddy birds. That noise came from something big, like a buzzard or something."

"Usually buzzards only come this far north in summer. In any case, they don't sing."

Tammy feigned a yawn. "I know an adorable little spot." She pointed with her free hand to a bluff some way around the shoreline, its top covered in black oak trees.

"How many times have you been up here?" he enquired, surprised by her knowledge of the terrain.

She puckered her lips. "First time was summer before last. Since then, quite a few. It's so beau-ti-ful."

At the base of the bluff there was a lacuna in the rock which widened into a warm hollow overhung by dense thickets of American hazelnut, spotted with tiny red flowers and pendulous catkins. In the centre was a wedge-shaped slab of yellow sandstone.

"Say, how did you find this place?" he asked. "It's like we're at the bottom of a well."

"A friend showed me," Tammy said coyly, and pulled the top over her head.

"What are you doing?" asked Robert, going wide-eyed and suddenly becoming aware of the not inconsiderable number of used condoms scattered about the rocky ground.

She laughed reaching back to unfasten her bra. "What do you think, soldier? You're going to fuck me." Before he could say anything, she grabbed the front of his shorts and pulled him towards her. "I can feel it in there," she said, stroking him through the fabric. "Mmm, it's going hard."

She stopped and stepped back, allowing her bra to fall from her breasts.

"Take your shirt off," she ordered, tossing the bra down beside her top.

He looked round. "What if someone is watching?"

"So what if they are? I like an audience."

His breathing was growing ragged. Quickly he unbuttoned his shirt and threw it aside.

"Well, Robert, let's see how you perform. I like it hard and deep, up against that rock." She tweaked his nipples, then moved in to kiss him. As her lips met his, she stuck her tongue into his mouth, and at the same time unbuckled his shorts, letting them fall about his ankles. She pulled away for a moment, appraising him.

"You kiss OK ... for a virgin."

Again she stroked him through his underwear, bringing him to a full erection.

"That's a biggy," she said. "Come on, I'm doing all the work here. Feel me up."

Robert had already realised that this was not what he wanted. Tammy was not what he wanted: she was entirely the wrong shape; her hips stuck out unattractively; she was too soft, her shoulders weren't broad enough; the angles of her face and chest were all wrong; she didn't even smell right. She was a girl and – most importantly – she wasn't Jack. Clumsily, he put both hands on her breasts, but as he did so his penis began to soften.

"Jeez, you are green," she said, taking his left hand and pushing it down the front of her shorts. He could feel the wetness through her panties.

"Now, finger it," she said.

"I'm stuck," he said, feeling Tammy's waistband squeezing his knuckles.

She huffed and pulled off her shorts and underwear in one go, then stood with her legs apart. Her pubic area had been razored to a brown stubble; the lips of her vagina were engorged and parted, and were leaking copious amounts of fluid.

"Go on," she said, "put a finger or two in; it won't hurt."

"I don't like it," he said, seeing what – to his eyes – was a shapeless mass of pinky-red flesh.

She looked scornfully at him. "The last one wanted it so much he spilled himself before he'd even touched me."

"I'm not like that," he explained, feeling foolish with his shorts round his ankles and a withered erection in his jockeys. "We're not married. It's a sin."

Tammy laughed in his face. "That's not the reason, is it?"

Robert bent to pull up his shorts. "It's wrong."

She began to gather up her clothes. "But you would have been all right with a hand job, wouldn't you? But as soon as you had to give a bit back, you couldn't stomach it, could you?"

He picked up his shirt. "Think what you like."

"You're a fag."

"And you're a whore," he said.

She slapped him across the face. "Faggots revolt me."

He wanted to hit her back, but he merely held his sore cheek and stared at her.

"Have you got a boyfriend in England?" she asked scornfully. "Do you lick his dirty ass?"

He was tempted to say yes just to spite her, but he merely turned and made off through the gap.

***

The feeling of wretchedness had not left him by the time he walked back into the car park. It was not so much the humiliation, but what it told him about himself.

He found Greg leaning back, arms folded, against the Cadillac.

"Where's Tammy?" he asked, yawning. "You've been a long time. We ate hours ago."

Hours ago! Robert thought and noticed that the shadows had already begun to lengthen. "What time is it?" he asked.

"I noticed you weren't wearing a watch," replied Greg, pityingly. "I suppose they don't have watches in England."

Before they could say more, Rosa, Chris and Katie came towards, them chattering away happily, having just bought ice lollies. Chris threw one at Greg. "Sorry, Robert, we didn't know you were back. Where's Tammy?"

Rosa frowned, seeing the dour expression on Robert's face. "What's happened?"

"As if you didn't know," he replied.

"I don't know. What are you talking about?"

Immediately he was sorry to have spoken so abruptly. Perhaps she really didn't know what her sister got up to on these trips to the park. Chris and Katie exchanged puzzled glances.

"What's the matter, Robert?" asked Chris.

"I want to go back," he said.

"We can't go until Tammy returns, now can we?" replied Greg with heavy sarcasm.

I wish we could leave her here. I hope she gets set upon by twenty men on the way back down the trail. Dear Lord Jesus Christ, forgive me for having such bestial thoughts, but I am confused and scared.

"Here she comes," said Katie brightly.

They all turned to watch as Tammy stomped across the car park. She simpered at Greg. "I've lost my heel and all this gentleman did was go on without me!"

Greg looked disapprovingly at Robert. "Time we were making tracks, I think."

"Why is everyone in a bad mood?" asked Katie.

"I'm not in a bad mood. I've had a great time," said Chris.

Katie stamped her foot. "Christopher Foster, you're completely oblivious to the ambience."

Rosa had been looking on silently through all these exchanges. Now, she went over to Robert and spoke quietly. "Sit next to me if you want."

"Well, no one else will want to sit next to him, will they?" said Tammy.

Rosa turned to her sister. "How many times have you pretended to lose your heel in the woods?"

Tammy seemed about to give Rosa a mouthful of invective, but instead she took Chris by the arm and smiled sweetly. "Will you escort me to the car, Christopher dear?"

"Sure thing, Tammy," he spluttered, flattered by the attention.

"Homeward, folks, I think," said Greg.

So much for spiritual renewal, thought Robert.

***

By the time they arrived back at the Millers' house, it was dusk and he had calmed enough for a partial plan to have formed in his mind. After perfunctory goodbyes to Greg and company, he went straight up to his room, where he began to pack.

A quiet knock came on his door. When he opened it, Rosa was standing on the threshold with a solicitous expression on her face. "Can I come in?"

He held the door open for her. "I'm leaving."

"But where will you go?"

He shut the door quietly then walked over to the bed where his suitcase lay. "To my Auntie Una's, I think." He turned to her. "I'm sorry I snapped at you in the park."

She chuckled and threw herself backwards onto the bed beside his case, putting her hands behind her head. "No, you were right really. My sister is an open book to me, but one I don't care to read." Robert said nothing and turned away to continue sorting his clothes. Rosa regarded him.

"So you didn't like what she had to offer."

"What do you mean by that?" he asked sharply.

"I think you know."

"I don't," he replied.

"She hurt you, didn't she?"

He made a scornful noise. "Hurt me?... No."

"I don't mean physically, dork."

"She thought I was easy," he said, tight-lipped.

"So, you didn't rise to her charms?"

Despite the string of innuendos, he no longer felt threatened by Rosa. "I guess I didn't meet her expectations."

"You seem disappointed in yourself, rather than her."

Robert realised this was true, and turned to face her. "I am..."

"Gay," completed Rosa.

He blenched. "No!"

She looked up at him. "It must be very difficult for a person like you to come out, even to yourself."

"Why do you think I am... like that?"

Rosa smiled an upside-down smile. "I see it in your eyes. You're not interested in girls. You're so sweet and nice, Robert, if you were straight you could have any girl you wanted, including me."

He did a double take.

She laughed and sat up. "There, I've let on more than I should."

"I think we both have," he said.

She narrowed her eyes at him. "You know something, you haven't mentioned God or the Lord Jesus Christ once since we started this conversation."

"And you think that's a good thing?"

"Yes, siree Bob!" she snorted and stood up. "Now, can I do anything to make amends for having the sluttiest bitch this side of the Panhandle in the family?"

"If you could try to help me find my aunt in Oklahoma City, that would be good. I don't know her home address, but I know she works as a school crossing guard."

The girl was already on her feet before he'd finished. "What's her name?"

"Una Page, unless she's taken her partner's name, but I can't remember what that is."

"Well, let's hope, then..." She led him along the landing to her bedroom where she sat at the computer. After a two-minute search she had the address and telephone number of the one and only Una Page in Oklahoma City. 107, Briar Lane, Del City.

Rosa printed out the information for him, then went to get him the house telephone while he waited on the landing. Moments later, he could hear her arguing with Tammy, and so he retreated to his bedroom to continue packing, but left the door open.

"Here, catch!" she said, a little later, pretending to throw the phone. "I wish I was going with you."

"Where to, the City or England?"

"Who cares, as long as it's away from here..." She handed him the phone. "I'll leave you to sweet-talk your aunt."

Robert locked the door behind her then sat in the window seat. Outside, dark storm clouds were spreading in from the south-west. As he dialled the number, his hand trembled and sweat beaded his forehead. The phone rang at the other end. A man's voice answered, sounding distant and decidedly impatient, with an accent he didn't immediately recognise.

"Hello, could I speak to Una Page, please?"

"Who is this?"

"It's Robert, Robert Crittenden, her nephew."

There was a pause, he assumed while the information sank in, then a child squawked momentarily very loudly into the mouthpiece.

The man's voice returned, this time more focused, but with an undertone of tiredness. "Hello, Robert, this is Tom Sanchez, Una's partner. Listen, I'm sorry, you obviously haven't heard, but your aunt passed away in March."

Robert gasped. The one person he had liked and respected and who might have understood what he was going through could no longer help him.

"Hello? Are you still there?" the voice said.

"Yes..."

"I'm sorry to spring it on you like that. It came as a shock to all of us."

Robert sobbed. "Nobody told me."

"Where are you, Robert? The last I heard, you were in England."

"I'm in Tyree, but I fly back on Wednesday. I was going to ask Auntie Una if I could visit..."

"Yes, you ought to come. There's something I'm sure she'd want you to have."

"I'll come tomorrow..." He could barely get the words out.

"Phone me when you arrive. I'll pick you up."

"Thank you."

"Goodbye, Robert. I'll see you soon."

Some of the weight that had lifted from his shoulders during his talk with Rosa now fell heavily back into place.

***

That night, they ate their dinner of beef brisket with barbecue sauce, mashed potato and baked root vegetables to the accompaniment of the flash, crack and drum roll of a thunderstorm. Hailstones pattered on the roof and the chandelier lights above the table dimmed and brightened.

"I apologise, Mrs Miller," said Robert, unable to finish his apple dumplings and ice cream. "It was a real nice meal."

"Don't worry, dear, you've had a nasty shock."

"Why, Robert, we're all so sorry to hear about your aunt. And she with two lovely half-caste children, born out of wedlock by a bean— I mean, Latino." Tammy oiled her words with honeyed sweetness to point up their insincerity.

"Redneck hag!" mouthed Rosa across the table to Robert.

"Bruce will drive you to the bus station first thing tomorrow, won't you, dear?"

"It'll have to be early, Robert. I have to be in the office by eight."

"Yes, sir. My bus is at eight as well."

***

89: Tuesday 23rd April. 11.45 a.m. Mallaig, west coast of Scotland.

JACK

Jack sat crossed legged on the beach, dressed in white T-shirt and blue cargo shorts, trying to bury his unloved toes in the pearl white sand. The holiday had been much more enjoyable than he had expected, due in no small part to the unseasonably warm weather. The sea was far out now, shimmering in the near cloudless sky, leaving rivulets of fresh water to meander across the sand. Mikey was a mini figure in the distance, decked out only in speedos, merrily running to and fro with bucket and spade collecting sea shells from rock pools. There was not another soul in sight. Jack looked up to his right to where their caravan was perched on a wide ledge safely out of reach of the highest tide and sheltered in the lee of cliffs from the westerly wind. It was still a mystery to him how the owners had managed to get it up there.

Dan emerged from the caravan in his new black swim jammers with red and white side stripes, a towel slung over his shoulder. He picked his way cautiously in bare feet down a flight of wooden steps onto the beach. Jack smiled ruefully to himself; his brother was getting to be a very handsome young man who would undoubtedly far outshine him. He waved and Dan made a beeline for him.

"Hey, LB, are you going in?"

The boy crouched down beside him. "Thinking about it. What about you?"

"Well, I'll see you first. Aren't Mum and Dad back?"

"Nah! I expect Mum's dragging Dad around all the junk shops in town."

Jack cocked his head towards his brother. "Am I mistaken, or is that a bit of armpit fuzz I can see?"

Dan lifted his arm proudly and brushed the sprinkling of hair. "Some. It's a lot lighter than yours, though. Can I see your treasure trail?"

Jack lifted his T-shirt and pushed down the hem of his shorts.

"Jeez, it's all joined up!" said Dan, inspecting it closely. "Sophie wants me to grow one."

"Oh, yeah, and why is that?"

Dan sniggered and blushed at the same time. "So she can follow it down to my jewel box, she said."

Jack laughed. "If you ask me, you're fast becoming the super-stud of Swanford."

"I wish you'd laugh more," said Dan.

Jack gave a small shake of his head. "I wish I could too."

The boy sat down beside his older brother and stretched out his legs. "I already told you, you can tell me anything, didn't I?"

"Yeah, but it's not that easy."

"I can keep a secret."

"I trust you, LB, but..."

"You've been unhappy for so long now. Why not just tell me?"

Jack gave a long sigh. "LB, would you believe I'm in love with someone?"

Dan gave a huge grin. "But Jesus, that's way cool! So what's the problem?"

"The love isn't returned."

Dan knelt up, his eyes wide, and spoke in a confidential whisper. "But who is she?"

Jack looked hard at his brother. "It's not a she."

There was silence. Dan's eyes seemed to go dim for a moment, before becoming hard and fixed. He fell back and began to scrabble away from his brother, his face flushed and twisted.

"No! I don't want to know that. It's sick. You're sick! You're gay! How can a professional footballer have a fag for a brother?"

"LB..."

"Don't call me that! Don't ever call me that again! You must never tell anyone about this. I'll be crucified on the team if they knew!" He stood up and began to walk away, then he stopped and turned. "It's that fucking American, isn't it? I should have known. Fuck me. I don't want to speak to you again, ever! It's disgusting. Just keep the fuck away from me as well! Keep your fucking faggoty fingers to yourself!"

266

Jack watched his brother storm off towards the caravan, his swim forgotten. Despondency enveloped him and he put his head in his hands.

His bout of self-pity didn't last long, however, as with a jolt he realised he hadn't been looking out for Mikey. He gazed towards the rock pools under the cliffs to right and left, but there was no sign of him. Panic seized him. He got to his feet. And a little figure suddenly bobbed up in the dead centre of the beach, smiling and running towards him, bucket and spade in hand. Relieved beyond measure, Jack waved and the boy raised his spade, then tripped, falling flat on his face, his bucket of shells scattering across the sand.

Jack ran down the beach, hearing Mikey's cries. When he reached the boy, the sand that had stuck to his face was streaked with tears. "My shells," he sobbed.

Jack knelt down beside him and gently stroked his head, knowing it was the shock of falling more than anything. "It's all right. We can pick them up." Quickly he gathered up a good number and put them back into the bucket.

"They're sandy," whimpered Mikey.

"I know they're sandy, they're just like you. Shall we go and wash them off?"

The little boy nodded and made a little whiny noise.

"And would you like me to carry you?"

The little boy nodded again and made a slightly louder, but less whiny, noise.

"Come on, then." Jack hoisted him up and put him into the crook of his arm. "You big lump."

Mikey put his arms round Jack's neck. "Why is Dan watching us?"

Jack looked over towards the caravan, where his brother was standing with his hands on hips, staring back at them. It was too far away to see his expression, but it was not hard to guess. "He probably saw you fall and was worried," he said.

"I'm cold," complained Mikey.

"I can feel you're cold. It's time we got you back for a hot shower."

"Will you carry me all the way?"

"Yes, unless I fall down dead from exhaustion, then you'll have to carry me."

Mikey relaxed against his brother's chest and gave him a kiss on the cheek.

"At least someone still loves me," said Jack.

***

90: Tuesday, 23rd April. 11.45 a.m. Oklahoma City.

ROBERT

The art deco bus station on West Sheridan Avenue had long since lost its charm. It was not a welcoming place, nor was it a place to stay long. Robert had phoned Tom Sanchez's number. There was no answer, so he left a message. Now, he sat huddled on a plastic seat, taking sips from a bottle of water, surrounded by his expensive luggage and feeling vulnerable. He fiddled with his backpack and was surprised to find a piece of printed notepaper had been inserted into one of the pockets.

Fag, you better not say anything about IT or I'll make sure everyone gets to know you're a dirty fudge-packer. I'm told that spics hate queers; I hope that's right. I pray to God that you and your boyfriend get AIDS.

He read it two or three times without emotion, just a sense of irony about the assumption of a boyfriend. If she only knew that the person he really wanted wasn't like that...

"Robert?"

He jumped up, almost standing to attention. A tall, olive-skinned man in a checked shirt and corduroy jacket gave him a smile and offered his hand. He had the tiredest eyes the boy had ever seen. Still holding the note and the bottle, he hesitated, then stuffed the paper into one of the compartments of his suitcase, before grasping the rough and calloused hand.

"Sir."

"Call me Tom."

The battered station wagon was at least twenty years old, and the right front bumper hung lopsidedly.

"Not what you're used to," Tom said as they sped along Reno Avenue.

Robert couldn't deny it, but didn't want to offend.

The Latino glanced at him. "If you're open with me, I'll be open with you. I don't know you, and you don't know me, but Una was very fond of you, I do know that."

"Do you mind talking about her?" asked Robert tentatively.

"I'm pleased to. I loved her a lot and I don't get many opportunities to let my feelings be known." Tom gripped the steering wheel more tightly. "It happened not far from here. She was on crossing patrol and had a stroke. Just like that. Gone." He sighed. "A month and a half ago, that's all, yet in some ways it seems like years."

"Do my parents know?" asked Robert pointedly.

"A letter was sent to your church."

The boy let this information sink in before speaking again. "Her last email was a bit critical of me."

"Ah, I remember that! It took her so long to decide to send it."

"I'm glad she did."

"Why do you say that?"

"I'm ashamed," said Robert, "that boy tried to kill himself..."

"Madre de Dios...!" Tom crossed himself and the car swerved slightly.

They crossed the river, entering Del City from the north-west. Everything Robert had been told about this area was negative, from the high crime rate to the poor general health of the population. "I've heard it's a bit rough in these parts," he said.

Tom smiled in amusement. "I think it's safe to say that it's not the best area in town, but where we live is fairly quiet."

"Have you had to skip work to pick me up?"

"Not really. I had to switch to part-time work after Una passed on. The kids, you know, particularly Susie with her breathing. Barney's OK, he started the Pre-K class at Epperly Heights last fall."

"How do you manage?"

"I don't, Robert. I get by most days. I've let things slide, but you'll find that out when we get home. Look..." he said, bending his head. His thick blue-black hair was streaked with tiny ribbons of white. "All that since March."

They turned right off Tinker Diagonal Street into a residential area of ranch-style 1960s properties. "Nearly there," the Latino said, slowing the station wagon as it bounced along the uneven concrete road, which was criss-crossed with asphalt repairs. "I haven't mentioned my grandmother," he continued, making it sound like a guilty secret.

Robert looked askance at him. "Your mother's mother?"

"My papa's mother..."

The boy nodded, not sure where this was going.

"She came to stay for a few days after the funeral, and stayed, and stayed."

"She must be quite old..."

"Yeah, I've never dared to ask, but I guess she's in her seventies."

"That is old..."

Tom chuckled. "She can be cranky, but take no notice of her."

Robert nodded, even more slowly than before.

A short distance along Briar Lane, they turned into the driveway of one of the smaller houses, coming to rest before an incongruous double garage. The front garden was dominated by a red oak tree adorned in spring leaves which towered over the residence, casting it into almost permanent shade.

"Welcome to number 107," said Tom, hauling himself out of the wagon.

A small barefoot boy dressed only in denim dungarees came flying from the house, oblivious of the stony ground. "Papá, papá!"

"Meet my little muchacho," said Tom, grasping his son and setting him down in front of Robert.

"¿Quién es este?" the boy asked.

"English, Barney, please... This is your cousin, Robert. Robert, meet Barney."

Robert squatted down. "Snap," he said, bending his head forward, because although the little boy had the same dark complexion as his father, on the top of his head was an untidy thatch of red hair. The little boy put out his not-altogether-clean hand and touched his cousin's pate. "Crespo!" he squeaked with delight.

"English!" cried Tom.

"Sí, papá."

They manhandled the luggage from the boot of the station wagon and entered the house. "Lita está de mal humor, papá," whispered Barney, putting his index finger to his lips.

Across the drab living room was the kitchen diner, where worn carpet gave way to scuffed tiles. Robert knew about poverty, but had never experienced it at first hand until now. Grandma Sanchez was standing in front of an old electric coil stove, stirring a steaming aluminium saucepan. The pleasant aroma of cooking could not hide the pervasive mushroom smell of dry rot.

"Abuela," called Tom, "come and meet Robert."

"I can see him well enough from here."

"The food smells real nice, Mrs Sanchez."

"Ay! It has to last us three days," she said, "so when you're flying off in your plane think of us scraping the bottom of the saucepan."

Tom raised his eyes heavenward. "Abuela, where's Susie? At least she has good manners and knows how to treat a guest."

Grandma Sanchez regarded him, using her wooden spoon as a baton. "Where do you think? She is lying down on her bed, gasping for breath because you can't afford to buy her medicines."

"¡Ay, Dios mío!" murmured Tom.

Robert felt a tug on his sleeve and looked down to see Barney smiling at him. "Crespo, por favor!" He knelt, allowing the small boy to run his fingers through his hair again. This seemed to delight him, making him shiver and stamp his little feet.

"Hey, Barney," said Tom, "you go out to play now and stop pestering our guest.

Follow me, Robert, I'll show you to your room."

In the centre of the house was a short flight of steps down to a tiny cellar which had been converted to a utility room with a rectangular window at ceiling height to give a small amount of illumination. Now the space had been cleared and an army surplus cot bed had been laid on the concrete floor with a sleeping bag and pillow.

"It's the best I could do," said Tom, switching on the light.

"It's great," said the boy. "But I am causing you a lot of trouble..."

"No, Robert, you're not causing any trouble. Abuela and I don't get on, so whatever I do is wrong."

"I've got some money. I can pay for my board, if that's any help?" Robert said, blushing.

The Latino squeezed the boy's arm. "I am not a proud man, but asking my children's fifteen-year-old cousin to pay for a night's stay is out of the question."

"There must be something..."

"Tomorrow, when I drive you to the airport, we can take Barney and Susie, if she's well enough, and you can buy them a Big Mac at the drive-thru on Shield's Boulevard, if you like. They'll think that's really cool."

"OK. Er, can I ask you what's wrong with Susie?"

"Asthma... though they won't say it's asthma at her age. It's a worry, if you must know. We are not in a good environment here. Abuela won't stand any nonsense from her, and so she can administer the drugs better than I..."

***

91: Wednesday, 24th April. 1.30 p.m. South Shields Boulevard, Oklahoma City.

ROBERT

There was still an hour and a half before Robert had to check in for his flight, and so they decided to eat inside the McDonald's restaurant. Robert had failed to win over Grandma Sanchez sufficiently for her to accompany them, but she did waver, actually speaking to him directly before he left, though her words were in no way conciliatory.

"Your family has brought us nothing but trouble, young man, and now they ignore their own flesh and blood in their time of need. Why is that? We may go to different churches, but we still worship the same God!"

The words were still fermenting inside Robert's head as they walked across the car park. He would have much thinking to do on the flight back to England.

"This is your cousin Robert's treat," announced Tom to his two children.

Barney skipped around him excitedly while Susie merely stared, as if he had just landed from another planet.

"You can have anything you like," said Robert, "and you too, Tom, please."

"As long as you eat it all," warned their dad.

Susie was like a little ghost: pale and waif-like with jet-black hair and the same soulful, tired eyes as her father. Each breath was an audible wheeze and whether it was necessary or just a habit, she cleared her throat each time she spoke.

"Can I order?" said Barney in English with a barely perceptible accent. He had found out soon enough that he could communicate better with this new person in his life if he used standard American.

"You sure can. I'll have a deluxe quarter pounder with fries and coke."

While they sat munching away, Tom took out two CD cases and an envelope from his jacket and laid them before Robert.

"Una would have wanted you to have these," he said. "I found this letter in a drawer. It is a matter for your family, not mine."

Robert stopped eating.

"Mommy's gone to heaven," breathed Susie.

"We're still sad," said Barney.

The children were sitting either side of him and he gave them both a hug. "Your mom looked after me when I was ten. She was very kind."

"You've probably guessed," continued Tom. "These are CDs of photographs Una took while still in Tyree. When she and your folks were close."

"There are some of me and Aaron, aren't there? I remember her coming with her new digital camera, while my dad was still using Kodak."

"Yes, those were sunny days for her," said Tom. "Robert, though you'll be thousands of miles away, I hope we can keep in touch."

Robert nodded and tucked the items into his pockets. "I intend to."

***

92: Thursday 25th April. 2.50 p.m. 25 miles from Swanford.

ROGER

They broke the five-hundred mile journey from Mallaig with an overnight stop at a hotel in Sedbergh. It was meant to have been a pleasant and relaxing detour to the small market town in the Yorkshire Dales National Park, but the arguments had started as soon as they arrived. Dan had refused to occupy the same room as his older brother and so Mikey and he swapped, pleasing the little boy who got a big bed all to himself, but infuriating Dan, who was relegated to a small cot in his parent's room.

On the second day the atmosphere was just as tense and for the last hundred miles of the journey, barely a word was spoken. Then, some thirty-five minutes from home, Roger, in the front passenger seat, turned to face his children.

"Well, I hope you two are satisfied!"

Jack gazed out of the window and Dan set his jaw, staring into the middle distance. Only Mikey, perched in the booster seat between them, actually looked at his dad.

"I'm talking to you two!"

"It's got nothing to do with me," mumbled Jack.

"It's got everything to do with you!" said his dad.

"Just keep him away from me, that's all." said Dan.

"What has got into you, Daniel Moseley?" said his mother from the driver's seat.

"Ask him!"

"Do you want me to tell them?" said Jack in the most sarcastic tone he could muster.

Dan pulled himself up and tried to throw a punch at Jack over Mikey's seat, but Roger grabbed him by the wrist. "Don't you ever do that!" he exclaimed.

The boy wrenched his hand away and shrank back into his seat.

"I've had an accident," Mikey sobbed. "I don't like it when everyone's angry."

Roger slapped his forehead. "This family is going to pieces!" he declared.

***

93: Thursday 25th April, Virgin Atlantic Flight 104.

<u>ROBERT</u>

The stewardess has just asked me if there's anything the matter. Of course, I said no, but that's not really true. Everything's the matter! I wish now I'd spoken to Rosa as much as I did to Tammy – she seemed to understand me better than I do myself. Just before I left Tyree she gave me an envelope to open on the flight to England. She told me to look up all these people on the internet and choose which one I'm most like.

I know who they are: homosexuals, gays as she calls them. Both my mom and dad hate that word. Gay, to them, means what it was like in the antebellum period of our history. If she's right, if I am one of these people, then I have nothing: no family, no church, I don't even have Jack, who started off all these thoughts in my head. But that's a lie. Jack didn't start off the thoughts; they were already there. I just couldn't bring myself to fish them out until he came along.

And now this! This other letter to my aunt from my dad. Tom must have read it; he must have known the effect it would have on me. That's not fair, though – he had to give it to me. In any case, it answers quite a few of the questions I've never had explanations for. It's just that I feel I'm being bombarded from all sides at the moment. It was written five years ago when I was ten. Ten! I've read it several times already and every time I read it I find something new, something worse in it.

Tulsa, Oklahoma,
Friday, October 3rd

Dear Una,
I am grateful for the support you are giving the family in our darkest hour. Maybelle is a voluntary patient and should be home before Thanksgiving. I have decided that for her sake

I shall remove the physical evidence of his existence and would be obliged if you would make sure that Robert's mementoes are likewise destroyed.

I shall now speak for the first – and final – time on the other matter that has so concerned you. When I made a full confession of my sin to Maybelle, at your behest, I included the fact that you had knowledge of all my dalliances. I also made it clear that her own frigidity was to blame for my need to seek relief elsewhere. This, of course, she accepted. What she found more difficult to accept was her own sister's complicity in my sinful deeds.

Clearly the timing of my confession could not have been worse since a few days later my younger son died and Maybelle concluded that this was God's punishment on the family. I thought when I married your sister that she was a strong woman who would not suffer from any of the more emotional feminine conditions, but in my youthful naivety I was proved wrong.

To the case in point, I do not intend to have any legal action brought against me, therefore I have made generous provision for the woman and her child up to its eighteenth year – on condition that I never see or hear of them again.

As far as I am concerned, both these matters are now closed, and I think a respectful silence on all sides should be observed. In addition, I expect you to destroy this letter as soon as you have read it.

Yours,
Frank

So what have I learned from my 'spiritual renewal', my 'spiritual reawakening', the 'recharging of my spiritual batteries'? My Aunt Una, my friend and comforter, is dead. My dad is an adulterer. My mother spent a period in a psychiatric hospital. Somewhere in America, I have a half-brother or sister who I shall never meet. And I may as well admit it, I do not want to have sex with a girl, especially one like Tammy Miller – gross! But I could have sex with a boy, especially a certain English boy. In fact, I already have, in my dreams. Therefore I am a homosexual, like Kieran Scott, the boy who tried to hang himself and who I called a disgusting pervert.

In this new upside-down world, did anything good come out of my time in America? Yes: Rosa, Tom and the kids. Will I ever be able to talk about any of this to Mom and Dad? No! To be honest, I feel as if I don't really know them any more. And as for church, what is the point of going to a place that hates me and what I am? If I'm damned to the eternal lake of fire, I sure as hell want to enjoy myself before I get there. But how? I'm tied to my present life for the foreseeable future.

The stewardess has just brought me a bottle of fruit juice. She said I looked as if I needed a drink, but they can't give me alcohol. We had a little laugh about that. She's gone back to her station now and I've got three hours before we land at Heathrow to think about what a miserable SOB I am. There, I've even started swearing!

***

94: Saturday 4th May. 11.30 a.m. 15 Leighton Lane.

JACK

A letter addressed to Mr J. Moseley with a first-class stamp arrived on the mat just as his parents were leaving to go shopping. The script in blue fountain pen reminded him of his nan's careful but wavery writing.

Jack took it upstairs to read, frowning at the sudden increase in volume of the music coming from his brother's room. He ripped open the envelope and withdrew the single sheet of paper from inside.

Linden Lee Nursing Home,
3 Carisbrooke Drive,

3rd May

Dear Jack,

I was given your name by Mr Ray, the kind gentleman in the newsagent's on the high street. He informed me that you were the young man whose diligence I have to thank for saving me from certain death. I had slipped in the bath and was lying, in something of a state, for a best estimate of five days before you raised the alarm.

Being 83 years of age has no doubt been the cause of my slow rate of recovery, because I have been in hospital and then this nursing home for the best part of three months. Now, however, with a new hip joint and no longer needing crutches, I am ready to return home.

I have been liaising with an interior designer to sort out my requirements and next week, after the May Day bank holiday, workmen will begin the much-needed renovation of my old house to make it 'user friendly' (I think that is the modern term) for someone of my great age. Then it will be a matter of finding someone I trust to take on some of the burden of looking after me, hopefully as a live-in tenant, as I have ignored my inevitable decline for too long.

All the improvements should be finished by the middle of June, and I should be very pleased if you would call in sometime after that so that we could meet.

Once again, thank you for your assistance: you are a prince among paper boys.

Yours very sincerely,

Elspeth Chambers.

Jack read the letter several times over, feeling a certain amount of panic as the message sank in. He just had three days' grace to get Stewart out of the house and find him somewhere else to live. This letter was clearly a wake-up call for them both. At least it would give him something to do and take his mind off his own problems.

Jack entered his brother's room without knocking; in any case, the music was so loud he probably wouldn't have been heard. He was surprised to find Justin Walker there, and even more surprised to see that he must have been there for a sleepover, judging by the camp bed under the window. It was a mark of how out of touch he was with his brother's life.

"Hi, Jack," said Justin with a friendly smile. He was ten days younger, and half an inch shorter, than Dan, sturdy, with his fair hair clippered short and the top spiked with gel.

"Hey Justin, how long now?"

"I had a letter telling me to report to the Woolgrove Academy on the twenty-ninth of July, subject to my medical on the twenty-third."

"The twenty-third – that's the last day of term."

"Why are you in here?" interrupted Dan, the first words he'd spoken directly to his brother since the holiday.

"I want your phone."

Dan's gritted his teeth. "No."

"You can borrow mine," said Justin, taken aback by the enmity between them.

"Thanks, but I may need it for a while."

"No," repeated Dan.

"I need it and I'm going to have it," replied Jack simply and without rancour. "I'll make sure you get all your messages and texts."

His brother's face flushed.

"No!" he exclaimed.

Jack turned.

"Justin, I have something to tell you..."

"Bastard!" cried Dan and threw his phone down onto the bed.

"Thank you," said Jack. "Where's the charger?"

95: Saturday 4th May. 12.45 p.m. 41 Westbury Avenue.

JACK

The gate was unlocked when he arrived and Stewart was waiting for him in the kitchen, the remains of breakfast still on the table. Jack gave him a hug, then handed over the letter, which he read through twice before sighing disconsolately.

"So that's it, then."

"Let's sit down and talk," said Jack.

Stewart led the way into the dining room at the back.

Instead of the seven-foot ceilings Jack was used to, in this house they were ten feet high and seemed to tower above him. Two huge single-glazed windows with a French door between them gave a panoramic view of the garden while retaining complete privacy. Considering its size, the room was sparsely furnished. It contained an old square table, draped with a green oilcloth; a darkly grim utility sideboard; two armchairs from the 1970s, and an ancient gas fire surrounded by a 1930s tiled mantelpiece. The only saving grace were the many framed black-and-white photographs hanging from the picture rail on light gold chains.

"I don't know how she stuck it, living alone in this place."

"I've stuck it," replied Stewart.

"You're not eighty-three."

"I love looking at these photos, Jack." The boy paused before a studio-quality portrait of a girl sitting in front of a painted backcloth of an Indian temple. "She's about our age."

"Was, you mean."

Stewart flopped down into the big armchair nearest the window and Jack noticed that the true dark colour of his hair and eyebrows was beginning to show.

"Stewy, we need to find your mother – your real mother. It's the only way out. You can't go on like this."

The boy picked at his trousers.

"But I don't know where she lives. I can hardly remember what she looks like, and in any case she didn't want me and she'll have forgotten all about me."

"Would you like to meet her?"

Stewart gave a non-committal shrug, but his expression told a different story.

"Can you remember her name?"

"Anne, Anne with an 'e' is what she always said." He smiled at the recollection.

"When was the last time you saw her?"

"I was at school; she came to say goodbye."

"Which school?"

"Heathfield..."

"That was my school. So why didn't I know you then?"

Stewart shrugged.

"No one notices me."

"Was she actually married to your dad?"

"Jack, I don't know anything. I was only seven when she went away. My dad said she was a prostitute, that she didn't want me and that I was to forget about her. I didn't even know what a prostitute was when he told me."

Jack realised he was upsetting his friend.

"Sorry, Stewy, I'm being a prick."

The boy wiped his eyes on the back of his hand.

"I suppose I just ought to go to the police and get it over with."

"No! We've still got a couple of days, and in any case, I don't trust them. There's something fishy going on there."

"But what if we find her and she still hates me? What if she thinks I'm a skank?"

"No one in their right mind would think that, and I bet she never hated you. In any case, you're cute." Jack blushed. he had meant to say, everyone thinks you're cute.

Stewart smiled shyly.

"Cute? That is such a gay thing to say."

That was far too near the knuckle. Jack looked down into his lap while his heart thumped in his chest.

"Jack, are you gay?"

There it was, the $64,000 question. Jack stole a glance at his friend sitting impassively in the old armchair and it seemed, by the way he emphasised the question, that he already knew the answer. A certain defiance flared inside him.

"Do you want me to deny it?" he asked.

"I want you to trust me, like I trust you."

Jack scratched an itchy spot on his forehead where he had begun to sweat.

"My brother said exactly the same."

"I'm not your brother."

"Do you think I'm gay because I called you cute?"

"No, I know you don't fancy me."

"Why, then?"

Stewart shrugged.

"I think a lot of people think you are, but because you're not obvious and everyone likes you and respects you, no one says it."

Jack thought for a while.

"I'm not a fag, then?"

"I'll never use that word again, I promise, not even in fun."

"Yes, then, I am."

Stewart gave a little chuckle.

"And shall I tell you how I know you don't fancy me?"

"Go on, then."

"Because you're in love with someone else."

"Stewy, no! This is too much. We're not going there. I think we should get back on subject."

His face fell. "You mean, finding my mum?"

"Yes, of course that's what I mean!" Jack got up and handed Stewart his phone. "You keep this. I've borrowed my brother's so we can keep in touch. It's all set up and fully charged."

"What are you going to do?"

Jack smiled, grateful to his friend for his easy acceptance.

"I've had enough interrogation for one day, but I'll give you a ring later."

Stewart walked with him to the back door, and as he was about to leave touched him on the arm.

"I'll tell you what they did to me one day soon," he murmured.

***

96: Saturday 4th May. 2 p.m. 14 Edward's Lane.

JACK

Alan Henderson was in the driveway of his parents' house, practising on his skateboard, when Jack rode up on his bike. The thirteen-year-old was fully decked out in purple and yellow helmet and matching pads.

"Hey!" said Jack, parking his bike against the wooden pole that displayed the UK Majority Party poster for the forthcoming election. "You voting on Thursday?"

The boy got off his board and stared at him.

"I can't vote," he said. "I'm too young."

"Oh, I thought any dimwit could," Jack said, walking past him.

Alan frowned, uncertain whether he'd been insulted or not. "My dad's party is going to win," he said.

"Well, as I said, any dimwit can vote." Jack smiled, pleased to see there were no cars or vans about. "Your mum in?"

"What do you want with her?"

"It's all right; you're not in trouble," answered Jack, ringing the bell with a confidence he did not feel.

An elegant middle-aged woman answered. She had sun-bleached blonde hair styled into a bob and was dressed in a smart blue suit with matching silk scarf. This was someone who looked unused to housework or the rigours of parenthood.

"Mrs Henderson?"

"Yes."

"I'm Jack Moseley, a friend of Stewart's..."

Her subtly made-up face fell, and some of her poise slipped in the process.

"I just wondered whether you had any news..."

"You'd better come in," she said, warily glancing around and about.

He toed off his trainers in the passageway and was taken into a long, rectangular living room. The light colours of the walls, carpet and fabrics were offset by dark rosewood furniture. Everything was so spick and span that it was hard to believe that five boys lived here.

Mrs Henderson sat him down on the sofa while she positioned herself opposite on a chaise longue, tucking her legs neatly together with both feet facing the same way. Her hands too were held tightly in check, but this could not disguise the tremor that ran through them.

"You're the first young person to come and enquire about him," she said. "I thought he had no friends."

Jack had not expected this. She was genuinely distressed that no one had been to visit, and seemed to have no idea why. "Everyone liked, I mean likes, Stewart."

"There is a difference between liking someone and being their friend," she said.

"I haven't been before because it didn't seem right," he answered, surprised to be put on the defensive. "But I am his friend."

"We have had no news," she relented. "The police don't seem to have a clue, even after arresting those people."

Jack decided to be forthright. "Do the police think he was actually taken, or did he run away?"

"There was no reason for him to run away, therefore he must have been abducted," she replied, though he detected a certain ambivalence in her tone.

"Does his mother – I mean, his real mother – know he's missing?"

She stared at him, but whether it was because she thought him insightful or merely impertinent, he wasn't sure.

"What did he tell you about his mother?" she asked.

"Well, I know her name was Anne Henderson and Stewy was about seven when he last saw her and, from what I could gather, he had happy memories of her." The noise of a vehicle pulling up outside made him shift nervously in his seat.

"Her name wasn't Anne Henderson; it was Anne Baxter. We decided it would be best for Stewart to have no contact with her from the day she left."

The front door opened and a set of unwelcome voices could be heard in the hall.

"Do you know where she went?" he asked, wanting to get as much information as he could in the short time left to him.

"She gave a forwarding address in Basingstoke, but we don't know if she's still there. I very much doubt if she's heard about Stewart."

"Maybe I could contact her," he suggested, hearing footsteps approach.

"But it's all ancient history to her. Seven years! She has probably married and had children; made a new life for herself."

Derek entered the room. "What are you doing here, Moseley?" He turned to his stepmother. "Lisa, don't you know that this is the troublemaker we talked to Dad about?"

Jack wished he was like Si at the gym, big and strong enough to face up to him and preferably punch him in the mouth. "Mrs Henderson, do you have the exact address in Basingstoke?"

"Get out of here, Moseley, before I give your gob another knuckle sandwich."

"Derek!" said his stepmother, rising from her seat, but stumbling as she did so.

"Alan!" he called, not giving her a second look. "Here, now!"

Alan Henderson appeared in the doorway.

"Why did you let this faggot into the house?"

The thirteen-year-old stared up mutely at his brother.

"Tit!" snarled Derek then he turned and shouted. "John! That brown-nose Moseley is queering our house!"

Jack didn't struggle as they manhandled him through the house, though he did fall heavily onto his hands and knees as they pushed him out onto the driveway. He sat, giving himself time to recover, and realised his trainers were still inside. Alan came out, pulling the helmet over his head.

"Trainers," said Jack, brushing grit from his hands.

"I don't help faggots," sneered the boy.

Jack stared at him. "Do you want to survive in school next week?"

The boy blinked a few times as though switches were going on and off in his brain. Then, wordlessly, he went back inside and threw the trainers out onto the drive.

"Thanks." Jack put them on without tying his laces, then retrieved his bike. "Maybe next time I could borrow that helmet of yours. After all, purple is a really faggoty colour, isn't it?"

Alan blushed, then backed away several steps before he spoke.

"Fuck off, Moseley, or I'll set my brothers on you."

Jack laughed. "Have a good election, pussy boy," he called, putting up two fingers as he rode off down the road.

***

97: Saturday 4th May. 3.15 p.m. 15 Leighton Lane.

JACK

When he arrived home, Roger stopped him in the kitchen. "Where have you been, young man?"

"Out," said Jack.

"Why is your room a tip?" said his dad, stepping into his path.

Jack made a face that was supposed to convey incomprehension, but it came out as a scowl.

"You're not doing anything, or going anywhere, until it's been tidied up."

His room was always a tip, so why would anyone be bothered about it right now, just when he had other matters to attend to?

"Is this some sort of stupid new rule?"

"Just do as you're told!"

"And why are you going in my room in the first place?" Jack shouted and stormed upstairs, racing into his bedroom and slamming the door behind him. Only then did he see what his father had been talking about. The mattress was halfway off the bed; drawers were pulled out, clothes scattered; his laundry basket was upside-down; his wardrobe door was open and many of its contents lay in a tangled heap in the bottom.

It was obvious who had done this, but he had more important things to do than lose his temper again. A quick computer search for Anne Baxter in Basingstoke brought up no results. Then, for the next half an hour, he tried Google, Facebook, Twitter and the telephone directories, eventually widening his exploration to the whole of Great Britain, still without any success.

"Hi!" said Mikey, coming uninvited into the room.

"Don't you knock, pest?"

"Mummy wants to know if you want anything to eat?"

"No."

"Mummy says you don't eat enough and you'll make yourself ill."

"What are you, her brainless echo?"

"Jack, why is your room in a mess?"

"Ask your brother."

"I'll help you tidy up if you like," the little boy said in a serious voice.

Jack swivelled in his chair until he was facing Mikey, then beckoned him over with his index finger. "Why are you being nice to me when I'm being nasty to you?" He held out his bag of coconut mushrooms.

"Silly," said the little boy with a smile, taking a sweet.

"I want it back, now!" Dan was standing in the open doorway, holding on to the frame.

"Better scoot, chum," said Jack to Mikey.

The little boy ran under his brother's arm and away down the stairs.

"Thanks for turning over my room."

Dan strode over to him. "You've stolen my phone, now give it me back!"

"I can't just at the moment; I need it. It's important. I can't tell you why."

"I'll take something of yours."

"Have anything you like."

"I don't want any of your faggot stuff."

"Why are you being such a total prick, Dan?"

"They've firebombed some old queers out of their house in Gainsford Crescent."

"Really? Then I'm surprised you weren't up there, fanning the flames."

"Justin lives on Gainsford Crescent. His house could have been burned down too."

"So, if the fire had spread to Justin's house, these two old men would have been responsible for that, not the bombers?"

"Partly, yes, and that's what'll happen to us, if they learn about you."

"We'll just have to make sure they don't, then..." said Jack levelly. "Anyway, I'd like to continue this crazy talk, but as you can see I've got a lot of tidying up to do, unless you'd care to help, of course."

Dan turned on his heels and stalked out, almost bumping into his mother.

"My, I am popular today, aren't I?" said Jack.

Pam frowned at the state of the room. "A boy just delivered this for you; he said it was important." She handed him a sealed envelope with his name on it.

For a moment, Jack's heart leaped, thinking it might be Robert, but when he looked closely the handwriting was completely different. "Who was it?"

"I don't know, but he seemed a nice, polite little boy. He had on a purple and yellow cycle helmet."

So much for old people's judgement, he thought, signalling for her to leave by holding the door open in the most obvious way he could muster.

"I'll tidy my room, then come and have a sandwich," he said in a placatory tone.

On the threshold, she turned to him.

"Jack, everything you do these days makes us suspicious."

He shut and locked the door, then tore open the envelope.

Dear Jack,

This is the last known address and contact number of Anne Baxter, sometimes known as Anne Waverly: 34 Farnsfield Road, Basingstoke, Hampshire. Tel.: 01256 084381.

L. Henderson

It took him ten minutes to make his room presentable and five more to eat a ham and tomato sandwich which he didn't really want. Then he phoned Stewart to tell him he was on his way. In the meantime, he caught sight of the Swanford Mail on the kitchen table with a picture of a beaming Kenneth Anderson on the front. The story beneath read:

Mr Anderson, the Police and Crime Commissioner, was quoted as saying: "Of course, we don't approve of people taking the law into their own hands, but the public has a right to be angered by these so-called gays flaunting themselves at a time when a young boy has been abducted."

Meanwhile, Ms Sarah Heath MP, who will be seeking a further five-year term in next week's general election, said in a statement that: "People who become vigilantes have no place in a democratic society and should be prosecuted to the full extent of the law."

Mr Lawrence Hyde, prospective United Kingdom Majority Party candidate for the Woolgrove constituency, said Ms Heath was "merely pandering to the discredited human rights lobby, of which she is a long-term sympathiser".

***

98: Saturday 4th May. 5 p.m. 41 Westbury Avenue.

JACK

The boys sat adjacent to one another at the table in the back room, their phones lying in front of them on the green oilcloth.

"I think your stepmum guessed what I was on about, Stewy."

The boy looked again at the note from Lisa Henderson. "I don't think she'll tell. She's afraid, but more for Alan than me."

"How close are you to him?"

"He's just an annoyance, like all little brothers."

"What about letting him know you're safe, so he can tell your mum?"

"Too dangerous, Jack. He'd rat on me to my brothers, just to suck up to them."

"OK then, let's make the call to Basingstoke..."

"I'm too scared," said Stewart. "Can't you phone her for me and I'll listen."

Jack shook his head. "It's your show, Stewy. In any case, what's the worst that could happen?"

First they connected with each other, then with trembling fingers Stewart punched in the numbers. Jack could feel his own heart beating rapidly, and could only imagine how his friend must be feeling. The number rang, and rang again, then there was a click.

"Hello, Anne speaking... Hello?"

"Hello, this is Stewart... your son..." He had barely got the words out before tears were streaming from his eyes and nose, and his voice was lost in a series of sobs and sniffs.

"Hello, I'm Jack Moseley, a friend of Stewart's. Please don't hang up."

"Is that really my son, Stewart?" came the faltering voice.

"Yes..." Jack knew that Anne would hardly be calm herself now.

The boy could barely hold the phone, his hand was shaking so much. "Mum!"

"Stewart, darling, I've missed you so much!"

Stewart put the phone down, unable to control himself. It seemed that many weeks, perhaps months or years, of bottled-up yearning were coming out all at once.

"Mrs Waverly. Can you give him a minute?" said Jack.

"Of course. I think I need one myself."

Jack held tightly on to Stewart, allowing him to cry out his emotions. When it was over, not one but five minutes had passed.

"All right now?" asked Jack, finding a tissue in his pocket to give to Stewart.

The boy nodded and they went back to their phones. Anne had not heard of Stewart's disappearance, but she told him she had never stopped thinking about him and wanted to meet him.

They learned a little of her circumstances; that she currently worked as a freelance hairdresser and had a son, Alex, now aged three, from a marriage that had ended in divorce. Stewart told her that the police were searching for him, but that he wouldn't go home because he was being bullied by his older brothers. Jack butted in to say that, from Tuesday, Stewart would have nowhere to live and explained his current circumstances were. When Anne said she would drive up to Swanford on the bank holiday Monday, Stewart's eyes shone with excitement. Jack put his phone on hold, but forgot about the other one.

"You'll want to be on your own, Stewy?"

"No! Please be there, Jack, in case something goes wrong. In any case, I want you to meet my mum."

"OK," he said and switched his phone back on.

Anne gave a little laugh. "I heard you, Jack. I think you should be there too. You sound like a very good friend."

"He's the best," said Stewart, causing Jack to wonder why others didn't think the same.

***

99: Monday 6th May. 9.15 a.m. 15 Leighton Lane.

DAN

I can hear him downstairs, now, my fag brother arguing with Mum and Dad. They thought it would be a nice idea if we all went out for the day, it being the bank holiday and good weather, but the fag's got other plans. I heard him talking on the phone – my phone – just now, probably arranging to meet his boyfriend or something. I don't usually listen through walls, but since he stole my phone I've really wanted to get back at him, and now I've done it.

That was the back door slamming. Mum and Dad are arguing with each other now and Mikey's crying, wimping over his big brother, I expect. I'm in the fag's bedroom, eating his coconut mushrooms and looking out of his window, because I'm just about to get a really big laugh. I let the fag's tyres down and hid his pump, so he won't be going anywhere – at least, not for a while.

Yeah! He's picked up his bike and is wheeling it to the gate. The stupid fuck's not noticed yet. Now he has! Oh God, he's practically crying. What a fag! He's noticed there's no pump, and is just standing there like a blockhead. He looks such a crazy fuck these days.

He's got my phone out again. No, he's put it back. What's he doing now? Better lie low for a sec, or he'll see me!

293

P'raps it would be even funnier if I pointed at him through the window and laughed my socks off. The trouble is, he's bigger than me and I'm not sure I could deck him, even though he is just a fag.

Jesus! You know what he's gone and done? He's got my bike out of the shed. Why didn't I think of that? I've got to try to stop him, before it's too late!

***

100: Monday 6th May. 9.30 a.m. 41 Westbury Avenue.

<u>JACK</u>

The boys spent an hour tidying the old house, and when they left even put the door key back under the mat. Stewart wanted to look as much like his real self as possible and so had consigned the sticky tape and glasses to the bin and had washed his hair with baby shampoo the previous night, so that by the morning nearly all the natural darkness had returned. He put on a hooded top for safety's sake, because they were going to have to make a journey of two miles or more through town to reach the rendezvous point.

"That's a smart bike," said Stewart, when he saw it propped against the pergola.

"LB's."

"Are you friends again?"

"Hardly. I took it. Mine got two flats from somewhere. He tried to chase after me, but I'd got too much of a start."

"He's angry with you."

"Angry, and then some. I was thinking of buying him a football or games magazine to... you know."

"Is he angry because you told him?"

Jack gave a perfunctory nod.

"Strange how some people react."

"He totally lost it."

294

They left through the front gates, and Stewart looked back at the house that had been his home for over a month. "I never found out what was in that garage," he said.

"Probably empty, if the rest of the house is anything to go by."

The two boys mounted Dan's bike and set off. They had arranged to meet Anne Waverly at the covered entrance to the cemetery on the Malton Road at eleven o'clock, but they made good time and arrived ten minutes early.

"Nervous?" asked Jack, propping the bike against the wall.

Stewart pulled his hood down and began to pace along the grass verge. "What happens if a funeral comes along at the same time as my mum?"

"Why? Do you think we might be asked to carry the coffin?"

Stewart barely smiled. He was too pent up, like an athlete about to run a race. As each car came along the road from the south-east, he stopped pacing to watch it go by.

Ten minutes went by. "We forgot to ask her what car she'd be driving," said Jack conversationally.

Stewart breathed deeply, trying to calm himself. "Not that sort," he said as a Jaguar XJ saloon went by. "It'll probably be a little car."

"She has to get her hair equipment in it, though."

"It's after eleven, she's not coming," replied Stewart.

"It's two minutes past and she's got an eighty-mile journey in bank holiday traffic. Anyway, she would have phoned."

"Do you think she won't like me because I'm small?"

"Stewy, you just want me to call you cute again."

A Honda Civic hatchback slowed and turned into the Sheepway, a side road running along the town side of the cemetery. It stopped. They both watched. A woman emerged from the driver's seat and crossed the road to the verge.

"Hello," she called, her eyes on Stewart.

He looked at her, hesitated, then ran to her.

"I remember you!" he cried.

They embraced. "Stewart, my lovely boy! I've thought about you so often..."

Jack turned away as the reunion took place. He had expected Anne to be the same age as his mother, but she was at least ten years younger with a face similar in shape to Stewart's, but with larger eyes and much fairer hair. He realised that she couldn't have been that much older than he was now when she became pregnant.

A little boy with very fine curly blond hair sat in the back of the Civic, perched up in a booster seat. He was watching his mother with rapt curiosity.

"Would you get him out for me?" smiled Anne, briefly diverting her attention from her new-found son.

Jack smiled back and scurried across to the car.

"Hey, I'm Jack," he said. "What's your name?"

The little boy eyed him uncertainly. "Alex," he said.

"Would you like me to get you out of that contraption?" asked Jack amused at seeing the same jug ears as on Stewart. When the boy gave his consent, he clicked open the seat belt and, checking for traffic, lifted him out. "Do you want to walk or be carried?"

"Carry me to Mummy," ordered Alex, pointing with his index finger.

"You're used to children," said Anne as he set the boy down beside her.

"Two younger brothers," he answered.

She held out her hand. "Pleased to meet you, Jack, and you must call me Anne."

He smiled and gave a brief shake. "Have you any plans?"

Stewart knelt in front of Alex. "I'm your brother," he said.

The little boy cocked his head on one side, gazing with a perplexed expression at his sibling.

"I hope he likes me," said Stewart, looking up at Jack.

"Everyone likes you, Stewy," replied his friend.

"If I didn't know, I'd think you two were brothers," said Anne.

"I wish he was!" exclaimed Stewart.

Anne paused as if to give consideration to the remark, before she turned to Jack. "To answer your question about plans: is there somewhere we can sit and talk? I've brought us all a picnic."

Jack pointed. "In the middle of the cemetery there's a sort of little square surrounded by trees with seats and statues. We could go there. There's no church here; it's the overflow for the town."

"A picnic with the dead," said Anne. "Well, there's a first time for everything."

The small sanctuary was deserted and the ideal place to sit and talk, with just the sounds of birdsong and a gentle breeze blowing through the leaves. It was as if the seven intervening years had been a fleeting moment, as mother and son accepted each other without question. Stewart agreed to live with Anne in Basingstoke, where he would have a roof over his head. All the implications of such a move and the fallout from his disappearance would be dealt with in the coming days. Stewart asked to borrow Jack's phone for a little longer, promising to keep him informed of events, but gave back his Post Office debit card, admitting he had spent over £100 on it. Anne made a fuss about this, but Jack insisted that he didn't want to be paid back.

Then they sat and ate, after which Stewart felt so relaxed he began to get sleepy. Meanwhile, little Alex amused himself by running, stopping, looking at something, chatting to himself, then repeating. Jack felt that it was time for him to depart but, before he did, he handed the letter he had received from Elspeth Chambers to Anne, pointing out the last paragraph, where she referred to looking for someone to live with her as a home carer.

"You've thought this through very carefully, haven't you, Jack?"

"If you went for this, it would mean Stewy could stay on at Swanford School. It's a huge house; there's plenty of room."

"And what do you think, Stewart?" asked Anne.

"Good plan," he said, his eyelids drooping.

Anne looked at Jack. "You seem a very together young man."

"I'm not..."

"I was going to say, you do look a bit peaky."

"Jack's in love," murmured Stewart.

"Stewy!" warned Jack.

Stewart opened one eye and gave his friend a knowing smile.

"I'd better go; I've got to make peace with my brother."

"Buy him some magazines," yawned Stewart.

***

101: Monday 6th May. 4.30 p.m. 15 Leighton Lane.

DAN

I'm in my bedroom now, grounded, even though it was the fag who stole my phone and my bike. Dad caught me coming out of the shed with the pump I'd hidden, and asked me what I was doing, and like a stupid fuck I went red and it all came out. Then it got worse because I'd already been in the front garden and put nails in his tyres, but only because he stole my bike and phone and because he's a fag. So now I'm not only grounded, but I've lost my games console as well, and have to either repair the fag's tyres or buy some new ones.

The only consolation is that the fag's going to be grounded too, for going off on my bike and having a hissy fit. I hope he gets mad and they take away his internet connection and do a search on him and find my phone.

He's back and I'm waiting for the big row, but I don't hear anything. So what's happening? I go to the door and open it and listen, then he comes up the stairs, all calm-like, and I'm standing there like a dork, and he's surprised to see me, but then he shoves these two mags into my hands and says that he needs my phone for just one more week and it doesn't matter about the tyres, then he goes into his room and shuts the door. And I'm left feeling like I'm in the wrong when it's him that's wrong, because he stole my bike and my phone, and he's a fucking fag. Then I feel like ripping up the mags, but I can't because I want them, and I've got nothing else to do for a week.

***

102: Tuesday 7th May. 8.45 p.m. 15 Leighton Lane.

PAM

"All quiet on the western front?" asked Roger, looking up from his newspaper.

"Sulking, I expect," replied Pam, sitting down beside him on the settee.

"What's that you've got?"

"Election leaflets. I thought I'd read through them all and decide."

"Aren't you going to vote for the Monster Raving Loony Party as usual?"

"Be serious, Roger."

"Why? The result's the usual foregone conclusion, isn't it?"

"Not this time. You should hear them in the post office going on about Edward Helms and how he will set the country straight."

"The UKMP? I don't even know what it stands for."

"The United Kingdom Majority Party. According to their candidate, Lawrence Hyde, the country should be returned to its traditional values and not held to ransom by 'vociferous and unrepresentative minorities'."

"What am I then, a minority or a majority?"

"You're definitely a minority of one, Roger," said Pam, squeezing his arm.

"Thank you, my love."

"Listen to this: married couples are going to get an extra £1,000 tax allowance, and the income tax and National Insurance threshold will be £13,500. That's good for us, isn't it?"

"Promises, promises," said Roger, "and who's going to pay for it?"

"Well, by leaving the EU and cutting the foreign aid budget."

"So, are they getting your vote?"

"Hmm, they do also say that they want councils to outsource their services to a designated list of private companies."

"That's already happened in Swanford, thanks to Councillor Henderson and his cronies, so I doubt if the UK Majority Party will be getting my vote."

***

103: Wednesday, 8th May. 7.25 a.m. Pear Tree Cottage, the Ropewalk.

ROBERT

Dad came home last night from his trip to Africa in a good mood and so he probably didn't notice the tension between me and Mom. No doubt Mom will have filled him in by now, and so I'm not looking forward to breakfast.

Why didn't you tell me Aunt Una had died? It was the first question I asked her on the drive home from the airport, which probably wasn't such a good idea. She clammed up immediately and things have been frosty ever since. She may be mad at me, but I'm doubly mad at them. Grandma Sanchez was right when she said the Crittendens are hypocrites. I know she didn't exactly say that, but that's what she meant.

I went to the mall at Prestleigh last Saturday afternoon on the bus and bought myself a cell of my own. It's a Nokia pay-as-you-go and cost £50, which is $63. I used the left-over money from my trip plus some of my wages from Mrs Annesley. She used to give it to me in an envelope, but now she just hands it to me straight out of the cash register, which is strange, as she's always out back 'doing the books'.

On Sunday, after church, I went to the Jewel to set up my phone and get a Gmail account. Unfortunately, he came in, but he didn't look at me and I tried not to look at him. He was with the gang. Mandy mussed my hair, but the rest just nodded. I guess I went as red as a beet.

I wish I could talk to him. No, I want to do more than that, but if I did, he'd probably kill me. You see... I love him, there I've said it. I can't help myself. I'm going crazy and I'm going to Hell, but I don't care. There must be something wrong with me, and I'm worried that there's something wrong with him because he looks all washed out. I'll say it again, I'll never ever tell my parents, Pastor Fisher or anyone else from church about this. That's not going to happen.

I've sent an email to Tom, asking for the dates of Barney and Susie's birthdays and thanking him for putting me up. I thanked Grandma Sanchez as well, but I expect she'll think I'm insincere. I haven't had a reply yet.

I sent a text to Rosa, as well, just to say hi. And I got one in return. It ended "the b**ch is on heat again so I'm trying to find a German Shepherd that'll f**k her", which made me laugh.

Funny that, a week or two back I'd probably have been shocked and disapproving. I've changed since my trip to the States, but I don't think my folks would think it was for the better.

Everything looks normal in the lounge. It's bright and tidy and breakfast is laid out as neat as ever on the tablecloth, which is white and crisp.

"Good morning, son," says my dad, looking up from his paper, while I stand waiting for the bomb to drop. "We expect to do well in the election tomorrow. Helms might even become Prime Minister."

No bombshell. "I didn't know you were interested in English politics, Dad."

"I'm very interested. For the first time in a quarter century, there's a chance to stop this island's decline into depravity."

I sit down. "What do you think will happen in Swanford?"

"Well, our man Hyde will give them a run for their money. If it was just the town we'd romp home, but the whole of the Woolgrove constituency is another matter."

"Good morning, Robert," says Mom in that disapproving voice, and she looks at Dad for support.

He notices but when he speaks his tone isn't harsh. "Son, we have to have a serious discussion about your attitude to your mother while I was away. You probably know what I'm talking about?"

"Yes, sir."

"But not right now," he adds. "There are times when we must keep our eyes on the bigger picture."

I guess he's talking about the election.

"I'll get your breakfast," says Mom, and I can tell she's miffed at Dad for not raking me over the coals.

***

104: Thursday 9th May. 7.45 p.m. The Jewel Café, Swanford town square.

JACK

There were more people than normal in the Jewel on election night. Voting was still going on, but the council building across the square was already preparing for the ballot boxes to arrive and the big count to begin. Usually, Woolgrove prided itself on being one of the first constituencies to declare, but tonight the opinion polls pointed to the strong possibility of a recount – which hadn't happened in the town for fifty years.

The ceiling fans were going full tilt when Jack and his friends from the gym entered the café and walked round to their usual booth by the toilets. Already, Mandy was ensconced in her seat, imperiously sucking a banana milkshake through a straw and defying anyone to muscle in on her realm.

"Manners, you're looking as radiant as ever," said Max, slipping into the seat beside her and kissing her on the lips.

"Which is more than can be said for you fucking load of sad sacks," she replied. "Especially you, Moseley."

Jack took the criticism without comment.

"Isn't Babs here yet?" asked Charlie.

Mandy narrowed her eyes. "Why do you have to ask such fucking stupid questions, Masefield? If she was here, she'd be here."

"Now, Manners," said Max, "what's got you into such high dudgeon?"

She slammed the election leaflet for the UK Majority Party down onto the table.

"Are the English totally as thick as shit, to be taken in by these moronic little Hitlers?"

Jack closed his eyes and yawned, listening to the background hum in the café.

"Five per cent pay rise," smiled Charlie.

"What?" asked Mandy.

"That's what Edward Hyde promised the police and army if the UKMP form the new government. Dad and Mum were practically running to the polling station."

Mandy shook her head in disbelief. "Listen to this. Moseley, pay attention!"

Jack opened his eyes tiredly. "What's it got to do with us? We can't vote and elections never affect us anyway."

Charlie nudged Jack and smirked. "Here's someone it might affect."

Andy Venables walked up, ready to take their order. "What can I get you, folks?"

"A strawberry milkshake for me, please, Andy," said Max. "And I'm sure Manners would like a top-up."

"Only if you're paying, Maxxy."

Max nodded.

"Coke for me, thanks," said Jack.

"Coke, burger with onions and fries for me," said Charlie. "I'm celebrating – and don't forget the relish."

The three boys paid and Andy retreated to the kitchen to attend to their order.

"What did you mean?" asked Jack of Charlie.

The boy smiled smugly. "You mean about Mr Venables or about the celebration?"

"I'll tell you what the supercilious cloth-eared cunt means," said Mandy, picking up the election leaflet once more. "I quote: 'UKMP will pass legislation making it illegal to intentionally promote homosexuality, or publish material with the intention of promoting homosexuality, or to promote the teaching in any maintained school of the acceptability of homosexuality as a form of family relationship. Pupils who have already become inculcated with this lifestyle will receive suitable counselling'."

"I say, that's a bit harsh, isn't it?" said Max. "Poor Andy."

"My dad says they've had it coming," stated Charlie. "All the police love UKMP."

Mandy sniffed. "What about this one, then? This affects us all. UKMP will ensure that schools fulfil the statutory obligation to assemble pupils for a corporate act of worship of a Christian nature, with suitable opt-out arrangements. British history and discipline will be taught in schools. The history curriculum should reflect the United Kingdom's rich cultural heritage. As education teaches critical thinking and encourages questions, so the science curriculum should include the

304

evidence of creation and design in the Universe, presenting evolution as an alternative hypothesis rather than falsely depicting it as a proven fact. Schools will be given the freedom not to employ staff who do not agree with the school's ethos."

"So?" said Charlie.

"That sounds like Robert Crittenden's territory," observed Max. "Yeehaw!"

"Let's hope they don't win, then," said Jack.

Mandy regarded him suspiciously. "Sometimes, Moseley, you are a riddle, wrapped in a mystery, inside an enigma..."

"Blimey, Manners, you've summed up Jack to a tee."

"Not me, Maxxy – Winston Churchill. I was quoting from a speech he made in 1939 about Russia, our new ally and trading partner if the UKMP get in."

***

105: Friday, 10th May. 7.15 a.m. 15 Leighton Lane.

PAM

Pam came downstairs in her dressing gown and went about her first task of the morning, opening the curtains. What was unusual about this day was that she paused in the lounge to switch on the television.

SLTV news briefing: Seen here in the town hall as the result is announced, Woolgrove constituency MP Sarah Heath breathes a sigh of relief after two recounts confirm her re-election as Member of Parliament for a second consecutive term. Her majority was slashed from 5,000 votes to just 450 in an election with a high turnout of 84 per cent. Lawrence Hyde of the UK Majority Party, who just a few months ago wasn't even expected to retain his deposit, was second. Now his party under the leadership of Edward Helms is set to be the major partner in a coalition government...

"Goodness!"

"I just heard it on the radio," said Roger, coming up behind her. "Councillor Henderson will be over the moon. His party got two hundred and twenty-four seats, an increase of guess how many over last time?"

"Yes, I can work it out – two hundred and twenty-four. We're certainly going to find some interesting things happening in this country over the next few months." said Pam.

"Did you actually vote for this shower?" asked Roger.

His wife smiled seraphically.

"Why isn't breakfast ready?" asked Jack, putting his head round the lounge door.

"I'm not your slave, you know," replied Pam.

"I just want a mother," said Jack.

Pam turned to face him, her jaw set. "And if you'd behave like a son, instead of a spoiled arrogant monster, things might be better round here."

"Fine! I'll get my own," he said and stomped off.

"Calm," said Roger, "deep breaths..."

***

106: Saturday 11th May. 10.30 a.m. Folly Farm.

<u>ALAN</u>

This is awesome! Derek wants me to learn how to drive the van, and so here I am with my hands on the wheel, waiting. It must be because everyone's in such a good mood after the election. Dad says that although Mr Hyde didn't win in Swanford, it won't be long before he is the Woolgrove MP. I don't know what that means – I thought elections were held every five years unless someone dies.

I have driven dirt bikes and quads, but they're just for kids, and this is real. Why does it give me such a buzz? It's like being on drugs, only better, because it doesn't give me a bad stomach and a headache.

I'm in a paddock normally used by stupid little girls on stupid little ponies to jump over stupid little fences, but I've been here since six taking all of them down. I've pushed the seat forward as far as it'll go, because I'm only four foot ten, but I'm growing. The other day, in PE, Neil Cunliffe said I was getting a burger belly like my brother Ben, so I flattened him. Well, I tripped him up, actually, but it's the same thing.

Ben and John are rubbish drivers and know nothing about mechanics. Derek and I are the only ones who can even change a wheel. I'm going to join an F1 team as soon as I leave school. Dad says he knows someone who can get me a job. It probably won't be much to start with, but I expect I'll be the youngest F1 driver ever. World champion by the time I'm twenty, that'll be me!

I can't be fat, though, else it's not going to happen. Imagine Ben trying to get behind the wheel of a Ferrari! They'd need a can opener to get him out. Mum says it's just puppy fat and I'm normal for my age. But why, if I am normal, have I got nothing down there? All the boys that matter have got something, and their voices have broken too. It's not fair. I know some of them have started calling me Alana, but not to my face!

I hate school, anyway. The only books I like are about cars. But Dad says if I'm going to join an F1 team, I've got to stick it out, even though he left school at fourteen and Derek never went again after he turned fifteen. I'd prefer to spend my time in a garage or on my skateboard or in the gym. I've really got to get this fat off; it's driving me nuts.

Dad and Derek have got a thing about those Moseleys, especially with them helping Stewart to go off like that and find his real mum. My mum really got it in the neck for talking to Jack Moseley. I heard Dad say that he's a shirt-lifter for sure, which means he's a fag. It's his fault I sometimes don't wear my helmet and knee pads when skateboarding, because he said purple was gay. I know he only said it to dis me, because I chose that colour.

Derek and Dad are right about the Moseleys. Dan and his friend Justin Walker have started picking on me. They didn't used to, but every time they see me now they give me hassle. It's not fair, because they're both built and Dan has even got the start of a six-pack. He's the worst of the two. He called me a fag to my face the other day in front of the whole second year, just because I said I watch body-building programmes. Me, a fag! I think he wanted me to curl up and start crying, but I didn't! Everyone laughed, though. I really hate him for showing me up like that.

Derek calls that whole family the 'Faggoleys' and says they're going to be sorted out, but he hasn't said how. I was shittin' myself, worrying that he might find out I delivered the letter about Stewart's mum to them, but my mum didn't grass. One good thing came out of it, though. I found out that Dan Moseley lives in a pathetic little house with no decent equipment anywhere, not even a satellite dish.

My brother, Stewart, was always a saddo; all of us hated him. He never joined in anything the family did. John used to call him 'the whining monkey' because of his jug ears and the fact that he was always locked in the toilet crying and shitting himself. I thought he might be gay, because he cried a lot and Derek called him his little pansy, but then I found some pictures of naked women on his mobile... not that I was being nosey or anything! After that, I used to borrow his mobile to look at the dirty pictures, which proves I'm not gay. There were some pictures of men and women together too, but not many, and the men were mostly old and fat. When Dad was in his Bible phase he told us about this King Saul who hated his son because he was a fag. His son's name was Jonathan and he had a boyfriend called David who used to wait for him behind this Stone of Ezel, so the king wouldn't see him. Dad said that if he had been King Saul he would have cut their balls off with a blunt knife, which I think he said to frighten us into not being gay. Personally, I'm glad Stewart's gone.

Derek's coming over now. He's promised me a lesson every day and if I don't foul up, by this time next week, I'll be driving round Swanford!

***

107: Tuesday 14th May. 7.55 p.m. 15 Leighton Lane.

JACK

Why is it, now that's Stewart's life is getting back on track, mine is going down the tubes again? He keeps looking at me with those big sad eyes, and it's turning me over. It's ever since he came back from his trip to America. Why doesn't he aim his religious freakery at some other poor sucker? I looked up his church on the internet and they say no man can love another man as a man loves a woman, so he can never understand how I felt about him. No, how I feel! Whatever it is he's up to, he's making my life hell, which is probably what his religion tells him to do.

I haven't heard anything from Stewart since Friday when we had a chat just before he was due to go to the police station in Basingstoke to make a statement. His mum has already got a solicitor working on the case, so it should be all right. Stewy said he's never going to tell the police about what was done to him. I told him that was a mistake, because they may start bullying Alan, but he could be right too, because I think the Hendersons have a lot of influence in Swanford.

Maybe my phone – the phone Stewy's got – is dead, because I can't get through to him any more, or perhaps he just wants to put everything behind him and start a new life. In any case, I've decided to give Dan his phone back, then at least he won't have anything to moan about. He's started football practice again tonight so I'll just stick it on his desk before he comes back, but first I'll delete all the stuff between me and Stewart.

309

108: Wednesday, 15th May. 3.55 p.m. 15 Leighton Lane.

<u>DAN</u>

There's no one home and the outside door was unlocked. I'm worried. My fag brother's not here either, but that's not unusual, because he finishes school later than I do. In any case, I wouldn't care if he never came back. I looked at my phone, but there are no messages, then I tried ringing Mum, but there's no reply. So I'm in my bedroom lying on my bed, trying not to wimp out. Oh yeah, I found my mobile on my desk yesterday. It had £15 worth of credit on it, £10 more than when he took it off me two weeks ago, but I know he's just trying to get round me for his own fag reasons. There was one text he hadn't wiped off. It said Arrived Basingstoke ~ SH, which is a real fag type message.

I caught Alan Henderson checking me out in the changing rooms today. His tongue was practically hanging out. I knew the little fat freak was a fag, just like my brother. His cannonball head went so red I thought it was going to explode. I made sure everyone got to know what he did, and now they're calling him Alana Henderfag. Freddie pulled his towel off him which he always wraps tight round his pot belly. Now I know why. His dick is so small you need a microscope to see it, and there's not a single pubic hair on him. We spent a good five minutes laughing at him and flicking him with the towel. Then Justin and I threw all his clothes into the shower, turned the water on and left him crying, stark-bollock naked in the middle of the changing rooms. What a fag!

I put the games magazine in the recycling so my fag brother would see I'd thrown it out, but I'm still deciding what to do with the football magazine, because there's some things in it I want to show Justin when he next comes round.

I'm not grounded any more and I went to football training last night. Except for a break in April, we do it all year round.

310

Coach Brennan said I was crap – well, that's not exactly what he said, but that's what he meant. I couldn't seem to get any rhythm going and all the fellows were giving me a hard time for not putting any effort in. Sophie told me I'm not as much fun as I used to be, either, which really cheered me up.

It's the fag's fault. Why can't things be like they were before he became a fag? For one thing, he looks like something dead that's been washed up on the beach. He's got spots on his forehead; they're disgusting red-and-black scabby things, like he's got a disease or something. Mum told him to put some lotion on them, but he just looks at her like there's no one in. His grades have gone right down, which means I'm officially cleverer than him for the first time, which is something, I suppose – if being cleverer than a fag means anything, which I doubt. He can't be doing his homework, though, because his school bag is always left unopened by the kitchen door. All he does is moon around all day, probably thinking about that American.

Now and again I see that tall Yankee ginger streak in the playground, standing on his own looking worried, like he doesn't know what time of day it is either. I can't tell if he's a fag too. Sometimes I wish— no, I can't say it...

My brother, the fag, is in his bedroom. I didn't hear him come in. Perhaps he knows where Mum and Mikey are, but I can't go and ask him, because I told him to keep away from me and never speak to me again, and though he has spoken to me, I haven't spoken to him except to dis him. But I am quite scared at the moment, because I don't know what's going on.

I just heard him outside on the stairs. I'd better go and see what's going on.

Mum's back. I can hear her voice, they're rowing. So what's new? I'll creep downstairs while I'm listening...

"Why are you opening my bank statements?"

"Why haven't you done what I ask?"

"What are you talking about?"

"Your brother is in hospital, and all you can do is act as if you don't care!"

"Which brother? What's happened? I don't know anything!"

"I sent you a text and a voicemail because your phone was off. I sent Dan the same and told both of you to pass the message on!"

"I lent my phone to someone; it's been off for days. What's happened to Mikey?"

I'm standing in the hall doorway now looking into the kitchen. The fag's got his back to me, but Mum looks dishevelled and red in the face and I can tell she's been crying. Why are they rowing when Mikey's in hospital?

"What's wrong with Mikey?" I shout. Oh God! My voice sounds like a girl's.

"Why didn't you pass the message on to your brother, or did you get a message and because of your stupid pride didn't pass it on?" She's screaming at me.

"I didn't get a message." I say, but I feel guilty because I haven't actually checked, but the phone didn't ring, I'm sure of it.

"Do you think he wouldn't tell me if Mikey was in hospital? You probably didn't forward it properly."

For some reason, my fag brother is defending me. Why is that?

"Your father and I need to have a long talk with you, Jack Moseley. We know what you've been doing!"

"By opening my private letters?"

They're at it again, rowing, and I still don't know what's happened to Mikey.

"You're still under eighteen and we're responsible for you!"

"What's happened to Mikey?" That's me screaming now. I definitely am turning into a girl. They both turn their attention my way. Jesus! My fag brother's looking more like Skull Kid with spots every day.

***

312

109: Wednesday, 15th May. 4.25 p.m. 14 Edward's Lane.

<u>ALAN</u>

This has been the worst day of my life. I came home from school soaking wet, and not because it was raining. Something happened, but I can't say what. Except that I hate Dan Moseley and Justin Walker.

There was no one around when I got home, which for once I was glad about. I don't know where Mum is. She's probably in her room, asleep. I've told her she takes too many pills, but she won't listen.

I'm going to have to pretend to be sick or, if that doesn't work, I'll have to bunk off school. I can't go back after what happened today – ever.

But what if Dan Moseley decides to split on me to my brother Ben? That means Derek will get to know and then he won't give me any more driving lessons and they'll all start picking on me. Even worse, what if my dad finds out? I'll either be put out on the street or he'll use that blunt knife on me, because he'll never have a fag for a son, that's for sure. Even though I'm definitely not one.

I haven't missed a single lesson so far, and Derek's promised me that he'll let me drive all the way from here to Folly Farm at the weekend. That's miles! With power steering and being high up, Transits are much easier to drive than you might think. You've just got to mind the wheelbase. If Dad or my brothers ever find out about me, I'll steal the van and drive so far away that they'll never be able to track me down. I might take my mum as well, but I'm not sure.

When I'm world champion and have loads of money, I'm going to open a motor museum like the one in the New Forest, except mine will only be for cars with running boards. Does that sound stupid? Maybe I'll include limousines without running boards as long as they were made before 1960, because they were pretty cool too. My all-time favourites are the British Salmsons because they were manufactured for only about five years in the 1930s, but they were so weirdly wicked, especially the 20/90 sports saloon.

Derek's got a new air rifle. It must have cost a bomb. It's got telescopic sights and everything. On Monday he shot a bird from the van while I was driving. That's how much he trusts me. When we got out to have a look, he had to stamp on it because it wasn't quite dead. I'm hoping he might let me have a go. With those sights, I bet I could knock a bird out of a tree from a mile away, but I don't want to have to stamp on it...

Why couldn't I have been called Jayden or something, instead of stupid Alan? My kids are all going to have good names. I really hate Dan Moseley. He thinks he's the number-one guy, but I'll show him! That is, unless he tells on me, then I may as well be dead...

**

110: Wednesday, 15th May. 6.40 p.m. 15 Leighton Lane.

JACK

Mikey's in hospital. He had an argument with his best friend Mike about who was to play Pinocchio in the end of term concert. They started to fight, and Mike pushed Mikey off the stage. He's having a brain scan and they think he's broken his leg. Everybody's shouting at me at home as if it's my fault, just because I didn't get a message to take a quiche out of the freezer: can you believe that? But I don't care, they can shout as much as they want.

They've cornered me in my room now and they're going to give me a hard time about things they know nothing about.

"Why did you make those withdrawals from your bank account?" asked Dad.

"It's my money. I can do what I like with it."

"£200 in a week and nothing to show for it?"

"Why can't you tell us, Jack?" asked Mum.

"Because it's none of your business, and you opened my private letter."

"It's because we're worried about you; look at the state you're in."

"We think you're buying drugs!" exclaimed Dad.

You have to laugh, don't you, especially as one of those entries is for shopping at Tesco.

"In case you hadn't noticed, our local drug dealer was sent down for three years last week."

"There are others," said Mum.

"I'm not buying, selling or dealing in drugs, and if you don't believe me, tough."

"Everything! Everything that's gone wrong with this family in the last three months is down to you!" shouted Dad. "And all we get for trying to help is abuse and cheek!"

"Really, so how is it I'm just fifteen years old and your son, and you're supposed to be the big man of the house?"

"So help me, for two pins I'd hit him," Dad said to Mum.

"Rog! We agreed we'd do this calmly. I think we should leave him to it now. In any case, you've got to take me to the hospital."

Well, that was a good show of parental responsibility, wasn't it? The fact is, I don't care. They can throw me out with the waste if they want. Everything they said is true, though; I am no good to anyone. I try not to think about anything, because if I do think, I think about him and then I feel terrible. I am such a feeble arse.

***

111: Thursday, 16th May, 3.50 p.m. Junction of Leighton Lane and Knowles Road.

DAN

Guess who I saw on my way home this afternoon? He's supposed to be off sick and he comes boarding down Knowles

Road, dressed in all his expensive kit as if it's a Saturday. I try to ignore him, but he comes tearing up to me, tail drags, turns, flips his skateboard with his foot, catches it and tucks it under his arm all in one go. It makes me sick that a faggy little freak can do that and make it look easy.

I can see he wants to say something, but he just stands there, so I pretend to be bored.

"What do you want, Alana?"

This makes him uncomfortable and he clams up even more, so I roll my eyes again and repeat the question.

"What do you want, Alana?"

"You won't tell Ben, will you?" he says at last in his faggy whine.

Of course I hadn't even thought of telling that Neanderthal anything, since I never speak to him and never want to. In any case, people have moved on from what happened in the changing rooms, because that was yesterday. But now he's said it, I decide to have some fun since I'm dealing with a fag and a dumb one at that.

"I don't like my junk being checked out by fags, Alana. Especially when they're always trying to hide their own, which isn't difficult for you, is it?"

I got him on three counts there for the price of one.

"Everyone's different, and you're older than me," he says, then he blurts out, "My dad'll kill me if he finds out. Honestly, he'll throw me out, he will!"

I can see he's upset now; he's shaking, not like trembling, but doing these jerky spasmy movements, as though someone's giving him electric shocks. And I want to make him feel worse. "You should have thought of that before you started gagging for my dick, Alana." Then I have an idea which will really piss him off. "But I'll tell you what I'll do. I won't tell Ben you're a fag – if you give me your skateboard."

His board is excellent: custom-made and must have cost a bomb. The deck has a really cool picture of a leopard making claw marks. But I don't want it. To tell the truth, I'm a really poor skateboarder and I'm jealous of the fag because for a pudgy little guy he's pretty awesome. In any case, what would Mum say if she caught me with it?

The next thing I know, the skateboard is in front of me and he's walking off back up Knowles Road. This really annoys me, for some reason.

"Hey!" I call out to him, "I don't want your fucking faggy skateboard, dickhead."

He turns round but won't look at me and I know he's crying. "I used to think you were all right, Dan Moseley," he snivels. "But you're just a prick." Then he runs off on his little faggy legs, so I pick up the skateboard and hurl it over the nearest hedge into someone's garden.

***

I'm just moping about my room now feeling pretty low.

You know when you've been playing a computer game and you come back to the real world, but still think you can replay what's just happened? I wish...

There's a real buzz about having power over someone, isn't there? It's no surprise there are so many dictators in the world. I'll probably be in trouble over the skateboard. I wonder if he went back for it? Maybe I should go and look, if I can remember which garden I threw it in. But I can't because we've got to go to the hospital to see Mikey in a minute.

When did I turn into this low-life scuzzbag? It's my fag brother's fault. Why can't he just be normal?

***

112: Saturday, 18th May. 10 a.m. Fruit and Flower, Swanford High Street.

ROBERT

Mrs Annesley has just told me that Mikey Moseley is in hospital having a brain scan and I'm in a cold sweat about it. He's just the same age as Aaron was...

"Why, Robert, you've gone very pale."

I take some deep breaths. "Sorry. I'm all right really. Did you hear what was wrong?"

"An accident at school, so Mrs Adams told me. Her son is in the same class as Jack Moseley, but where she got it from I don't know."

But I didn't hear anything about it at school. Mandy never mentioned it. Perhaps it's not true. I'd better get back to my post; there are people to serve.

I can't concentrate, I'm making silly mistakes with the money. I wonder how Jack is? I wish I was with him, but what's the use of thinking what might have been?

Oh! Jack's mom just came into the shop. I've only seen her in here once before. Mrs Annesley seems to know her, though; maybe she shops in the week. She's just brought some grapes and a bunch of flowers. What does that mean? I must find out!

There's a lull now, so I can ask.

"Mrs Annesley, excuse me, did Mrs Moseley say anything about Mikey?"

"They get the scan results today and if they are clear, then he'll be discharged on Monday, they think. He's got a full-length cast on his leg. Mrs Moseley said he's very miserable and in quite a bit of pain."

***

113: Sunday, 19th May. 6 p.m. 15 Leighton Lane.

JACK

I'm here on my own. The others have gone to the hospital, but they don't want me there, as I'm just a wet blanket and they think I'll make Mikey even more miserable

318

than he is already, which is probably true. The brain scan was normal – well, normal for a pest – but his leg's broken which means he'll be in plaster for four weeks or so.

There was an article in this week's paper about Stewy, on page four, would you believe? "Missing Boy Found Safe and Well" was the headline.

"A missing fourteen-year-old boy who cannot be named for legal reasons..." What bullshit! His name was all over the paper when they thought he'd been kidnapped! "...has been found safe and well, living with his natural mother in Basingstoke. Police and Crime Commissioner Ken Anderson told the Mail that he was very satisfied with the police response to what had first appeared to be a case of abduction. He said that, as far as he was concerned, the case had been resolved and all parties were now happy with the status quo. A statement from the boy's father said that his son was a typical rebellious teenager, and that he was quite happy for him to live with his mother if that is what his son wants to do. Solicitor Bryan Smith, speaking for the boy's mother, asked that the family be left in peace to enable them to resume a normal life."

It was on the local radio too, for two seconds. Total crap, of course. Derek and John Henderson get off scot-free while all those people who got arrested, and that boy who tried to hang himself, and those two old geezers who got their house firebombed, are all forgotten. It makes me sick, but so what?

I'm glad that Stewy has settled in with his mother, though I wish I knew how he was getting on. It's better that I don't try to get in touch, because he probably wants to forget about his old life and I would just bring up bad memories.

I just heard something come through the letterbox. I'd better go and see, though it's probably from a pizza delivery service or something interesting like that.

There's a card from him, addressed to Mikey. I'm going to open it, because he shouldn't have done it. It's of a boy all in bandages kicking off his bed clothes and shouting 'Get me out of here! It's a good card, as you'd expect from him, and it's signed: To Mikey, with love from Robert. And it makes me hate him, because he's put love on it, but not to me! How dare he! In any case, how does he know about Mikey, and what business is it of his anyway?

I've ripped it up and I'm going to put the pieces on his desk at school tomorrow, because I want to hurt him, like he hurts me. Jeez, what sort of hypocrite am I? I complain about Mum and Dad opening my letter, but at least they didn't destroy it.

***

114: Monday, 20th May, 8.55 a.m. Swanford Community School.

JACK

I'm just making a pile of his card in the middle of his desk. My hands are shaking; I don't know why. I brought the pieces in a plastic bag. Some of the class are watching me, but no one has said anything yet. Everyone tries to avoid me as much as possible these days, which I'm glad about because I've got nothing to say to anyone.

"What are you doing, Moseley, you div?"

It's Mandy Simpkins. She can't help talking to anyone, including me. I look at her, but I can't meet her gaze. The spots are itching on my forehead and I'm sweating.

"Moseley, you shifty-eyed cunt, I asked you what you're doing?"

She nearly made me cry then, calling me that.

He'll be here in a minute. I don't know if I can go through with this.

I'm trying to get my anger up against him again, but I can't. I pick up most of the pieces and put them back in the bag. Then I see him watching me from the door. I try to get the rest of the pieces into the bag, but some of them scatter on the floor. Mandy's still staring at me. I can't stand this. I'm going to have to go to the toilets to calm down...

***

115: Tuesday, 21st May. 8.15 p.m. 15 Leighton Lane.

JACK

Mikey's in his own room lying on his bed with his leg in plaster; it goes from his thigh right down to his foot so that only his toes are visible. He's as miserable as sin and doesn't want to talk to anyone, just like me. Even thirty get-well cards from school haven't cheered him up. Tomorrow they're getting him a wheelchair, one that'll keep his leg out straight, so he can come downstairs. They think that'll buck him up, but I think there's more to it than that.

Dan is back from football practice and he's in his room too, with a face like a wet weekend. I heard him tell Dad that he might not go to football any more, because the others are telling him he's playing like crap and not really trying, which must mean they're all retards, because he's the best player in the squad by miles, and that includes Justin Walker.

I go down to the lounge and Mum and Dad are sitting there in front of the television like zombies. I only stay for a few seconds. They don't really want me in there, and I don't blame them. This whole family would be better off without me...

***

116: Thursday, 23rd May. 7.45 p.m. 15 Leighton Lane.

DAN

I took Mikey out for a ride earlier in his wheelchair, but he won't talk to me. I don't understand what's going on in his tiny mind. Perhaps the fall did damage his brain. He's wetting

321

himself more than ever, as well, and I have to take turns in changing him now with his cast on, which is not what a teenage boy should have to do. Mum says I'm better at it than anyone, which is no excuse for Dad – who never does it.

I've been lying on my bed for the last half hour, thinking. I'm sick of it all. We're all so miserable and I want things to be back to where they were before we went on holiday to Scotland, but I don't know how. Except I'm not going to call him a fag any more, even though he is one. It makes me sound such a dick, repeating that word over and over.

Sophie's going to chuck me if I'm not careful, and that would make me about as popular as Alana – I mean, Alan – Henderson. I'm worried that something's happened to him. He hasn't been back to school, so I don't even know if he got his skateboard back. I think I hate myself for what I did to him.

When we pick teams for practice games, no one wants to be on my side any more. I just can't concentrate properly. Even Justin makes comments, and it's all because I'm worried about what will happen if they find out my brother is a you-know-what.

Am I sad or what? It shouldn't make any difference to me, should it? I still haven't figured it out. There's something I'm missing— Oh, that's my phone, I'd better get it. It's probably Justin or Freddie...

The phone says: Jack Moseley calling, but it can't be – he's in his room...

"Hello?"

"Hello, is that Jack?"

"No, it's Dan. Who is this?"

"It's Stewart, Stewart Henderson. Is Jack in?"

I'm going to have to lie, because otherwise... "Hello, Stewart. No, he's out at the moment. How are you doing? I heard about you on the radio."

"I'm fine. I would have rung earlier but I've only just found a way to charge this thing. I'm coming up to Swanford on Monday, and I thought I'd call in, if that's all right?"

"I'm sure it will be."

"I'll bring Jack's phone and Mum wants me to give a letter to your parents, explaining how he helped me."

"How he helped you?"

"Yes. If it wasn't for Jack, I'd probably be dead in a ditch by now, or be in some police cell. Hasn't he said anything?"

"Er, things are difficult at the moment."

"Yes, he said you totally freaked when he told you he was gay."

Oh God, he knows! I thought it was going to be a secret for ever. "He told you?"

"Yeah, but it was pretty obvious the way he's all moony over Robert. Those two should be together, they're so in love with each other, but they just don't see it."

I'm going to die. He's talking as if this is all normal. "Stewart, you're freaking me out now too."

"Dan, I know you and your brother were close. He loves and admires you so much and you really hurt him when you rejected him. Jack's been so kind to me, better than any of my brothers have ever been. Can't you see what you've got there?"

I can't speak, because if I do I'm going to blub. He's making me feel like a gutless loser.

"Are you still there, Dan?"

"Yeah. Listen, Stewart, I'll see you on Monday, OK?"

"OK, see you Monday. Bye!"

That's what the message was about on my phone: Arrived Basingstoke ~ SH, and I'm just too thick to have put two and two together. What time is it? It's eight o'clock. I think I'll go to bed now. I don't feel very well.

***

It's dark and that's Mikey crying. I suppose I'll have to see to him. What time is it? Twenty past three! I've been asleep for nearly seven hours. Maybe all that stuff with Stewart Henderson was just a bad dream. Who am I kidding?...

Listen... What a relief, Jack's with him... I've started calling him by his name again.

"It hurts."

That's whiny Mikey talking.

"I know, a broken leg does hurt. Just let me check your pill status."

"I'm wet..."

"You know what we're going to have to do with you, don't you?"

"What?"

"Attach you to a little hose with the other end out of the window so you can water the flowers."

Mikey's giggling now. I wish I could do that. They're so alike, those two. I'm the odd one out of the three of us. They're always fighting and always making up. I'm just constant, or at least I was until I... Go on, admit it! I let him down. I told him he could tell me anything, and when he trusted me, I stabbed him in the back.

I've just realised. The missing piece. It all fits now. I really am a gutless loser. That's why I failed to get into the Football Academy. I'm not a physical coward; I'm a mental coward, but isn't there another word for that?

That's Jack's bedroom door. He must have settled Mikey. Let's hope it'll do for the rest of the night. My brother isn't a mental coward. How can he be when at the same time as everyone was treating him like dirt, he was being a real friend to Stewart Henderson? And while he's giving a helping hand to one Henderson, I'm being a complete jerk-off to another. It was the same when I freaked out on the beach and made Jack feel like a reject, and five minutes later he was giving Mikey a helping hand to pick up his fucking shells. And that's why Stewart thinks he makes such a great brother and why I'm so worthless, as a brother, as a friend and as a team mate.

***

It's half past seven, almost time to get up. It's the last day before half term and I've decided what I'm going to do. I don't know if it'll work and, if it doesn't, things could be even worse, if that's possible. But it'll be my first chance to prove that I don't have to be a mental coward, and that I can support my brother and not act like a shallow piece of chicken shit.

Oh, and I've just thought of that word: I should change 'mental' to 'moral'.

***

117: Friday, 24th May. 8 a.m. 15 Leighton Lane.

JACK

There were more wet sheets outside Mikey's open bedroom door. Jack thought about popping his head in, but decided against it, and instead tramped slowly down the stairs, listening to his mother's raised voice coming from the kitchen.

"This has nothing to do with a broken leg. He's been doing it every single night for weeks. It's just that the leg is making it worse because he's having water with his pills. You know he was coming home from school with his pants and trousers sopping wet too."

"The doctor said it'll stop. He said the same about Dan's eczema, and he was right."

Dan, who was sitting quietly at the table eating cereal, looked up.

"I still get a patch now and then."

"You can put ointment on eczema," said his mother. "You can't do the same for bed-wetting! We'll have to start thinking about nappies at this rate."

"Good idea," said Dan.

"No!" said his dad firmly. "He's far too old for night nappies."

"But you never change him! It doesn't affect you!" said his mother and Dan nodded his agreement.

"This is not Mikey's fault; it's all the hassle being caused by your other sons, particularly your eldest."

Jack walked into the kitchen. "So, now I'm to blame for Mikey pissing the bed every night, am I? Is there anything I'm not to blame for in this house?"

Roger looked at him. "You're making everyone's life a misery, including Mikey."

Jack looked towards Dan, who was staring into space with a steely-eyed expression.

"Come and have some breakfast, Jack," said his mother.

"I'm not hungry."

"There you go," said Roger. "A typical drama-queen response."

"Why doesn't everyone just shut up for once!" shouted Dan suddenly, throwing down his spoon. "I'm off to school for a bit of peace." He got up and went to put on his jacket and collect his bags.

"I'm off too," said Roger, rising from the table. "There, Jack, in a minute you'll have the whole place to yourself to act out in!"

Jack went round the table to put on his shoes and pick up his bag, which had lain unopened on the floor since the previous day.

"You look terrible!" said Pam. "And you look dirty. How long is it since you had a shower and hair wash?"

"What do you care how I look?" snapped Jack, pulling open the outside door. "Goodbye! I probably won't bother coming back!"

***

118: Friday, 24th May. 9.15 a.m. Swanford Community School, Class 4S.

JACK

Mr Colt sighed. He'd asked the class for silence while they read through their latest essays before handing them in for marking, but someone was making an annoying knocking noise. His eyes came to rest on Jack Moseley, who was sitting with his head bowed, massaging his forehead with one hand while tapping rhythmically on the desktop with the fingers of the other.

"Mr Moseley..." said his teacher quietly. There were a few snickers when Jack continued, oblivious to the summons.

"Mr Moseley..." he repeated in a slightly louder voice.

Jack's head went up as though he had been woken from sleep. "Yes, sir?" he replied automatically.

"Have you read through your essay?"

"I haven't done it, sir," he said quietly.

Mr Colt inclined his head. "Jack, do you think you ought to go and see the nurse?"

The quiet classroom became even quieter, as everyone listened for the reply.

"I don't know, sir."

"Mr Seddon, would you mind escorting Mr Moseley to the nursing station?"

Max rose and took Jack, unprotesting, from the classroom. The rest of 4S remained silent while Mr Colt sat thoughtfully, almost in the pose that Jack had assumed when caught tapping. After a time, he leaned back in his chair and gazed round his class.

"What is wrong with Jack?" he asked rhetorically.

***

At the end of assembly the headmaster read out the list of notices, knowing full well that the pupils were more interested in how much break they would lose if he didn't finish soon. Only the very last announcement had any effect, and even that was reserved for a small corner of the hall.

"And will Jack Moseley of class 4S come to my office immediately after assembly..."

327

"Oh crikey," whispered Max, "what's he been up to now?"

"Stupid fucker," murmured Mandy, and gave Max's hand a squeeze.

"Where is he?" asked Charlie as they filed out into the playground.

"I left him with the nurse and I haven't seen him since," answered Max.

"Don't you think we ought to find him?" said Barbara.

"There's the silly cunt who should be looking out for him," declared Mandy, pointing across the playground at Robert.

"What do you mean by that?" demanded Charlie.

"Isn't that Moseley junior talking to him?" said Max.

"Middle Moseley's quite the little hottie, isn't he?" asserted Barbara.

"Babs, really!" scolded Charlie. "He's just a child."

Jack had heard the announcement standing at the back of the hall and like an automaton had made his way down the corridor to the headmaster's study. He knocked on the door but, receiving no reply, sat down on a chair outside to wait.

The door opened. A heavyset, jowly man he had never seen before beckoned him inside.

"Sit," the man said, indicating the hard chair in front of the headmaster's desk.

Jack recognised the only other person in the room. It was PC Wren, who had taken notes when he was last interviewed by the police, only this time there wasn't even a ghost of a smile for him.

The man sat on the corner of the desk, so close that Jack could smell stale tobacco on his suit.

"Is this your handiwork?" he said, drawing a piece of neatly typed A4 paper off his desk.

Jack scanned the sheet, but the words were just a blur.

"Well?"

"Yes, I suppose," he mumbled.

Suddenly the man was on his feet. He grabbed Jack by the hair, pulling him back so that the chair was balanced on its two back legs. Before he had time to protest, the man covered his mouth with his hand. "But it is a pack of lies, isn't it? Soiled tracksuits and sordid insinuations of sodomy."

Jack whimpered, shocked and scared. How could this be happening to him in school? In the headmaster's study, of all places?

"Well, you spotty, greasy freak, it's a pack of lies, right?"

The man let go and the chair righted itself with a clatter. Instinctively, Jack put his feet down hard on the floor to prevent himself being catapulted forward. His scalp burned and tingled as if his hair had actually been pulled out by the roots.

"Now sign this..." The man tapped another piece of paper on the desk and held out a pen. "Go on, sign!"

Jack's hand shook as he took the pen and scratched his name at the bottom.

"PC Wren, will you witness this retraction?"

She nodded and with her own pen put her signature to the document.

The man stapled the papers together. "Now get out of here, you little skunk. Accusing respectable people of disgusting crimes! You'd better watch it in future. Times have changed and we've got our eyes on you!"

Jack was bundled out of the headmaster's study. The bell rang, but muffled, as if he was hearing it from underwater. He swayed and for a moment thought he might faint.

"What are you doing here, Jack Moseley?" It was Miss Chawner, the school secretary, returning to her office, her voice ringing muddily in his ears. "Go on! It's time you were in class."

He fled past her. The corridors were fast emptying of pupils. 4S, period three, Mr Thompson, science, practical chemistry. Just the thought of the smells, and of being surrounded by a room full of people, was too much. He ran out of the school building and down onto the playing fields, where he slumped onto the grass and retched, but nothing came up.

The next thing he remembered was sitting on the grass, crying soundlessly, his head in his hands. The school was completely quiet. He dried his eyes on a tissue and wiped his nose on his jacket, leaving a string of snot on the sleeve.

The toilets in the base of the science block stairwell were deserted, as was usual during lessons. He filled a bowl with cold water and began to splash his face, then wiped the snot off his sleeve with a paper towel. It calmed him somewhat, but when he looked at his reflection in the mirror, his heart sank and all he felt was despair. He gripped the edge of the bowl.

"I can't do this any more," he sobbed.

Hands gently took hold of his wrists. "Jack..."

He jumped and tried to break free, but Robert held on tighter.

"I'm not letting you go."

"Please!" cried Jack. "Leave me alone."

"I think you might hurt yourself."

"So what? Why should you care?" said Jack, again attempting to break free.

Robert manoeuvred him round so they were facing each other. "Because I love you."

Jack closed his eyes. Was this more torture?

"I love you," repeated Robert, pushing him up against the tiled wall. "I can't help myself. I love you. I love you so much."

The English boy moaned. "How did you know I was here?"

"Because I've been looking for you, of course."

"Let me go."

"Not until you tell me whether you love me or not."

Jack opened his eyes, but it was as if he were looking through a veil. Robert's face was so close in front of him that he could feel the warmth of his breath and smell his distinctive aroma, but still his features were blurred and insubstantial. I don't want him to let me go, do I?

330

"Do you love me?" repeated the American.

Jack blinked and the veil lifted enough for him to focus on the two intensely bright eyes peering at him. As earnest and beautiful as ever, he thought. "I love your eyes," he whispered, noticing that they were not black but a rich chocolatey brown. "I've always loved you."

Immediately, Robert let go his grip and enfolded him in his arms, brushing his lips against Jack's.

A little of the tension drained from Jack. That fleeting kiss made him feel a little bit more alive, made his heart beat that much more strongly. He grasped the American, allowing himself to relax and be supported by the firm, upright body.

"I've been so unhappy... "

"We both have," said Robert.

Gently they began to caress each other, soothing and comforting the hurt and heartache they felt.

"Jack, we need to go someplace else. I've gotta straighten things out. I've gotta tell you what a mess I made of things..."

They emerged from the science block and ran quickly across the playing fields. Jack led Robert over a fence into Woolgrove Wood, a fragment of ancient woodland, bordered on two sides by a brook, beyond which meadows stretched for as far as the eye could see. In the centre was a glade encircled by old beech trees only now coming into full leaf.

"Are we safe here?" enquired Robert.

"As houses. Unless you wade through the brook, you can't get in except from the school."

The boys cast their jackets aside and sprawled on the springy turf. The intense green and dappled shade under the peaceful blue sky worked like a magical balm on them. They drew in deep breaths of the fragrant air and gazed at one another.

"Jack, forgive me."

The English boy smiled.

"Please, Jack, it's very important to me."

Jack put out his hand and touched Robert's hair. "I love ginger," he said. "We've both been arseholes." He leaned forward and kissed him on the cheek. "There, I forgive you."

"You're a kind person," said Robert, "a loving person."

Jack was feeling that life was worth living again.

"Do you remember your first day, when you were stuck in the school entrance answering those questions from the little kids? I've been in love with you since then."

"Seriously... right from then?"

Jack took Robert's hand and put it to his face. "Maybe making each other miserable was a kind of test. We're just kids, after all. We still don't know much about how to do this."

"It was your brother who told me how you felt. I was never really certain, you see."

"Dan?"

"He cornered me in the playground this morning. Gee, he was all fired up! He said I didn't deserve you and that I was a gutless swine with no business being loved by someone as good as you."

"He said that?"

Tears began to trickle out of Robert's eyes. "Yes, and I couldn't say anything, because it was all true!"

Jack held Robert close. "But we both know how we really feel now, and nothing else matters."

The American pulled a clean handkerchief from his pocket and wiped his eyes and nose. "He really wanted to beat the crap out of me, I can tell you that."

"I told him how I felt about you when we were in Scotland, but he just couldn't take it. We haven't spoken for weeks, except to row."

"So that's why he kept saying and I'm as bad as you!"

Jack kissed Robert. "Thanks for telling me."

"Anything for my best friend."

"Am I your boyfriend as well as your best friend, then?"

"You're everything to me."

"Even with spots?"

"I don't see spots; I just see you."

"You know, I ripped up your get-well card to Mikey, because I was jealous."

The American smiled at him. "I do know. I saw you trying to get all the pieces back in the bag."

"I wanted to hurt you."

"And when I saw what you were doing, it made me want to put my arms around you and protect you."

Jack kissed Robert on the cheek. "You're lovely, you know that?"

"I love making up, I know that."

"What about making out?"

"Hmm!"

Jack nestled comfortably against Robert. The American relaxed too, feeling the warm grass on his back. "I just didn't know how good this would be, Jack."

"Robert Crittenden, will you snog me?"

"You mean, like Charlie and Barbara?"

"Yes... only more!"

The American cupped Jack's head in his hands and kissed him on the forehead, then on the bridge of his nose, and then on the mouth.

"Wow! Where did a good Christian boy learn to kiss like that?"

"Movies," replied Robert, "and...Tammy..."

He felt himself blush.

"Hmm, Tammy? Secrets, huh?" mused Jack, noticing his colour rise.

The American gave a heartfelt sigh. "Jack, it's been horrible..." And suddenly it was all pouring out of him: Tammy, his church, Pastor McKellan, Kieran Scott, Aunt Una, his parents and his brother, Aaron and finally the letter...

"Robert..." whispered Jack, holding him tightly in his arms. "I'm sorry, so sorry. I didn't know anything... I'm such a fool."

"I've been bottling up all that for so long. You're the only one I could tell; the only one I wanted to tell. It's such a relief..."

Jack kissed him on the lips and Robert responded, urgently and passionately. Their tongues entwined and this time it was a completely natural and pleasurable experience for Robert. His hand went down to gently fondle Jack, who felt himself growing hard, very hard. Moments later, he had to pull away.

"I'm going to come," he said, breathlessly.

"Please let me see!" cried Robert.

Jack quickly unfastened his trousers and only just had time to lift his shirt and boxers before he was pumping semen out across his stomach.

"Oh God! My turn... Quick!"

Jack undid Robert's belt and tugged both trousers and underpants down around his thighs, then watched a jet of fluid gush from the tumescence.

Jack stared admiringly.

"Jesus, it's a beast," he said and ever so carefully took the still heavy penis in his hand and gently inspected it. "I love it!" he murmured, running the tips of his fingers through the thick bush of gingery pubic hair.

Robert groaned.

"Sorry, am I hurting?"

The American shook his head. "No. I've dreamed about us doing this."

"Have you?" said Jack, surprised and flattered.

"But doing it for real is so much better."

"You'd better tuck it away before I get excited again."

"Would you like my handkerchief," asked Robert, "to, you know... clean..."

The English boy chuckled. "We can try, but I don't think it's going to be quite big enough for both of us."

A calm descended on them. Jack lifted himself onto one elbow and looked into Robert's eyes. "You're so fucking gorgeous," he said, sensing his lips begin to part once more. "I love you so much it hurts, here." He thumped his chest.

"It can't be wrong, can it?" said Robert.

"What?"

"This... us."

"You're talking about your church again, aren't you?"

"I guess so."

"I've no time for people who preach hate in the name of love."

"Jack, I'm no longer lying to myself, but I shall have to live an even bigger lie now."

"Come and live with me, then," smiled Jack.

"Hey, that's just like the poem Mr Colt was reading. 'Come live with me and be my love', et cetera..."

"Etcetera? I can't remember etcetera being in any of the poems Mr Colt set us."

Robert chuckled. "I'd love you to kiss me again, please," he said, lifting his head.

And Jack did so, softly and gently, in a tender affirmation of his love.

***

They lay in the quiet solitude of Woolgrove Wood for a long time, curled against one another, occasionally sharing a kiss or just staring at each other. All of the dark despair that had clouded their lives for so long had lifted and had been replaced by an intense rapture: a closeness between themselves and with the natural beauty all around them.

"Shall we go back?" asked Jack at length.

"You're hungry, aren't you?"

"Famished. I could eat a horse."

"So could I, and that means more than one of your English mini-meals."

"That's why Americans are so fat."

"I'm not fat."

"You have got a little belly mound."

"Have I?"

"We could exercise it off together."

"You're quite sassy on the quiet, aren't you, Jack Moseley?"

"I might well be when it comes to a certain American."

Robert stood up, unbuttoned and dishevelled, and offered Jack a hand.

"Better go, or we'll be in the most frightful trouble, as you English folks say."

"If they saw us like this, we'd be in more than frightful trouble."

"Is there anywhere to freshen up?"

Jack guffawed. "Is that what you Americans call wiping off dried spunk?"

Robert knotted his brow. "I've sure got a lot of adjusting to do."

"We'd better start adjusting by washing in the stream over there," said Jack.

Robert nodded, then looked round and up through the trees. "Say, how d'ya get out of here?"

***

There was still five minutes before the bell when they got back, and the canteen was deserted. Jack went through the line of dinner ladies first and was served roast lamb with mashed potatoes, gravy, peas and a rice pudding. He didn't speak, except to say thank you. Then it was Robert's turn, and when he came to stand before the tray of macaroni bake, the dinner lady automatically plopped the requisite spoonful onto his plate. The boy hesitated and then said in a low voice, "Please, ma'am, can I have some more?"

In all her fifteen years of serving, no one had ever dared ask this particular beady-eyed dinner lady for anything, despite the fact that she only came up to Robert's shoulder. With bird-like swiftness, she looked to her left and then to her right, checking that no members of staff were in sight, then she turned back to the nervous American.

"What?" she shrieked, bringing up her spoon as if to strike him.

Robert steeled himself: "Please, ma'am, may I have a little more?"

She leaned forward and whispered confidentially, "Of course you can, my love. You only have to ask in that darling accent." She heaped another, larger, spoonful on Robert's plate.

"Jesus!" said Jack, on seeing Robert's tray. Every dinner lady had given him extra.

"It's my darlin' accent," he said. "The one on the end called me Oliver, for some reason."

The bell rang and shortly the canteen was a hive of activity. Trays in hand, Max and Charlie made for their regular table, but stopped short, simultaneously doing a double take.

"Am I seeing things?" asked Max.

"No, but they're not seeing us," replied Charlie.

"There's something suspiciously different about them."

"They're sitting together – that's different."

"True, but I mean how they look."

"They look like... dunno, unstressed."

"They look," said Max emphatically, "like the cats who got the cream."

"Maybe that's what they've been doing, then, creaming each other."

"Please! I'm about to have my dinner, douche!"

They managed to get right up to the table and could have sat down as well without being noticed, but Max decided politely to clear his throat.

"Oh, hi, guys," said Jack.

"Hello, fellas," added Robert, "nice of you to join us."

"What do you mean, nice of us to join you?" exclaimed Max, putting his tray down. "We actually sit here, Robert Crittenden; this is our place!"

"What's up with him?" Jack asked.

Charlie smirked. "Didn't get his first choice." He sat down and immediately began to shovel food.

Max eyed the two boys across the table. "So, what's happened?"

337

"What do you mean?" asked Jack, blinking innocently.

"Don't be obtuse," retorted Max.

Robert felt Jack's hand stroking his knee.

"Stop it!" he giggled.

Max turned his gaze on the American. "Stop what?"

"Stop asking jackass questions," interjected Jack. "Oh, by the way, would you mind swapping desks with Robert, please, Max?"

"You know, this musical desks obsession will have to stop!"

"Wouldn't you prefer to sit next to Mandy?" questioned Robert.

"Tell me something, Pastor Crittenden," said Max, leaning across the table and eyeballing the American. "Doesn't the Good Book, the one you hold most dear, say: lead us not into temptation?...Yet here you are, trying to pimp me."

"We're all sinners," replied Robert. "Me especially."

"Max," said Jack, "can I tell you something?"

"I suppose you're going to defend this reprobate."

"No."

"What then?"

"Your tie has soaked up half your gravy."

"Oh, shit!"

"Serves you right," said Charlie, throwing his knife and fork down and reaching for his rice pudding. "So, you two have kissed and made up, have you? About fucking time. It's been like Doomsville, Arizona, around here."

"Doomsville?" said Robert. "I know that place."

Charlie chuckled. "The Yank's getting funny as well."

Max loosened his tie and drew it over his head. "I'm going to have to soak this, and I didn't want shitty roast lamb in the first place, but all the maca—" He stopped, goggle-eyed, pointing at Robert's plate. "What is that?"

"I was given a double portion, because the dinner lady loves my darlin' accent."

"Oh, the injustice!" Max said.

338

"Would you like some?" asked Robert, not expecting his offer to be taken up.

"Jesus, yes," said Max. "Macaroni bake's my favourite and, if you let me have some of that jelly and custard as well, I'll move the desks myself."

***

119: Friday, 24th May. 3.15 p.m. Swanford Community School, Class 4S.

JACK

What a difference six hours can make.

Mr Colt looked up, and he didn't usually look up until his two minutes of coming to order had passed. But this afternoon, in this second and final period before half term, his teacher radar had picked up a change, a significant change, for above the usual scraping of chairs and squeaking of desk lids and the normal buzz of conversation, he heard two voices speaking quietly to one another as they hadn't done in weeks – no, months. And there they were, second row back, oblivious to everyone and everything except themselves, and they appeared totally at ease, and they were sitting so close that their knees sometimes touched. And there was something about their glances and smiles which reminded him of a pair of...

It was if an arc lamp of illumination had been turned on inside Mr Colt's brain, but the revelation so totally dumbfounded him that he wasn't prepared yet to fully accept it. Oh, but Lord! How he cringed at the thought of the talk he had had with Jack when he had returned from suspension. He already knew it had been one of the least edifying of his long teaching career, and now it was also very likely that he had made a complete ass of himself.

Still there was work to be done.

"Well, class, we have reached the halfway point of this spring term and from tomorrow you have a week of grace in which to appreciate the beauty of a sunlit May, away from the confines of school."

A score of happy faces nodded in agreement and, for the first time in weeks, Jack's smile lit up the classroom and his glance towards Robert and the shy glance of pleasure back spoke volumes and finally convinced Mr Colt of what he had suspected. Oh bliss, he thought, two blithe spirits. Please may it continue...

"But class!" he waited for the groan, "but class, under the revised arrangements, your mock GCSEs in the compulsory subjects, id est Maths, English and science – the latter for some meaning separate exams in physics, chemistry and biology – will begin the first week back. The result of this is, I'm afraid, that you must give up a part of your hedonistic leisure time to the less immediately interesting, but in the end more rewarding, practice of revision." More groans. "Yes! Now, I know full well that your addled adolescent brains aren't capable of coherent thought...""

A knock at the door interrupted Mr Colt's flow, and Mr Colt never liked his flow being interrupted.

He was about to shout a testy, "Enter!" when the school secretary walked in, looking stern and resolute. This meant only one thing: trouble.

"Miss Chawner, what a delightful surprise," Mr Colt said, recovering his composure and standing politely.

"Good afternoon, Mr Colt. May I have a word with you... outside?"

Although this was phrased as a request, it was in fact an order, for Miss Chawner did not tread the corridors of the school of her own volition, but at the behest of the headmaster.

"Certainly, Miss Chawner. Class: Coriolanus, Act V, scene II, the Volscian Camp. We are not far from the denouement, ladies and gentlemen."

"Thank fucking Christ for that," Mandy Simpkins said when Mr Colt was safely out of earshot.

"Amen," retorted Robert loudly, causing a burst of laughter.

"What does de-new-ment mean, Mandy?" asked Carol Manning.

"It means the end, you fucking ignorant slag."

"Zooks! Can anyone tell what's going on out there?" called Max, feeling isolated at the back of the class.

Mandy patted his wrist. "Never mind, chuck, we're back in harness now."

"Oh crikey!" wailed Max and then he turned and grinned at her.

Meanwhile Jack had his eyes fixed on the door panel, where he could make out the two heads talking animatedly through the lightly frosted glass.

"It's about us," he said quietly to Robert.

As the American turned to look, teacher and school secretary walked off purposefully down the corridor.

"Have you two been naughty boys again?" asked Barbara Carter.

"I know what they've been up to," said Charlie in a confidential manner so that everyone could hear.

"Go on," said Barbara,

Charlie rose from his desk and peered hard at Robert. "Don't worry," he said, like a dentist about to perform a filling, "This won't hurt."

The American blinked as Charlie reached out and picked something from his hair. "There, I got it."

"What is it?" asked Robert, taken aback.

"Nothing much," Charlie said, holding out his fingers and wiping over them with his thumb. "Just a dry bit of Jack's cum."

There was a stunned silence. Robert blushed purple, and for a few moments, Charlie watched his embarrassment with mounting hilarity.

"Joke!" he said, at last, and turned to his audience. "Joke, boys and girls!"

Barbara thumped Charlie on the arm.

"You are so gross, I don't know why I bother with you."

"Because I'm gorgeous, Babs."

"I thought you were for real, Charlie," said Colin Messom.

"You would, bone-head! But Jack's not a stallion like me, he couldn't possibly shoot it up that far."

Max gagged. "You are one sick mother, Masefield."

In due course, the classroom door was opened just noisily enough to gain everyone's attention. Mr Colt strode to his desk, as a silence fell. He stared round at the anxious faces.

"What's the matter?" he said eyeing his audience with the surprised gaze of a true thespian.

"Who's got the chop, sir?" Carol asked.

"Jack thinks it's him, sir," said Charlie.

"There's a minor matter of discipline which I have to take up at the end of class, but it is far less important than what I said about you all knuckling down to some half-term revision." There were more groans all round. Mr Colt held up his hand. "Meanwhile, in the closing pages of this half term, we must not neglect our favourite play, which I trust you have been studying during my short absence. Starting at Act V, scene II, Mandy will you begin? You are First Guard."

Twenty minutes later. "Have a good and productive holiday, class. Mr Moseley, Mr Crittenden, will you stay behind, please?"

So this was it, as expected. Jack and Robert stood together in front of Mr Colt's desk and waited while their form teacher gathered his books together.

He eyed each of them in turn. "The headmaster has decided to give me the task of reprimanding you for bunking off science this morning. I am to reprimand you also for the even more serious offence of straying outside the school boundary during school hours, id est, Woolgrove Woods. You were apparently seen by our esteemed groundsman, Mr Peebles."

The boys bowed their heads.

"Sorry, sir," said Jack.

"I am very sorry, Mr Colt."

"So you should be."

342

The boys waited in silence... and waited.

Jack looked up. "Sir?"

Mr Colt paused from packing books into his briefcase. "Are you two still here? I thought you'd be out enjoying the sunshine. Do try to make the best of the good weather, boys, and please do some revision – your work has suffered terribly in the past month or so."

"But our punishment, sir?"

"I just gave it to you, boy. Now, be off with you..."

The boys glanced at each other.

"Mr Colt," drawled Robert, after a moment's hesitation. "You are a very nice man."

"Thank you, sir," whispered Jack. "And I'm sorry about... everything."

"The way to thank me is to do well in your upcoming exams, and to get up to date with your work, Jack. Now..." Their form teacher paused and looked askance at them, wondering how mature these two really were. He stroked his chin thoughtfully.

"Perhaps you could delay your departure until I've told you a little story?"

"Is this our punishment, sir?" asked Jack with the smile that only Jack could give.

Mr Colt chuckled, which he rarely did in front of pupils. "Yes, it is. It means you have to listen to what I have to say and not react and at the end leave without any question or comment. Is that clear?"

"Yes, sir."

"When I was a young man – no, not a young man, a child really, younger than you, there were two older boys in the school where I was a pupil who became surrounded in scandal. Rumour and speculation said that they had been caught holding hands and kissing and probably more, and even when reprimanded and told to desist, refused to be separated and refused to promise not to see each other again. For this they were disgraced and expelled, and who knows what happened to them.

"Now, as a good, obedient pupil, I probably thought they got their just deserts, but as I've grown older I have never forgotten that incident and have come to view what happened to those two boys as a travesty, an injustice, and an appalling way to treat young people. Fortunately, a sizeable swathe of society has also travelled a good distance with me since those days. So much so, that we now have the redoubtable Ms Lane to put us in our place should we stray from the path of equality."

Mr Colt became serious and he eyed each of the boys in turn.

"However, we have just had an election, and its results do not bode well for minorities like yourselves. There are many people, some now in high places, who don't think in the same way, and for one reason or another, usually through fear or ignorance, or a twisted religious conviction, or simply a lust for power or money, are openly hostile to people like you."

Their form tutor shifted his position, as if to ease a tension. "Now, if either of you has any problems, you can come to me, or if you think my previous attempts at counselling were the disaster I do, Jack, there is always the redoubtable Ms Lane. She possesses something which I have never had, boys."

"What's that, sir?" asked Jack quietly, forgetting not to ask questions.

Mr Colt looked over his glasses. "Balls, dear boy, balls... Thank you both. Have a good holiday and come back with those revision notes in your hot little hands."

Jack was about to open his mouth again, but Robert pulled him away and, without a word between them, scurried, first to their lockers and then out of school, into the bright afternoon sunshine.

Only then did Jack fall to his knees and allow the well of tears to finally fall from his eyes, for he was relieved beyond measure and uncertain whether he was laughing or crying.

"Balls, dear boy! Balls! Priceless!" He beat the ground with his fists, while Robert looked on in bemused amusement.

At last, Jack rose to his feet and wiped his face on his jacket sleeve, then looked seriously at Robert. "He got us out of the shit, didn't he?"

"Big time."

"He knows about us."

"Yes, and we've got those two boys he's had in his mind since he was a little fella to thank for his attitude."

"They'll be ancient now, like him."

"He's a good and kind man, Jack."

"I know it... I wish we could thank him properly."

"Do well in our exams, is what he said."

"We could revise together," said Jack then, looking under his brows at Robert, added, "and perhaps mix business with a little pleasure."

"You are a wicked boy."

"We could be very wicked together, if you want."

Robert blushed. "I think I do want..."

They parted with a quick kiss, not caring if anyone was watching, having swapped numbers again and arranged for Jack to visit the veg shop the following morning. They needn't have worried about being seen. The school had already emptied of pupils and most of the staff, all anxious to be away at the start of their half-term holiday.

***

120: Friday, 24th May. 4 p.m. 15 Leighton Lane.

PAM

A despondent Pamela Moseley watched Jack walk up the garden path towards the house. Ahead there loomed a full week in which she could only envisage more depression and misery, yet more frayed tempers and bad feeling. Hell could be no worse, she thought. She looked round at her youngest sons, sitting anxiously at the table, their drinks and biscuits untouched. The door opened.

345

"Hello, dear," she said, as brightly as she could muster.

Jack threw his bag down by the door and smiled at her. "Hey," he said quietly, then turned to Dan and their eyes locked.

"LB," he whispered and burst into tears.

Dan rocketed out of his seat and came round the table.

"Jack," he cried and they embraced. "Sorry, sorry, sorry," he wept. "I love you."

Jack kissed him on the cheek. "Thank you, thank you so much. I love you."

So surprised were they by this turn of events that both Pam and Mikey could only stare, transfixed, at this show of brotherly affection.

"I want a kiss," said Mikey, the first to recover.

"Come on, then," said Jack, holding out his arm.

The little boy scooted round in his wheelchair and hugged his brothers, who both kissed him on the top of the head.

"Well then, what about me?" said Pam.

Jack smiled and went to give his mum a peck on the cheek. "What's for tea? I'm starving."

Five minutes later, Pam was out in the back garden collecting in the washing and revelling in the afternoon sunshine. The world had suddenly come right again. She didn't know why, and to be honest she didn't really care. She was simply so grateful that a great burden had been lifted from her shoulders. She felt ten years younger.

***

121: Friday, 24th May. 4.15 p.m. 15 Leighton Lane.

JACK

Jack had finished changing out of his school things and was reading the instructions on a tube of Clearasil when there came two light taps on his door.

"Come in, LB." He smiled as the once familiar words passed his lips again.

Dan entered, wearing a green-and-white checked T-shirt and fluorescent yellow shorts with matching ankle socks. His brow was furrowed. "I've got to tell you something," he said.

"Well, you can start by telling me where you got that outfit from; it's so cool."

Dan went and sat on the bed in his usual place. "It's not too bright, is it? I got most of it online from Zee & Co."

"I think it'll knock 'em dead, but I'm right for bright colours, don't forget."

The younger boy didn't get the reference; he was too concerned with what he was about to say.

"Jack, I've been a real low-down loser and probably would still be if Stewart Henderson hadn't rung last night."

"Stewy?"

Dan offered his mobile.

"I think you should ring him. He wants to come up on Monday."

Jack's face lit up and he took the phone.

"This has been the best day of my life, thanks to you, LB."

Dan sobbed and covered his eyes.

"Hey," said Jack, "this is happy days, remember? Here, have one of my wanky hankies and a jelly baby."

Dan snickered, taking a tissue and wiping his eyes. "Jelly baby?"

"Yeah, you can have any colour except black – they're special."

Dan dipped his fingers into the bag and withdrew an orange one.

Jack's brow furrowed.

"LB, I've just remembered something that happened this morning concerning Stewy. It was unreal..." He described to the younger boy his meeting with the police officers in the headmaster's office and how he'd signed a piece of paper.

"But they assaulted you!" said Dan, incredulously.

"I don't know what's going on. That policewoman seemed all right before."

"Did you get his name?"

"If it was mentioned, I didn't notice. I wasn't in a fit state to take much in."

"What are we going to do about it?"

Jack smiled at the use of the word we.

"I don't think there's anything we can do, except tell Stewy. Only, be aware of the threat. It affects you."

Dan's eyes went wide. "But it's quite exciting, really."

"Yeah, maybe. Now, are you free tomorrow morning?"

"Unless I'm forced to go shopping with Mum and Dad."

Jack frowned. "We've got something more important to do than that..."

***

Jack made arrangements with Stewart for Monday, then both boys went downstairs to the lounge where Mikey was sitting, bored and disconsolate, in his wheelchair, despite being surrounded by a room full of cards.

"Hey," said Jack, "are you watching TV?"

The little boy shook his head and stuck out his bottom lip. Dan picked up the remote and switched off the TV before joining his brother on the sofa. Jack turned the wheelchair round so that Mikey was facing them, then the elder brothers folded their arms in unison and narrowed their eyes at him.

"So, baby bro, what's eating you?"

The little boy put his chin on his chest.

"Tell us."

No response.

"Tell us or we'll put itching powder down your cast," said Jack, drawing out a cylinder of pepper that he had taken from the kitchen.

"No!" cried Mikey.

"So," said Dan, "if we guess, will you tell the truth?"

Jack held up the pepper in a threatening manner.

The little boy nodded.

"Can you spell?" enquired Jack.

"Yes," said Mikey, insulted.

"If we spell out the correct word for why you're unhappy, you have to tell us, OK?"

The little boy nodded again.

"M," said Jack.

"I," said Dan.

"K," said Jack.

"E," said Dan.

Two large tears rolled down Mikey's cheeks.

"He hasn't been to see me," he said. "He hasn't sent me a get-well card. I'm lonely."

"Do you know where he lives?" asked Dan.

"In a green house," whimpered Mikey.

The two older boys chuckled. "In a greenhouse?" said Jack.

"Are his parents tomatoes?" asked Dan.

Mikey screwed his face up at them.

"Wherever he lives, we're going to take you to see him tomorrow," said Jack.

Mikey thought for a moment then smiled. "In my wheelchair?"

"No, in a space rocket," said Dan.

"I've got something else to tell you too," said Jack. "You had a get-well card from Robert, but I ripped it up."

The little boy frowned. "Why?"

"Because I was jealous."

"Was it a nice card?"

"Very nice. It said love from Robert."

Two more tears rolled out of Mikey's eyes.

"Sorry, Mikey. Do you forgive me?"

The little boy had to think for a long time about that before he nodded.

"Here you are then, piglet," said Jack, holding out a black jelly baby between thumb and forefinger. "Open wide."

122: Friday, 24th May. 6 p.m. 15 Leighton Lane.

ROGER

When Roger arrived home from work, the elder boys were back in their rooms while Mikey was in the lounge, sorting through his cards and thinking about tomorrow. Pam was busy around the kitchen preparing tea, a quickly devised special of egg, sausage and home-made chips followed by Tesco apple and blackberry crumble and Bird's custard.

"What have I done to deserve this?" he asked with a tired smile.

She came over and kissed him, for a little longer than usual.

"Well, I must have done something right," he concluded.

"Not you," she said softly, not wanting to break any spell that might have been cast over them. "He's back to normal. Just like that. I can't believe it." There were tears in her eyes. "Oh, Rog, it was lovely to see Jack and Dan make up. They cried just like they were little boys, but they were so grown-up about it too."

"So, what's brought about this miracle?"

"Not a clue. Perhaps we'll find out later."

Roger saw a warning expression on her face.

"Why are you looking at me like that?"

"I just don't want you to say or do anything that might alter things. I don't know how fragile this change is."

"All I've ever want is a quiet life. I shall be the soul of tact and discretion," he said and kissed her again.

Ten minutes later, Pam called them all in for tea. At once, Roger saw the change, as Jack and Dan came along the hall pushing Mikey, smiling and chatting, as best friends do.

"Hello, boys," said Roger. "Special tea tonight."

"Hey, Dad," said Jack, manoeuvring Mikey into position. "Smells great."

"Hi," said Dan. "Looking good."

"Hi!" squeaked Mikey, as Roger bent down to give him a hug.

They ate mostly in convivial silence, enjoying the relaxed atmosphere. Roger stole glances at his eldest son, marvelling at how the sallow, hollow-cheeked creature he had almost got used to was transforming back into the radiant boy with shiny dark hair and beautiful rosy skin, before his eyes. When they had cleared the last morsels from their plates and they were waiting for the crumble to appear from the oven, he thought a tentative question would be in order.

"How are you feeling, Jack?"

"I'm great, Dad, thanks. Can Robert come over on Monday for the day?"

"Yeah, Robert!" screeched Mikey, clapping his hands.

Roger looked over at Pam, who nearly dropped the crumble.

"Robert? You mean the American boy?"

"Yes," said Jack.

"Oh!" said Dan innocently. "Have you made friends again?"

"Fine by me," said Roger. "In any case, I shall be at work. The council doesn't run to half-term holidays."

"I've got a shift from two till five-thirty," said Pam, putting the crumble on the table then going to fetch the jug of custard, "so you'll have to look after Mikey."

"No problem. We've got a lot of studying to do."

Dan sniggered. "Me, Justin and Freddie are going fishing, but we'll be back for tea."

"Fishing?" said Roger. "Since when?"

"Well, actually it's my first time. Freddie Hall's dad is lending me a rod. We're cycling down to the Teme at Larch Farm."

"That's a long way," said Pam, serving up the crumble into bowls while trying to make sense of it all.

"Four miles is not a long way."

"Nearer five, and you be careful. Leighton Lane is busy, especially near the Prestleigh turn-off."

"We're not boneheads, Mum," said Dan, pouring custard over his crumble. "And you'll thank me when you have a freezer full of trout."

"We could have a barbecue in the evening – invite Justin, Freddie and Stewart," said Jack, accepting the jug from Dan. "Cook some trout, have a few beers..."

"No beers, dear," said Pam.

"Stewart?" questioned Roger.

"You know – Stewart Henderson."

"Stewart?" said his mother. "You mean the boy who went missing?"

"Yes," said Jack, as if perplexed by the questions. "He's been before."

"Oh, and we want to take Mikey to see Mike tomorrow morning," said Dan.

Jack nodded. "And if all's well, Mike could come to the barbecue too."

"Yeah!" shouted Mikey.

Roger looked hard at his youngest son.

"But Mike pushed you off the stage at school. He's the reason you've got a broken leg."

"He didn't mean to," said Mikey, rolling his eyes as if the idea was preposterous.

"We'll phone before we go, to make sure they're in," stated Jack, thinking that perhaps he should have done that first, "if you've got the number."

"It's in the book," said Pam absent-mindedly, rightly suspicious that they were being presented with a fait accompli. "And who's going to organise this big barbecue?"

"Me and Robert, of course."

"And me!" shouted Mikey, forgetting his leg was in plaster.

"And him," said Jack.

Pam looked at Roger, who shrugged, remembering her warning about not upsetting the apple cart.

"If the weather's fine, why not? Though I expect a garden full of boys will have the neighbours running for the hills."

"There'll be some girls there too," said Dan. "Don't worry, Dad. Everything will be under control."

***

123: Friday, 24th May. 11 p.m. Pear Tree Cottage, The Ropewalk.

ROBERT

"Hello?" said Robert, bleary-eyed.

"Hey, sleepy, did I wake you?"

"Jack! New phone?"

"I borrowed Dan's. What you doing?"

"Lying in bed, thinking of you."

"Can you send me a vid? No, just a picture. I want to see you."

There was a pause. "How's that?"

"Good, but it would be perfect if you were here with me right now. I'm sending..."

"I've just got a picture of this really cute boy called Jack Moseley who I fancy something rotten."

"Isn't that an English expression?"

"Yes, I heard Henry use it in school."

"Every thing's set for Monday. Can you come early?"

"I can't help coming early when you're around."

"Naughty."

"How about ten?"

"How about nine?"

"Nine thirty."

"Till late?"

"As late as you want."

"I love you."

"Sappy."

"I know."

353

"I love you, Jack."

"I'll see you at the veg shop tomorrow morning."

"Yeah?"

"Can you wear your apron?"

"I always wear my apron."

"I mean – and nothing else."

"I could do, but what would Mrs Annesley say?"

"I don't care what Mrs Annesley says; it's just so sexy."

"You're not getting a stiffy, are you?"

"It's been like a rocket since I started talking to you; now it's ready to go off. I'd show you, but I don't know who else might be watching..."

"I'd better go. I'm having problems down there myself now."

"Is it rampant, then?"

"Oh, Jesus, Jack, I gotta go! Kiss."

"Kiss! Night, night, my beauty and his beast..."

The End
of
Book One

SATAN'S LEGIONS